The Ancient English Romance of Havelock the Dane : Accompanied by the French text

Frederick Madden Esq.

THE ANCIENT ENGLISH ROMANCE OF Havelok the Dane;

ACCOMPANIED BY

THE FRENCH TEXT:

WITH

AN INTRODUCTION, NOTES, AND A GLOSSARY,

BY FREDERICK MADDEN, ESQ.

F. A. S. F. R. S. L.

SUB-KEEPER OF THE MSS. IN THE BRITISH MUSEUM.

PRINTED FOR THE

Roxburghe Club.

LONDON.

W. NICOL, SHAKSPEARE PRESS, MDCCCXXVIII.

EARL SPENCER, K. G. PRESIDENT.

THE DUKE OF DEVONSHIRE, K. G.
THE DUKE OF MARLBOROUGH.
EARL OF CARLISLE.
EARL GOWER.
VISCOUNT ALTHORP.
VISCOUNT CLIVE.
HON. AND REV. G. NEVILLE GRENVILLE
SIR EGERTON BRYDGES, BART.
SIR WALTER SCOTT, BART.
SIR FRANCIS FREELING, BART.
SIR JOSEPH LITTLEDALE, KNT.
WILLIAM BENTHAM, ESQ.
WILLIAM BOLLAND, ESQ.
REV. WILLIAM HOLWELL CARR.
REV. THOMAS FROGNALL DIBDIN, D.D. *V.P.*
REV. HENRY DRURY.
GEORGE HENRY FREELING, ESQ.
JOSEPH HASLEWOOD, ESQ.
RICHARD HEBER, ESQ.
GEORGE HIBBERT, ESQ.
EDWARD LITTLEDALE, ESQ.
JOHN ARTHUR LLOYD, ESQ.
JAMES HEYWOOD MARKLAND, ESQ.
JOHN DELAFIELD PHELPS, ESQ.
THOMAS PONTON, ESQ.
GEORGE WATSON TAYLOR, ESQ. M. P.
PEREGRINE TOWNLEY, ESQ.
EDWARD VERNON UTTERSON, ESQ.
ROGER WILBRAHAM, ESQ.
VENERABLE ARCHDEACON WRANGHAM.

INTRODUCTION.

INTRODUCTION

The ancient English Metrical Romance of Havelok, which is now for the first time submitted to the press, was discovered by accident in a volume preserved among the Laudian Mss. in the Bodleian Library. Of its value, not only in a Glossographical point of view, or as an accurate picture of the manners and customs of former times, but also as serving in a singular manner to illustrate the history and progress of our early poetry, there can be but one opinion, and on each and all of these accounts, it must certainly be considered as a highly interesting addition to the specimens we already possess of ancient English metrical composition.

Among our modern writers on the subject, Tyrwhitt appears to have been the first to lament the loss of the 'Rime' concerning Gryme the Fisher, the founder of Grymesby; Hanelok [Havelok] the Dane, and his wife Goldeburgh, daughter to a King Athelwold, "who all now," adds the same ingenious author, "together with their bard,

—— illacrymabiles
Urgentur ignotique longâ
Nocte ——

Diss. p. 53. n. (51.) Ed. 8vo. 1822.

These words are re-echoed by Ritson in his Dissertation on Romance and Minstrelsy, p. lxxxviii. but with his accustomed research and accuracy, he points out several of the early historians who notice the story, particularly Gaimar, Knyghton, Warner, and Camden, all of whom will be hereafter separately considered. He concludes however: "whether this poem were originally composed in English, or were no more than a translation from the French, cannot be now ascertained, *as it seems to be utterly destroyed.*"—It forms the greatest satisfaction of the present Editor, to have been the humble means of retrieving from oblivion a poem so long supposed to have perished, and by its publication to throw some few rays of light on the obscurity deplored by the preceding writers, as well as on the conjectures advanced by them. To effect this, it is proposed to divide the present Introductory Memoir into three heads, stating I. The Historical and Traditional evidence on which the Story is founded; II. Remarks on the originality and style of the English Poem, compared with the French text, and on the period of its composition; III. Account of the Mss. from which both the English and French Texts are now published.

I. In endeavouring to trace the channels through which the traditions respecting Havelok and Grim have descended, we must of necessity acknowledge the superior antiquity of the French text of this Romance. That the tradition itself existed from the Saxon times, is warranted by a high degree of probability, and at least, may be believed, without any great claim on our credulity. The earliest shape, however, in which the story is now known to us, is certainly that presented by the French Romance, whether we regard it in its separate and original form, or as subsequently abridged by Geoffrei Gaimar. Now, as this poet is generally allowed to have written some years anterior* to the time of Waće,

* Gaimar mentions his having obtained the lòan of a book containing the history of the British Kings, [the Latin translation of Geoffrey of Monmouth, made about 1138.] from Robert, Earl of Gloucester, through the favor and intercession of Dame Constance Fitz-Gilbert, and Walter Espec, Baron of Helmeslac [Helmsley, co. York.] Therefore, as Robert, Earl of Gloucester, died in 1147. and Walter Espec in 1153. [Ritson says, 1140. Diss. Rom. p. xl.] the Abbe De la Rue very justly concludes, that Gaimar must be esteemed anterior to Wace, whose work was completed in 1155. *Archæolog.* V. xii. p. 207. It will at least prove Gaimar to have undertaken his own historical poem before that period. His Chronicle originally began with the Expedition of Jason, as we learn from the concluding lines, but in all the copies which remain, it constantly appears as a Continuation of Wace, commencing only with the arrival of Certiz

and as the Chronicle of the latter was finished in the year 1155. we are at once authorised to place the original composition of the poem within the first half of the 12th century;—an antiquity, which, we believe, no other French Romance extant (not on a religious subject) can, with equal certainty, challenge. In three, out of the four, copies of Gaimar known to exist, an abridgement of the Romance is inserted into, and forms a part of, his Metrical Chronicle, but in the remaining copy, viz. that preserved in the Heralds' College, it is annexed to the Chronicle, whilst the introductory lines of Gaimar, and the account given of himself and his work at the close, are wholly omitted. That the poem as it thus appears preserves the form in which it was first written, is proved by the discovery of its separate existence in another Ms. in the possession of Sir Thomas Phillipps, Bart. where it is intitled *Le Lai de Aveloc*, and corresponds accurately with the copy in the Heralds' College, excepting those verbal variations which always occur in the collation of Mss. From its being called expressly a *Lay*, and also from the assertion of the poet, v. 21.

> Qe vn *lai* en firent *li Breton*,
> Si l'appellerent de son non,
> Et Haueloc & Cuarant.

repeated again, v. 1102.

> *Li auncien* par remenbrance
> Firent vn *lai* de sa victoire,
> Qe touz iors en soit memoire.
> Ceo fut le *lai de Coarant*.

it is impossible not to ascribe the origin of the poem to the same quarter, whence Marie of France derived her *Lais*, and which in the French fragment of Kyng Horn, Ms. Harl. 527. supplies Lenburc with the Lay of Batolf, the son of Hunlaf. From the

or Cerdic, A. D. 495. The reference made in the beginning to a preceding narrative, is certainly to a former part of the work now lost, for the circumstances mentioned are not found either in Wace, or Geoffrey of Monmouth.

same country also emanate the Lays of Emare, Sir Orpheo, Erl of Toulouse, Sir Gowther, and some few others, in English, to which may be added the evidence of Chaucer, in the Prologue to his Frankelein's Tale.* It is not intended here to enter more fully on the question, whether Armorica were really the cradle of these fictions, as Leyden contends, or, on the other hand, to deny, with Ritson, such fables ever to have existed in the language of that country; but there is some reason to believe, that by *Breton* traditions, all those stories are meant, whether clothed in the garb of history, or pure invention, which were promulgated by Nennius, the Pseudo-Gildas, Geoffrey of Monmouth, Caradoc of Llancarvan, or any other writer, pretending to follow British or Armoric originals.†

* See on this subject Tyrwhitt's Introd. Disc. n. (24.) Rits. Note to Emare, v. 1030. Price's Note to Warton, Hist. Engl. Poet. V. I. p. lxxiv. sq. and De la Rue, Archæolog. V. xiii. p. 36. sq.

† In the text of the Romance, the Bretons mentioned v. 21. are the subjects of Arthur, and consequently natives of Britain. And in Gaimar, v. 73. *Bretaigne* is equally spoken of Britain, as including Colchester and Hoiland. Alsi is said in the Romance to be *Bret par lignage*, v. 200. (copied by Gaimar, v. 61.) in distinction to Ekenbright, who was of Danish descent, and in v. 313. where the councillors of Alsi advise him to send away Argentille, they say,

Fetes la loignz enmener
En *Bretaigne dela la mer*,
Et a vos parenz comander.

Britain is here evidently distinguished from England, but may still refer to Wales. In the lines *Li auncien par remembrance*, &c. we may either understand the Armoric Britons, or the Britons of Wales, as will appear by a comparison of the parallel passages in Marie.

Del aventure de ces treis
Li auncien Bretun curteis
Firent le Lai pur remembrer,
Que hum nel deust pas oblier.
Lai d'Eliduc, v. 1171.

De lur amur e de lur bien
Firent un lai *li Auncien*.
Lai de Milun, v. 23.

If we now turn to Gaimar, and compare his account of Havelok with the French Romance, in its separate form, there will be little difficulty in acknowledging the former to have been certainly abridged from the latter, and often in the same words; but with the insertion of some particulars which do not appear in the original. Gaimar, however, quotes Gildas as his authority for the tale:

Si co est veir ke GILDE *dist,*
En la geste troua escrit,
Ke dous Reis, &c.—v. 41.

If by the Gildas here mentioned, we are to understand the author of the "Epistle," and the "Lamentations," who actually lived at the period to which the story refers, we must believe some other work of his to have existed, which is now lost, and indeed some such work is often ascribed to him. But it is most probable, that the Annals referred to under his name, are nothing more than the History of Nennius, which is frequently assigned to Gildas in the Mss. and in which no trace of the story exists, any more than in the metrical version of Geoffrey of Monmouth, attributed to Gildas, Ms. Cott. Jul. D. xi. In the confusion existing with regard to writers of this name, of whom no less than *seven* are enumerated by Bibliographers, and justly ridiculed by Ritson,* no argument can with certainty be drawn, and the difficulty must be left as we find it. Gaimar's original is again referred to in another passage,

We may also allege the lines in the Romance, corresponding so much to the style of Marie,

Cuaran l'appelloient tuit,
Car ceo tenoient *li Breton*
En lur language *quistron.*—v. 258.

We have examined the Celtic dictionaries in vain, (and in our research have been kindly assisted by Mr. Douce) to ascertain the etymology here offered. The only words given by Lhuyd to express *Scullion*, are *Guâs kegin* (i. e. Cook's boy) *guâs karr, hoeg-uesyn,* and how near these approach to *Cuaran* or *Cuherant.* the reader may himself judge.

* Life of King Arthur, p. 65. n.

in which it is said, after the defeat of Edulf [Hodulf] in Denmark by Havelok,

> Grant feste tint, e grant baldoire,
> *Si cum nus dit la verai estoire.*—v. 757.

This feast is not mentioned in the French Romance, but is detailed at length in the English version, which would seem to prove some still more ancient authority to have existed, common both to Gaimar and the writer of the English text. Traditional authority is also alleged, v. 95. *Si com dit l'antine gent*, and contributes to establish the wide reception and popularity of the story. The additions in Gaimar not found in the French Romance, are chiefly the mention of Gunter (the Father of Havelok,) being married to Alvive, daughter to King Gaifer, v. 403. (an incident borrowed by the interpolator of Robert of Brunne, as will subsequently appear) and of Hodulf being the brother of Aschis, v. 524. who was slain whilst fighting against Mordred, on the side of Arthur. This Aschis is the same with the Achilles of Geoffrey of Monmouth, and Aschis of Wace, who is said to have held the crown of Denmark when Arthur visited the kingdom, to whom he did homage; but in the Romance, and in Gaimar, Gunter is stated to have been King at that period, and to have been treacherously murdered by Hodulf, to whom Arthur delivers the throne. Whether these additions are to be traced to the *bon livre de Oxeford*, the *Estorie de Wincestre*, the *liuere Engleis de Wassingburc*, [Wassingburgh, co. Lincoln,] or to any other of the authorities cited by Gaimar, it is now impossible to ascertain, and as the evidence of Master *Nicole de Trailli*, to whom all sceptics are referred by the Chronicler, is unfortunately lost, we must be content to wait, until some future discovery shall enlighten us.

But it may be objected, and with some reason, that the entire story of Havelok and Argentille, as engrafted upon the Chronicle of Gaimar, is an interpolation by a later hand. In reply to this, it must indeed be owned, that the abrupt introduction of the story and its want of connexion, either with what precedes, or follows, are circumstances which would induce us to yield the point, did not the frequent references to Havelok subsequently occurring in the Chronicle, seem to indicate on the part of the writer, a testimony to some preceding account given by himself. Thus, after his relation of the combats between the Britons and Saxons under the command of Cerciz [Cerdic] and his son Chenriz [Kynric] he proceeds to tell us:

En Norfolc erent les Daneis
Del tens ke HAUELOC fu Reis.*
Si defendeient cel pais
E cel ki fu al reis ‡EDELSIS. &c.
Ms. Reg. 13. A. XXI. f. 117. c. 2.

‡ *Alsis*, Ms. Coll. Fec.

In another passage is related the arrival of the Danes, and their claim to the country, in the time of Bertriz [Bertric, A. D. 784—800. Sax. Chr.] King of Wessex, and this invasion is the same as that described in the Saxon Chronicle, under the year 787.

En Bretaigne voldrent venir,
As Engleis la voldrent tolir,
Car entr'els eurent esgardé,
E dit ke co est lur herité,
Et mulz homes de lur linage,
Vrent le regne en heritage,
Ainceis ke Engleis i-entrast,
Ne home de Sessoigne i-habitast,
Li Reis Danes tint le regnez,
Ki de Denemarch fu nez.
Si fist §AILBRITH *e* HAUELOC,
Et plus en nomerent ouoc.
Purquai il distrent pur verité
Bretaigne ert lur dreit herité.†—f. 124. c. 1.

§ *Edbright*, Ms. Coll. Fec.

* Constantine, in whose reign Havelok is previously placed, is supposed to have succeeded to Arthur A. D. 542. and to have held the crown three years, whilst the reign of Kynric is fixed to A. D. 534-560. (Sax. Chr.)

† Similar claims of the Danes to ancient sovereignty in England, are found in their Historians and Sagas. Saxo Grammaticus, who died in 1204. would place

And again, in the last year of the reign of Ethered [871. Sax. Chr.] at the battle of Esenesdone, or Ashdown in Wiltshire, the Danish army is stated to have been divided. In the one half commanded the Kings Basing and Halfdene:—

En l'altre eschele Contes out
Sydroc le veil, ki ferir sout,
E od lui le iouene Sydroc,
Ki fu parent le rei HEUELOC.*—f. 129. b. c. 1.

With these repeated allusions to the tradition, it would be hazardous to reject the abridgement inserted in Gaimar, as not proceeding from his own hand; and should a complete copy of his work ever be discovered, it may probably appear, that it is owing to some portion having perished, the transition from the reign of Constantine to the arrival of Cerdic appears so sudden.

A long interval elapses after the time of Gaimar, before we again collect any notice of the Romance. The great stream of our early Historians seem to have neglected it, either because

Danish Kings in Britain previous to the Christian æra; and even Snorro, a writer of equal antiquity, and more to be depended on, names Ivar Vidfadme and Haralld Hyldetand as Kings of Northumbria, at the close of the 6th century and beginning of the seventh. See Yngl. Sag. c. xlv. p. 54. Herv. Sag. c. xix. p. 293. and Turner's Hist. Ang. Sax. V. I. p. 450. 4th Ed. We shall find that the same claim on account of Havelok, is ascribed by some of the English Historians to the Danish King who brought over Colbrand, in the reign of Athelstan, and also to Canute, as a lineal descendant from the same hero. It must be remarked also, that at a subsequent period to the time referred to in the Chronicle, the district of East Anglia, comprising Norfolk and Suffolk, is always fixed on as the Danish province, and was assigued to Guthrum by King Alfred in the year 878. which was apparently founded on some tradition of their former sovereignty. It continued, in fact, with part of Lincolnshire and Northumbria, the seat of the Danish settlers, until their final expulsion.

* The Saxon Chronicle under the year 871. notices both the Earls Sidroc, together with the Kings *Bagsac* and Healfdene, but omits any mention of Havelok. According to the same authority, both these Earls were slain at Ashdown.

they regarded it unworthy of credit, or, what is more probable, from not being acquainted with the traditions peculiar to that tract of country formerly subject to the Danish sceptre. It is in the French Chronicle of Peter de Langtoft (so named from Langtoft in the county of York) that we next meet with the story. Of this writer, whose Chronicle is an abridgement of Geoffrey of Monmouth, continued down to the death of Edw. I. in 1307. we know nothing, except that he was a Canon of the Austin Priory of Bridlington in Yorkshire, and probably died soon after the completion of his work. The lines alluded to occur under the reign of Alfred.

Taunt cum vers le North Alfred est alez
Gounter̃ le pere Hauelok, de Danays Ray clamez,
Of grant chiualerye est Engleterre entrez,
Destrut ad les viles, & arses les cytez.
Les Norays s'atyrent, le Ray les ad maundez,
Of le Ray Gounter̃ en chaump sunt encountrez.
Les clers saint Chuthbert sun cors vnt leuez,
Hors del sepulture, ou fust entoumbez;
VII. anz parmy la terre le corsaint fu portez,
Dunt le Rays Alfrede fu souent confortez.
Kant Alfred & Gounter̃ ensemble ount guerrez,
Gounter par aide de Deu chaunge voluntez,
Le Rays Alfred, pur veirs, de founte li ad leuez,
Trent des melz vayllaunz of ly sunt baptisez,
Retournent Cristyens ke vindrent renaez.

Ms. Cott. Jul. A. v. f. 60.*

This is, we believe, the earliest attempt, after Gaimar, to engraft the tradition on the page of history, and to present to us, under the form of a well authenticated personage, a character which originally appears to have been wholly fictitious. The only trace

* This is a good copy, on vellum, contemporary with the author. The other Mss. we have consulted which contain the same passage, are Mss. Reg. 20. A. II. 20. A. XI. and Ms. Harl. 114.

of the Romance preserved in this account, is the name of *Gounter*, which is apparently taken from the Gunter of the French text, v. 25. Gaimar, v. 403. but instead of being assigned, as before, to the period of Arthur, and forming one of the heroes in a Dano-British cycle of fable, we find ourselves transported at once to Saxon ground, and the father of Havelok identified with the Northern invader, who entered England with the sons of Lodbrog, in the year 871. and who, under the varied names of Godrum, Gudrum, Guthrum, Gurmound,* &c. is stated by all our historians to have been defeated by Alfred at Æthandune [Heddington,

* '*Rex Godroun*, quem nos *Gurmound* vocamus.' Ingulph. p. 494. Ed. 1596. '*Gudrun*, quem nostri *Gurmundum* vocant.' W. Malmesb. p. 43. Ed. Frankf. 1601. There is some reason to believe this Guthrum to be the same with the *Gormo Enski*, or *Anglicus* of the Danish Chroniclers, who is said to have been baptised in England. Langeb. V. I. p. 158. Mr. Turner inclines also to this opinion. He is probably identical with, but often distinguished from, *Gorm hin Gamle* (Senior) who is reported to have married Thyra Denmarkebot, daughter of King Ethelred; from whom successively descended Harald, Sweyne, and Cnute. V. Langeb. V. I. p. 11. 16. 19. 22. 29. 37. 66. Chron. Erici, p. 158. Sveno Agg. p. 48. 50. Chron. P. Olai, p. 115. Chron. Tho. Gheysmer, V. II. p. 345. It must be remarked also, that Guthrum is called Gormo by Verstegan. The period of his death is very uncertain. The Saxon Chronicle places it in 890. Ethelweard, Florence of Worcester, and the Chronicle of Mailros, in 891. The Chronicle of Hamsfort in 881. that of Eric in 950. and P. Olaus in 936. (al. 926.) Our own Annals are the most to be depended on. Assuming Gunter and Gormo to be identical, Havelok should then correspond with Harald-Blatan, his son and successor, but the whole story is involved in such obscurity and fable, that it is not worth while seriously to attempt to reduce it to the data of true history. It is scarcely worth noticing in addition, that in one list of the Danish Kings, composed about the middle of the 13th century, Gorm is surnamed *Loke*, and in the Chronicle of Sveno, *Loghæ*, which according to Langebek, signifies *Desides, ignavus*. We learn from Weever, *Anc. Funeral Monum.* fol. Lond. 1631. p. 741. that a tradition existed at Hadley in Suffolk, of Guthrum's having been there interred, and a monument still shewn as his, in the same manner as the vulgar tradition at Grimsby ascribes the tomb of Sir Tho. Haslerton to the supposed founder of the place, Grime. After noticing the battle of Æthandune, Weever adds, p. 749. "This battell, and the

in Wiltshire] A. D. 878. and to have received baptism shortly afterwards. In the translation of the above passage by Robert of Brunne,* not many years subsequent to its composition, (the

baptising of Gutron and his Lords, I have also out of an ancient namelesse manuscript in my owne custody, thus deliuered:

Than *Gunter* that fader was of *Haueloke*,
Kynge of Denmarke, was than of mykle myght,
Arevyd so than in Ingylond wythe hys floke
Of Danes, fell, cruyll, myghty, and wyght;
Wyth whom the kyng full strongly than dydd fyght
And hem venquyste," &c.

The same precise lines are quoted by Gervase Holles in his account of Grimsby (Ms. Harl. 6829.) and ascribed to Robert of Gloucester. The passage, however, does not occur in Hearne's Ed. nor in any Mss. of that author, as proved by a printed copy preserved in the Bodleian library, collated with the Mss. by Dr. Waterland. The rhythm too is different from that of Rob. of Gloucester. But on comparing the lines with the French of Peter Langtoft, it is perfectly clear they are a mere translation of his words, and hence there is reason to conclude, another version existed besides that of Robert of Brunne, in whose translation the passage is rendered differently, in both the Ms. copies which exist of it.

* It appears very extraordinary, that Hearne, the publisher of Robert of Brunne, Bridges, Burton, Warton, Ellis, Ritson, and a host of others, have been so mistaken in their account of this writer. The only particulars known of his life are derived from notices given by himself, in the Prologues to his translation of the *Manuel des Pechés* [began in 1303.] and of Peter Langtoft's Chronicle [finished in 1338.] In the former he writes thus:

To alle crystyn men vndir sunne,
And to gode men of Brunne,
And speciali alle be name
The felaushepe of Symprynghame,
ROBERD OF BRUNNE greteth zow,
In al godenesse th[t] may to prow,
Of Brymwake yn Kesteuene,
Syxe myle be syde Sympryngham euene,
Y dwelled yn the pryorye,
Fyftene zere yn cumpanye,
In the tyme of gode dane Jone
Of Camelton, that now ys gone,

translation being completed in 1338.) we read as follows, p. 25. Ed. Hearne:

De Guntero patre Hauelok, sicut dicit Petrus.

Zit another Danes kyng in the North gan aryue.
Alfrid it herd, thider gan he dryue.
*Hauelok** fader he was, *Gunter* was his name.
He brent citees & tounes, ouer alle did he schame.

In hys tyme was y ther ten zeres,
And knewe and herde of hys maneres;
Sythyn w[t] dane Jone of Clyntone,
Fyue wyntyr wyth hym gan y wone;
Dane Felyp was mayster that tyme
That y began thys Englysshe ryme.
The zeres of grace fyl than to be
A thousind and thre hundred and three.
Ms. Harl. 1701. f. 1.

In his Prologue to the Chronicle we read:

Of Brunne I am, if any me blame,
Robert Mannyng is my name.—
In the thrid Edwardes tyme was I
Whenne I wrote alle this story;
In the hous of Sixille I was a throwe,
Danz Robert of Maltone, that ze know,
Did it wryte for felawes sake,
Whenne thai wild solace make.
Ed. Hearne, App. p. ci.

From these passages (which it was necessary to produce, in order to trace their connexion) we are told by his biographers, that he was *at first* a Canon in the house of Sixhille, a *Gilbertine priory* in Lincolnshire, and *afterwards* a Canon of Brunne (Bourn) an *Austin monastery* near Depyng, in the same county; that he was born at *Malton* in Yorkshire, or Lincolnshire, and that he called himself *Robert of Brunne, Robert Mannyng*, and *Danz Robert of Malton!* Cf. Hearne Pref. P. Langt. p. xxxii. xxxvi. cii. Pref. R. Glouc. p. lx. Gloss. p. 706. Warton, Hist. Engl. Poetr. V. i. p. 62. 79. Ellis, Spec. Engl. Poetr. V. i. p. 112. Ed. 1811. Ritson, Bibliogr. Poet. p. 31. Ritson, indeed, in his Observations on Warton, p. 7. pointed out the inaccuracy of supposing his birth-place

---

* *Hanelok* in Hearne, throughout, but undoubtedly *contra fidem* Mss.

Saynt Cutbertes clerkes tho Danes thei dred.
The toke the holy bones, about thei tham led.
Seuen zere thorgh the land wer thei born aboute,
It comforted the kyng mykelle, whan he was in doute.
¶ Whan Alfrid & Gunter had werred long in ille,
Thorgh the grace of God, Gunter turned his wille.
Cristend wild he be, the kyng of fonte him lift,
& thritty of his knyghtes turnes, thorgh Godes gift.
Tho that first were foos, and com of paien lay,
Of Cristen men haf los, & so thei wend away.

This is the whole that appears in the original, but after the above lines immediately follows, in the language of Robert of Brunne himself (as noted also by Hearne, Pref. p. lxvii.) the following curious, and to our inquiry, very important passage:

Bot I haf grete ferly, that I fynd no man,
That has writen in story, how Hauelok this lond wan. *De Hauelok.*

to have been Malton, and Ellis, in a stricture on the same writer, rightly conjectured his residence at Sixhille must have taken place during the reign of Edw. III. But it appears to us, from a long and attentive consideration of the above passages, that Robert Mannyng was *born at Brunne,* but was never a Canon in any monastery of that place, for he equally calls himself of Brunne soon after the year 1303. and in 1338. It appears also, that he was a Canon of the *Gilbertine Order,* and for fifteen years, i. e. from 1288. to 1303. professed in the *Priory of Sempryngham,* and it is from this circumstance he alludes so repeatedly to the foundation, Chron. pp. 111. 200. 243. that he afterwards removed to *Brymwake, in Kestevene,* six miles distant from Sempryngham, where he wrote the Prologue to his first work. What became of him for some time after this we have no means of ascertaining, but between the years 1327. and 1338. he tells us he completed his translation of Langtoft, and *during that period* was a short time in the House of Sixhille (hence his mention of it, Chron. p. 243.) another *Gilbertine priory,* (for Robert of Brunne *never changed his Order*) in the same county, the Prior of which, *Dan Robert of Malton,* CAUSED *the work to be undertaken.* We should apologise for the length of this note, did we not conceive it a service to literature, to remove an error of such long duration, and so carelessly adopted by many of our best informed writers. Should the list of Priors of Sempryngham and Brunne ever be discovered, the truth or error of the above statement will be rendered decisive.

Noither *Gildas*, no Bede, no Henry of Huntynton,
No William of Malmesbiri, ne Pers of Bridlynton,
Writes not in ther bokes of no Kyng Athelwold,
Ne Goldeburgh his douhtere, ne Hauelok not of told,
Whilk tyme the were Kynges, long or now late,
Thei mak no menyng whan, no in what date.
Bot that thise *lowed men vpon Inglish tellis*,
Right story can me not ken the certeynte what spellis.
Men sais in Lyncoln castelle ligges zit a stone,
That Hauelok kast wele forbi euerilkone
& zit the chapelle standes, ther he wedded his wife,
Goldeburgh the Kynges douhter, *that saw is zit rife.*
& of Gryme a fisshere, *men redes zit in ryme,*
That he bigged Grymesby Gryme that ilk tyme.
Of alle stories of honoure, that I haf thorgh souht,
I fynd that no compiloure of him tellis ouht.
Sen I fynd non redy, that tellis of Hauelok kynde,
Turne we to that story, that we writen fynde.

There cannot exist the smallest doubt, that by the " Ryme" here mentioned " that lowed men vpon Inglish tellis," the identical English Romance, now first published, is referred to. It must therefore certainly have been composed prior to the period at which Robert of Brunne wrote, (a proof rendered almost unnecessary by the age of the Ms. itself) in whose time the traditions respecting Havelok at Lincoln were so strongly preserved, as to point out various localities to which the story had affixed a name, and similar traditions connected with the legend, as we shall find hereafter, existed also at Grimsby. The doubts expressed by the Chronicler, as to their authenticity, or the authority of the " Ryme," are curious, but only of value so far as they prove he was ignorant of the existence of a French Romance on the subject, or of its reception in Gaimar's historical poem.

But on consulting the Lambeth copy of Rob. of Brunne, in order to verify the passage as printed by Hearne from the Inner

Temple Ms. we were not a little surprised to ascertain a fact hitherto overlooked, and indeed unknown, viz. that the Lambeth Ms. (which is a folio, written on paper, nearly a century later than the Temple copy, and imperfect both at the beginning and close) does not correspond with the Edition, but has evidently been revised by a later hand, which has abridged the Prologues, omitted some passages, and inserted others. The strongest proof of this exists in the passage before us, in which the Lambeth Ms. entirely omits the lines of Rob. of Brunne respecting the authenticity of the story of Havelok, and in their place substitutes an abridged outline of the story itself, copied apparently from the French Chronicle of Gaimar. The interpolation is so curious, and so connected with our inquiry, as to be a sufficient apology for introducing it here.

¶ Forth wente Gounter & his folk, al in to Denmark,
Sone fel ther hym vpon, a werre styth & stark,
Thurgh a Breton kyng, th[t] out of Ingeland cam,
& asked the tribut of Denmark, th[t] Arthur whylom nam.
They wythseide hit schortly, & non wolde they zelde,
But rather they wolde dereyne hit, wyth bataill y the felde.
Both partis on a day, to felde come they stronge,
Desconfit were the Danes, Gounter his deth gan fonge.
When he was ded they schepe bryng, al his blod to schame,
But Gatferes doughter the kyng, *Eleyne* was hure name,
Was kyng Gounteres wyf, and had a child hem bytwene,
Wyth wham scheo scapede vnethe, al to the se with tene.
The child hym highte HAUELOK, th[t] was his moder dere, *De Hauelok.*
Scheo mette with Grym atte hauene, a wel god marinere,
He hure knewe & highte hure wel, to helpe hure with his might,
To bryng hure saf out of the lond, wythinne th[t] ilke night.
When they come in myd se, a gret meschef gan falle,
They metten wyth a gret schip, lade wyth outlawes alle.
Anon they fullen hem apon, and dede hem mikel peyne,
So th[t] wyth strengthe of their assaut, ded was quene Eleyne.

But zyt ascapede from hem Grym, wyth Hauelok and other fyue,
& atte the hauene of Grymesby, ther they gon aryue.
Ther was brought forth child Hauelok, wyth Grym and his fere,
Right als hit hadde be ther own, for other wyste men nere.
Til he was mykel & mighti, and man of mykel cost,
Th^t for his grete sustinaunce, nedly serue he most.
He tok leue of Grym & Seburc, as of his sire & dame,
And askede ther blessinge curteysly, ther was he nought to blame.
Thenne drow he forth northward, to kynges court Edelsie,
Th^t held fro Humber to Rotland, the kyngdom of Lyndesye.
Thys Edelsy of Breton kynde, had Orewayn his sister bright
Maried to a noble kyng, of Norfolk Egelbright.
Holly for his kyngdam, he held in his hand,
Al the lond fro Colchestre, right in til Holand.
Thys Egelbright th^t was a Dane, and Orewayn the quene,
Hadden gete on Argill, a doughter hem bytwene.
Sone than deyde Egelbright, & his wyf Orewayn,
& therfore was kyng Edelsye, bothe joyful & fayn.
Anon their doughter & here eyr, his nece dame Argill,
& al the kyngdam he tok in hande, al at his owene will.
Ther serued Hauelok as quistron, & was y-cald Coraunt,
He was ful mykel & hardy, & strong as a geaunt.
He was bold curteys & fre, & fair & god of manere,
So th^t alle folk hym louede, th^t auewest hym were.
But for couetise of desheraison, of damysele Argill,
& for a chere th^t the kyng sey, scheo made Coraunt till,
He dide hem arraye ful symplely, & wedde togydere bothe,
For he ne rewarded desparagyng, were mani on ful wrothe.
A while they dwelt after in court, in ful pore degre,
The schame & sorewe th^t Argill hadde, hit was a deol to se.
Then seyde scheo til hure maister, of whenne sire be ze?
Haue ze no kyn ne frendes at hom, in zoure contre?
Leuer were me lyue in pore lyf, wythoute schame & tene,
Than in schame & sorewe, lede the astat of quene.
Thenne wente they forth to Grymesby, al by his wyues red,
& founde th^t Grym & his wyf, weren bothe ded.

But he fond ther on Aunger, Grymes cosyn hend,
To wham th^t Grym & his wyf, had teld word & ende.
How th^t hum stod wyth Hauelok, in alle manere degre,
& they hit hym telde & conseilled, to drawe til his contre.
T'asaye what grace he mighte fynde, among his frendes there,
& they wolde ordeyne for their schipynge, and al th^t hem nede were.
When Aunger hadde y-schiped hem, they seilled forth ful swythe,
Ful-but in til Denemark, wyth weder fair & lithe.
Ther fond he on sire Sykar, a man of gret pousté,
Th^t hey styward somtyme was, of al his fader fe.
Ful fayn was he of his comyng, & god help hym behight,
To recouere his heritage, of Edulf kyng and knyght.
Sone asembled they gret folk, of his sibmen & frendes,
Kyng Edulf gadered his power, & ageyn them wendes.
Desconfyt was ther kyng Edulf, & al his grete bataille,
& so conquered Hauelok, his heritage saunz faille.
Sone after he schep him gret power, in toward Ingelond,
His wyues heritage to wynne, ne wolde he nought wonde.
Th^t herde the kyng of Lyndeseye, he was come on th^t cost,
& schop to fighte wyth hym sone, & gadered hym gret host.
But atte day of bataill, Edelsy was desconfit,
& after by tretys gaf Argentille, hure heritage al quit.
& for scheo was next of his blod, Hauelokes wyf so fayr,
He gaf hure Lyndesey after his day, & made hure his eyr.
& atte last so byfel, th^t vnder Hauelokes schelde,
Al Northfolk & Lyndeseye, holy of hym they helde.

Ms. Lamb. 131. f. 77.

Our next reference, (which in point of chronological accuracy, with the one that follows, ought to have preceded Robert of Brunne) occurs in a French prose Chronicle, compiled in the year 1310. by *Meistre Rauf de Boun*, at the request of Henry de Lacy, Earl of Lincoln, intitled: *Cy comence le Bruit D'Engleterre, q̃ vous dirra de Roy en autre, Payne et Chrestien, ickis Roy Edward de Carnaruan, qe ore est, solome la ordinaunce Meistre Rauf de Boun, q̃ a la requeste Monsr. Henry de Lacy, Count de Nichole, ceste chose ad nouelment abbreggé, hors du Grant Bruit, en l'an du reigne nostre seignur le Roy Edward de Carnaruan le tiers en entraunt*, &c. It is called also at the close *Le Petit Bruit*, and is written on paper in a hand of the 16th century, preserved in Ms. Harl. 902. Although said to be taken from the *Grand Bruit*, by which is generally understood Geoffrey of Monmouth, or his translator Wace, it has scarcely any connexion with either, but is a collection of historical notices chiefly derived from apocryphal sources, and put together in so confused and ignorant a manner, in defiance of chronology, as to baffle all ingenuity to reconcile them to each other. The Chronicler commences, as usual, with Brute, B. C. 2000. and after taking us through the succeeding reigns to the time of Cassibelin, who fought with Julius Cæsar, informs us, that after Cassibelin's death came Gurmound out of Denmark, who claimed the throne as the son of the eldest daughter of Belin, married to Thorand, King of Denmark. He occupies the kingdom 57. years, and is at length slain at *Hunteton*, called afterwards from him *Gurmoundcestre*. He is succeeded by his son Frederick, who hated the English, and filled his court with Danish nobles, but who is at last driven out of the country, after having held it for the short space of 71. years. And then, adds this miserable History-monger: " Et si entendrez vous, que par cel primer venue de auant dit Roy Gormound, et puis par cele hountoux exile de son fitz Frederick, si fu le rancour de Daneis vers nous en pendaunt, et le regne par cel primer accion vers nous enchalangount plus de sept C. ans apres, *iekis a la venue Haueloke, fitz le Roy Birkenbayne de Dannemarche, q̃ le regne par mariage entra de sa femme*."—f. 2. b.

After a variety of equally credible stories, we come to Adelstan II.* son of Edward [the Elder] who corresponds with the real

* The Chronicler writes of him, f. 6. " Il feu le plus beau bachelier q̃ vnqes reigna en Engleterre, *ceo dit le Bruit*, par quoy ly lays ly apellerunt *King Adelstane with gilden kroket*, pour ce q'il feu si beaus." We have here notice of another of those curious historical poems, the loss of which can never be

King of that name, A. D. 925-941. He is succeeded by his son [brother] Edmund, who reigned four years [A. D. 941-946.] and is said to have been *poisoned* at Canterbury; after whom we have ADELWOLD, whose identity with the Athelwold of the English Romance, will leave no doubt as to the source whence the writer drew great part of his materials in the following passage:

" Apres ceo vient Adelwold son fitz q̃ reigna XVI. et demie, si engendroit ij. feiz et iij. filis, dount trestoutz murrirent frechement fors q̃ sa pune file, le out a nom [1] *Goldburgh*, del age [2] de VI. aunz kaunt son pere Adelwold morust. Cely Roy Adelwold quant il doit morir, comaunda sa file a garder [3] a vn Count de Cornwayle, al houre kaunt il quidoũie (sic) hountousement auoir deparagé, quant fit *Haueloke*, fitz le Roy Byrkenbayne de Denmarche, esposer le, encountre sa volunté, q̃ primis fuit Roy D'Engleterre et de Denmarch tout a vn foitz, [4] par quele aliaunce leis Daneis queillerunt g̃ndr̃ (sic) mestrie en Engleterre, et long temps puise le tindrunt, *si cum vous nouncie l'estorie de Grimesby*, come *Grime* primes nurist Haueloke en Engleterre, depuis cel houre q'il feut chasé de Denmarche &c. deqis al houre q'il vint au chastelle de Nichole, q̃ cely auaunt dit traitre *Goudriche* out en garde, en quel chastel il auauntdit Haueloke espousa l'auauntdite Goldeburgh, q̃ fuit heir D'Engleterre. Et par cel reson tynt cely Haueloke la terre de Denmarche auxi come son heritage, et Engleterre auxi par mariage de sa femme; et si entendrez

sufficiently deplored. The term *crocket* (derived by Skinner from the Fr. *crochet*, uncinulus) points out the period of the poem's composition, since the fashion alluded to of wearing those large rolls of hair so called, only arose at the latter end of Hen. III. reign, and continued through the reign of Edw. I. and part of his successor's.

[1] *Goldusbourgh*, H. de Knyghton. [2] vi. *annorum et dimidii*, Id.

[3] *cuidam Godrico, Duci Cornubie, qui maritavit eam cuidam Hauelec, filio Birkelani regis Dacie, apud Lincolniam, qui postea regnavit tam in Anglia quam in Dacia simul, in Dacia jure hereditario, et Anglia, jure hereditatis uxoris sue.* Id.

[4] *Inde Dani sumpserunt nimiam audaciam in Anglia, et suppeditaverunt Anglos longo tempore.* Id.

vous, q̃ par la reson q̃ ly auauntdit Gryme ariua primez, kaunt il amena l'enfaunt Haueloke hors de Denmarche, par meyme reson reseut cele vile son nom, de Grime, quel noun ly tint vnquore Grimisby.

Apres ceo regna meyme cely Haueloke, q̃ mult fuit prod homme, et droiturelle, et bien demenoit son people en reson et ley. Cel Roy Haueloke reigna [5]xli. aunz, si engendroit [6]ix. fitz et vii. filis, dount trestoutz murreroumt ainz q̃ furunt d'age, fors soulement iiij. de ses feitz, dont l'un out a noun Gurmound, cely q̃ entendy auoir son heir en Engleterre; le secound out a noun Knout, quen fitz feffoit son pere en le regne de Denmarche, quant il estoit del age de xviii. aunz, et ly mesme se tynt a la coroune D'Engleterre, quel terre il entendy al oeps son ainez fitz Gurmound auoir gardé. Mes il debusa son col auxi [7]comme il feu mounte vn cheval testous q̃ poindre volleyt, en l'an de son regne xxiij. entrant. Le tiers fitz ont a noun Godard, q̃ son pere feffoit [8]de la Seneschacie D'Engleterre, q̃ n'auo᷉ut (sic) tante come ore fait ly quart. Et le puisnez fitz de toutz out a noun [9]Thorand, [1]q̃ espousa la Countesse de Hertouwe en Norwey. Et par la reson q̃ cely Thorand feut enherité en la terre de Norwey, ly et ses successours [2]sont enheritez iecis en sa p̃ce (sic) toutdis, puis y-auoit affinité de alliaunce entre ceulx de Denmarche et ceulx de Norway, a checun venue q̃ vnkes firent en ceste terre pur chalenge ou clayme mettre, iekis a taunt q̃ lour acc᷉on feut enseyne destrut par vn noble chevallere *Guy de Warwike,** &c. Et tout en sy

[5] xxxi. *annis, et rexit populum suum cum ingenti honore,* Id.

[6] xv. *filios et filias,* Id.

[7] *ascenso equo indomito, volens magistralia attemptare,* Id.

[8] *in Senescaria Dacie et in mercimoniatu Angl'.* Id.

[9] *Thoraldus,* Id.

[1] *qui duxit uxorem comitissam de Hertowe,* Id. *comitis* a s. m.

[2] *cujus affinitas in Northwegia perseverat usque ad præsens,* Id.

[3] *jacet London' apud Sanctum Paulum,* Id.

* This connection of the story of Havelok, and the claim of the Danes, through him, to England, with the legend of Guy of Warwick, is curious, and enables us to form another link in the chain of Dano-Saxon traditions. The legend itself may be found in Robert of Brunne; in the *Petit Bruit,* referred to above; in the rhimes of Girardus Cornubiensis, (said by Tanner to be extracted from Girald. Cambrensis, c. xi. Hist. Reg. West. Sax.) printed by Hearne, ad calc. Annal. Dunst. No. xi. and translated by Lydgate; in the Chronicles of Knyghton, Rudburn, Fabyan, and Hardyng, in the *Liber de Hida,* Ms. Sloane, 717. and in

feffoit Haueloke sez quatre fitz: si [3]gist a priorie de *Grescherche** en Loundrez."—f. 6. b.

The *Estorie de Grimesby* therefore, referred to above, is the identical English Romance before us, and it is no less worthy of remark, that the whole of the passage just quoted, with one single

Dugdale's Hist. of Warwickshire, p 374. In all these authors, the Kings of Denmark and Norway, who are said to have brought over Colbrand, are named *Anelaphus* and *Conelaphus*, but in the old metrical Romance of *Guy of Warwick*, printed by W. Copland, before 1567. *Coll. Garrick*, K. 9. (which Warton, V. 1. p. 91. conjectures to have been written by Walter of Exeter, a Franciscan friar of Carocus in Cornwall, about 1292.) the names are corrupted as follows:

But or Guy went that man him tolde,
That the King was in cares colde,
The King of Denmarke HANELOCKE [HAVELOCKE]
And the King of Norway Conelocke,
Both be come into this lande,
With doughty knightes a thousande.—sign. Hh. iii. 6.

And below:

And king Athelstone swore than,
If Colbrand ouercame his man,
He and all his lynage,
Should doe King *Henelock* [Hevelok] homage.—sign. Ii. i.

In a Ms. English Chronicle, Harl. 63. which we shall again have occasion to refer to, the Danish King who brought over Colbrand, A. D. 927. is called *Gaufride*, (the Guthfrith of the Saxon Chronicle). "And Adelstone lay at Wychestre, and the kyng of Denmarke sent vnto hym an harowde of Armes, to witte wheder he wold fynde a man to fighte w[t] Colbrande for the righ[t]e of the Kyngdom of Norhumbr̃, *that the Danes had claymed byfore by the title of kyng* Haueloke, *that wedded Goldesburghe* the kyngis daughter of Northumbr̃." —f. 19.

To those who may feel disposed from the above lines in the Romance of Guy of Warwick, to identify Havelok with the well known Danish king Anlaf, in the reigns of Athelstan, Edmund, and Edred, the following curious coincidence in sound with Havelok's epithet of *Cuaran*, may appear of weight. "A°. 949. Her com *Anlaf Cwiran* on Northymbra land," Sax. Chron. which Professor Ingram converts into Anlaf *Curran*.

* Apparently the same with the *Gristischurche* mentioned subsequently as the burial-place of St. Edmund.

variation of import, has been literally translated by Henry de Knyghton, and inserted in his Chronicle. Of the sources whence the information respecting Havelok's sons is derived, we are unable to offer any account, as no trace of it occurs either in the French, or English texts of the story.

About the same time at which Rauf de Boun composed his Chronicle, was written a brief Genealogy of the British and Saxon Kings, from Brutus to Edward II. preserved in the same Ms. in the Heralds' College, which contains the French text of the Romance. The following curious rubric is prefixed:—*La lignée des Bretons et des Engleis, queus il furent, et de queus nons, et coment Brut vint premerement en Engleterre, et combien de tens puis, et dont il vint. Brut et Cornelius furent chevalers chacez de la bataille de Troie,* M. CCCC. XVII. *anz deuant qe dieus nasquit, et vindrent en Engleterre, en Cornewaille, et riens ne fut trouee en la terre fors qe geanz, Geomagog, Hastripoldius, Ruscalbundy, et plusurs autres Geanz.* In this Genealogy no mention of Havelok occurs under the reign of Constantine, but after the names of the Saxon Kings Edbright and Edelwin, we read: "ATHELWOLD auoit vne fille *Goldeburgh,* et il regna vi. anz. HAUELOC esposa meisme cele Goldeburgh, et regna iij. anz. ALFRED le frere le Roi Athelwold enchaca Haueloc par Hunehere, et il fut le primer Roi corone de l'apostoille, et il regna xxx. anz."—fol. 148. b. By this account Athelwold is clearly identified with Ethelbald, King of Wessex, who reigned from 855. to 860. whilst Havelok is substituted in the place of Ethelbert and Ethered.

Not long after the same period was written a Metricle *Chronicle of England,* printed by Ritson, Metr. Rom. V. II. p. 270. Two copies are known to exist, the first concluding with the death of Piers Gavestone, in 1313. [Ms. Reg. 12. C. XII.] and the other continued to the time of Edw. III. [Auchinleck Ms.] The period of Havelok's descent into England is there ascribed to the reign of King Ethelred [978—1016.] which will very nearly coincide with the period assigned by Rauf de Boun, viz. A. D. 963—1004.

Haueloc com tho to thes lond,
With gret host & eke strong,
Ant sloh the kyng Achered,
At Westmustre he was ded,
Ah he heuede reigned her
Seuene an tuenti fulle zer.
Ms. Reg. 12. C. XII.

This date differs from most of the others we have adduced, and appears founded on the general notion of the Danish invasions during that period; the Chronicler adopting the name of Havelok as one that was well known, or in mistake for Anlaf, as we have before remarked.

We next come to the well known Prose Chronicle called the BRUTE, which from its extreme popularity, and its having subsequently formed the basis of Caxton's Chronicle, added to the frequent continuation of it by different hands, has been involved in some little obscurity, the removal of which by the examination of a great number of Mss. the Editor has endeavoured in some degree to accomplish.

The original Chronicle is in French, and appears to have been composed at the commencement of Edw. III. reign, for all the early Ms. copies unite in bringing the History down to the battle of Gaskmore, in 1332. or of Halidon-Hill, in 1333. It is chiefly founded on Geoffrey of Monmouth, but borrows also from other sources, and in the later part, contains a considerable portion of original matter. Of its first author we are completely ignorant, unless we admit with Mr. Douce (Illustr. Shakesp. V. I. p. 423.) and Dr. Dibdin, (Ames, V. I. p. 90.) the authority of an anonymous note written in one copy of the English translation, Ms. Harl. 4690. as follows: *The Memorālle Cronicke, written by John Douglas, Munke of Glastonburye Abbaye,*—but this is too vague to bear the character of direct evidence, and most probably only refers to the scribe of the Ms. In other copies of the English version, Ms. Harl. 24. and Ms. Digb. 185. we are told in the

Preface: "The wiche gestis and Romayns, as it folowith here after, mani dyuers goode men and grete clerkes, and namely men of relygion, as in Abbais, Priouries of Englande, haue compilede and wretone, that befelle in here tyme, and made therof grete Bookes and Remembrances to alle men that com after hem, to hire and to se what byfelle afor, and was doone in this lande, and lette calle hem *Cronicles*, and [to] seye the sothe, in this lande haue bene with this Brute vnto kyng Edwarde the thirde after the Conquest CXXXII. kyng[es] whos lyues, actes, and dedes bene alle compilede shortly in this Booke here folowyng, the which conteyneth CCXXXVIII. chapitours, withoute the Protegolle othir Prologe."* So also in the copies Harl. 1337. 6251. Hatton 50. is written at the conclusion: "*Here endith a booke callyd the Cronic̄les of Englonde, made & compiled by notabil Clerkis, of aventuris of kyngis that were in this londe, and how they died.*" From these passages it would result, that the name of the original composer was never avowed, or at least, not known, but the whole work considered as a mere compilation from the Chronicles of the earlier Historians.

The greater part of the Ms. copies of the English version of this Chronicle come down to the siege of Rouen, in 1418. but others are continued to the 6th or 8th year of Hen. VI. and even later. From one of these later Mss. Caxton undoubtedly printed. It would seem, however, from the passage quoted above from Ms. Harl. 24. that the translation originally concluded with the death of Edw. III. [1377.] and in Bennet College Library at Cambridge, is another copy (No. 174.) ending in the same year. But it must at the same time be observed, that no Ms. exists of any portion of this English version and continuation, older than the 15th century, nor will the language permit us to believe the first portion was

* In reality the Ms. Harl. contains 244. chapters, and concludes, like the other copies, with the siege of Rouen, 6. Hen. V. [1418.] but the 238th chapter closes with the death of Edw. III. a manifest proof of the addition of the latter part.

translated at an earlier period. The translator's name is, like that of the compiler, for some reason concealed, but from some lines added to the Harleian copy 2279. apparently by a hand of the 16th century, we may be enabled to gain some little accession to our knowledge on this head.

This English booke that is present,
was made to a good entent,
For hem that Englishe vnderstonde
of the Cronicles of Engelonde.
This was translated by god avyse,
owt of French into Englyse,
By Sire John the Maundevyle,
that hath ben person but a whyle
In Brunham Thorp, that little tone,
God graunt him hise benysone.
The yeer of Henry I vnderstonde
The sexte Kyng of Engelonde,
After the Conquest, soth to seyne,
1435. *The* xiii. *yere of hise reygne.*
He that sitt in Trinite,
One god and persons three,
Save the kyng from all mischaunce,
Bothen in Engelond and in Fraunce.

Thes verses written in the end of this mans translac̄on, which doth somewhat vary from this translac̄on out of ye first originall frenche.

Warton, V. i. p. 67. n. merely alludes to this note (which he learnt from the printed Catalogue,) but makes no remark on it. It is certain, however, from Blomfield's Norfolk, V. iii. Ed. 1769. that in the year 1427. *John Maundevile* was presented by the King to the Rectory of Burnham Thorp, and held it till the year 1441. This period will exactly suit the age of the Mss. both as to style and writing, and it is very clear from the lines above quoted, that *Sire* John the Maundevyle (so stiled by the usual courtesy towards a Priest) was the author of an English version of the Chronicle in question, in the year 1435. The words added in prose might seem to intimate there were *two* translations, but this is disproved by the numerous Mss. remaining, all of which essentially agree with each other, but contain more or less variation in the phraseology, as we have proved by the collation of several of the best copies. We would therefore conclude, that the writer of this remark, finding these variations in his own copy from the copy in which the verses were written transcribed by him, might easily suppose there were two translations, whereas that was not the fact, but only one single translation, made by *Sire John the Maundevyle.*

The identity of this Ms. English Chronicle with that afterwards printed by Caxton, and very absurdly called by his name, (since he could only have been the author of some of the last chapters,) has already been proved by Lewis, who states truly, "that they are the same without any interpolations [but the Mss. sometimes *fuller*, towards the latter part] only the old and obsolete language is sometimes altered to make it more intelligible."*

Having thus cleared in some measure the history of this famous Chronicle (which well deserves to be reprinted)† we come now to

* Life of Caxton. Pref. p. XI. XII. and App. No III. 8vo. 1737. The Edd. used by Lewis were of W. de Worde, 1497. and 1520. and Jul. Notary, 1515. By the permission and liberal kindness of the Earl Spencer, we have been enabled to compare the Edd. in his Lordship's valuable library, and the following notice of the series may be of service. The first Ed. is that of Caxton, 1480. intitled *The Cronycles of Englond,* which was reprinted by W. de Machlinia, *s. a* and at Antwerp, by G. de Leew, 1493. This Ed. ends with the accession of Edw. IV. in 1460. Next appeared the *Fructus Temporum* or *Frute of Tymes,* printed at St. Alban's, 1483. which is often confounded with Caxton's Chronicle. It consists of a reprint (or very nearly so) of Caxton, with the addition of a General History, prefixed as a first part, and some other additional chapters of Popes and Emperors, taken from Martinus Polonus, and other writers, and said to have been compiled "by one sometime scole mayster of Saynt Alban's." After this is the Ed. of W. de Worde, 1497. intitled *Cronycle of Englonde, wyth the Frute of Tymes,* which is nearly a reprint of the St. Alban's Ed. and the same may be stated of the subsequent Edd. of Julian Notary, [1504] 1515. Pynson, 1510. W. de Worde 1502. [1515] 1520 and 1528.

† Hearne intended to reprint it, as appears from a note inserted at the close

the object for which these remarks have been made. In this Chronicle, in all its various shapes, is contained the Story of Havelok, *engrafted on the British History of Geoffrey of Monmouth,* and in its detail, following precisely the French text of the Romance. The only variation of consequence is the substitution of the name of Birkabeyn (as in the English text) for that of Gunter, and in some copies, both of the French and English Mss. of the Chronicle, the name of *Goldeburgh* is inserted instead of *Argentille;* which variations are the more curious, as they prove the absolute identity of the story. For the sake of a more complete illustration of what has been advanced, we are induced to copy the passage at length, as it appears in the French Chronicle, taken from a well written Ms. of the 14th cent. Ms. Reg. 20. A. III. collated with another of the same age, Ms. Cott. Dom. A. x. and a third of the 15th cent. Ms. Harl. 200. intitled *Les Cronikes de tout Engleterre.*

Des Rois Adelbright & Edelfi. Cap. IIII^xx. XIX.

[1]Apres le Roi Constantin estoient deux Rois en graunt Brutaigne, dount li vns out a noun [2]Aldelbright, & fust Danois, & [tint[3]] tut le païs de Norff' & de Suffolk, & ly altre out a noun [4]Edelfi, q̃ fust Brittone, & tint Nicole & Lindeseie, & tote la terre desqes a Humbre. Ceux deux Rois soi entregueroierent, [& moult s'entrehaierent[5]] mais puis furent il entre acordez & soi entreamerent, taunt com s'il vssent estee freres de vn ventre neez. Le Roi Edelfi out vne soer, [6]Orewenne par noun, & la dona par grant [7]amour al Roi Aldelbright a femme. Et il engendra de ly vne fille q̃ out a noun [8]Argentille. [9]En le tiercz an apres vne greue maladie ly [1]suruint, si deuereit morrir, & [2]maunde par vn

of a Ms. copy in the Rawlinson collection, No. 190. He erroneously ascribes it to the " scolemaster of St. Alban's."

[1] *En temps cesti R.* Cott. Harl. [2] *Athelbright, Ethelbright,* C. H. pass.
[3] Mss. C. H. [4] *Edelsy,* H. pass. [5] Mss. C. H.
[6] *q'auoit a noun Orwenne,* C. H. [7] *admiralté,* C. *admirabilité,* H.
[8] *Goldeburgh,* C. [9] *& le quinte an,* C. H. [1] *prist,* C. H.
[2] *maunda le Roi E.* C. *maunda a Roy Edelsy q'il vensist,* H.

iour al roi Edelfi, soun frere en lei, q'il venist a ly parler, [3]& cil ly emparla volentiers. Donqe ly pria le Roi Aldelbright et ly coniura en le noun [de[4]] Dieu, q'il apres sa mort preist Argentille sa fille, & sa terre, & q'il la feist [5]honestement garder [& nurrir[6]] en sa chambre, & quant ele serreit de age, q'il la [7]feist marier al plus fort hom & plus vaillaunt q'il porroit trouer, [8]& q̃ a donqe ly rendist sa terre. Edelfi ceo graunta, & par serment afferma sa priere. Et quant Adelbright fust mort, & enterree, Edelfi prist la damoysele, & la [9]norrist en sa chambre, si deuynt ele la plus beale creature q̃ hom porreit trouer.

Coment le Roi Edelfi maria la damoisele Argentille a vn quistroun de sa quisine. Cap. C.

Le Roi Edelfi, [1]q̃ fust vncle a la Damoysele Argentille, pensa fausement coment il porreit la terre sa nece auoir pur touz iours, & malueisement countre son serment [2]pensa a deceuire la pucelle, si la maria a vn quistroun de sa quisyne [3]q̃ fust apellée Curan, si esteit il le plus haut, le plus fort, & le plus vaillaunt de corps, [4]q̃ hom sauoit nulle part a cel temps, & la quidoit hountousement [5]marier, pur auoir sa terre a remenant, mais il fust deceu. Car cest Curan fust [le Roi[6]] Hauelok, filz le Roi [7]Kirkebain de Denemarche,[8] & il conquist la terre sa femme, [en Bretaigne[9]] & occist le Roi Edelfi, vncle sa femme, & [1]conquist tote la terre, *si com aillours est trouée plus pleinement,* [*en l'estorie*[2]] & il ne regna q̃ [3]treis aunz. Car Saxsouns & Danoys le occirent, & ceo fust grant [4]damage a tote la grant Brutaigne. Et les Brittouns le porterent a Stonhenge, & illoeqes ly enterrerent a grant honour."

[3] *& il vint* vol. C. H. [4] Mss. C. H. [5] *bien*, C. H.
[6] Mss. C. H. [7] *dust*, C. H. [8] *& la rendisist donqe*, C. H.
[9] *fist nurrir*, H. [1] *son oncle, pensa traiterousement en son qoer*, coment, C. H.
[2] *la pensa deceiure & trahir, &* la m. C. H.
[3] *q'auoit a noun Cuaran*, C. *Guarran*, H.
[4] *de qi home oist parler* n. p. *en* cele t. C. H. [5] *auer marie*, C. H.
[6] Ms. C. [7] *Birkebein*, C. *Birkebyn*, H.
[8] *qe puis fu Roi de Damarz &* conq. C. H. [9] Mss. C. H.
[1] *auoit*, C. Verba *et occ—terre*, desunt H.
[2] Mss. C. H. In H. post *lestorie* inseritur, *& occist le Roy Edelsy, vncle sa femme.* [3] xx. *anz*. C. [4] *doel*, C. H.

With the above may be compared the English version, as extant in Ms. Harl. 2279. 24. 753. all of which agree with the Ed. of Caxton, except in the occasional substitution of one word for another. The copy in Ms. Harl. 4690. differs rather more, and appears on the whole to be the most correct. The more important variations are annexed.

Ms. Harl. 2279. f. 45. *Of the kinges Albright & of Edelf.* Ca° IIII^xx. XI°.

[1]After̃ kyng Constantinus deth, ther were ii. kynges in Britaigne, [2]that one men callede [3]Adelbright, [4]that was a Danoys, and helde the cuntray of Northfolk and Southfolk, that other̃ hight [5]Edelf, and was a Britoñ & helde [6]Nichole, Lindeseye, and alle the lande vnto Humber. Thes ii. [7]kynges faste werred togedere, but afterward [8]thei were acorded, and louede togedere as thei had ben [9]borne of o bodie. The kyng Edelf had a suster̃ that [1]men called Orewenne, and he yaf here [2]thurgh̃ grete frenship̃ to kyng [3]Adelbright to wif, and he begate on here a doughter̃ that [4]men callede Argentille, and in the [5]iii. yeer̃ after̃ him come vppoñ a [6]strong sekenesse [7]that nedes he muste die, and he sent to kyng Edelf, his brother̃ in lawe, that he shulde come and speke with him,[8] and he come to him with good wille. Tho prayed he the kyng and coniurede also in the name of God, that after [9]whan he were dede, he shulde take

[1] *After the king Constantine wer*, Harl. 4690.
[2] *that me called*, Harl. 24. 753. *oone hight*, H. 4690. *was callyd*, Caxt.
[3] *Aldelbrighte*, H. 4690. *Albryght*, 753.
[4] *the wiche was a Dane*, H. 4690. [5] *Edolfe*, Id. *Edel*, Caxt.
[6] *Lincolne*, H. 4690. [7] *kynges werreden togeder*, Id.
[8] *thei loveden togider*, Id. [9] *bretheren of oone body ybore*, Id.
[1] *me called*, H. 24. 753. *was callyd*, Caxt. *hete*, H. 4690. [2] *for*, Id.
[3] *Aldebrighte*, Id. [4] *me called*, H. 24. 753. *was callid*, Caxt. *hete*, H. 4690.
[5] *fourth*, Caxt. *thyrde*, Jul. Not. 1515.
[6] *greuous maladye*, H. 4690. *gret sykenesse*, H. 753.
[7] *that he most be dede*, H. 4690.
[8] *and anone he come right gladdely, & he praied him in the name*, Id.
[9] *his dethe*, Id.

Argentil his doughter, and the lande, and that he [1]kepte hir wel, and noreshed in his chambre; and when she were of age he shulde done here be mariede to the strongest and [2]worthiest man that he myzt fynde, and than he shulde [3]yelde vp her lande ayen. Edelf hit grauntid, and bi othe hit confermede his prayer. And whan Adelbright was dede and enterede, Edelfe toke the damesel Argentil, and noreschid her in his chambre, and she become the fayrest creature [4]th[t] myzt lif, or eny man finde.

How kyng Edelf mariede the damysel Argentil to a knaue of his kichyn.
Ca° IIII[xx.] XII.

This kyng Edelf, that was vnele to the damesel Argentil, [5]bithought how that he myzte [6]falsliche haue the lande from his nece for [7]euermore, and [8]falsly ayens his othe thouzte to desceyue the damysel, and [9]marie here to a knave of his kichon, [1]that men callede Curan, and he become the worthiest and strengest man of bodie that eny man wist in eny lande that tho leuede. And to him he thouzt here shendfully haue mariede, for to haue had here lande afterward; but he was clene desceyuede. For this Curan that was Hauelokis son that was kyng of Kirkelane in Denmark, and this Curan conquerede his wifes landes, and slow kyng Edelf, that was his wifes vncle, and had alle here lande, as in another [2]stede

[1] *schulde kepe her well in his gouernaunce w[t]ynne his housholde into the tyme that sche myght be mariedde*, Id. [2] *most worthi*, Id.

[3] *yeue with her alle the londe. Edolfe graunted to do alle this, and therto he made an othe, and wan Aldebrighte*, Id. *bi oth confermed it*, H. 24. 753.

[4] *that eny manne might a see*, H. 4690. *became as fayre as ony myghte be*, Jul. Not. 1515. [5] *falselye thoughte*, H. 4690.

[6] Deest H. 4690. [7] *euerre*, Id. [8] *maliciously*, Id.

[9] *so he maried her to a qwestron*, Id.

[1] *that me called*, H. 24. 753. *was called*, Caxt. *the wiche hete Curan, but this qwestron was a comely yong man and the moste myghty th[t] men knewen, & afterward most worthy of his body. And so were, as the king semed, that he had maryed the damsell schamfully, so to haue hadde alle the londe, he was deceyved, for thatt questron, Curan be name, was the kingges sone Hauelokke, the king of Kirkelane in Dennemarke, and afterwarde he conq.* Id.

[2] *place hit*, H. 24. 753. Caxt. These words are omitted in H. 4690.

hit telleth more openly, and he ne regnede but iii. yeer for Saxones and Danoys [3]him quelde, and that was grete harme to al [4]Britaigne, and Britouns [5]bere hym to Stonehenge, and ther thei him interede [6]with mochel honour and solempnite.

It must not be concealed, that in some copies, viz. in Mss. Harl. 1337. 6251. Digb. 185. Hatton 50. Ashm. 791. 793. the story is altogether omitted, and Conan made to succeed to Arthur. In those copies also of the English Polychronicon, the latter part of which resembles the above Chronicle, the passage is not found.

Among the Harl. Mss. (No. 63.) is a copy of the same Chronicle in an abridged form, in which the name of *Goldesburghe* is substituted for that of *Argentille*, and the corrupt paragraph in the common copies is thus given :—"for when Goldesburghe come to the age of XIIII. yere, he maryed here to a scolyone of his kechyn, that was called Hauelok, & kept the lande to hym selffe. *Of kyng Haueloke.* And so it appenyd that Haueloke be rythe of of his wiffe was ryghte heir to the kyng of Denmarke, and went to Denmarge, and there was made kyng, and after he come agayn w^t^ moche people, and slewe Edelff, and was made kyng of this lande, and regnyd III. yere, and liethe at Stonehynge."—f. 15. b.

It is to this popular and well known book of Caxton's press, and of his followers, that Warner was indebted for the tale of *Argentile and Curan*, which he has introduced into his Poem intitled *Albion's England*, Book IV. chap. 20. published in 1586. In the shape of a ballad it met with so much praise, as to induce Bishop Percy to reprint it separately in the *Reliques of Anc. Pop. Poetr.* V. II. p. 231. Ed. 1765. This elegant scholar, however, errs widely from the truth, when he writes: "The story of Argentile and Curan is, I believe, the poet's own invention; *it is not mentioned in any of our Chronicles.*" Warner strictly adheres to his copy, even to the corruption of the King's name into the kingdom

[3] *slew him*, Id. *hym kylled*, H. 24. [4] *the Britounes*, H. 4690.
[5] *ladden his body*, Id.
[6] *with grete worshipp*, Id. *with moch honour*, H. 24. 753. Caxt.

he governed:—" At *Kirkland* is my father's court." The admiration bestowed on his performance induced another writer, not many years afterwards, to publish a larger poem on the same subject, in stanzas of six lines, intitled: *The most pleasant and delightful historie of Curan, a prince of Danske, and the fayre princesse Argentile, daughter and heyre to Adelbright, sometime king of Northumberland,* &c. by Will. Webster, 4to. Lond. 1617. which, as we learn from Bishop Percy, was only a paraphrase of the preceding poem by Warner. At a more recent period it descended into the shape of a common street ballad.

It was, in all probability, to this Chronicle also, in its original form, that Thomas Gray, the author of the *Scala Cronica* (or *Scale Cronicon*), a Chronicle in French prose, composed between the years 1355. and 1362.* is indebted for his knowledge of the tale. As we have not been able to inspect the *unique* Ms. of this work, preserved in Bennet College library, Cambridge, our notice of it must be confined to the excerpts given by Leland, *Collectan.* V. I. pt. 2. p. 509. sq. who translates the passage relative to Havelok in the following manner:

" Sum say that in Constantine King of Britons tyme, that Ethelbright and Edelsy were smaul Kinges under hym, where of the first was King of Norfolk and Southfold (sic) and the other of Lindesey. And these 2. Kinglettes encresid, and Ethelbright toke to wife Orwenne, the Syster of Edelsy, of whom he got a Doughter *caullid Argentile in Brutisch, and*

* Cat. Mss. C.C.C.C. No. CXXXII. 2. Sæc. 14. Nasm. p. 208. The name of the author is discovered from the Prologue, in which it is expressed by numbers. He speaks of himself frequently in the course of the work, and at the time of its composition, was a prisoner in Edinburgh. It is asserted by Leland, that Gray composed his Chronicle from a metrical work in French, and in a note prefixed to a copy of Peter Langtoft, Ms. Cott. Jul. A. v. goes so far as to assert, " Hunc P. Langtoft in Gallicam prosam vertit Auctor Scalæ Cronicæ." This is not true, as may be found on comparing the extracts taken from Gray with Langtoft's Chronicle. And Gray himself, in his Prologue, cites as authorites not only Langtoft, but Joannes Anglicus, and Otterbourne, both of whose Chronicles were in prose.

Goldesburg in Saxon. And this Goldeburge was after left with her Uncle Edelsy on this Condition, that he that yn Feates of Chevalry might be found most noble, that he shoulde have his Doughter. And she was after maried to one Havelok, that was Sun to a King of Dennemark, but conveyid by slaite into England, and after, the Treuth knowen, was restorid in Denmark as trew Heire.

One Cuaran, Sun to Grime, a strong and a mighty young Felow, cam to Edelsy's Court in to Lindesey, and ther was first a Turner of Broches yn the Kechyn, and after by valiant Deades rose to greate Name.

Cuaran Sun to Gryme, a poor Fisschar, not able to kepe hym for Poverty.

Gryme had Haveloc (by Commaundement of the king of Denmark Stuard) to be drownid; but having Pite on hym, he conveyid hym yn to Lindesey, in England, to a Place syns caullid of his Name Grymesby. But this Historie ys countid of sum but as an Acocriphe. (sic) And sum say, that Sweyn of Denmark (Father to King Knut) first attempted Lindesey by the firste cumming thither and Mariage of Haveloc."

Grimsby unde.

How completely this account corresponds with the story in the preceding sources, and with the English Romance, is evident, but Leland, apparently, was not aware of the identity of Cuaran and Havelok, and from that cause has represented them as if they were distinct persons.

The next authority we shall cite is Henry de Knyghton, a canon of Leicester Abbey, who florished in the time of Rich. II. at the end nearly of whose reign (1395.) he concludes his History.* He professes to follow the seventh Book of Higden, from the Conquest downward, but with the addition of some Chapters prefixed on the early Saxon and Danish History. From the situation of the Abbey, and its proximity to the county of Lincoln, the tradition of Havelok was probably well known there, and may have existed in the *Historiæ in Abbatia,* cited by him as his guides. But we are fortunately enabled to point out the very source from which Knyghton in the present instance copies, viz. the French Chronicle of Rauf de Boun, previously quoted by us. He introduces his translation of the passage thus: " Inter cetera videamus quam

* Two copies remain in Ms. Cott. Tib. E. VII. and Claud. E. III. It is printed by Twisden, int. Dec. Scriptt. fol. Lond. 1652.

ob causam et qua racione Canutus venit in Angliam, et misit clamium in regno Anglie. Fuit quondam in Anglia quidam rex Egelwoldus nomine, et genuit ij. filios et iij. filias, &c." almost in the words of his original, except in the notice of Havelok's burial place, which Knyghton fixes at St. Paul's, whilst De Boun places it in *Grescherche*.* The minuter variations of Knyghton's text have been already subjoined to the passage from De Boun.

The last mention of Havelok we have met with in our ancient Chroniclers, appears in a short Historical compilation, from Brutus, A. C. 2000. to the reign of Hen. VI. in Ms. Cott. Cal. a. II. f. 107. b. "Idem Lucius Rex habuit filiam Yng castam (sic) et ad evacuandam (sic) effusionem sanguinis, Anglia fuit bipartita (sic) inter quinq. reges, et sic per cccc. [annos] *et fuerunt reges medio tempore de quibus non fit mencio,* de Glouc, qui fecit Gloucester, Bedwin, qui fecit Bedford, *Gormond,* qui fecit Chester, &c. *Ethelwolde,* qui generavit filiam de (sic) *Haueloke* de Denmarke, *per quem Danes per cccc. annos postea fecerunt clameum Anglie,*" &c.

The blunder of the scribe is apparent, and the passage is only noticed, as forming another proof of this ancient tradition respecting the Conquest of England by Havelok, and the Danish claims subsequently founded on that event, having been constantly retained in the fabulous Chronicles of England, and not only admitted from the 12th to the 15th centuries as an historical fact, but mingled in the same stream which has brought down to our own times the actions of an Alfred and an Edward.

Among our more modern Compilers of History, the story seems to have been neglected by common consent. John Fabyan is the only writer who has at all noticed it, in his *Concordance of Historyes,* printed in 1516. His authority is the *Englysshe Cronycle*

* An odd tradition is mentioned by Hentzner respecting the "Kings of Denmark, that reigned in England," buried in the Temple Church. The Editor of the private reprint, 4to. Reading, 1807. metamorphoses the two Inns of Court, Gray's Inn, and Lincoln's Inn, into the names of the Danish Kings, "*Gresin* and *Lyconsin*"!! This is the greatest blunder we ever recollect to have met with.

(described above) and after briefly alluding to the narrative of *Adelbryght* and *Edill*,(whose names he conjectures to have been borrowed from Ethelbert, King of Kent, and Ella, King of Northumbria) he adds: " Of thyse tway kynges ye sayd Englisshe Cronycle tellyth a longe processe, the which, *for I fynde noon auctor of auctorite y^t^ wrytith or spekyth of the same,* I passe it ouer." Ed. Ellis, p. 82. 4to. 1811.

We now arrive at the period, when the tale first began to be noticed by our Topographers, among whom Camden takes the lead (for Leland we have already disposed of.) In his notice of Grimsby, he thus alludes to the tradition: " Et postea Grimesby, quod Sabini nostri, qui quod volunt, somniant, a *Grimo* mercatore sic dictum volunt, qui quod *Hauelocum*, regium Danorum puellulum expositum educaverat, *fabellis decantatur,* cum Haueloco illo pupillo, qui in Regis coquina primo lixa, et postea Regis filiæ nuptiis, ob heroicum fortitudinem honoratus, nescio quæ facinora gessit, illis dignissima qui anilibus fabulis noctem protrudere solent."—p. 353. Ed. 8vo. Lond. 1587.

This contemptuous opinion of Camden has been called in question by later writers, particularly by Gervase Holles, (whose words we shall presently have occasion to quote,) who defends the authenticity of the legend on two separate grounds, first, the ancient connexion of Grimsby with Denmark, and secondly, the local traditions of the town. On each may be offered a few remarks.

We have taken considerable pains to ascertain if the story of Havelok exists in any of the Scandinavian writers, and with that view, have gone over the greater part of the ancient Chronicles and Sagas, but without success. A slight coincidence, indeed, but merely in name, occurs in Snorro's account* of young Haco's being brought to England, in the time of Athelstan, by *Hauk Habrok,* a person selected by Harald-Harfager, King of Norway, on account of his courage, and long experience in maritime affairs; but in no other respect does this relation resemble the one we are examining.

* See Snorro, Hist. Reg. Septent. V. I. p. 119. Ed. Stockh. 1697. Torf. Hist. Reg. Norv. Pt. 2. p. 64.

Failing in our own attempts to discover a trace of Havelok in the Northern Historians, we addressed a communication on the subject to Professor Rask, of the University Library, Copenhagen, who, in his reply, refers us to Suhm's *Kritiske Historie af Danmark*, Bind III. p. 850—860. 4to. 1776. This writer, after quoting P. Langtoft, Knyghton, and Weever, (a proof, by the way, that he was not aware of the existence of any Scandinavian authorities) expresses his opinion that it is a true history, as to the ground work, but that several of the Danish Kings are confounded in the person of Havelok, especially Svend [Sweyn, circ. 994—1014.] and Hardeknud. " In fact," adds the Professor, " there is an Icelandic fragment published at the end of *Jomsvikinga-saga ok Knytlinga*, &c. 8vo. Copenh. 1828. p. 417.* stating (on the authority of Adamus Bremensis) that *Svend Treskæg* was expelled from Denmark by a King of Sweden, and found a refuge in Scotland, from which he afterwards returned, and became again King of Denmark, as also of England, by conquest. Perhaps this might be the foundation of the story; at all events, Havelok is likely to be a surname given him (and perhaps all the Danish kings) by the English. It has no meaning, as far as I know, in Danish."

The ancient communication also between the port of Grimsby and the North of Europe may probably be adduced in favor of the legend. In the *Orkneyinga Saga*, p. 152. it is related that Earl Kali, about the middle of the 12th century, accompanied some merchants to an emporium (*kaupstadar*) in Britain, called *Grimsbær*, to which place resorted an immense multitude from the Orcades, Scotland, and the Western Isles. It is to this passage Macpherson alludes in his *Annals of Commerce*, V. I. p. 391. and it is corroborated by the *Landnamaboc*, and by Snorro (who wrote towards the close of the 12th cent.) who tells us, that many places in England had names of Danish origin given to them, such as

* It is also printed in Langebek, V. I. p. 148. from a Ms. written in 1313. The same story is in Saxo, p. 188. Adam Bremensis (who wrote about A. D. 1077.) mentions the expulsion of Svend, but does not say he went to Scotland. p. 21. 23. Ed. Lindenbrog. ED.

Grimsboer, *Hauksfliot*, and many others. V. I. p. 129. But it will easily be remarked, that the 12th century, to which period these passages refer, is long posterior to the supposed epoch of Grim and Havelok, and therefore no very great stress can be laid on the circumstances mentioned. Despairing therefore of obtaining any further clue to our inquiry from the Northern Chronicles, let us turn to the claims presented by the local traditions of Grimsby. These will be best stated in the words of Gervase Holles, (the well known patriot and antiquary in the reign of Charles I.) who, in his Mss. Collections for Lincolnshire, preserved in Ms. Harl. 6829. thus speaks of the story we are examining.*

"And it will not be amisse, to say something concerning ye Common tradition of her first founder Grime, as ye inhabitants (with a Catholique faith) name him. The tradition is thus. *Grime* (say they) a poore Fisherman (as he was launching into ye Riuer for fish in his little boate upon the Humber) espyed not far from him another little boate, empty (as he might conceaue) which by ye fauour of ye wynde and tyde still approached nearer and nearer unto him. He betakes him to his oares, & meets itt, wherein he founde onely a Childe wrapt in swathing clothes, purposely exposed (as it should seeme) to ye pittylesse [rage] of ye wilde & wide Ocean. He moued with pitty, takes itt home, & like a good foster-father carefully nourisht itt, & endeavoured to nourishe it in his owne occupation: but ye childe contrarily was wholy denoted to exercises of actiuity, & when he began to write man, to martiall sports, & at length by his signall valour obteyned such renowne, y^t^ he marryed ye King of England's daughter, & last of all founde who was his true Father, & that he was Sonne to ye King of Denmark; & for ye comicke close of all; that *Hauelok* (for such was his name) exceedingly aduanced & enriched his foster-father Grime, who thus enriched, builded a fayre Towne neare the place where Hauelocke was founde, & named it Grimsby. Thus say some: others differ a little in ye circumstances, as namely, that Grime was not a Fisherman, but a Merchant, & that Hauelocke should be preferred to ye King's kitchen, & there liue a longe tyme as a Scullion: but

* His account has been printed in the *Topographer*, V. I. p. 241. sq. 8vo. 1789. We follow, as usual, the Ms. itself, p. 1.

however ye circumstances differ, they all agree in ye consequence, as concerning ye Towne's foundation, to which (sayth ye story) Hauelocke ye Danish prince, afterward graunted many immunityes. This is ye famous Tradition concerning Grimsby wch learned Mr. Cambden gives so little creditt to, that he thinkes it onely *illis dignissima, qui anilibus fabulis noctem solent protrudere.*"

Holles, on the contrary, does not think the story deserves utterly to be exploded as fabulous, and proceeds to state his reasons:

" First, ye etimology of ye word (Grimsby) will carry a probability, ye termination *By* signifying in ye Danish tongue *habitatio*, a dwelling, so as I know noe reason, why Grimsby should not import ye dwelling of Grime,* & receaue this denomination from him, as well as *Ormes-by* from Orme, and *Ketels-by* from Ketell, two Danish captaines under Canute, in the dayes of King Ethelred, which Capt. Henry Skipwith affirmed unto me, & that he could prove itt, not onely out of ye legend of Nun-Ormesby, but from other good & unquestionable Records. Secondly, that there was such a Prince as Hauelocke, take old Robert of Gloucester for proofe, who speakes him ye sonne of Gunter, or Gurthrum, Gutron, or Gurmond (for all those foure names I fynde given him, Kinge of Denmarke.

Than Gunter, that fader was,† &c.

Thirdly, that Hauelocke did sometymes reside at Grimsby, may be gathered from a great blew Boundary-stone, lying at ye East ende of Briggowgate, which retaines ye name of *Hauelock's-Stone* to this day. Agayne ye great priviledges & immunities, that this Towne hath in Denmarke above any other in England (as freedome from Toll, & the rest) may fairely induce a Beleife, that some preceding favour, or good turne called on this remuneration. But lastly (which proofe I take to be *instar omnium*) the Common Seale of ye Towne, & that a most auncient one," &c. [Here follows a description of the Seal.]

* Skinner also gives this etymology, in v. " Forte a quodam *Grimo* conditore." Mr. Oliver states, but we know not on what authority, that Grim originally came from *Souldburg*. Mon. Antiq. Grimsb. p. 12.

† Vid. ante, p. xiii. n.

The subsequent conjecture of Holles, that Grim, the reputed founder of Grimsby, was the same person as the *Grimus* mentioned by Pontanus, is very wide of the mark, and intitled to no consideration. The name of Grim was far from uncommon,* and neither the chronology, nor the relation of Pontanus will at all bear reference to the tradition before us. Holles concludes, p. 3. "He that is not satisfyed with this, let him repayre to *Dicke Jackson's famous manuscript concerning this matter*, where he shall fynde a great deale more, to as little (if not less) purpose. Who 'Dick Jackson' was, or what is become of his 'famous manuscript,' we have been unable to discover.

The singular fact, alluded to by Holles, of the Burgesses of Grimsby being free from toll at the Port of Elsineur, in Denmark, is confirmed by the Rev. G. Oliver, in his *Monumental Antiquities of Grimsby*, 8vo. Hull. 1825. who is inclined from that, and other circumstances, to believe the story is not "so totally without foundation."—p. 15. In addition also to the boundary-stone between the parishes of Grimesby and Wellow, mentioned by Holles, (and which still exists under the same appellation) is a place of safe anchorage for ships within the Spurn Point, near the site of the ancient town of Ravenspur, which retains the name of "The Hauk Roads," probably, as Mr. Oliver conjectures, from the exposure of young Hauk or Havelok in that place. Another extravagant legend preserved among the lower classes at Grimsby, is only worthy of notice, as it evinces how fiction gradually usurps the place of truth, whenever an event is transmitted by the organ of popular credulity. It was kindly communicated to us by the Rev. G. Oliver.

"The Church at Grimsby has a broad tower, at *one* angle of which is an elevated turret. It is said originally to have had a similar turret at

* The Grimus in Pontanus, Rer. Dan. Hist. p. 28. fol. Amst. 1631. is called *Norvegiæ clarum pugilem*, and placed in the reign of Haldan II. [A. D. 554.] A *Grim athleta* occurs in Saxo, p. 70. b. See the mention of other persons of this name in Orkneyinga Saga, p. 186. Antiq. Celto-Scand. p. 27. Landnamaboc, p. 24. Kemp Dater, p. 20. fol. Stock. 1737. Hist. Wilkinens. and Torf.

each angle, and the following absurd story is gravely told to account for the present deficiency. *Old Grime,* as he is familiarly denominated, being once upon the summit of this tower on the *look out* for his piratical vessels, he beheld some of them in danger of a hostile attack from a squadron of superior force, and, in the violence of his anxiety and rage, he kicked one of the turrets into the sea, and it fell amongst the enemy's shipping. Gratified by his success, he made a second attempt, but his strength being much exhausted by the first effort, the next turret fell short, and dropped in Wellowgate, forming the boundary called *Havelok's Stone.* It appears that Grime had sufficient energy for a third attempt, but it was so completely powerless, that though he succeeded in breaking it from its position, the turret fell within the enclosure of the Churchyard, where it yet remains in the form of a *stump Cross.* His strength being now wholly exhausted, Grime descended from the tower, without being able to interfere with the fourth turret, which still elevates its head on the S. W. angle of the tower ! !"

To the same gentleman we are indebted for an impression of the ancient and very curious Seal of Grimsby, (referred to by Holles), an engraving from which is annexed.

Much importance is naturally attached to so singular an illustration of the legend on which the Romance is founded, since we are enabled, with the greatest confidence, to pronounce the Seal to be, at least, as old as the time of Edw. I. and consequently contemporary with the English text of the Romance. In the Ms. of Holles is a very spirited outline copy of it, which was most wretchedly engraven in the *Topographer*. Mr. Oliver caused it again to be copied in his work on Grimsby, but not accurately enough to give an adequate idea of the original; the spirit and execution of which, we confess, even in our own engraving, has scarcely been treated with justice. We here see Grim represented as a man of gigantic stature (according to the French text, which pictures him as a *Vikingr*, and also in the spirit of one of the local traditions of Grimsby), brandishing a massive sword in his right hand, and in his left a shield of unusual make and proportions, purposely designed as it would seem, by the draughtsman, to represent armor of an archaic description. Behind the figure is his name in capital letters GRYEM. Beneath, on the right, is a young man, with a crown over his head, to denote his royal descent and sovereignty, and in his hand the hatchet he is described in the Romance to have used so effectually. Above him we read HABLOC. On the opposite side stands the Princess, regally crowned, whose name GOLDEBVRGH is placed immediately above her. The legend round the Seal is thus: SIGILLVM COMUNITATIS GRIMEBYE, in a character, which after the year 1300. fell into disuse, and was succeeded by the black letter, or *Gothic*. Mr. Oliver, however, in his search among the Corporation Records of Grimsby, could find no document to which it was affixed of greater antiquity than the reign of Hen. VII. The original matrix is now in private hands, and probably will never again be accessible to the Corporation, but the Grimsby Haven Company (incorporated about 1800.) have caused it to be re-cut, and adopted it as their official devise.

Such is the evidence to authenticate the Story of **Havelok the Dane.** The Editor conceives it wholly unnecessary for him to bestow a moment on the task of confirming or controverting the opinions already advanced. The demarcations of Fiction and History, now so rigorously observed, were at that early period unknown or neglected. The rhyming Chronicler, and the monkish Historian who wrote in prose the events of ancient times, received with the same degree of credence every circumstance handed down to them by document or tradition, and not possessing the means or the judgement to discern between truth and falsehood, admitted into the sober page of History legends founded on the wildest efforts of imagination. Hence it is, to use the language of Percy, that the historical narratives of the North so naturally assume the form of a regular Romance. To this cause must we ascribe the romantic traditions preserved concerning Ragnar Lodbrog and the huntsman Bruno Brocard, in all its variations; the singular legends respecting Guy and Colbrand, and Bevis of Southampton; the no less curious Histories of King Attla, and of King Alefleck, and of his travels to India and Tartary; (all of which, with several more in existence, might form a Dano-Saxon cycle of Romance highly worthy the attention of the poetical antiquary), to which we may add the interesting Romance of Moris and Constance, inserted by Nicolas Trivet in his Chronicle,* and the curious gest of Dan Waryn, mentioned by R. de Brunne, and partly still preserved in the story of Fulco Fitz Warin, quoted by Leland, and exstant in a Ms. of the Royal Library.† In all these may probably be traced some real historical personages and events, mingled with a mass of fable and invention. In the Romance before us, in like manner, the names of real personages seem to have been adopted, without any regard to the time of their existence, and some slight circumstance actually occurring in History, might have been esteemed a sufficient basis for the superstructure subsequently raised by imagination. Thus, for instance, Æthelwolf, Æthelbright, and Guthrum, might be transported into the Athelwold, Athelbright, and Gunter of the Romance, whilst the marriage of Ethered's daughter to Gormo, as asserted by the

* Ms. Soc. Reg No. 56. † Ms. Reg. 12. C. xii.

Danish Historians, might be converted into the fiction of Goldeburgh's marriage with Havelok. The local traditions of Lincoln and Grimsby, most certainly, lend a certain degree of support to the story, and must have been founded on transactions which we cannot wholly reject as fabulous. At all events, whether we regard the tale at present as a web of mingled truth and fiction, or as a pure creation of fancy, we must admit that for ages it was chronicled and read, and in the immediate province to which it so particularly refers, was considered quite as much intitled to belief, as any other portion of our National Annals.

II. The preceding extracts have extended to such a length, as to preclude us from offering many remarks on the Poem itself. We have already admitted the superior antiquity of the French text. This, in itself, may be considered nearly as great a curiosity as the English Romance, both from its being the most ancient French Romance (properly authenticated) existing on a subject not sacred, and also from its being the *first* ever published in this country.* Without at present entering too deeply into the question of French or English originality of invention, we are willing to allow, the composer of the English story had probably read, and might also have copied, in some passages (which are pointed out in the Notes) the legend as it existed in the Norman language. But from the variations in the tale, the complete change of time and action, the dissimilarity of the names, and the variety of circumstances and amusing details introduced so graphically by the English poet, and not exstant in the French, there is quite as much claim to originality as in the Romance of Sir Tristrem, which was unquestionably preceded by a French prototype.

The opinion, however, of Tyrwhitt, repeated by Ritson, Warton, Ellis, and Sir W. Scott, that no English Romance existed prior to the days of Chaucer, which is not a translation of some

* The late lamented and elegant scholar, the Rev. J. J. Conybeare, privately printed an analysis of the French Romance of *Octavien*, 8vo. 1816. from Ms. Hatton, 100. but did not publish the entire text.

earlier French one, must be received with considerable modification. The ancient Romance of Kyng Horn is decidedly of English growth, and this opinion, first advanced by Percy, is confirmed* by the superior judgement of Conybeare (Illustr. of A. S. Poetr. p. 237. and Price (Warton's H. E. P. V. I. p. 46.). But it may justly be asked, why should nearly all the writers on the subject of English Poetry, have united to deprive our countrymen of the merit of invention or original composition, and so constantly have referred us to a foreign source for the patterns they imitated for nearly 200 years? Is it not far more consonant to propriety and reason, to believe, that the Romances founded on English history and tradition, the scene of which is laid in Britain, such as Merlin, Morte Arthur, Sir Tristrem, Lancelot, Kyng Horn, Havelok, Guy of Warwick, &c. should be the production of English authors writing in French, rather than of Norman poets, who (as Sir W. Scott observes) can scarcely be supposed, without absurdity, to have visited the remote corners of the kingdom merely to collect or celebrate the obscure traditions of their inhabitants. Tyrwhitt is the only writer who has ventured to make this suggestion,† and he has given a long list of names of those Englishmen who are known to have written in French during the reigns of Hen. III. Edw. I. II. and III. among whom are enumerated Robert Grosthead, Peter de Langtoft, Helis de Guincestre, Hue de Roteland, and Wauter de Byblesworthe, to whom we may add Thomas of Kent, John Hoveden, Robert Bikez, Wauter de Henleye, William de Widington, Robert de

* Ritson's opinion of the antiquity of the Ms. Harl. 527. containing a portion of the French Romance, assigning it to the 12th century, is too unguardedly admitted by Price. (H. E. P. I. p. 191.) It is of the same age as Mr. Douce's Ms. containing a further portion, and both may safely be attributed to the latter half of the 13th cent.

† Essay on Chauc. p. 58. n. (55.) We had ourselves formed this opinion long previous to our knowledge of Tyrwhitt's sentiments, and propose at some future period, to examine the question more at large, by an analysis and illustrations of the French Romances on English traditions, still remaining in Ms.

Graham, the author of the Life of St. Tobias, and many others. Hue de Roteland is avowedly the author of the French text of Ypomedon;* Thomas of Kent is quoted as one of the authors of the French Romance of Alexander, in De Bure's *Catal. de La Valliere*, T. II. p. 158. and we cannot help suspecting, that the same person was the author of the French Sir Tristrem, and of the French Kyng Horn, in both of which a *Tomas* is named as the author, and in the latter are many proofs of its being written by an Englishman.† In the highly curious and unique Latin Romance of Waldiff, King of East Anglia, or (as it is elsewhere called) King Attla, preserved in Bennet College library, No. CCCXXIX. (Sæc. 15.)‡ the translator, Johannes Bramis, monk of Thetford, positively asserts it to have been originally composed in English, and thence turned into French verse (a copy of which is in Mr. Heber's library); but considerable liberties having been taken with the English text, the author of the Latin version was induced to translate it again from the English. It is sufficient therefore on these grounds to conjecture, that the French text of Havelok might also have been composed by a native of Britain.

The writer of the English text was undoubtedly a native of the district formerly comprised under the name of Mercia. We can even advance one step further, and assert him to have been an inhabitant of Lincolnshire, as appears not only from the phraseology, founded upon what Dr. Whitaker calls the Mercno-Saxon, but also from the evidence of the writer, in which he says of Lincoln:

> And hwan he cam unto the borw,
> Shamelike ben led ther thoru,
> Bi southe the borw, unto a grene,
> That thare is yet, als Y wene.—v. 2826.

The age of the poem is the next consideration, and we think it

* Ms. Cott. Vesp. A. VII.

† See Notes, p. 192. and Gloss. in v. WITE.

‡ V. Nasm. p. 348. He calls it "Historia fabulosa, in qua, tempore Britonum, Normanniæ et Saracenorum mentio." There might very probably be found some mention of Havelok in it, if examined.

will be admitted, without difficulty, to rank among the earliest specimens of our Romance-Poetry, and to possess equal claims to antiquity with Kyng Horn or Sir Tristrem. The great names of Hickes and Warton have unfortunately been the cause of so many errors in forming an opinion of the relative age of our early poetry, that we must still deplore the want of a work on the subject, supported by the authority of Mss. and founded on a sober and patient investigation of the progress of the English language. The notices by which we are enabled to trace the rise of our national poetry from the Saxon period to the end of the 12th century, are few and scanty. We may, indeed, comprise them all in the Song of Canute recorded by the monk of Ely,[1] (who wrote after 1166.) the words put into the mouth of Aldred, Archbishop of York, who died in 1069.[2] the verses ascribed to St. Godric, the hermit of Finchale, who died in 1170.[3] the few lines preserved by Lambarde and Camden, attributed to the same period,[4] and the prophecy said to have been set up at Here, in the year 1189. as recorded by Benedict Abbas, Roger Hoveden, and the Chronicle of Lanercost.[5] To the same reign of Hen. II. are to be assigned the metrical compositions of [6]Layamon and [7]Orm, and also the legends of St. Katherine, St. Margaret, and St. Julian,[8] with some few others, from which we may learn with tolerable accuracy the state of the language at that time, and its gradual formation from the Saxon to the shape it subsequently assumed. From this period to the middle of the next century, nothing occurs to which we can affix any certain date, but we shall probably not err in ascribing to that interval the poems ascribed to John de Guldevorde,[9] the Biblical History,[1] and poetical Paraphrase of the Psalms,[2] quoted by Warton, and the Moral Ode published by Hickes.[3]

[1] Hist. Elyens. p. 505. ap. Gale
[2] W. Malmesb. De gest. Pont. l. 3. p. 271.
[3] Rits. Bibliogr. Poet.
[4] Rits. Anc. Songs, Diss. p. xxviii.
[5] Rits. Metr. Rom. Diss. p. lxxiii.
[6] Ms. Cott. Cal. A. ix. and Otho, C. xiii.
[7] Ms. Jun. 1
[8] Ms. Bodl. 34.
[9] Mss. Cott. Cal. A. ix. Jes. Coll. Oxon 29.
[1] Ms. Bennet, Cant. R. 11.
[2] Mss. Cott Vesp. D vii. Coll. Benn. Cant. O. 6. Bodl. 921.
[3] Mss. Digb. 4. Jes. Coll. Oxon 29.

Between the years 1244. and 1258. we know, was written the versification of part of a meditation of St. Augustine, as proved by the age of the Prior who gave the Ms. to the Durham library.[4] Soon after this time also were composed the earliest songs in Ritson and Percy, (1264) with a few more pieces it is unnecessary to particularise. This will bring us to the close of Henry III. reign, and beginning of his successor's, the period assigned by our poetical antiquaries to the Romances of Sir Tristrem, Kyng Horn, and Kyng Alisaunder, and which we think Havelok, on very fair grounds, is intitled to claim. But as the language could not perceptibly change within twenty or thirty years, we should have no objection to fix its composition between the years 1270—1290. and there are some circumstances in the poem (explained in the Notes) which would strengthen this probability.

It is rather a singular circumstance, and worthy of remark, that the same names found in the Romance of Havelok are also found in the French Fragments of Kyng Horn. Thus, Aaluf is said to be the nephew of Bauderolf, by his daughter *Goldeburc*, v. 258. and the wife of king Gudereche of Ireland bears the same name, v. 2382. one of whose daughters is called *Leiuiue* (Comp. Havelok, v. 2914.) The name of Horn's mother is *Samburc*, or *Suanburc*. (Comp. Hav. v. 411.) A king *Houlac* is also mentioned in *Horne Childe*, ap. Rits. Metr. Rom. v. 3. These coincidences might at first lead us to suppose some connexion existed between the Romances of Horn and Havelok, but an attentive examination of both has convinced us to the contrary.

The popularity of the Romance of Havelok must have been considerable, since we not only find it quoted by several of the early Chroniclers (as we have before shewn), but also by the anonymous translator of Colonna,* ranked together with the most famous Romances of antiquity.

[4] Ms. Eccl. Dun. A. III. 12. and Bodl. 42.

* Ms. Laud. 595. (Sæc. 15.) It is falsely, by a recent hand, attributed to Lydgate, from whose Troy Book it totally differs.

Many speken of men that romaunces rede,
That were sumtyme doughti in dede,
The while that God hem lyff lente,
That now ben dede, and hennes wente.
Off Bevis, Gy, and of Gauwayn,
Off kyng Richard & of Owayn,
Off Tristram & of Percyuale,
Off Rouland Ris and Aglauale,
Off Archeroun and of Octauian,
Off Charles & of Cassibaldan,
Off HAUELOK, Horne, & of Wade,
In Romaunces that of hem ben made,
That gestoures often dos of hem gestes
At mangeres and at grete festes.
Here dedis ben in remembraunce
In many fair Romaunce, &c.—f. 1.

This Romance, in all probability, was addressed to the same class of people for whom Robert of Brunne wrote his Chronicle, and composed also by one not conversant with the Court; for, as Sir W. Scott has remarked, the English language when first adapted to the purposes of poetry, was abandoned to the peasants, whilst the nobles listened to the Lais, Romances, and Fabliaux of Norman(?) trouveurs. Hence we may understand why Robert of Brunne speaks of it as written by "lowed men." It constitutes, perhaps, its greatest singularity and value, that it presents the only instance exstant of a Romance written for the "comonalty," exhibiting faithfully, in the vernacular dialect, the language, habits, and manners of the period. In this respect it is of infinitely greater importance to the Glossographist, than either Sir Tristrem or Kyng Horn, and also infinitely more amusing, and in either view will prove no small addition to our present stock of ancient English literature. In point of style, the Romance will bear comparison with any other composition of that age, and is, in many respects, superior to every specimen we possess prior to the time of Langland and Chaucer. The minuteness of detail is not such as to weary, while the attention is continually kept up by the change of person or scene. As a fair specimen of the author's real poetical feeling, may be adduced the following lines:

> The heu is swilk in here ler,
> So the rose in roser,
> *Hwan it is fayr sprad ut newe*
> *Ageyn the sunne, brith and lewe.*—v. 2918.

with which may be compared the verses of Chaucer, *Compl. of the Black Knight:*

> And that the flowers of mani divers hue
> Upon her stalkes *gonne for to spread*
> *And for to splaye out her leves in brede*
> *Again the sun,* gold-burned in his sphere,
> That downe to hem cast his beames clear.

The orthography of Havelok approaches very nearly to that of Sir Tristrem and Kyng Horn, as will be evident on comparing the Glossaries of each. Similar liberties are also taken in the rhythm, and in the elision of letters, which characterise the English poetry of the 13th and 14th centuries, and serve to mark its progress from the accentuated prose of the Saxons. The more striking peculiarity is the omission of a final letter, as *d* in *shel, hel, hon, bihel,* &c. *r* in *the, neythe, othe, douthe,* &c. *l.* in *mike,* &c. From the same license arises the frequent repetition of such rhythm as *riden* and *side,* where the final *n* seems to have been suppressed in pronunciation. Cf. v. 29. 172. 253. 954. 1102. 1179. 2237. &c. and hence we perceive how readily the infinitive verbal Saxon termination glided into its subsequent form. The broad pronunciation of the dialect in which the poem was written, is also frequently discernible, as in *slawen,* v. 2496. and *knaue,* v. 946. which rhyme to *Rauen* and *plawe.* So likewise, *bothe* or *bethe* is, in sound, equivalent to *rede,* v. 200. 360. 430. 1496. Cognate letters are sometimes analogous in pronunciation, as *yer* and *del,* v. 1329. *feld* and *swerd,* v. 1640. 2455. A stranger license is taken in the instance of *fet* and *ek,* v. 1300. but may be explained on similar principles.

See Gloss. in v. KAYN. Many words also are strongly aspirated, as *held, hevere, hend, hinne, his, hwan, wrobberes,* &c. which will be more particularly noticed in the Glossary.

III. It now remains to describe the Mss. which have been followed in editing the contents of the present Volume. The English text of Havelok forms a portion of a Ms. among the Laudian Collection in the Bodleian library, formerly marked K. 60. and at present No. 108. It is a folio, written very fairly on vellum, and to judge from the character, about, or a few years previous to, A. D. 1300. In the old printed Catalogue it is described merely as *Vitæ Sanctorum,* (which is one cause of the Romance being so long overlooked), and indeed the greater part of the Ms. is occupied by those Metrical Legends, (compiled probably in imitation of the *Aurea Legenda* of Jacobus de Voragine,) which Hearne, rather wildly, conjectured to have been written by Robert of Brunne, and which, with the exception of the Lives of St. Margaret and St. Winifred, printed by Hickes and Bishop Fleetwood, and the excerpts given by Hearne, and Warton, are yet unpublished. If we might hasard a conjecture as to the author, we would rather fix on the person who wrote the Chronicle called Robert of Gloucester's,* than any other, so far as identity of style enables us to judge. At all events, they were not written much earlier than 1290. but certainly not later. The only internal evidence is presented by the Lives of St. Edmund of Pounteneye, and St. Dominic. The former died in 1242. and was canonised in 1248. His metrical history is translated from the Latin legend written by Robert Riche, the Archbishop's brother. In the Life of St. Dominic, he is falsely stated to have died in 1281 This date, however, is corrected in three other

* Tho. Hearne, and all his followers, " servile pecus," fix the death of Rob. of Gloucester soon after 1278. which is the latest date they could find in his Chronicle. But it is singular how they could all contrive to overlook the express mention in p. 531. of the Canonisation of St. Louis, which did not take place till 1297. consequently the work must have been completed after that period.

(but all more recent) copies we have examined, (Laud. 463. Bodl. 779. and Ms. Vernon.) to the real time of his death, 1221. But as mention is made in the legend of the son of Simon de Montfort, slain at the Battle of Evesham in 1264. it is clear to us, that the anachronism was originally made through ignorance, and the alteration of the date has only made the blunder more apparent. These Lives or Festivals are 61. in number, in the Laudian Ms. 108. (with a list of 31. omissions added by a recent hand) written in long Alexandrine verse. Then succeed the Sayings of St. Bernard, and the Visions of St. Paul, both in six line stanzas; the *Disputatio inter Corpus et Animam,* the **English Romance of Havelok,** the Romance of *Kyng Horn,* and some additions in a hand of the 15th century, including the Lives of St. Blaise, St. Cecilia, and St. Alexius, and an alliterative poem intitled *Somer Soneday,* making in all the Contents of the Volume to amount to 70. pieces.

The character of the Ms. may be judged of better from the annexed fac-simile of the first sixteen lines of the folio on which Havelok commences, written in double columns. The rubric has been nearly cut off by the Vandal who bound the Ms.

... aueloc quondam Rex Anglie. ... Et Denemarchie.

Herknet to me gode men	Of red gold upon hys lac
Wiues maydnes and alle men	In a male with hoz blac
Of a tale yat ich you wile telle	Ne funde he non yat him misseyde
Wo so it wile here and yer-to duelle	With iuele on hond leyde
Ye tale is of Hauelok i-maked	Yane micthe chapmen fare
Wil he was litel he yede ful naked	Yuruth englond wit here ware
Hauelok was a ful god gome	And balde bije and selle
He was ful god in eueri trome	Oueral yer he wilen dwellen

* Other copies are in Mss. Harl. 2277. Ashm. 507. Trin. Coll. Oxon. 57. Bennet Coll. Cant. 145.

The French text of the Romance is transcribed from a Ms. in the Herald's College, marked E. D. N. No. 14. 4to. vell. written in double col. at the commencement of Edw. II. reign, and containing the Brut of Wace, with the Continuation of Gaimar, to which the Romance is annexed; together with some other pieces it is unnecessary to enumerate. A Ms. of Sir Thomas Phillipp's, Bart. of Middle Hill, Gloucestershire, contains the same text, with two other uniqne Poems, intitled *Le Lai del Desire*, and the *Romanz des Cles*. It is written on vellum, about the same period as the last, and is conjectured to have once belonged to Wilton Abbey. The original we have not seen.

The abridgement of this Text by Gaimar, is taken from Ms. Reg. 13. A. xxi. in the British Museum, which is a folio, on vell. written in double col. about the middle of the 13th century. The Ms. is unfortunately defective where the Romance commences, but the passages wanting have been supplied from copies of the same Chronicle preserved in the Cathedral libraries of Lincoln and Durham. Ritson had noticed the story from the Royal Ms. and calls it " a great curiosity, though too imperfect" to publish. This deficiency being now remedied, its value may be estimated proportionately higher.

In copying from these Mss. the Editor has scrupulously adhered to the orthography of each, and has only assumed the liberty, authorised by every one who has preceded him in the task, of introducing marks of punctuation, of dividing or uniting words improperly connected or disjoined by the scribe, of occasionally correcting the errors occasioned by a letter manifestly false, as, in the English Romance, *th* (þ) for *w* (ƿ), *y* for *th* (þ), and *vice versa*, and of substituting Capital letters for smaller ones, when required. The Saxon forms also of ẏ, ƿ, and þ have been replaced by the more modern equivalents of *y*, *w*, and *th*, as tending to render the English poem more intelligible, and less difficult to read. With these exceptions, the transcripts will be found to correspond literally with their respective originals.

A few words are necessary on the mode of compilation adopted in the Glossary, in which it has been the Editor's object to follow, as far as possible, the examples of Tyrwhitt and Chalmers, and to produce what might be considered an additional contribution towards that great desideratum A DICTIONARY OF THE OLD ENGLISH LANGUAGE. With the above writers, Etymology has been considered as a pursuit exceeding the bounds prescribed to a Glossarist, unless fixed on some firm and certain basis, and on that account it has been deemed sufficient simply to indicate the root, (except in doubtful or rare cases of its use), and in instances where the derivation is uncertain, it has been left to the researches of future Glossographers. The use of a Glossary formed on a grammatical basis, and illustrated by examples, has long been known to the writer, but the difficulties of composing it must be obvious to all who have ever made the attempt, and on that account some indulgence is craved for the present performance. A few terms still remain, the sense of which is left unexplained. Some of these are doubtless to be attributed to the blunders of the scribe, but there are others, which, until our knowledge of the ancient English language becomes more extended, must be still reserved for the discoveries of future laborers in the same path with ourselves.

In conclusion, the Editor has to express his grateful sense of the obligations laid on him by the kindness of the Rev. BULKELEY BANDINEL, D. D. and the Rev. PHILIP BLISS, D. C. L. Librarians of the Bodleian, as well for the permission to transcribe the English Text of the Romance, as for the unvaried attention and assistance he has ever experienced, in the course of his researches in the Bodleian and Collegiate libraries. To THOMAS YOUNG, Esq. York Herald, and Registrar of the College of Arms, his thanks are not less due for the facility granted in inspecting the historical Mss. there deposited, and the liberty to copy the French Romance. To HENRY PETRIE, Esq. Keeper of the Records in the Tower, for the loan of his collations of the Durham and Lincoln Mss. the Editor begs his sincerest acknowledgements. To Sir THOMAS PHILLIPPS,

Bart. for the similar loan of a transcript of a Ms. in his possession containing the French Text; to FRANCIS DOUCE, Esq. for leave to transcribe the very curious French fragment of Kyng Horn, in his valuable library; to the Rev. G. OLIVER, for the donation of his publication on Grimsby, for impressions of the ancient Corporation Seals, and for the communication of some interesting local traditions; to Professor RASK, of Copenhagen, for information relating to the Scandinavian Historians; and to the Rev. Dr. D'OYLY, Librarian to his Grace the Archbishop of Canterbury, for permission to inspect the Ms. of Rob. of Brunne, in the Lambeth library;—to all and each the Editor feels he is materially indebted for the illustration and improvement of his undertaking.

Lastly, to the Members of **The Roxburghe Club**, to whose liberal encouragement of Ancient English Literature the present publication owes its appearance, the Editor most respectfully offers his thanks, conscious as he is, that whatever curiosity or value the volume may possess, it is wholly to their patronage he is indebted for the opportunity of now presenting it to the world.

F. MADDEN.

British Museum,
July 11, 1828.

HAVELOK.

Incipit vita Hauelok, quondam Rex Anglie et Denemarchie.

[fol. 204. col. 1.]

Herknet to me gode men,
Wiues, maydnes, and alle men,
Of a tale that ich you wile telle,
Wo so it wile here, and ther to duelle.
The tale is of Hauelok i-maked;
Wil he was litel he yede ful naked:
Hauelok was a ful god gome,
He was ful god in eueri trome,
He was the wicteste man at nede,
That thurte riden on ani stede.
That ye mowen nou y-here,
And the tale ye mowen y-lere.
At the [1]beginning of vre tale,
Fil me a cuppe of ful god ale;
And wile drinken her Y spelle,
That Crist vs shilde alle fro helle!

[1] Beginnig, Ms.

Krist late vs heuere so for to do,
That we moten comen him to,
And wit that it mote ben so!
Benedicamus domino!
Here Y schal biginnen a rym,
Krist us yeue wel god fyn!
The rym is maked of Hauelok,
A stalworthi man in a flok;
He was the stalwortheste man at nede,
That may riden on ani stede.
It was a king bi are dawes,
That in his time were gode lawes
He dede maken, an ful wel holden;
Hym louede yung, him louede holde,
Erl and barun, dreng and kayn,
Knict, bondeman, and swain,
Wydues, maydnes, prestes and clerkes,
And al for hise gode werkes.
He louede God with al his micth,
And holi kirke, and soth, ant ricth;
Rirth-wise men he louede alle,
And oueral made hem for to calle;
Wreieres and wrobberes made he falle,
And hated hem so man doth galle;
Vtlawes and theues made he bynde,
Alle that he micthe fynde,
And heye hengen on galwe-tre;
For hem ne yede gold ne fe.

In that time a man that bore
[Wel fyfty pundes, Y woth, or more,][2]
[col. 2.] Of red gold upon hijs bac,
In a male with or blac,
Ne funde he non that him misseyde,
N[e] with iuele on hond leyde.
Thanne micthe chapmen fare
Thuruth Englond wit here ware,
And baldelike beye and sellen,
Oueral ther he wilen dwellen,
In gode burwes, and ther fram;
Ne funden he non that dede hem sham,
That he ne weren sone to sorwe brouth,
An pouere maked, and browt to nouth.
Thanne was Engelond ath ayse;
Michel was svich a king to preyse,
That held so Englond in grith!
Krist of heuene was him with.
He was Engelondes blome;
Was non so bold lond to rome,
That durste upon his bringhe
Hunger, ne here wicke thinghe.
Hwan he felede hise foos,
He made hem lurken, and crepen in wros;
The hidden hem alle, and helden hem stille,
And diden al his herte wille.

[2] Supplied from conjecture. Cf. v. 653. 787. A few more instances will be found where a similar liberty has been taken, for the purpose of completing the sense.

Ricth he louede of alle thinge,
To wronge micht him no man bringe,
Ne for siluer, ne for gold :—
So was he his soule hold.
To the federles was he rath,
Wo so dede hem wrong or lath,
Were it clerc, or were it knicth,
He dede hem sone to hauen ricth ;
And wo diden widuen wrong,
Were he neuere knicth so strong,
That he ne made him sone kesten,
And in feteres ful faste festen ;
And wo so dide maydne shame
Of hire bodi, or brouth in blame,
Bute it were bi hire wille,
He[3] made him sone of limes spille.
He[4] waste beste knith at nede,
That heuere micthe riden on stede,
Or wepne wagge, or folc vt lede ;
Of knith ne hauede he neuere drede,
That he ne sprong forth so sparke of glede,
[f. 204. b. col. 1.] And lete him of hise hand dede
Hw he couthe with wepne spede ;
And other he refte him hors or wede,
Or made him sone handes sprede,
And " Louerd, merci !" loude grede.
He was large, and no wicth guede ;
Hauede he non so god brede,

[3] Ke, Ms. [4] Ke, Ms.

Ne on his bord non so god [5]sbrede,
That he ne wolde thorwit fede,
Poure that on fote yede;
For to hauen of him the mede
That for vs wolde on rode blede,
Crist, that al kan wisse and rede,
That euere woneth in ani thede.
The king was hoten Athelwold,
Of word, of wepne he was bold;
In Engeland was neure knicth,
That betere hel the lond to ricth.
Of his bodi ne hauede he eyr
Bute a mayden swithe fayr,
That was so yung that sho ne couthe
Gon on fote, ne speke wit mouthe.
Than him tok an iuel strong,
That he we[l] wiste, and underfong,
That his deth was comen him on:
And seyde, " Crist, wat shal Y don!
Louerd, wat shal me to-rede!
I woth ful wel ich haue mi mede.
W shal nou mi douhter fare?
Of hire haue ich michel kare;
Sho is mikel in mi thouth,
Of me self is me rith nowt.
No selcouth is thou me be wo;
Sho ne kan speke, ne sho kan go.

[5] *F.* shrede. *V. Gloss.*

Yif scho couthe on horse ride,
And a thousande men bi hire syde;
And sho were comen intil helde,
And Engelond sho couthe welde;
And don hem of thar hire were queme,
An hire bodi couthe yeme;
Ne wolde me neuere iuele like,
Me thou ich were in heuene riche!"
Quanne he hauede this pleinte maked,
Ther after stronglike [he] quaked.
He sende writes sone onon
[col. 2.] After his erles euere ich on;
And after hise baruns, riche and poure,
Fro Rokesburw al into Douere.
That he shulden comen swithe
Til him, that was ful vnblithe;
To that stede the he lay,
In harde bondes, nicth and day.
He was so faste wit yuel fest,
That he ne mouthe hauen no rest;
He ne mouthe no mete hete,
Ne he ne mouchte no lythe gete;
Ne non of his iuel that couthe red;
Of him ne was nouth buten ded.
Alle that the writes herden,
Sorful an sori til him ferden;
He wrungen hondes, and wepen sore,
And yerne preyden Cristes hore,

That he turnen him
Vt of that yuel that was so grim!
Thanne he weten comen alle
Bifor the king into the halle,
At Winchestre ther he lay:
"Welcome," he seyde, "be ye ay!
Ful michel thank kan [Y] yow
That ye aren comen to me now!"
Quanne he weren alle set,
And the king aueden i-gret,
He greten, and gouleden, and gouen hem ille,
And he bad hem alle ben stille;
And seyde, "That greting helpeth nouth,
For al to dede am ich brouth.
Bute nov ye sen that I shal deye,
Nou ich wille you alle preye
Of mi douther that shal be
Yure leuedi after me,
Wo may yemen hire so longe,
Bothen hire and Engelonde,
Til that she winan of helde,
And tha she mowe yemen and welde?"
He ansuereden, and seyden anon,
Bi Crist and bi seint Ion,
That therl Godrigh of Cornwayle
Was trewe man, wituten faile;
Wis man of red, wis man of dede,
And men haueden of him mikel drede.

[fol. 205. col. 1.]

" He may hire alther-best yeme,
Til that she mowe wel ben quene."
The king was payed of that rede;
A wol fair cloth bringen he dede,
And ther on leyde the messebok,
The caliz, and the pateyn ok,
The corporaus, the messe-gere;
Ther on he garte the erl suere,
That he sholde yemen hire wel,
Withuten lac, wituten tel,
Til that she were [6] tuelf winter hold,
And of speche were bold;
And that she covthe of curteysye
Gon, and speken of luue drurye;
And til that she louen mithe,
Wom so hire to gode thoucte;
And that he shulde hire yeue
The best man that micthe liue,
The beste, fayreste, the strangest ok:—
That dede he him sweren on the bok.
And thanne shulde he Engelond
Al bitechen into hire hond.
Onanne that was sworn on his wise,
The king dede the mayden arise,
And the erl hire bitaucte,
And al the lond he euere awcte;
Engelonde eueri del;
And preide, he shulde yeme hire wel.

[6] *Qu.* tuenti. *Cf.* v. 259.

The king ne mowcte don no more,
But yerne preyede Godes ore;
And dede him hoslen wel and shriue,
I woth, fif hundred sithes and fiue;
An ofte dede him sore swinge,
And wit hondes smerte dinge;
So that the blod ran of his fleys,
That tendre was, and swithe neys.
[7]And sone gaf it euere il del;
He made his quiste swithe wel.
Wan it was gouen ne micte men finde
So mikel men micte him in winde,
Of his in arke, ne in chiste,
In Engelond that noman wiste:
For al was youen, faire and wel,
That him was leued no catel.
Thanne he hauede ben ofte [8]swungen,
[col. 2.] Ofte shriuen, and ofte dungen,
In manus tuas, [9]loude he seyde,
Her that he the speche leyde.
To Ihesu Crist bigan to calle,
And deyede biforn his heymen alle.
Than he was ded there micte men se
The meste sorwe that micte be;
Ther was sobbing, siking, and sor,
Handes wringing, and drawing bi hor.

[7] Some lines appear to be wanting here.
[8] Swugen, Ms.
[9] *Qu.* Louerde.

Alle greten swithe sore,
Riche and poure that there wore;
An mikel sorwe haueden alle,
Leuedyes in boure, knictes in halle.
Quan that sorwe was somdel laten,
And he haueden longe graten,
Belles deden he sone ringen,
Monkes and prestres messe singen;
And sauteres deden he manie reden,
That God self shulde his soule leden
Into heuene, biforn his sone,
And ther wituten hende wone.
Than he was to the erthe brouth,
The riche erl ne foryat nouth,
That he ne dede al Engelond
Sone sayse intil his hond;
And in the castels lechhe do
The knictes he micte tristen to.
And alle the Englis dede he swere,
That he shulden him ghod fey beren.
He yaf alle men, that god thoucte,
Liuen and deyen til that him moucte,
Til that the kinges dowter wore
Tuenti winti hold, and more.
Thanne he hauede taken this oth
Of erles, baruns, lef and loth,
Of knictes, cherles, fre and thewe,
Justises dede he maken newe,

Al Englelond to faren thorow,
Fro Douere into Rokesborw.
Schireues he sette, bedels, and greyues,
Grith-sergeans, wit longe gleyues,
To yemen wilde wodes and pathes
Fro wicke men, that wolde don scathes;
And for to hauen alle at his cri,
At his wille, at his merci;
[f. 205. b. col. 1.] That non durste ben him ageyn,
Erl ne barun, knict ne sweyn.
Wislike for soth, was him wel
Of folc, of wepne, of castel.
Sothlike, in a lite thrawe
Al Engelond of him stod awe;
Al Engelond was of him adred,
So his the beste fro the gad.
The kinges douther bigan thriue,
And wex the fayrest wman on liue.
Of alle thewes [1]w she wis,
That gode weren, and of pris.
The mayden Goldeboru was hoten;
For hire was mani a ter i-groten.
Quanne the Erl Godrich him herde
Of that mayden, hw we[l] [2]he ferde;
Hw wis sho was, w chaste, hw fayr,
And that sho was the riche eyr
Of Engelond, of al the rike:—
Tho bigan Godrich to sike,

[1] *Qu.* was she. [2] *F.* she.

And seyde, " Wether she sholde be
Quen and leuedi ouer me?
Hwether sho sholde al Engelond,
And me, and mine, hauen in hire hond?
Datheit hwo it hire thaue!
Shal sho it neuere more haue.
Sholde ic yeue a fol a therne,
Engelond, thou sho it yerne?
Datheit hwo it hire yeue,
Euere more hwil I liue!
Sho is waxen al to prud,
For gode metes, and noble shrud,
That hic haue youen hire to offte;
Hic haue yemed hire to softe.
Shal it nouth ben als sho thenkes,
Hope maketh fol man ofte blenkes.
Ich haue a son, a ful fayr knaue,
He shal Engelond al haue.
He shal [ben] king, he shal ben sire,
So brouke I euere mi blake swire!"
Hwan this trayson was al thouth,
Of his oth ne was him nouth.
He let his oth al ouer ga,
Therof ne yaf he nouth a stra;
But sone dede hire fete,
[col. 2.] Er he wolde heten ani mete,
Fro Winchestre ther sho was,
Also a wicke traytur Iudas;

And dede leden hire to Doure,
That standeth on the [3]sei soure;
And ther hinne dede hire fede
Pourelike in feble wede.
The castel dede he yemen so,
That non ne micte comen hire to
Of hire frend, with to speken,
That heuere micte hire bale wreken.
Of Goldeboru shul we nou laten,
That nouth ne blinneth for to graten,
Thet sho liggeth in prisoun:
Ihesu Crist, that Lazarun
To liue broucte, fro dede bondes,
He lese hire wit hise hondes;
And leue sho mo him y se
Heye hangen on galwe tre,
That hire haued in sorwe brouth,
So as sho ne misdede nouth!
Sa we nou forth in hure spelle,
In that time, so it bifelle,
Was in the lon of Denemark
A riche king, and swythe stark.
Th[e] name of him was Birkabeyn,
He hauede mani knict and sueyn;
He was fayr man, and wicth,
Of bodi he was the best knicth
That euere micte leden uth here,
Or stede onne ride, or handlen spere.

[3] se is oure, Ms.

Thre children he hauede bi his wif,
He hem louede so his lif.
He hauede a sone, douhtres two,
Swithe fayre, as fel it so.
He that wile non forbere,
Riche ne poure, king ne kaysere,
Deth him tok than he bes wolde
Liuen, but hyse dayes were fulde;
That he ne moucte no more liue,
For gol ne siluer, ne for no gyue.
Hwan he that wiste, rathe he sende
After prestes fer an hende,
Chanounes gode, and monkes bothe,
Him [4]for to wisse, and to rede;
[fol. 206. col. 1.] Him for to hoslon, an for to shriue,
Hwil his bodi were on liue.
Hwan he was hosled and shriuen,
His quiste maked, and for him gyuen,
His knictes dede he alle site,
For thorw hem he wolde wite,
Hwo micte yeme hise children yunge,
Til that he kouthen speken wit tunge;
Speken and gangen, on horse riden,
Knictes and sweynes bi [5]hete siden.
He spoken ther offe, and chosen sone
A riche man was, under mone
Was the trewest that he wende,
Godard, the kinges oune frende;

[4] fort, Ms. [5] *Qu.* here. Cf. v. 127.

And seyden, he moucthe hem best loke,
Yif that he hem vndertoke,
Til hise sone mouthe bere
Helm on heued, and leden vt here;
In his hand a spere stark,
And king ben maked of Denemark.
He wel trowede that he seyde,
And ou Godard handes leyde;
And seyde, "Here biteche I the
Mine children alle thre,
Al Denemark, and al mi fe,
Til that mi sone of helde be;
But that ich wille, that tho suere
On auter, and on messe-gere,
On the belles that men ringes,
On messe bok the prest on singes,
That thou mine children shalt we[l] yeme,
That hire kin be ful wel queme,
Til mi sone mowe ben knicth,
Thanne biteche him tho his ricth,
Denemark, and that thertil longes,
Casteles and tunes, wodes and wonges."
Godard stirt up, and sweor al that
The king him bad, and sithen sat
Bi the knictes, that ther ware,
That wepen alle swithe sare
For the king that deide sone:
Ihesu Crist, that makede mone

On the mirke nich to shine,
Wite his soule fro helle pine;
And leue that it mote wone
[col. 2.] In heuene riche [6]wrth Godes sone!
Hwan Birkabeyn was leyd in graue,
The erl dede sone take the knaue,
Hauelok, that was the eir,
Swanborow, his sister, Helfled, the tother,
And in the castel dede he hem do,
Ther non ne micte hem comen to
Of here kyn, ther thei sperd were;
Ther he greten ofte sore,
Bothe for hunger and for kold,
Or he weren thre winter hold.
Feblelike he gaf hem clothes,
He ne yaf a note of his othes;
He hem [ne] clothede rith, ne fedde,
Ne hem ne dede richelike be bedde.
Thanne Godard was sikerlike
Vnder God the moste swike,
That eure in erthe shaped was,
Withuten on, the wike Iudas.
Haue he the malisun to day
Of alle that eure speken may!
Of patriack, and of pope!
And of prest with loken kope!
Of monekes, and hermites bothe!

[6] *Qu.* with. *V. Gloss.*

And of the leue holi rode,
That God him selue ran on blode!
Crist warie him with his mouth!
Waried wrthe he of north and suth!
Offe alle man, that speken kunne!
Of Crist, that maude mone and sunne!
Thanne he hauede of al the lond
Al the folk tilled intil his hond,
And alle haueden sworen him oth,
Riche and poure, lef and loth,
That he sholden hise wille freme,
And that he shulde him nouth queme,
He thouthe a ful strong trechery,
A trayson, and a felony,
Of the children for to make:
The deuel of helle him sone take!
Hwan that was thouth, onan he ferde
To the tour ther he woren sperde,
Ther he greten for hunger and cold:
The knaue that was sumdel bold,
Kam him ageyn, on knes him sette,
[f. 206. b. col. 1.] And Godard ful feyre he ther grette;
And Godard seyde, " Wat is thw?
Hwi grete ye and goulen nou?"
" For us hungreth swithe sore:"—
Seyden he wolden more,
" We ne haue to hete, ne we ne haue
Herinne neyther knith ne knaue,

That yeueth us drinken, ne no mete,
Haluendel that we moun ete.
Wo is us that we weren born!
Weilawei! nis it no korn
That men micte maken of bred?
[7]Ths hungreth, we aren ney ded."
Godard herde here wa,
Ther offe yaf he nouth a stra,
But tok the maydnes bothe samen,
Also it were up on hijs gamen;
Also he wold with hem leyke,
That weren for hunger grene and bleike.
Of bothen he karf on two here throtes,
And sithen hem al to grotes.
Ther was sorwe wo so it sawe!
Hwan the children bith wawe
Leyen and sprauleden in the blod:
Hauelok it saw, and the bi stod.
Ful sori was that seli knaue,
Mikel dred he mouthe haue,
For at hise herte he saw a knif,
For to reuen him hise lyf.
But the [8]knaue, that litel was,
He knelede bifor that Iudas,
And seyde, "Louerd, merci nov!
Manrede, louerd, bidd I you!
Al Denemark I wile you yeue,
To that forward thú late me liue;

[7] *Qu.* Us. [8] kaue, Ms.

Here hi wile on boke swere,
That neure more ne shal I bere
Ayen the, louerd, shel ne spere,
Ne other wepne bere, that may you dere.
Louerd, haue merci of me!
To day I wile fro Denemark fle,
Ne neuere more comen ageyn:
Sweren Y wole, that Bircabein
Neuere yete me, ne gat:"—
Hwan the deuel [9]herde that,
[col. 2] Sumdel bigan him for to rewe;
Withdrou the knif, that was lewe,
Of the seli children blod;
Ther was miracle fair and god!
That he the knaue nouth ne slou,
But to rewnesse him thit drow.
Of Auelok rewede him ful sore,
And thouche he wolde that he ded wore,
Buton that he nouth wit his hend
Ne drepe him nouth, that fule fend,
Thoucte he, als he him bi [1]shod,
Starinde als he were wod:
" Yif Y late him liues go,
He micte me wirchen michel wo.
Grith ne get Y neuere mo,
He may waiten for to slo;
And yf he were brouct of liue,
And mine children wolden thriue,

[9] hede, Ms. [1] *Qu.* stod.

Louerdinges after me,
Of al Denemark micten he be.
God it wite, he shal ben ded,
Wile I taken non other red;
I shal do casten him in the [2]se,
Ther I wile that he drench be;
Abouten his hals an anker god,
That he ne flete in the flod."
Ther anon he dede sende
After a fishere that he wende,
That wolde al his wille do,
And sone anon he seyde him to:
"Grim, thou wost thu art mi thral,
Wilte don mi wille al,
That I wile bidden the,
To morwen shal maken the fre,
And aucte the yeuen, and riche make,
With than thu wilt this child take,
And leden him with the to nicht,
Than thou sest se mone lith,
Into the se, and don him ther inne,
Al wile [I] taken on me the sinne."
Grim tok the child, and bond him faste,
Hwil the bondes micte laste;
That weren of ful strong line:—
Tho was Hauelok in ful strong pine.
Wiste he neuere her wat was wo:
[fol. 207. col. 1.] Ihesu Crist, that makede to go

[2] she, Ms.

The halte, and the doumbe speken,
Hauelok the of Godard wreken!
Hwan Grim him hauede faste bounden,
And sithen in an eld cloth wnden,
A keuel of clutes ful unwraste,
That he [ne] mouthe speke, ne fnaste,
Hwere he wolde him bere or lede:
Hwan he hauede don that dede,
Hwan the swike him hauede hethede,
That he shulde him forth [lede]
And him drinchen in the se;
That forwarde makeden he.
In a poke, ful and blac,
Sone he caste him on his bac,
Ant bar him hom to hise cleue,
And bitaucte him dame Leue,
And seyde, "Wite thou this knaue,
Also thou with mi lif haue;
I shal dreinchen him in the se,
For him shole we ben maked fre,
Gold hauen ynou, and other fe;
That hauet mi louerd bihote me."
Hwan dame [Leue] herde that,
Vp she stirte, and nouth ne sat,
And caste the knaue adoun so harde,
That hise croune he ther crakede
Ageyn a gret ston, ther it lay:
Tho Hauelok micte sei, "Weilawei!

That euere was I kinges bern!"
That him ne hauede grip or ern,
Leoun or wlf, wluine or bere,
Or other best, that wolde him dere.
So lay that child to middel nicth,
That Grim bad Leue bringen lict,
For to don on his clothes:
"Ne thenkeste nowt of mine othes
That ich haue mi louerd sworen?
Ne wile I nouth be forloren.
I shal beren hem to the se,
Thou wost that houes me;
And I shal drenchen him ther inne;
Ris up swithe, an go thu binne,
And blou the fir, and lith a kandel:"
Als she shulde his clothes handel
[col. 2.] On for to don, and blawe [3] the fir,
She saw ther inne a lith ful shir,
Also brith so it were day,
Aboute the knaue ther he lay.
Of hise mouth it stod a stem,
Als it were a sunne bem;
Also lith was it ther inne,
So ther brenden cerges [4] inne:
"Ihesu Crist!" wat dame Leue
"Hwat is that lith in vre cleue!
[5] Sir up Grim, and loke wat it menes,
Hwat is the lith as thou wenes?"

[3] ther, Ms. [4] *Qu.* tenne. Cf. v. 2125. [5] *Qu.* stir, *or* stirt.

He stuten bothe up to the knaue,
For man shall god wille haue,
Vnkeuelede him, and swithe unbounden,
And sone anon him funden;
Als he tirneden of his serk,
On his rith shuldre a kyne merk;
A swithe brith, a swithe fair:
" Goddot!" quoth Grim, " this ure eir
That shal [ben] louerd of Denemark,
He shal ben king strong and stark;
He shal hauen in his hand
A[l] Denemark and Engeland;
He shal do Godard ful wo,
He shal him hangen, or quik flo;
Or he shal him al quic graue,
Of him shal he no merci haue."
Thus seide Grim, and sore gret,
And sone fel him to the fet,
And seide, " Louerd, haue merci
Of me, and Leue, that is me bi!
Louerd, we aren bothe thine,
Thine cherles, thine hine.
Lowerd, we sholen the wel fede,
Til that thu cone riden on stede,
Til that thu cone ful wel bere
Helm on heued, sheld and spere.
He ne shal neuere wite, sikerlike,
Godard, that fule swike.

Thoru other man, louerd, than thoru the,
Sal I neuere freman be.
Thou shalt me, louerd, fre maken,
For I shal yemen the, and waken;
Thoru the wile I fredom haue:"
[f. 207. b. col. 1.] Tho was Haueloc a blithe knaue.
He sat him up, and crauede bred,
And seide, "Ich am ney dede,
Hwat for hunger, wat for bondes,
That thu leidest on min hondes;
And for keuel at the laste,
That in mi mouth was thrist faste.
Y was the with so harde prangled,
That I was the with ney strangled."
"Wel is me that thu mayth hete:
Goddoth!" quath Leue, "Y shal the fete
Bred an chese, butere and milk,
Pastees and flaunes, al with suilk;
Shole we sone the wel fede,
Louerd, in this mikel nede.
Soth it is, that men seyt and suereth:
Ther God wile helpen, nouth ne dereth."
Thanne sho hauede brouth the mete,
Haueloc anon bigan to ete
Grundlike, and was ful blithe;
Couth he nouth his hunger mithe.
A lof he het, Y woth, and more,
For him hungrede swithe sore.

Thre dayes ther biforn, I wene,
Et he no mete, that was wel sene.
Hwan he hauede eten, and was fed,
Grim dede maken a ful fayr bed;
Vnclothede him, and dede him ther inne,
And seyde, "Slep sone, with muchel winne;
Slep wel faste, and dred the nouth,
Fro sorwe to ioie art thu brouth."
Sone so it was lith of day,
Grim it undertok the wey
To the wicke traitour Godard,
That was [6] Denemak a stiward,
And seyde, "Louerd, don ich haue
That thou me bede of the knaue;
He is drenched in the flod,
Abouten his hals an anker god;
He is witerlike ded,
Eteth he neure more bred;
He lith drenched in the se:—
Yif me gold, other fe,
That Y mowe riche be;
And with thi chartre make fre,
[col. 2.] For thu ful wel bihetet me,
Thanne I last spak with the."
Godard stod, and lokede on him
Thoruthlike, with eyen grim;
And seyde, "Wiltu ben erl?
Go hom swithe, fule, drit, cherl;

[6] *Qu.* Denemarkes.

Go hethen, and be euere more
Thral and cherl, als thou er wore.
Shal [thou] haue non other mede;
For litel ig do the lede
To the galues, so God me rede!
For thou haues don a wicke dede.
Thou mait stonden her to longe,
Bute thou swithe ethen gonge."
Grim thoucte to late that he ran
Fro that traytour, tha[t] wicke man;
And thoucte, "Wat shal me to rede?
Wite he him on liue, he wile bethe
Heye hangen on galwe tre:
Betere us is of londe to fle,
And berwen bothen ure liues,
And mine children, and mine wiues."
Grim solde sone al his corn,
Shep wit wolle, neth wit horn,
Hors, and swin wit berd,
The gees, the hennes of the yerd;
Al he sold, that outh douthe,
That he eure selle moucte,
And al he to the peni drou:
Hise ship he greythede wel inow,
He dede it tere, an ful wel pike,
That it ne doutede sond ne krike;
Ther inne dide a ful god mast,
Stronge kables, and ful fast,

[7] *Qu.* his, *i. e.* is.

Ores god, an ful god seyl,
Ther inne wantede nouth a nayl,
That euere he sholde ther inne do:
Hwan he hauedet greythed so,
Hauelok the yunge he dide ther inne,
Him and his wif, hise sones thrinne,
And hise two doutres, that faire wore,
And sone dede he leyn in an ore,
And drou him to the heye se,
There he mith alther-best fle.
Fro londe woren he bote a mile,
[fol. 208. col. 1.] Ne were neuere but ane hwile,
That it ne bigan a wind to rise
Out of the north, men calleth *bise*,
And drof hem intil Engelond,
That al was sithen in his hond,
His, that Hauelok was the name;
But or he hauede michel shame,
Michel sorwe, and michel tene,
And thrie, he gat it al bidene;
Als ye shulen nou forthwar [7] here,
Yf that ye wilen ther to here.
In Humber Grim bigan to lende,
In Lindeseye, rith at the north ende.
Ther sat is ship up on the sond,
But Grim it drou up to the lond;
And there he made a litel cote,
To him and to hise flote.

[7] *Qu.* lere. Cf. v. 1640.

Bigan he there for to erthe,
A litel hus to maken of erthe,
So that he wel thore were
Of here herboru herborwed there;
And for that Grim that place aute,
The stede of Grim the name laute;
So that GRIMESBI calleth alle
That ther offe speken alle,
And so shulen men callen it ay,
Bituene this and domesday.
Grim was fishere swithe god,
And mikel couthe on the flod;
Mani god fish ther inne he tok,
Bothe with neth, and with hok.
He took the sturgiun, and the qual,
And the turbut, and lax withal,
He tok the sele, and the hwel;
He spedde ofte swithe wel:
Keling he tok, and tumberel,
Hering, and the makerel,
The butte, the schulle, the thornebake:
God paniers dede he make
Ontil him, and other thrinne,
Til hise sones to beren fish inne,
Vp o-londe to selle and fonge;
Forbar he neythe tun, ne gronge,
That he ne to-yede with his ware;
Kam he neuere hom hand bare,

[col. 2.] That he ne broucte bred and sowel,
In his shirte, or in his couel;
In his poke benes and korn:—
Hise swink ne hauede be nowt forlorn.
And hwan he tok the grete laumprei,
Ful we[l] he couthe the rithe wei
To Lincolne, the gode borw;
Ofte he yede it thoru and thoru,
Til he hauede [8]wol wel sold,
And ther fore the peines told.
Thanne he com, thenne he were blithe,
For hom he brouthe fele sithe
Wastels, simenels, with the horn,
Hise pokes fulle of mele an korn,
Netes flesh, shepes, and swines,
And hemp to maken of gode lines;
And stronge ropes to hise netes,
In the se, weren he ofte setes.
Thus gate Grim him fayre ledde.
Him and his genge wel he fedde
Wel twelf winter, other more:
Hauelok was war that Grim swank sore
For his mete, and he lay at hom:
Thouthe [he] " Ich am now no grom;
Ich am wel waxen, and wel may eten
More than eure Grim may geten.
Ich ete more, bi God on liue,
Than Grim an hise children fiue!

[8] *Qu.* ful.

It ne may nouth ben thus longe,
Goddot! Y wile with the gange,
For to leren sum god to gete;
Swinken ich wolde for mi mete.
It is no shame for to swinken;
The man that may wel eten and drinken,
That nouth ne haue but on swink long,
To liggen at hom it is ful strong.
God yelde him ther ine may,
That haueth me fed to this day!
Gladlike I wile the paniers bere;
Ich woth, ne shal it me nouth dere,
They ther be inne a birthene gret,
Also heui als a neth.
Shal ich neuere lengere dwelle,
To morwe shal ich forth pelle."

[f. 208. b. col. 1.] On the morwen, hwan it was day,
He stirt up sone, and nouth ne lay;
And cast a panier on his bac,
With fish giueled als a stac;
Also michel he bar him one,
So he foure, bi mine [9]mone!
Wel he it bar, and solde it wel,
The siluer he brouthe hom il del;
Al that he ther fore tok
With held [1]ne nouth a ferthinges nok.
So yede he forth ilke day,
That he neuere at home lay.

[9] Cf. v. 1711. [1] *Qu.* he.

So wolde he his mester lere;
Bifel it so a strong dere
Bigan to rise of korn, of bred,
That Grim ne couthe no god red,
Hw he sholde his menie fede;
Of Hauelok hauede he michel drede:
For he was strong, and wel mouthe ete
More thanne heuere mouthe he gete;
Ne he ne mouthe on the se take
Neyther lenge, ne thornbake,
Ne non other fish that douthe
His meyne feden with [2]he mouthe.
Of Hauelok he hauede kare,
Hwilgat that he micthe fare;
Of his children was him nouth,
On Hauelok was al hise thouth,
And seyde, "Hauelok, dere sone,
I wene that we deye mone,
For hunger this dere is so strong,
And hure mete is uten long.
Betere is that thu henne gonge,
Than thu here dwelle longe;
Hethen thow mayt gangen to late;
Thou canst ful wel the ricthe gate
To Lincoln, the gode borw,
Thou hauest it gon ful ofte thoru,
Of me ne is me nouth a slo,
Betere is that thu thider go,

[2] *Qu.* here, *i. e.* their.

For ther is mani god man inne,
Ther thou mayt thi mete winne.
But wo is me! thou art so naked,
Of mi seyl Y wolde the were maked
A cloth, thou mithest inne gongen,
Sone, no cold that thu ne fonge."
[col. 2.] He tok the [3]shres of the nayl,
And made him a couel of the sayl,
And Hauelok dide it sone on;
Hauede [4][he] neyther hosen ne shon,
Ne none kines othe wede;
To Lincolne barfot he yede.
Hwan he kam the, he was ful wil,
Ne hauede he no frend to gangen til;
Two dayes ther fastinde he yede,
That non for his werk wolde him fede;
The thridde day herde he calle:
" Bermen, bermen, hider forth alle!"
Sprongen forth so sparke on glede,
[Of no man ne hauede he drede.][5]
Hauelok shof dun nyne or ten,
Rith amidewarde the fen,
And stute forth to the kok,
[Ther the herles mete he tok,]
That he bouthe at the brigge:
The bermen let he alle ligge,

[3] *Qu.* sheres. [4] *V. Gloss. v.* He.

[5] Cf. v. 90. Here and below an additional line seems requisite.

And bar the mete to the castel,
And gat him there a ferthing wastel.
Thet other day kepte he the ok
Swithe yerne the erles kok,
Til that he say him on the [6]bigge,
And bi him mani fishes ligge.
The herles mete hauede he bouth,
Of Cornwalie, and kalde oft:
" Bermen, bermen, hider swithe!"
Hauelok it herde, and was ful blithe,
That he herd " bermen" calle;
Alle made he hem dun falle,
That in his gate yeden and stode,
Wel sixtene laddes gode.
Als he lep the kok til,
He shof hem alle upon an hyl;
Astirte til him with his rippe,
And bigan the fish to kippe.
He bar up wel a carte lode
Of segges, laxes, of playces brode,
Of grete laumprees, and of eles;
Sparede he neyther tos ne heles,
Til that he to the castel cam,
That men fro him his birthene nam.
Than men haueden holpen him doun
With the birthene of his croun,
The kok stod, and on him low,
And thoute him stalworthe man ynow,

[6] *Qu.* brigge.

And seyde, " Wiltu ben wit me?
[fol. 209. col. 1.] Gladlike wile ich feden the;
Wel is set the mete thu etes,
And the hire that thu getes."
[7]"Goddot!" quoth he, " leue sire,
Bidde ich thou non other hire;
But yeueth me inow to ete,
Fir and water Y wile yow fete,
The fir blowe, an ful wele maken;
Stickes can ich breken and kraken,
And kindlen ful wel a fyr,
And maken it to brennan shir;
Ful wel kan ich cleuen shides,
Eles to curuen of here hides;
Ful wel kan ich dishes swilen,
And don al that ye euere wilen."
Quoth the kok, " Wile I no more;
Go thu yunder, and sit thore,
And Y shal yeue the ful fair bred,
And make the [8]broys in the led.
Sit now doun and et ful yerne:
Datheit hwo the mete werne!"
Hauelok sette him dun anon,
Also stille als a ston,
Til he hauede ful wel eten;
Tho hauede Hauelok fayre geten.
Hwan he hauede eten inow,
He kam to the welle, water up drow.

[7] Soddot, Ms   [8] *Or* broths.

And filde the a michel so ;
Bad he non ageyn him go,
But bitwen his hondes he bar it in,
A[l] him one to the kichin.
Bad he none him water to fete,
Ne fro [9] bigge to bere the mete,
He bar the turues, he bar the star,
The wode fro the brigge he bar ;
Al that euere shulden he nytte,
Al he drow, and al he citte ;
Wolde he neuere hauen rest,
More than he were a best.
Of alle men was he mest meke,
Lauhwinde ay, and blithe of speke ;
Euere he was glad and blithe,
His sorwe he couthe ful wel mithe.
[col. 2.] It ne was non so litel knaue,
For to leyken, ne for to plawe,
That he ne wode with him pleye :
The children that [1] yeden in the weie
Of him he deden al he[re] wille,
And with him leykeden here fille.
Him loueden alle, stille and bolde,
Knictes, children, yunge and holde ;
Alle him loueden, that him sowen,
Bothen heyemen and lowe.
Of him ful wide the word sprong,
Hw he was mike, hw he was strong,

[9] *Qu.* brigge. [1] yden, Ms.

Hw fayr man God him hauede maked,
But on that he was almest naked:
For he ne hauede nouth to shride,
But a kouel ful unride,
That ful [was,] and swithe wicke,
Was it nouth worth a fir sticke.
The cok bigan of him to rewe,
And bouthe him clothes, al span newe;
He bouthe him bothe hosen and shon,
And sone diden him dones on.
Hwan he was clothed, osed, and shod,
Was non so fayr under God,
That euere yete in erthe were,
Non that euere moder bere;
It was neuere man that yemede
In kinneriche, that so wel semede
King or cayser for to be,
Than he was shrid, so semed he;
For thanne he weren alle samen
At Lincolne, at the gamen,
And the erles men woren al thore,
Than was Hauelok bi the shuldren more
Than the meste that ther kam:
In armes him no man nam,
That he doune sone ne caste;
Hauelok stod ouer hem als a mast.
Als he was heie al he was long,
He was bothe stark and strong;

In Engelond [was] non hise per
Of strengthe that euere kam him ner.
Als he was strong so was he softe,
They a man him misdede ofte,
Neuere more he him misdede,
[f. 209. b. col. 1.] Ne hond on him with yuele leyde.
Of bodi was he mayden clene,
Neuere yete in game, ne in grene,
Thit hire ne wolde leyke ne lye,
No more than it were a strie.
In that time al Hengelond
Therl Godrich hauede in his hond,
And he gart komen into the tun
Mani erl, and mani barun;
And alle that liues were
In Englond, thanne wer there,
That they haueden after sent,
To ben ther at the parlement.
With hem com mani chambioun,
Mani with ladde, blac, and brown;
An fel it so, that yunge men,
Wel abouten nine or, ten,
Bigunnen the for to lake:
Thider komen bothe stronge and wayke;
Thider komen lesse and more,
That in the borw thanne weren thore;
Champiouns, and starke laddes,
Bondemen with here gaddes,

Als he comen fro the plow;
There was sembling inow:
For it ne was non horse-knaue,
Tho thei sholden in honde haue,
That he ne kam thider, the leyk to se:
Biforn here fet thanne lay a tre,
And putten with a mikel ston
The starke laddes, ful god won.
The ston was mikel, and ek greth,
And al so heui so a neth;
Grund stalwrthe man he sholde be,
That mouthe liften it to his kne;
Was ther neyther clerc, ne prest,
That mithe liften it to his brest:
Therwit putten the chaunpiouns,
That thider comen with the barouns.
Hwo so mithe putten thore
Biforn another, an inch or more,
Wore he yung, [or] wore he hold,
He was for a kempe told.
Al so the stoden, an ofte stareden
The chaunpiouns, and ek the ladden,
[col. 2.] And he maden mikel strout
Abouten the altherbeste but.
Hauelok stod, and lokede ther til,
And of puttingge he was ful wil,
For neuere yete ne saw he or
Putten the stone, or thanne thor.

Hise mayster bad him gon ther to,
Als he couthe therwith do.
Tho hise mayster it him bad,
(He was of him sore adrad,)
Therto he stirte sone anon,
And kipte up that heui ston,
That he sholde puten withe;
He putte at the firste sithe,
Ouer alle that ther wore,
Twel fote, and sumdel more.
The chaunpiouns that put sowen,
Shuldreden he ilc other, and lowen;
Wolden he no more to putting gange,
But seyde, [2]"Ye dwellen her to longe!"
This selkouth mithe nouth ben hyd,
Ful sone it was ful loude kid;
Of Hauelok, hw he warp the ston
Ouer the laddes, euerilk on;
Hw he was fayr, hw he was long,
Hw he was with, hw he was strong;
Thoruth England yede the speche,
Hw he was strong, and ek meke;
In the castel up in the halle
The knithes speken ther of alle,
So that Godrich it herde wel
The speken of Hauelok, eueri del,
Hw he was strong man, and hey,
Hw he was strong, and ek fri,

[2] Qu. We.

And thouthte Godrich, " Thoru this knaue
Shal ich Engelond al haue,
And mi sone after me;
For so I wile that it be.
The king Athelwald me dide swere
Vpon al the messe-gere,
That I shude his douthe yeue
The hexte that mithe liue,
The beste, the fairest, the strangest ok;
That gart he me sweren on the bok.
Hwere mithe I finden ani so hey
[fol. 210. col. 1.] So Hauelok is, or so sley?
Thou Y southe hethen into Ynde,
So fayr, so strong, ne mithe Y finde.
Hauelok is that ilke knaue,
That shal Goldeborw haue."
This thouthe [he] with trechery,
With traysoun, and with felony;
For he wende, that Hauelok wore
Sum cherles sone, and no more;
Ne shulde he hauen of Engelond
Onlepi forw in his hond,
With hire, that was therof eyr,
That bothe was god and swithe fair.
He wende, that Hauelok wer a thral,
Ther thoru he wende hauen al
In Engelond, that hire rith was;
He was werse than Sathanas,

That Ihesu Crist in erthe [3]shop:
Hanged worthe he on an hok!
After [4]Goldeborw sone he sende,
That was bothe fayr and hende,
And dide hire to Lincolne bringe,
Belles dede he ageyn hire ringen,
And ioie he made hire swithe mikel,
But netheles he was ful swikel.
He seyde, that he sholde hire yeue
The fayrest man that mithe liue.
She answerede, and seyde anon,
Bi Crist, and bi seint Iohan,
That hire sholde no man wedde,
Ne no man bringen to [5]hire bedde,
But he were king, or kinges eyr,
Were he neuere man so fayr.
Godrich the erl was swithe wroth,
That she swore swilk an oth,
And seyde, "Hwor thou wilt be
Quen and leuedi ouer me,
Thou shalt hauen a gadeling,
Ne shalt thou hauen non other king;
The shal spusen mi cokes knaue,
Ne shalt thou non other louerd haue.
Datheit that the other yeue
Euere more hwil I liue!
To [6]morwe ye sholen ben weddeth,
And maugre thin togidere beddeth."

[3] *Qu.* shok. [4] Goldebow, Ms. [5] *Qu.* hise. [6] mowe, Ms.

[col. 2.] Goldeborw gret, and thas hire ille,
She wolde ben ded bi hire wille.
On the morwen, hwan day was sprungen,
And day-belle at kirke rungen,
After Hauelok sente that Iudas,
That werse was thanne Sathanas:
And seyde, " Mayster, wilte wif?"
" Nay," quoth Hauelok, " bi my lif!
Hwhat sholde ich with wif do?
I ne may hire fede, ne clothe, ne sho.
Wider sholde ich wimman bringe?
I ne haue none kines thinge.
I ne haue hws, Y ne haue cote,
Ne I ne haue stikke, Y ne haue sprote,
I ne haue neyther bred ne sowel,
Ne cloth, but of an hold with couel.
This clothes, that ich onne haue,
Aren the kokes, and ich his knaue."
Godrich stirt up, and on him dong,
[With dintes swithe hard and strong.]
And seyde, " But thou hire take,
That Y wole yeuen the to make,
I shal hangen the ful heye,
Or Y shal thristen vth thin heie."
Hauelok was one, and was odrat,
And grauntede him al that he bad.
Tho sende he after hire sone,
The fayrest wymman under mone;

And seyde til hire, and slike,
That wicke thral, that foule swike:
" But thu this man understonde,
I shal flemen the of londe;
Or thou shal to the galwes renne,
And ther thou shalt in a fir brenne."
Sho was adrad, for he so thrette,
And durste nouth the spusing lette,
But they hire likede swithe ille,
Thouthe it was Goddes wille:
God, that makes to growen the korn,
Formede hire wimman to be born.
Hwan he hauede don him for drede,
That he sholde hire spusen, and fede,
And that she sholde til him holde,
Ther weren penies thicke tolde,
Mikel plente upon the bok:
He ys hire yaf, and she as tok.
[f. 210. b. col. 1.] He weren spused fayre and wel,
The messe he deden eueri del,
That fel to spusing, and god [7]clerk,
The erchebishop uth of Yerk,
That kam to the parlement,
Als God him hauede thider sent.
Hwan he weren togydere in Godes lawe,
That the folc ful wel it sawe,
He ne wisten hwat he mouthen,
Ne he ne wisten wat hem douthe;

[7] clek, Ms.

Ther to dwellen, or thenne to gonge,
Ther ne wolden he dwellen longe,
For he wisten, and ful wel sawe,
That Godrich hem hatede, the deuel him hawe!
And yf he dwelleden ther outh,
(That fel Hauelok ful wel on thouth,)
Men sholde don his leman shame,
Or elles bringen in wicke blame.
That were him leuere to ben ded,
For thi he token another red,
That thei sholden thenne fle
Til Grim, and til hise sones thre;
Ther wenden he alther-best to spede,
Hem for to clothe, and for to fede.
The lond he token under fote,
Ne wisten he non other bote,
And helden ay the rithe [wey]
Til he komen to Grimesby.
Thanne he komen there, thanne was Grim ded,
Of him ne haueden he no red;
But hise children alle fyue
Alle weren yet on liue;
That ful fayre ayen hem neme,
Hwan he wisten that he keme,
And maden ioie swithe mikel,
Ne weren he neuere ayen hem fikel.
On knes ful fayre he hem setten,
And Hauelok swithe fayre gretten,

And seyden, " Welkome, louerd dere!
And welkome be thi fayre fere!
Blessed be that ilke thrawe,
That thou hire toke in Godes lawe!
Wel is hus we sen the on lyue,
Thou mithe us bothe selle and yeue;
Thou mayt us bothe yeue and selle,
[col. 2.] With that thou wilt here dwelle.
We hauen, louerd, alle gode,
Hors, and neth, and ship on flode,
Gold, and siluer, and michel auchte,
That Grim ure fader us bitawchte.
Gold, and siluer, and other fe
Bad he us bitaken the.
We hauen shep, we hauen swin,
Bi leue her, louerd, and al be thin;
Tho shalt ben louerd, thou shalt ben syre,
And we sholen seruen the and hire;
And hure sistres sholen do
Al that euere biddes sho;
He sholen hire clothen, washen, and wringen,
And to hondes water bringen;
He sholen bedden hire and the,
For leuedi wile we that she be."
Hwan he this ioie haueden maked,
Sithen stikes broken and kraked,
And the fir brouth on brenne,
Ne was ther spared gos ne henne,

Ne the hende, ne the drake,
Mete he deden plente make;
Ne wantede there no god mete,
Wyn and ale deden he fete,
And made hem glade and blithe,
Wesseyl ledden he fele sithe.
On the nith, als Goldeborw lay,
Sory and sorwful was she ay,
For she wende she were bi swike
That shere yeuen unkyndelike.
O-nith saw she ther inne a lith,
A swithe fayr, a swithe bryth,
Al so brith, al so shir,
So it were a blase of fir.
She lokede [8]north, and ek south,
And saw it commen ut of his mouth,
That lay bi hire in the bed:
No ferlike thou she were adred.
Thouthe she, " Wat may this bi-mene!
He beth heyman yet, als Y wene,
He beth heyman er he be ded:"—
On hise shuldre, of gold red
She saw a swithe noble croiz,
Of an angel she herde a uoyz:
[fol. 211. col. 1.] "Goldeborw, lat thi sorwe be,
For Hauelok, that haueth spuset the,
He kinges sone, and kinges eyr,
That bikenneth that croiz so fayr.

[8] noth, Ms.

It bikenneth more, that he shal
Denemark hauen, and Englond al;
He shal ben king strong and stark
Of Engelond and Denemark;
That shal thu wit thin eyne sen,
And tho shalt quen and leuedi ben.
Thanne she hauede herd the steuene
Of the angel uth of heuene,
She was so fele sithes blithe,
That she ne mithe hire ioie mythe;
But Hauelok sone anon she kiste,
And he slep, and nouth it wiste.
Hwan that aungel hauede seyd,
Of his slep anon he brayd,
And seide, " Lemman, slepes thou?
A selkuth drem dremede me nou.
Herkne nou hwat me haueth met:
Me thouthe Y was in Denemark set,
Buton on the moste hil
That euere yete kam I til.
It was so hey, that Y wel mouthe
Al the werd se, als me thouthe.
Als I sat upon that lowe,
I bigan Denemark for to awe,
The borwes, and the castles stronge;
And mine armes weren so longe,
That I fadmede, al at ones,
Denemark, with mine longe bones;

And thanne Y wolde mine armes drawe
Til me, and hom for to haue,
Al that euere in Denemark liueden
On mine armes faste clyueden;
And the strong castles alle
On knes bigunnen for to falle,
The keyes fellen at mine fet :—
Another drem dremede me ek,
That ich fley ouer the salte se
Til Engeland, and al with me
That euere was in Denemark lyues,
But bondemen, and here wiues,
And that ich kom til Engelond,
[col. 2.] Al closede it intil min hond,
And Goldeborw Y gaf the :—
Deus lemman, hwat may this be?"
Sho answerede, and seyde sone:
" Ihesu Crist, that made mone,
Thine dremes turne to ioye!
That wite thw that sittes in trone!
Ne non strong king, ne caysere,
So thou shalt be, so thou shalt bere
In Englond corune yet;
Denemark shal knele to thi fet;
Alle the castles that aren ther inne,
Shaltow, lemman, ful wel winne.
I woth, so wel, so ich it sowe,
To the shole comen heye and lowe,

And alle that in Denmark wone,
Em and brother, fader and sone,
Erl and baroun, dreng an kayn,
Knithes, and burgeys, and sweyn,
And mad king heyelike and wel;
Denemark shal be thin euere ilc del.
Haue thou nouth ther offe douthe
Nouth the worth of one nouthe;
Theroffe withinne the first yer
Shalt thou ben king of euere il del.
But do thou als Y wile rathe,
Nim in with the to [9]Denemark bathe,
And do thou nouth onfrest this fare,
Lith and selthe felawes are.
For shal ich neuere blithe be
Til I with eyen Denemark se;
For ich woth, that al the lond
Shalt thou hauen in thin hon.
Prey Grimes sones alle thre,
That he wenden forth with the;
I wot, he wilen the nouth [1]weme,
With the wende shulen he yerne,
For he louen the hertelike,
Thou maght til he aren quike,
Hwore so he o-worde aren;
There ship thou do hem swithe yaren,
And loke that thou dwellen nouth:
Dwelling haueth ofte scathe wrouth."

[9] Denemak, Ms.   [1] *Qu.* werne.

Hwan Hauelok herde that she radde,
Sone it was day, sone he him cladde,
And sone to the kirke yede,
Or he dide ani other dede,
[f. 211. b. col. 1.] And bifor the rode bigan falle,
Croiz and Crist bi[gan] to kalle,
And seyde, " Louerd, that al weldes,
Wind and water, wodes and feldes,
For the hoh milce of you
Haue merci of me, louerd, now!
And wreke me yet on mi fo,
That ich saw biforn min eyne slo
Mine sistres, with a knif,
And sithen wolde me mi lyf
Haue reft, for in the se
Bad he Grim haue drenched me.
He [hath] mi lond with mikel onrith,
With michel wrong, with mikel plith,
For I ne misdede him neuere nouth,
And hauede me to sorwe brouth.
He haueth me do mi mete to thigge,
And ofte in sorwe and pine ligge.
Louerd, haue merci of me,
And late [me] wel passe the se!
That ihc haue ther offe douthe and kare,
Withuten stormes ouer fare,
That Y ne drenched [be] ther ine,
Ne forfaren for no sinne.

And bringge me wel to the lond,
That Godard haldes in his hond;
That is mi rith, eueri del:
Ihesu Crist, thou wost it wel!"
Thanne he hauede his bede seyd,
His offrende on the auter leyd,
His leue at Ihesu Crist he tok,
And at his suete moder ok,
And at the croiz, that he biforn lay,
Sithen yede sore grotinde awey.
[2] Hwan he com hom, he wore yare
Grimes sones for to fare
Into the se, fishes to gete,
That Hauelok mithe wel of ete.
But Auelok thouthe al another,
First he [3] kade the heldeste brother,
Roberd the Rede, bi his name,
Wiliam Wenduth, and [4] Rauen,
Grimes sones alle thre,
[col. 2.] And [5] seyde, " Lithes nou alle to me,
Louerdinges, ich wile yow sheue,
A thing of me that ye wel knewe.
Mi fader was king of Denshe lond,
Denemark was al in his hond
The day that he was quik and ded;
But thanne hauede he wicke red,

[2] In the Ms. the Capital letter is prefixed to the next line.
[3] *Qu.* kalde. [4] Hauen, Ms. Cf. v. 1868. [5] seye, Ms.

That he me, and Denemark al,
And mine sistres bitawte a thral:
A deueles lime hus bitawte,
And al his lond, and al hise authe.
For Y saw that fule fend
Mine sistres slo with hise hend;
First he shar a-two here throtes,
And sithen hem al to grotes,
And sithen bad in the se
Grim, youre fader, drenchen me:
Deplike dede he him swere
On bok, that he sholde me bere
Vnto the se, an drenchen ine,
And wolde taken on him the sinne.
But Grim was wis, and swithe hende,
Wolde he nouth his soule shende;
Leuere was him to be forsworen,
Than drenchen me, and ben forloren;
But sone bigan he for to fle
Fro Denmark, for to [6]berwen me,
For [7]yis ich hauede ther ben funden,
Hauede ben slayn, or harde bunden,
And heye ben henged on a tre,
Hauede go for him gold ne fe.
For thi fro Denemark hider he fledde,
And me ful fayre and ful wel fedde,
So that vnto this day,
Haue ich ben fed and fostred ay.

[6] beryen, Ms. Cf. v. 697. [7] *Qu.* yif.

But now ich am up to that helde
Cumen, that ich may wepne welde,
And Y may grete dintes yeue,
Shal I neuere hwil ich lyue
Ben glad, til that ich Denemark se;
I preie you that ye wende with me,
And ich may mak you riche men,
Ilk of you shal haue castles ten,
And the lond that thor til longes,
Borwes, tunes, wodes and wonges,"[8]

* * * * *
* * * * *
* * * * *
* * * * *

[fol. 212. col. 1.] "With swilk als ich byen shal:
Ther of biseche you nou leue;
Wile ich speke with non other reue,
But with the, that iustise are,
That Y mithe [9] seken mi ware
In gode borwes up and doun,
And faren ich wile fro tun to tun."
A gold ring drow he forth anon,
An hundred pund was worth the ston,
And yaf it Ubbe for to spede:—
He was ful wis that first yaf mede,
And so was Hauelok ful wis here,
He solde his gold ring ful dere,

[8] A folio has here been cut out of the Ms. containing 180 lines.

[9] *Qu.* sellen.

Was neuere non so dere sold,
For chapmen, neyther yung ne old:
That shoren ye forthward ful wel heren,
[1]Yif that ye wile the storie heren.
Hwan Ubbe hauede the gold ring,
Hauede he youenet for no thing,
Nouth for the borw euere il del:—
Hauelok bihel he swithe wel,
Hw he was wel of bones maked,
Brod in the sholdres, ful wel schaped,
Thicke in the brest, of bodi long;
He semede wel to ben wel strong.
"Deus!" hwat Ubbe, "qui ne were he knith?
I woth, that he is swithe with!
Betere semede him to bere
Helm on heued, sheld and spere,
Thanne to beye and selle ware.
Allas! that he shal ther with fare.
Goddot! wile he trowe me,
Chaffare shal he late be."
Netheles he seyde sone:
"Hauelok, haue thi bone,
And Y ful wel rede th[e]
That thou come, and ete with me
To day, thou, and thi fayre wif,
That thou louest al so thi lif.
And haue thou of hire no drede,
Shal hire no man shame bede.

[1] Yaf, Ms.

Sithe fey that Y owe to the,
Therof shal I me serf-borw be."
Hauelok herde that he bad,
And thow was he ful sore drad,
[col. 2.] With him to ete, for hise wif;
For him wore leuere that his lif
Him wore reft, than she in blame
Felle, or lauthe ani shame.
Hwanne he hauede his wille that,
The stede, that he onne sat,
Smot Ubbe with spures faste,
And forth awey, but at the laste,
Or he fro him ferde,
Seyde he, that his folk herde:
"Loke that ye comen bethe,
For ich it wile, and ich it rede."
Hauelok ne durste, the he were adrad,
Nouth withsitten that Ubbe bad;
His wif he dide with him lede,
Vnto the heye curt he [2]yede.
Roberd hire ledde, that was Red,
That haue tharned for hire the ded
Or ani hauede hire misseyd,
Or hand with iuele onne leyd.
Willam Wendut was that other
That hire ledde, Roberdes brother,
That was with at alle nedes:
Wel is him that god man fedes!

[2] yde, Ms.

Than he weren comen to the halle,
Biforen Ubbe, and hise men alle,
Vbbe stirte hem ageyn,
And mani a knith, and mani a sweyn,
Hem for to se, and for to shewe;
Tho stod Hauelok als a lowe
Aboven that ther inne wore,
Rith al bi the heued more
Thanne ani that ther inne stod:
Tho was Ubbe blithe of mod,
That he saw him so fayr and hende,
Fro him ne mithe his herte wende,
Ne fro him, ne fro his wif;
He louede hem sone to his lif.
Weren non in Denemark, that him thouthe,
That he so mikel loue mouthe;
More he louede Hauelok one,
Than al Denemark, bi mine wone!
Loke nou, hw God helpen kan
O mani wise wif and man.
Hwan it was comen time to ete,
[f. 212. b. col. 1.] Hise wif dede Ubbe sone in fete,
And til hire seyde, al on gamen:
"Dame, thou and Hauelok shulen ete samen,
And Goldeboru shal ete wit me,
That is so fayr so flour on tre;
In al Denemark [3]nis wimman
So fayr so sche, bi seint Iohan!"

[3] is, Ms.

Thanne [he] were set, and bord leyd,
And the beneysun was seyd,
Biforn hem com the beste mete
That king or cayser wolde ete;
Kranes, swannes, ueneysun,
Lax, lampreys, and gode sturgun,
Pyment to drinke, and god clare,
Win hwit and red, ful god plente.
Was ther inne no page so lite,
That euere wolde ale bite.
Of the mete for to telle,
Ne of the metes bidde I nout dwelle;
That is the storie for to lenge,
It wolde anuye this fayre genge.
But hwan he haueden the kiwing deled,
And fele sithes haueden wosseyled,
And with gode drinkes seten longe,
And it was time for to gonge,
Il man to ther he cam fro,
Thouthe Ubbe, "Yf I late hem go,
Thus one foure, withuten mo,
So mote ich brouke finger or to,
For this wimman bes mike wo!
For hire shal men hire louerd slo."
He toke sone knithes ten,
And wel sixti other men,
Wit gode bowes, and with gleiues,
And sende him unto the greyues,

The beste man of al the toun,
That was named Bernard Brun;
And bade him, als he louede his lif,
Hauelok wel [4]yemen, and his wif,
And wel do wayten al the nith,
Til the other day, that it were lith.
Bernard was trewe, and swithe with,
In al the borw ne was no knith
That betere couthe on stede riden,
Helm on heued, ne swerd bi side.
[col. 2.] Hauelok he gladlike understod,
With mike loue, and herte god,
And dide greythe a super riche,
Also he was no with chinche;
To his bihoue euer il del,
That he mithe supe swithe wel.
Also he seten, and sholde soupe,
So comes a ladde in a ioupe,
And with him sixti other stronge,
With swerdes drawen, and kniues longe,
Ilkan in hande a ful god gleiue,
And seyde, " Undo, Bernard the greyue!
Vndo swithe, and lat us in,
Or thu art ded, bi seint Austin!"
Bernard stirt up, that was ful big,
And caste a brinie up on his rig,
And grop an ar, that was ful god,
Lep to the dore, so he wore wod,

[4] ymen, Ms.

And seyde, " Hwat are ye, that are ther oute,
That thus biginnen for to stroute?
Goth henne swithe, fule theues,
For, bi the Louerd, that man on leues,
Shol ich casten the dore open,
Summe of you shal ich drepen!
And the other shal ich kesten
In feteres, and ful faste festen!"
" Hwat haue ye seid," quoth a ladde,
" Wenestu that we ben adradde?
We shole at this dore gonge
Maugre thin, carl, or outh longe."
He gripen sone a bulder ston,
And let it fleye, ful god won,
Agen the dore, that it to-rof:
Auelok it saw, and thider drof,
And the barre sone vt drow,
That was unride, and gret ynow,
And caste the dore open wide,
And seide, " Her shal Y now abide:
Gomes swithe vnto me![5]
Datheyt hwo you henne fle!"
" No," quodh on, " that shaltou coupe,"
And bigan til him to loupe,
In his hond his swerd ut drawe,
Hauelok he wend thore haue slawe;

[5] Vnto me datheit, Ms.—evidently the repetition of the first word in the succeeding line.

And with comen other two,
[fol. 213. col. 1.] That him wolde of liue haue do.
Hauelok lifte up the dore-tre,
And at a dint he slow hem thre;
Was non of hem that his hernes
Ne lay ther ute ageyn the sternes.
The ferthe that he sithen mette,
Wit the barre so he him grette,
Bifor the heued, that the rith eye
Vt of the hole made he fleye,
And sithe clapte him on the crune,
So that he stan-ded fel thor dune.
The fifte that he ouertok,
Gaf he a ful sor dint ok,
Bitwen the sholdres, ther he stod,
That he spen his herte-blod.
The sixte wende for to fle,
And he clapte him with the tre
Rith in the fule necke so,
That he smot hise necke on to.
Thanne the sixe weren doun feld,
The seuenthe brayd ut his swerd,
And wolde Hauelok riht in the eye;
And [6] hauele barre fleye,
And smot him sone ageyn the brest,
That hauede he neuere schifte of prest;
For he was ded on lesse hwile,
Than men mouthe renne a mile.

[6] *Qu.* Hauelok let the.

Alle the othere weren ful kene,
A red thei taken hem bitwene,
That he sholde him bi-halue,
And brisen so, that wit no salue
Ne sholde him helen leche non:
They drowen ut swerdes, ful god won,
And shoten on him, so don on bere
Dogges, that wolden him to-tere,
Thanne men doth the bere beyte:
The laddes were kaske and teyte,
And vn-bi-yeden him ilkon,
Sum smot with tre, and sum wit ston;
Sum putten with gleyue, in bac, and side,
And yeuen wundes longe and wide;
In twenti stedes, and wel mo,
Fro the croune til the to.
Hwan he saw that, he was wod,
And was it ferlik hw he stod,
[col. 2.] For the blod ran of his sides
So water that fro the welle glides;
But thanne bigan he for to mowe
With the barre, and let hem shewe,
Hw he cowthe sore smite,
For was ther non, long ne lite,
That he mouthe ouertake,
That he ne garte his croune krake;
So that on a litel stund,
Felde he twenti to the grund.

Tho bigan gret dine to rise,
For the laddes on ilke wise
Him asayleden with grete dintes,
Fro fer he stoden, him with flintes
And gleyues schoten him fro ferne,
For drepen him he wolden yerne;
But dursten he newhen him no more,
Thanne he bor or leun wore.
Huwe Rauen that dine herde,
And thowthe wel, that men misferde
With his louerd, for his wif,
And grop an ore, and a long knif,
And thider [7] drof al so an hert,
And cham ther on a litel stert,
And saw how the laddes wode
Hauelok his louerd umbistode,
And beten on him so doth the smith
With the hamer on the stith.
"Allas!" hwat Hwe, "that Y was boren!
That euere et ich bred of koren!
That ich here this sorwe se!
Roberd! Willam! hware ar ye?
Gripeth ether unker a god tre,
And late we nouth thise doges fle,
Til ure louerd wreke [we]
Cometh swithe, and folwes me!
Ich haue in honde a ful god ore:
Datheit wo ne smite sore!"

[7] dorof, Ms.

"Ya! leue, ya!" quod Roberd sone,
"We hauen ful god lith of the mone."
Roberd grop a staf, strong and gret,
That mouthe ful wel bere a net,
And Willam Wendut grop a tre
Mikel grettere than his thre,
And Bernard held his ax ful faste;
[f. 213. b. col. 1.] I seye, was he nouth the laste;
And lopen forth so he weren wode
To the laddes, ther he stode,
And yaf hem wundes swithe grete:
Ther mithe men wel se boyes bete,
And ribbes in here side breke,
And Hauelok on hem wel wreke.
He broken armes, he broken knes,
He broken shankes, he broken thes,
He dide the blode there renne dune
To the fet rith fro the crune,
For was ther spared heued non:
He leyden on heuedes, ful god won,
And made croune breke and crake,
Of the broune, and of the blake;
He maden here backes al so bloute
Als [8] he wombes, and made hem rowte
Als he weren kradel-barnes:
So dos the child that moder tharnes.
Datheit the recke! for he it seruede,
Hwat dide he thore weren he werewed;

[8] *Qu.* here.

So longe haueden he but and bet
With neues under hernes set,
That of tho sixti men and on
Ne wente ther awey liues non.
On the morwen, hwan it was day,
Ilc on other wirwed lay,
Als it were dogges that weren henged,
And summe leye in dikes slenget,
And summe in gripes bi the her
Drawen ware, and laten ther.
Sket cam tiding intil Ubbe,
That Hauelok hauede with a clubbe
Of hise [9]slawen sixti and on
Sergaunz, the beste that mithen gon.
" Deus !" quoth Ubbe, " hwat may this be !
Betere his I nime miself and se,
That this baret on hwat is wold,
Thanne I sende yunge or old.
For yif I sende him un to,
I wene men sholde him shame do,
And that ne wolde ich for no thing :
I loue him wel, bi heuene king !
Me wore leuere I wore lame,
Thanne men dide him ani shame,
[col. 2.] Or tok, or onne handes leyde,
Vnornelske, or same seyde."
He lep up on a stede lith,
And with him mani a noble knith,

[9] slawern, Ms.

And ferde forth unto the tun,
And dide calle Bernard Brun
Vt of his hus, wan he ther cam,
And Bernard sone ageyn nam,
Al to-tused and al to-torn,
Ner al so naked, so he was born,
And al to-brised, bac and the:
Quoth Ubbe, “ Bernard, hwat is the?
Hwo haues the thus ille maked,
Thus to-riuen, and al mad naked?”
“ [1] Louerd, merci,” quot he sone,
To nicht al so ros the mone
Comen her mo than sixti theues,
With lokene copes, and wide sleues,
Me for to robben, and to pine,
And for to drepe me and mine.
Mi dore he broken up ful sket,
And wolde me binden hond and fet.
Wan the gode men that sawe,
Hauelok, and he that bi the wowe
Leye, he stirten up sone onon,
And summe grop tre, and sum grop ston,
And driue hem ut, thei he weren crus,
So dogges ut of milne-hus.
Hauelok grop the dore-tre,
And [at] a dint he slow hem thre.
He is the beste man at nede,
That euere mar shal ride stede!

[1] Iouerd, Ms.

Als helpe god, bi mine wone,
A [2]thousend of men his he worth one!
Yif he ne were, ich were nou ded,
So haue ich don mi soule red;
But it is hof him mikel sinne;
He maden him swilke woundes thrinne,
That of the alther-leste wounde
Were a stede brouht to grunde.
He haues a wunde in the side,
With a gleyue, ful unride,
And he haues on thoru his arum,
Ther of is ful mikel harum,
[fol. 214. col. 1.] And he haues on thoru his yhe,
The vnrideste that men may se,
And othe wundes haues he stronge,
Mo than twenti swithe longe.
But sithen he hauede lauth the sor
Of the wundes, was neuere bor
That so fauth so he fauth thanne;
Was non that hauede the hern-panne
So hard, that he ne dede al to-cruhsse,
And al to-shiuere, and al to-frusshe.
He folwede hem so hund dos here,
Datheyt on he wolde spare!
That ne made hem euerilk on
Ligge stille so doth the ston:
And ther nis he nouth to frie,
For other sholde he make hem lye

[2] Thhousend, Ms.

Ded, or thei him hauede slawen,
Or al to-hewen, or al to-drawen.
Louerd, [3]haue I no more plith
Of that ich was thus grethed to nith.
Thus wolde the theues me haue reft,
But god thank he hauenet sure keft.
But it is of him mikel scathe:
I woth that he bes ded ful rathe."
Quoth Ubbe, " Bernard, seyst thou soth ?"
" Ya, sire, that I ne lepe oth.
Yif Y, louerd, a word leye,
To morwen do me hengen heye."
The burgeys that ther bi stode thore,
Grundlike and grete othes swore;
Litle and mikle, yunge and holde,
That was soth, that Bernard tolde.
Soth was, that he wolden him bynde,
And trusse al that he mithen fynde
Of hise, in arke, or in kiste,
That he mouthe in seckes thriste.
" Louerd, he haueden al awey born
This thing, and him self al to-torn,
But als God self barw him wel,
That he ne tinte no catel.
Hwo mithe so mani stonde ageyn,
Bi nither tale, knith or swein?
He weren bi tale sixti and ten,
Starke laddes, stalworthi men,

[3] haui, Ms.

And on, the mayster of hem alle,
That was the name Giffin Galle.
[col. 2.] Hwo mouthe [4]ageyn so mani stonde
But als this man of ferne lond!
Haueth hem slawen with a tre:
Mikel ioie haue he!
God yeue him mikel god to welde,
Bothe in tun, and ek in felde!
We is set he etes mete."
Quoth Ubbe, "Doth him swithe fete,
That Y mouthe his woundes se,
Yf that he mouthen holed be.
For yf he mouthe couere yet,
And gangen wel upon hise fet,
Mi self shal dubbe him to knith,
For thi that he is so with.
And yif he liuede tho foule theues,
That weren of Kaym kin and Eues,
He sholden hange bi the necke,
Of here ded datheit wo recke!
Hwan he yeden thus on nithes
To binde bothe burgmen and knithes.
For bynderes loue ich neuere mo,
Of hem ne yeue ich nouht a slo."
Hauelok was bifore Ubbe browth,
That hauede for him ful mikel thouth,
And mikel sorwe in his herte
For hise wundes, that we[ren] so smerte.

[4] agey, Ms.

But hwan his wundes weren shewed,
And a leche hauede knawed,
That he hem mouthe ful wel hele,
Wel make him gange, and ful wel mele,
And wel a palefrey bistride,
And wel upon a stede ride,
Tho let Ubbe al his care,
And al his sorwe ouerfare.
And seyde, "Cum now forth with me,
And Goldeboru, thi wif, with the,
And thine seriaunz all thre,
For nou wile Y youre warant be;
Wile Y nou, of here frend,
That thu slowe with thin hend,
Moucte wayte the [to] slo,
Also thou gange to and fro.
I shal lene the a bowr,
That is up in the heye tour,
Til thou mowe ful wel go,
[f. 214. b. col. 1.] And wel ben hol of al thi wo.
It ne shal no thing ben bitwene
Thi bour and min, also Y wene,
But a fayr firrene wowe;—
Speke Y loude, or speke Y lowe,
Thou [5]shalt ful wel heren me,
And than thu wilt, thou shalt me se.
A rof shal hile us bothe o-nith,
That none of mine, clerk ne knith,

[5] sahlt, Ms.

Ne sholen thi wif no shame bede,
No more than min, so God me rede!"
He dide unto the borw bringe
Sone anon, al with ioynge,
His wif, and his serganz thre,
The beste men that mouthe be.
The firste nith he lay ther inne,
Hise wif, and his serganz thrinne,
Aboute the middel of the nith
Wok Ubbe, and saw a mikel lith
In the bour that Hauelok lay,
Also brith so it were day.
"Deus!" quoth Ubbe, "hwat may this be?
Betere is I go miself, and se:
Hwether he sitten nou, and wesseylen,
Or of ani shotshipe to-deyle.
This tid nithes al so foles
Than birthe men casten hem in poles,
Or in a grip, or in the fen:
Nou ne sitten none but wicke men,
Glotuns, reures, or wicke theues,
Bi Crist, that alle folk onne leues!"
He stod, and totede in at a bord,
Her he spak anilepi word,
And saw hem slepen faste ilkon,
And lye stille so the ston;
And saw al that mikel lith
Fro Hauelok cam, that was so brith.

Of his mouth it com il del,
That was he war ful swithe wel.
" Deus!" quoth he, " hwat may this mene!"
He calde bothe arwe men, and kene
Knithes, and serganz swithe sleie,
Mo than an hundred, withuten leye,
And bad hem alle comen and se,
Hwat that selcuth mithe be.
[col. 2.] Als the knithes were comen alle,
Ther Hauelok lay, ut of the halle,
So stod ut of his mouth a glem,
Rith al swilk so the sunne-bem;
That al so lith wa[s] thare, bi heuene!
So ther brenden serges seuene,
And an hundred serges ok:
That durste hi sweren on a bok.
He slepen faste alle fiue,
So he weren brouth of liue;
And Hauelok lay on his lift side,
In his armes his brithe bride.
Bi the pappes he leyen naked:
So faire two weren neuere maked
In a bed to lyen samen:—
The knithes thouth of hem god gamen,
Hem for to shewe, and loken to,
Rith al so he stoden alle so.
And his bac was toward hem wend,
So weren he war of a croiz ful gent,

On his rith shuldre [6]swe brith,
Brither than gold ageyn the lith.
So that he wiste heye and lowe,
That it was kunrik that he sawe.
It sparkede, and ful brith shon,
So doth the gode charbucle ston,
That men mouthe se by the lith,
A peni chesen, so was it brith.
Thanne bihelden he hem faste,
So that he knewen at the laste,
That he was Birkabeynes sone,
That was here king, that was hem wone
Wel to yeme, and wel were
Ageynes uten-laddes here.
For it was neuere yet a brother
In al Denemark so [7]lith another,
So this man that is so fayr
Als Birkabeyn, he is hise eyr.
He fellen sone at his fet,
Was non of hem that he ne gret,
Of ioie he weren alle so fawen,
So he him haueden of erthe drawen.
Hise fet he kisten an hundred sythes,
The tos, the nayles, and the lithes,
So that he bigan to wakne,
[fol. 215. col. 1.] And wit hem ful sore to blakne,
For he wende he wolden him slo,
Or elles binde him, and do wo.

[6] *Qu.* swithe. Cf. v. 1252. [7] *F.* like.

Quoth Ubbe, " Louerd, ne dred the nouth,
Me thinkes that I se thi thouth.
Dere sone, wel is me,
That Y the with eyn se.
Manred, louerd, bede Y the,
Thi man auht I ful wel to be,
For thu art comen of Birkabeyn,
That hauede mani knith and sweyn;
And so shalt thou, louerd, haue,
Thou thu be yet a ful yung knaue.
Thou shalt be king of al Denemark,
Was ther inne neuere non so stark.
To morwen shaltu manrede take
Of the brune, and of the blake;
Of alle that aren in this tun,
Bothe of erl, and of barun,
And of dreng, and of thayn,
And of knith, and of sweyn.
And so shaltu ben mad knith
Wit blisse, for thou art so with."
Tho was Hauelok swithe blithe,
And thankede God ful fele sithe.
On the morwen, wan it was lith,
And gon was thisternesse of the nith,
Vbbe dide upon a stede
A ladde lepe, and thider bede
Erles, barouns, drenges, theynes,
Klerkes, knithes, [8]burgeys, sweynes,

[8] bugeys, Ms.

That he sholden comen anon,
Biforen him sone euerilkon,
Also he louen here liues,
And here children, and here wiues.
Hise bode ne durste he non at sitte,
That he ne [9]meme for to wite
Sone, hwat wolde the iustise:
And bigan anon to rise,
And seyde sone, " Lithes me,
Alle samen, theu and fre.
A thing ich wile you here shauwe,
That [1]ye alle ful wel knawe.
Ye witen wel, that al this lond
Was in Birkabeynes hond,
[col. 2.] The day that he was quic and ded;
And how that he, bi youre red,
Bitauhte hise children thre
Godard to yeme, and al his fe.
Hauelok his sone he him tauhte,
And hise two douhtres, and al his auhte,
Alle [2]herden ye him swere
On bok, and on messe-gere,
That he shulde yeme hem wel,
Withuten lat, withuten tel.
He let his oth al ouer go,
Euere wurthe him yuel and wo!
For the maydnes here lif
Refte he bothen, with a knif,

[9] *Qu.* come. Cf. v. 2282. [1] he, Ms. [2] henden, Ms.

And him shulde ok haue slawen,
The knif was at his herte drawen,
But God him wolde wel haue saue,
He hauede reunesse of the knaue,
So that he with his hend
Ne drop him nouth, that sor fend,
But sone dide he a fishere
Swithe grete othes swere,
That he sholde drenchen him
In the se, that was ful brim.
"Hwan Grim saw that he was so fayr,
And wiste he was the rith eir,
Fro Denemark ful sone he fledde
Intil Englond, and ther him fedde
Mani winter, that til this day
Haues he ben fed and fostred ay.
Lokes, hware he stondes her:
In al this werd ne haues he per;
Non so fayr, ne non so long,
Ne non so mikel, ne non so strong.
In this middelerd nis no knith
Half so strong, ne half so with.
Bes of him ful glad and blithe,
And cometh alle hider swithe,
Manrede youre louerd for to make,
Bothe brune, and the blake.
I shal mi self do first the gamen.
And ye sithen alle samen."

O-knes ful fayre he him sette,
Mouthe nothing him ther fro lette,
And bicam is man rith thare,
That alle sawen that there ware.
[f. 215. b. col. 1.] After him stirt up laddes ten,
And bicomen hise men;[3]
And sithen euerilk a baroun,
That euere weren in al that toun;
And sithen drenges, and sithen thaynes,
And sithen knithes, and sithen sweynes;
So that or that day was gon,
In al the tun ne was nouth on
That it ne was his man bicomen:
Manrede of alle hauede he nomen.
Hwan he hauede of hem alle
Manrede taken, in the halle,
Grundlike dide he hem swere,
That he sholden him god feyth bere
Ageynes alle that woren on liue;
Ther yen ne wolde neuer on striue,
That he ne maden sone that oth,
Riche and poure, lef and loth.
Hwan that was maked, sone he sende,
Vbbe, writes fer and hende,
After alle that castel yemede,
Burwes, tunes, sibbe an fremde,

[3] A word is added in the Ms. after *men*, apparently *beye*. Perhaps we should read: *hise heye men*.

That thider sholden comen swithe
Til him, and heren tithandes blithe,
That he hem alle shulde telle:
Of hem ne wolde neuere on dwelle,
That he ne come sone plattinde,
Hwo hors ne hauede, com gangande.
So that with inne a fourtenith,
In al Denemark ne was no knith,
Ne conestable, ne shireue,
That com of Adam and Eue,
That he ne com biforn sire Ubbe:
He dredden him so [4]thhes doth clubbe.
Hwan he haueden alle the king gret,
And he weren alle dun set,
Tho seyde Ubbe, " Lokes here,
Vre louerd swithe dere,
That shal ben king of al the lond,
And haue us alle under hond.
For he is Birkabeynes sone,
The king that was vmbestonde wone
For to yeme, and wel were,
[col. 2.] Wit sharp swerd, and longe spere.
Lokes nou, hw he is fayr;
Sikerlike he is hise eyr.
Falles alle to hise fet,
Bicomes hise men ful sket."
He weren for Ubbe swithe adrad,
And dide sone al that he bad,

[4] *Qu.* thes, *i. e.* thighs, *or* yhes, *i. e.* eyes; *or perhaps* theues.

And yet deden he sumdel more,
O-bok ful grundlike he swore,
That he sholde with him halde
Both ageynes stille and bolde,
That euere wode his bodi dere:
That dide [he] hem o-boke swere.
Hwan he hauede manrede and oth
Taken of lef and of loth,
Vbbe dubbede him to knith,
With a swerd ful swithe brith,
And the folk of al the lond
Bitauhte him al in his hond;
The cunnriche eueril del,
And made him king heylike and wel.
Hwan he was king, ther mouthe men se
The moste ioie that mouhte be:
Buttinge with sharpe speres,
Skirming with taleuaces, that men beres,
Wrastling with laddes, putting of ston,
Harping and piping, ful god won,
Leyk of mine, of hasard ok,
Romanz reding on the bok;
Ther mouthe men here the gestes singe,
The gleymen on the tabour dinge;
Ther mouhte men se the boles beyte,
And the bores with hundes teyte;
Tho mouthe men se eueril gleu,
Ther mouthe men se hw Grim greu;

Was neuere yete ioie more
In al this werd, than tho was thore.
Ther was so mike yeft of clothes,
That thou I swore you grete othes,
I ne wore nouth ther offe croud:
That may I ful wel swere, bi God!
There was swithe gode metes,
And of wyn, that men fer fetes,
Rith al so mik and gret plente,
So it were water of the se.
The feste fourti dawes sat,
[fol. 216. col. 1.] So riche was neuere non so that.
The king made Roberd there knith,
That was ful strong, and ful with,
And Willam Wendut, het his brother,
And Huwe Rauen, that was that other,
And made hem barouns alle thre,
And yaf hem lond, and other fe,
So mikel, that ilker twent[i] knihtes
Hauede of genge, dayes and nithes.
Hwan that feste was al don,
A thusand knihtes ful wel o-bon
With-held the king, with him to lede;
That ilkan hauede ful gode stede,
Helm, and sheld, and brinie brith,
And al the wepne that fel to knith.
With hem fiue thusand gode
Sergaunz, that weren to fyht wode,

With-held he al of his genge:
(Wile I na more the storie lenge.)
Yit hwan he hauede of al the lond
The casteles alle in his hond,
And conestables don ther inne,
He swor, he ne sholde neuere blinne,
Til that he were of Godard wreken,
That ich haue of ofte speken.
Hal hundred knithes dede he calle,
And hise fif thusand sergaunz alle,
And dide sweren on the bok
Sone, and on the auter ok,
That he ne sholde neuere blinne,
Ne for loue, ne for sinne,
Til that he haueden Godard funde,
And brouth biforn him faste [5]bunde.
Thanne he haueden swor this oth,
Ne leten he nouth for lef ne loth,
That he ne foren swithe rathe,
Ther he was unto the pathe,
Ther he yet on hunting for,
With mikel genge, and swithe stor.
Robert, that was of al the ferd
Mayster, he was girt wit a swerd,
And sat upon a ful god stede,
That vnder him rith wolde wede;
He was the firste that with Godard
[col. 2.] Spak, and seyde, [6]" Hede cauenard!

[5] birnde, Ms. [6] *Qu.* helde, *i. e.* old.

Wat dos thu here at this pathe?
Cum to the king, swithe and rathe.
That sendes he the word, and bedes,
That thu thenke hwat thu him dedes,
Hwan thu reftes with a knif
Hise sistres here lif,
An sithen bede thu in the se
Drenchen him, that herde he.
He is to the swithe grim:
Cum nu swithe unto him,
That king is of this kuneriche.
Thu fule man! thu wicke swike!
And he shal yelde the thi mede,
Bi Crist, that wolde on rode blede!"
Hwan Godard herde that ther threte,
With the neue he Robert sette
Biforn the teth a dint ful strong,
And Robert kipt ut a knif long,
And smot him thoru the rith arum:
Therof was ful litel harum.
Hwan his folk that saw and herde,
Hwou Robert with here louerd ferde,
He haueden him wel ner browt of liue,
Ne weren his two brethren and othre fiue,
Slowen of here laddes ten,
Of Godardes alther-best men.
Hwan the othre sawen that, he fledden,
And Godard swithe loude gredde:

"Mine knithes, hwat do ye?
Sule ye thus gate fro me fle?
Ich haue you fed, and yet shal fede,
Helpe me nu in this nede,
And late ye nouth mi bodi spille,
Ne Hauelok don of me hise wille.
Yif ye [7] id do, ye do to you shame,
And bringeth you self in mikel blame."
Hwan he that herden, he wenten ageyn,
And slowen a knit [8] and a sweyn
Of the kinges oune men,
And woundeden abuten ten.
The kinges men hwan he that sawe,
Scuten on hem, heye and lowe,
And euerilk fot of hem slowe,
But Godard one, that he flowe,
So the thef men dos henge,
[f. 216. b. col. 1.] Or hund men shole in dike slenge.
He bunden him ful swithe faste,
Hwil the bondes wolden laste,
That he rorede als a bole,
That he wore parred in an hole,
With dogges for to bite and beite:
Were the bondes nouth to leite.
He bounden him [9] fo fele sore,
That he gan crien Godes ore,
That he sholde of his hende plette,
Wolden he nouht therfore lette,

[7] *Qu.* it. [8] and and, Ms. [9] *Qu.* so.

That he ne bounden hond and fet:
Datheit that on that therfore let!
But dunten him so man doth bere,
And keste him on a scabbed mere,
Hise nese went unto the crice:
So ledden he that fule swike,
Til he was biforn Hauelok brouth,
That he haue ful wo wrowht,
Bothe with hungred, and with cold,
Or he were twel winter old,
And with mani heui swink,
With poure mete, and feble drink,
And swithe wikke clothes,
For al hise manie gret othes.
Nu beyes he his holde blame:
Old sinne makes newe shame:
Wan he was so shamelike
Brouht biforn the king, the fule swike,
The king dede Ubbe swithe calle
His erles, and hise barouns alle,
Dreng and thein, burgeis and knith,
And bad he sholden demen him rith:
For he knew, the swike dam,
Euerildel God was him gram.
He setten hem dun bi the wawe,
Riche and pouere, heye and lowe,
The helde men, and ek the grom,
And made ther the rithe dom,

And seyden unto the king anon,
That stille sat so the ston:
" We deme, that he be al quic slawen,
And sithen to the galwes drawe,
At this foule mere tayl;
Thoru is fet a ful strong nayl;
[col. 2.] And thore ben henged wit two fettres,
And thare be writen thise leteres:
This is the swike that wende wel,
The king haue reft the lond il del,
And hise sistres with a knif
Bothe refte here lif.
This writ shal henge bi him thare;
The dom is demd, seye we na more."
Hwan the dom was demd and giue,
And he was wit the prestes shriue,
And it ne mouhte ben non other,
Ne for fader, ne for brother,
That he sholde tharne lif;
Sket cam a ladde with a knif,
And bigan rith at the to
For to ritte, and for to flo,
And he bigan for to rore,
So it were grim, or gore,
That men mithe thethen a mile
Here him rore, that fule file.
The ladde ne let no with for thi
They he criede merci! merci!

That ne flow eueril del
With knif mad of grunden stel.
Thei garte bringe the mere sone,
[1]Skabbed and ful iuele o-bone,
And bunden him rith at hire tayl
With a rop of an old seyl,
And drowen him unto the galwes,
Nouth bi the gate, but ouer the falwes;
A tid henge thore bi the hals:
Datheit hwo recke! he was fals.

Thanne he was ded, that Sathanas,
Sket was seysed al that his was
In the kinges hand il del,
Lond and lith, and other catel,
And the king ful sone it yaf
Vbbe in the hond, with a fayr staf,
And seyde, "Her ich sayse the
In al the lond, in al the fe."
Tho swor Hauelok he sholde make,
Al for Grim, of monekes blake
A priorie to seruen inne ay
Ihesu Crist, til domesday,
For the god he haueden him don,
[fol. 217. col. 1.] Hwil he was pouere and we[l]o-bon.
And therof held he wel his oth,
For he it made, God it woth!
In the tun ther Grim was grauen,
That of Grim yet haues the name.

[1] Skabbeb, Ms.

Of Grim bidde ich na more spelle:
But wan Godrich herde telle,
Of Cornwayle that was erl,
That fule traytour, that mixed cherl,
That Hauelok was king of Denemark,
And ferde with him, strong and stark,
Comen Engelond with inne,
Engelond al for to winne,
And that she, that was so fayr,
That was of Engelond rith eir,
That was comen up at Grimesbi,
He was ful sorful and sori,
And seyde, "Hwat shal me to-rathe?
Goddoth! I shal do slou hem bathe.
I shal don hengen hem ful heye,
So mote ich brouke mi rith eie!
But yif he of mi lond fle,
Hwat wenden he to desherite me."
He dide sone ferd ut bidde,
That al that euere mouhte o-stede
Ride, or helm on heued bere,
Brini on bac, and sheld, and spere,
Or ani other wepne bere,
Hand-ax, sythe, gisarm, or spere,
Or alinlaz, and god long knif,
That als he louede leme or lif,
That they sholden comen him to,
With ful god wepne ye ber so,

To Lincolne, ther he lay,
Of Marz the seuententhe day,
So that he couthe hem god thank;
And yif that ani were so rang,
That he thanne ne come anon,
He swor bi Crist, and seint Iohan,
That he sholde maken him thral,
And al his ofspring forth withal.
The Englishe that herde that,
Was non that euere his bode sat,
For he him dredde swithe sore,
So runci spore, and mikle more.
[col. 2.] At the day he come sone
That he hem sette, ful wel o-bone,
To Lincolne, with gode stedes,
And al the wepne that knith ledes.
Hwan he wore come, sket was the erl thare,
Ageynes Denshe men to fare,
And seyde, "Lythes [2]me alle samen,
Haue ich gadred you for no gamen,
But ich wile seyen you for thi;
Lokes hware here at Grimesbi,
Hise uten-laddes here comen,
And haues nu the priorie numen;
Al that euere mithen he finde,
He brenne kirkes, and prestes binde;
He strangleth monkes, and nunnes bothe:
Wat wile ye frend her offe rede?

[2] mi, Ms. Cf. v. 2204.

Yif he regne thus gate longe,
He moun us alle ouer gange,
He moun vs alle quic henge or slo,
Or thral maken, and do ful wo,
Or elles reue us ure liues,
And ure children, and ure wiues.
But dos nu als ich wile you lere,
Als ye wile be with me dere;
Nimes nu swithe forth and rathe,
And helpes me and yu self bathe,
And slos up o-the dogges swithe:
For shal [I] neuere more be blithe,
Ne hoseled ben, ne of prest shriuen,
Til that he ben of londe driuen.
Nime we swithe, and do hem fle,
And folwes alle faste me,
For ich am he, of al the ferd,
That first shal slo with drawen swerd.
Datheyt hwo ne stonde faste
Bi me, hwil hise armes laste!"
"The lef the," couth the erl Gunter
"Ya!" quoth the erl of Cestre, Reyner.
And so dide alle that ther stode,
And stirte forth so he were wode.
Tho mouthe men se the brinies brihte
On backes keste, and late rithe,
The helmes heye on heued sette;
To armes al so swithe plette,

That thei wore on a litel stunde
[f. 217. b. col. 1.] Grathet, als men mithe telle a pund,
And lopen on stedes sone anon,
And toward Grimesbi, ful god won,
He foren softe bi the sti,
Til he come ney at Grimesbi.
Hauelok, that hauede spired wel
Of here fare, eueril del,
With al his ferd cam hem ageyn,
Forbar he nother knith ne sweyn.
The firste knith that he ther mette,
With the swerd so he him grette,
For his heued of he plette,
Wolde he nouth for sinne lette.
Roberd saw that dint so hende,
Wolde he neuere thethe wende,
Til that he hauede another slawen,
With the swerd he held ut drawen.
Willam Wendut his swerd vt drow,
And the thredde so sore he slow,
That he made upon the feld
His left arm fleye, with the [3]swerd.
Huwe Rauen ne forgat nouth
The swerd he hauede thider brouth,
He kipte it up, and smot ful sore
An erl, that he saw priken thore,
Ful noblelike upon a stede,
That with him wolde al quic wede.

[3] Cf. v. 1825. We should otherwise be tempted to read *sheld.*

He smot him on the heued so,
That he the heued clef a-two,
And that bi the shudre-blade
The sharpe swerd let wade,
Thorw the brest unto the herte,
The dint bigan ful sore to smerte,
That the erl fel dun anon,
Al so ded so ani ston.
Quoth Ubbe, "Nu dwelle ich to longe,"
And leth his stede sone gonge
To Godrich, with a god spere,
That he saw another bere,
And smote Godrich and G. him,
He[r]telike with herte grim,
So that he bothe felle dune,
To the erthe first the croune.
Thanne he woren fallen dun bothen,
Grundlike here swerdes ut drowen,
[col. 2.] That weren swithe sharp and gode,
And fouhten so thei woren wode,
That the swot ran fro the crune,
[To the fete there adune.][4]
Ther mouthe men se to knithes bete,
Ayther on other dintes grete,
So that with alther-lest dint
Were al to-shiuered a flint.
So was bitwenen hem a fiht,
Fro the morwen ner to the niht,

[4] Cf. v. 1904.

So that thei nouth ne blinne,
Til that to sette bigan the sunne.
Tho yaf Godrich thorw the side
Vbbe a wunde ful unride,
So that thorw that ilke wounde
Hauede ben brouth to the grunde,
And his heued al of slawen,
Yif God ne were, and Huwe Rauen,
That drow him fro Godrich awey,
And barw him so that ilke day.
But er he were fro Godrich drawen,
Ther weren a thousinde knihtes slawen
Bi bothe halue, and mo ynowe,
Ther the ferdes togidere slowe.
Ther was swilk dreping of the folk,
That on the feld was neuere a polk,
That it ne stod of blod so ful,
That the strem ran intil the hul.
Tho tarst bigan Godrich to go
Vpon the Danshe, and faste to slo,
And forth rith al so leuin fares,
That neuere kines best ne spares,
Thanne his gon, for he garte alle
The Denshe men biforn him falle.
He felde browne, he felde blake,
That he mouthe ouertake.
Was neuere non that mouhte thaue
His dintes, noyther knith ne knaue,

That he felden so dos the gres
Biforn the sythe that ful sharp is.
Hwan Hauelok saw his folk so brittene,
And his ferd so swithe littene,
He cam driuende upon a stede,
And bigan til him to grede,
And seyde, " Godrich, wat is the
That thou fare thus with me?
[fol. 218. col. 1.] And mine gode knihtes slos,
Sikerlike thou mis gos.
Thou wost ful wel, yif thu wilt wite,
That Athelwold the dide site
On knes, and sweren on messe-bok,
On caliz, and on [5]messe-bok,
That thou hise douhter sholdest yelde,
Than she were wimman of elde,
Engelond eueril del:
Godrich the erl, thou wost it wel.
Do nu wel withuten fiht,
Yeld hire the lond, for that is rith.
Wile ich forgiue the the lathe,
Al mi dede dede, and al mi wrathe,
For Y se thu art so with,
And of thi bodi so god knith."
" That ne wile ich neuere mo,"
Quoth erl Godrich, " for ich shal slo
The and hire for henge heye.
I shal thrist ut thi rith eye

[5] *Sic* Ms. *qu.* pateyn ok. Cf v. 187.

That thou lokes with on me,
But thu swithe hethen fle."
He grop the swerd ut sone anon,
And hew on Hauelok, ful god won,
So that he clef his sheld on two:
Hwan Hauelok saw that shame do
His bodi ther biforn his ferd,
He drow ut sone his gode swerd,
And smot him so upon the crune,
That Godrich fel to the erthe adune.
But Godrich stirt up swithe sket,
Lay he nowth longe at his fet,
And smot on the sholdre so,
That he did thare undo
Of his brinie ringes mo,
Than that ich kan tellen fro;
And woundede him rith in the flesh,
That tendre was, and swithe nesh,
So that the blod ran til his to:
Tho was Hauelok swithe wo,
That he hauede of him drawen
Blod, and so sore him slawen.
Hertelike til him he wente,
And Godrich ther fulike shente;
For his swerd he hof up heye,
[col. 2.] And the hand he dide of fleye,
That he smot him with so sore:
Hw mithe he don him shame more?

Hwan he hauede him so shamed,
His hand of plat, and yuele lamed,
He tok him sone bi the necke
Als a traytour, datheyt wo recke!
And dide him binde and fetere wel,
With gode feteres al of stel,
And to the quen he sende him;
That birde wel to him ben grim;
And bad she sholde don him gete,
And that non ne sholde him bete,
Ne shame do, for he was knith,
Til knithes haueden demd him rith.
Than the Englishe men that sawe,
That thei wisten, heye and lawe.
That Goldeboru, that was so fayr,
Was of Engeland rith eyr,
And that the king hire hauede wedded,
And haueden ben samen bedded,
He comen alle to crie merci,
Vnto the king, at one cri,
And beden him sone manrede and oth,
That he ne sholden, for lef ne loth,
Neuere more ageyn him go,
Ne ride, for wel ne for wo.

The king ne wolde nouth forsake,
That he ne shulde of hem take
Manrede that he beden, and ok
Hold other sweren on the bok;

But or bad he, that thider were brouth
The quen, for hem, swilk was his thouth,
For to se, and for to shawe,
Yif that he hire wolde knawe.
Thoruth hem witen wolde he,
Yif that she aucte quen to be.
Sixe erles weren sone yare,
After hire for to fare.
He nomen onon, and comen sone,
And brouthen hire, that under mone
In al the werd ne hauede per,
Of hende leik, fer ne ner.
Hwan she was come thider, alle
The Englishe men bigunne to falle
[f. 218. b. col. 1.] O-knes, and greten swithe sore,
And seyden, " Leuedi, K[r]istes ore,
And youres! we hauen misdo mikel,
That we ayen you haue be fikel,
For Englond auhte for to ben youres,
And we youre men and youres.
Is non of us, yung ne old,
That we ne wot, that Athelwold
Was king of this kunerike,
And ye his eyr, and that the swike
Haues it halden with mikel wronge:
God leue him sone to honge!"
[6] Quot Hauelok, " Hwan that ye it wite.
Nu wile ich that ye doun site,

[6] Guot, Ms. Cf. v. 1954.

And after Godrich haues wrouht,
That haues in sorwe him self brouth.
Lokes that ye demen him rith,
For dom ne spared clerk ne knith,
And sithen shal ich understonde
Of you, after lawe of londe,
Manrede, and holde othes bothe,
Yif ye it wilen, and ek rothe."
Anon ther dune he hem sette,
For non the dom ne durste lette,
And demden him to binden faste
Vpon an asse swithe unwraste,
Andelong, nouht ouerthwert,
His nose went unto the stert;
And so to Lincolne lede,
Shamelike in wicke wede,
And hwan he cam unto the borw,
Shamelike ben led ther thoru,
Bi southe the borw, unto a grene,
That thare is yet, als Y wene,
And there be bunden til a stake,
Abouten him ful gret fir make,
And al to dust be brend rith there;
And yet demden he ther more,
Other swikes for to warne,
That hise children sulde tharne
Euere more that heritage,
That hise was, for hise utrage.

Hwan the dom was demd and seyd,
Sket was the swike on the asse leyd,
And [7] him til that ilke grene,
[col. 2] And brend til asken al bidene.
Tho was Goldeboru ful blithe,
She thanked God fele sythe,
That the fule swike was brend,
That wende wel hire bodi aue shend,
And seyde, " Nu is time to take
Manrede of brune, and of blake,
That ich se ride and go:
Nu ich am wreke of mi fo."
Hauelok anon manrede tok
Of alle Englishe, on the bok,
And dide hem grete othes swere,
That he sholden him god feyth bere
Ageyn alle that woren liues,
And that sholde ben born of wiues.
Thanne he haueden sikernesse
Taken of more and of lesse,
Al at hise wille, so dide he calle
The erl of Cestre, and hise men alle,
That was yung knith wituten wif
And seyde, " Sire erl, bi mi lif,
And thou wile mi conseyl tro,
Ful wel shal ich with the do,
For ich shal yeue the to wiue
The fairest thing that is oliue.

[7] *Qu.* led.

That is Gunnild of Grimesby,
Grimes douther, bi seint Dauy!
That me forth broute, and wel fedde,
And ut of Denemark with me fledde,
Me for to burwe fro mi ded:
Sikerlike, thoru his red
Haue ich liued into this day,
Blissed worthe his soule ay!
I rede that thu hire take,
And spuse, and curteyse make,
For she is fayr, and she is fre,
And al so hende so she may be.
Thertekene she is wel with me,
That shal ich ful wel shewe the,
For ich giue the a giue,
That euere more hwil ich liue,
For hire shaltu be with me dere,
That wile ich that this folc al here."
The erl ne wolde nouth ageyn
The king be, for knith ne sweyn,
[fol. 219. col. 1.] Ne of the spusing seyen nay,
But spusede that ilke day.
That spusinge was god time maked,
For it ne were neuere clad ne naked,
In a thede samened two
That cam togidere, liuede so,
So they dide al here liue:
He geten samen sones fiue,

That were the beste men at nede,
That mouthe riden on ani stede.
Hwan Gunnild was to Cestre brouth,
Hauelok the gode ne forgat nouth
Bertram, that was the erles kok,
That he ne dide callen ok,
And seyde, "Frend, so God me rede!
Nu shaltu haue riche mede,
For wissing, and thi gode dede,
That tu me dides in ful gret nede.
For thanne Y yede in mi cuuel,
And ich ne haue[de] bred, ne sowel,
Ne Y ne hauede no catel,
Thou feddes and claddes me ful wel.
Haue nu for thi of Cornwayle
The erldom il del, withuten fayle,
And al the lond that Godrich held,
Bothe in towne, and ek in feld;
And therto wile ich, that thu spuse,
And fayre bring hire until huse,
Grimes douther, Leuiue the hende,
For thider shal she with the wende.
Hire semes curteys for to be,
For she is fayr so flour on tre;
The heu is swilk in hire ler,
So the rose in roser,
Hwan it is fayr sprad ut newe
Ageyn the sunne, brith and lewe."

And girde him sone with the swerd
Of the erldom, biforn his ferd,
And with his hond he made him knith,
And yaf him armes, for that was rith,
And dide him there sone wedde,
Hire that was ful swete in bedde.
After that he spused wore,
Wolde the erl nouth dwelle thore,
But sone nam until his lond,
[col. 2.] And seysed it al in his hond,
And liuede ther inne, he and his wif,
An hundred winter in god lif,[8]
And gaten mani children samen,
And liueden ay in blisse and gamen.
Hwan the maydens were spused bothe,
Hauelok anon bigan ful rathe
His Denshe men to feste wel
Wit riche landes and catel,
So that he weren alle riche:
For he was large and nouth chinche.
Ther after sone, with his here,
For he to Lundone, for to bere
Corune, so that it sawe,
Henglishe ant Denshe, heye and lowe,
Hwou he it bar with mikel pride,
For his barnage that was unride.

[8] Between this line and the next are inserted in the Ms. the words: *For he saw that he*, which have been subsequently struck out by the same hand, and the word *vacat* affixed.

The feste of his [9]coruning
Laste with gret ioying
Fourti dawes, and sumdel mo;
Tho bigunnen the Denshe to go
Vnto the king, to aske leue,
And he ne wolde hem nouth greue,
For he saw that he woren yare
Into Denemark for to fare,
But gaf hem leue sone anon,
And bitauhte hem seint Johan;
And bad Ubbe, his iustise,
That he sholde on ilke wise
Denemark yeme and gete so,
That no pleynte come him to.

Hwan he wore parted alle samen,
Hauelok bi lefte wit ioie and gamen
In Engelond, and was ther inne
Sixti winter king with winne,
And Goldeboru qūen, that I wene:
So mikel loue was hem bitwene,
That al the werd spak of hem two:
He louede hire, and she him so,
That neyther othe mithe be
For other, ne no ioie se,
But yf he were [1]togidere bothe;
Neuere yete ne weren he wrothe,
For here loue was ay newe,
[f 219. b. col. 1.] Neuere yete wordes ne grewe

[9] corunig, Ms. [1] togidede, Ms.

Bitwene hem, hwar of ne lathe
Mithe rise, ne no wrathe.
He geten children hem bitwene
Sones and douthres rith fiuetene,
Hwar of the sones were kinges alle,
So wolde God it sholde bifalle;
And the douhtres alle quenes:
Him stondes wel that god child strenes.
Nu haue ye herd the gest al thoru
Of Hauelok and of Goldeborw.
Hw he weren born, and hw fedde,
And hwou he woren with wronge ledde
In here youthe, with trecherie,
With tresoun, and with felounye,
And hwou the swikes haueden thit
Reuen hem that was here rith,
And hwou he weren wreken wel,
Haue ich sey you eueril del;
And for thi ich wolde biseken you,
That hauen herd the rim nu,
That ilke of you, with gode wille,
Seye a *pater noster* stille,
For him that haueth the rym maked,
And therfore fele nihtes waked;
That Ihesu Crist his soule bringe
Biforn his fader at his endinge.

AMEN.

THE FRENCH TEXT

OF THE

Romance of Havelok.

[E Mss. Coll. Fec. Arm. sign. E. D. N. No. 14.]

[fol. 125. b. col. 1.]

Uolenters deueroit l'om oir.
Et reconter & retenir.
Les nobles fez as anciens.
Et les prouesces & les biens.
Essamples prendre & remembrer.
Pur les francs homes amender.
Vilainies & mesprisions.
Ceo deuereit estre li sermons.
Dont l'om se deust chastier.
Car mult i-ad mauueis mester.
Chescuns se garde come pur soi.
L'auenture d'un riche roi.
Et de plusurs autres barons.
Dont ieo vus nomerai les nons.
Assez briefment le vus dirrai.
L'auenture vus conterai.
Haueloc fut cil roi nomé.
Et Cuaran est appellé.
Pur ceo vus voil de lui conter.
Et s'auenture remembrer.
Qe vn lai en firent li Breton.
Si l'appellerent de son non.

Et Haueloc & Cuarant.
De son piere dirrai auant.
Gunter out non, si fut Danois.
La terre tint, si estoit rois.
En icel tens qe Arthur regna.
Vers Danemarche mer passa.
La terre vout souz mettre a soi.
Et le treu auer del Roi.
Au roi Gunter se combati.
Et as Danois sis venqui.
Li rois meismes i-fut occis.
Et plusurs autres del pais.
Hodulf l'occist par traison.
Qui touz iors out le queor felon.
Quant Arthur out finie sa guerre.
Hodulf dona tote la terre.
Et les homages des barons.
Puis s'en ala od ses Bretons.
[col. 2.] Qe par destreit, qe par poour.
Hodulf seruirent li plusour.
Tieus i-out, li quistrent mal.
Par le consail Sigar l'estal.
Qui prodome fut & riche bier.
Et bien sauoit guerroier.
Cil auoit le corn a garder.
Qe nuls homs ne pout soner.
Si dreit heir ne fust del lignage.
Sur les Danois par heritage.

Einz qe li Rois Arthurs venist.
Ne od les Danois se combatist.
Gunter auoit vn soen chastel.
Sus la marine fort & bel.
De viande estoit bien garniz.
Dedenz mist sa femme & son fiz.
A vn baron de la contrée.
En ad la garde comandée.
Grim out non, mult le crei.
Leaument l'out touz tens serui.
Sur totes riens li comanda.
Son fiz qu'il forment ama.
Qe si de lui mesauenoit.
En bataille s'il morroit.
Q'a son poeir le garantist.
Et fors del pais le meist.
Qu'il ni fust ne pris ne trouez.
N'a ses enemis liuerez.
Li emfes n'estoit gaires granz.
N'auoit mie plus de .vii. anz.
Totes les houres q'il dormoit.
Vne flambe de lui issoit.
Par la bouche li venoit fors.
Si grant chalur auoit el cors.
La flambe rendoit tiel odour.
Onc ne sentit nul home meillour.
A grant merueille le tenoient.
Cil de la terre qui la veoient.

Puis qe li rois Gounter fut morz.
Et ses barons & son efforz.
[fol. 126. col. 1.] Hodulf chai & dechaca.
Tuz ceus q'il sout q'il ama.
La reyne grant poour out.
Et li prodoms qi la gardout.
Qui le chastel sus eus preist.
Et le fiz le Roi occeist.
N'ont mie force a eus defendre.
Autre consail lur estoet prendre.
Grim fet niefs apparailler.
Et de viande bien charger.
Fors del pais s'en uout fuir.
Pur le droit heir[1] de mort garrir.
La reyne merra od soi.
Pur la doute del felon roi.
Qui occis auoit son seignur.
Tost feroit a li deshonur.
Quant sa nief fut apparaillée.
Dedenz fist entrer sa meisnée.
Ses cheualers & ses serganz.
Sa femme demeine & ses enfanz:
La reyne mist el batel.
Haueloc tint souz son mantel.
Il meismes apres entra.
A Dieu del ciel se comanda.
Del hauene sont desancré.
Car il eurent bon orré.

[1] hoir, Ms.

Le trauers eurent de la mier.
Mes ne sieuent qu'en part aler.
Ou garder pussent lur seignur.
Malement lur auint le iour.
Car outlaghes les encontrerent.
Qui hautement les escrierent.
Mult durement les assaillirent.
Et cil forment se defendirent.
Mes il eurent poi desforz.
Li outlaghe les ont touz morz.
Ni remist nul petit ne grant.
Fors Grim, qui ert lur conoissant.
Sa femme & ses enfanz petiz.
Et Haueloc i-est garriz.
[col. 2.] Puis qe de eus furent eschapé.
Tant ont nagé & tant siglé.
Q'en vne hauene sont paruenu.
Et de la nief a terre issu.
Ceo fut el North a Grimesbi.
A icel tens qe ieo vus di.
Ni out onques home habité.
Ne cele hauene n'ert pas haunté.
Il i-adresca primes maison.
De lui ad Grimesbi a non.
Quant Grim primes i-ariua.
En .ii. moitez sa nief trencha.
Les chiefs en ad amont drescé.
Iloec dedenz s'est herbergé.

Pescher aloit sicome il soloit.
Siel vendoit & achatoit.
Tant q'il fut iloec bien seu.
Et des paisanz bien coneu.
Plusurs a li s'acompaignerent.
Sus le hauene se herbergerent.
Pur son non q'il eurent oi.
Le lui appellerent Grimesbi.
Li prodoms son seignur nurrit.
Et sa femme bien le seruit.
Pur lur enfant tuz le tenoient.
Car autre chose ne sauoient.
Grim li out fet changer son non.
Qe par tant nel conuist l'om.
Li emfes creut & amenda.
De cors de membres esforca.
Einz qu'il eust gaires de ée.
Ni trouast il home barbé.
S'encontre lui liuter vousist.
Qe li emfes ne la batist.
Mult fut forz & vertuous.
Et enpernant & airous.
A merueille s'en esioit.
Grim le prodome qi le nurrit.
Mes de ceo out le queor dolent.
[f. 126. b. col. 1.] Qu'il n'ert nurri entre tiele gent.
Ou il puist auqes entendre.
Et afetement aprendre.

Car il quidoit en son corage.
Qe oncore aueroit son heritage.
Grim l'appella vn iour a soi.
' Beau fiz,' fet il, ' entend a moi.
Ici manom mult soutiuement.
Od pescheours, od poure gent.
Qui se garrissent de pescher.
Tu ne siez rien de cel mester.
Ici ne poez sauer nul bien.
Tu ne gaigneras ia rien.
Va-t-en beau fiz en Engleterre.
A prendre sens & auoir querre.
Tes freres meine ensemble od toi.
En la curt a vn riche roi.
Te met beau fiz souz les serganz.
Tu es forz parcreuz & granz.
Si porras grant fes porter.
A tote gent te fai amer.
Si t'abandoune del seruir.
Quant tu porras en lui venir.
Et Dieu te dount si espleiter.
Qe auques i-puissez gaigner.'
Quant li prodoms l'out enseigné.
Et de draps apparaillé.
De lui le fist partir a peine.
Les .ii. valez od li ameine.
Tuit troi quidoient estre frere.
Sicome lur auoit dit lur piere.

Tant ont le droit chemin tenu.
Qu'il sont a Nichole venu.
Aicel tens qe ieo vus di.
Vn Roi q'ert nome Alsi.
Tenoit en la terre en sa baillie.
Nicole & tote Lindesie.
Cele partie vers le north.
Et Rotelande & Stanford.
Out cil Alsi en heritage.
Mes il estoit Bret par lignage.
[col. 2.] Le roiaume vers les Surois.
Gouernoit vns autres rois.
Ekenbright out cil rois a non.
Mult out en lui noble baron.
Il out la sorour Alsi.
Compaignon furent & ami.
Orewen vne dame vaillant.
Mes entre eus n'eurent enfant.
Mes qe vne fille bele.
Argentille out non la pucele.
Rois Ekenbright fut enfermez.
Et de grant mal forment greuez.
Bien siet n'en poet garrir.
Alsi fet a lui venir.
Sa fille li ad comandée.
Et sa terre tote liuerée.
Primerement li fet iurer.
Veiant sa gent & affier.

Qe leaument la nurrireit.
Et sa terre lui gardereit.
Tant q'ele fust de tiel age.
Qe suffrir porroit mariage.
Quant la pucele seit granz.
Par le consail de ses tenanz.
Au plus fort home la dorroit.
Qe el reaume troueroit.
Qu'il li baillast ses citez.
Ses chasteus & ses fermetez.
Sa niece en garde & sa sorour.
Et tuz les homes de lonur.
Mes la reyne en maladit.
Puis qe Ekenbright finit.
Hastiuement refut finie.
Lez son seignur fut enfouie.
De eus estoet ore ci lesser.
De Haueloc voil auant conter.
Rois Alsi qui donc regna.
Et les .ii. regnes gouerna.
Bone curt tient & grant gent.
A Nicole manoit souent.
[fol. 127. col. 1.] Cil Haueloc a sa curt vint.
Et vn keu le roi le retint.
Purceo qe fort le vist & grant.
Et mult le vist de bon semblant.
Merueillous fes pocit leuer.
Busche tailler, ewe porter.

Les esquieles receuoit.
Et apris manger les lauoit.
Et quantqu'il poeit purchacer.
Piece de char ou pain enter.
Mult le donoit volentiers.
As valez & as esquiers.
Tant estoit franc & deboneire.
Qe tuz voloit lur pleisir fere.
Pur la franchise q'il out.
Entre eus le tenoient pur sot.
De lui fesoient lui deduit.
Cuaran l'appelloient tuit.
Car ceo tenoient li Breton.
En lur language quistron:
Souent le menoient auant.
Li cheualer & sergant.
Pur la force q'en li fu.
Desqu'il seurent sa grant vertu.
Deuant eus liuter le fesoient.
As plus forz homes q'il sauoient.
Et il trestouz les abatit.
Et si nuls de eus le mesdeisist.
Par dreite force le lioit.
Tant le tenoit & iustisoit.
Qu'il li auoit tut pardoné.
Et qu'il restoient acordé.
Li rois forment s'esmerueilloit.
De la force q'en lui veoit.

Dis des plus forz de sa meson.
N'eurent vers li nule fuison.
.xii. homes ne poeient leuer.
Le fes qu'il poeit porter.
En la curt fut lungement.
Dici q'un assemblement.
[col. 2.] Qe li baron a la curt vindrent.
Qui de Ekenbright lur terre tindrent.
Et lors tenoient de Argentille.
La meschine qu'ert sa fille.
Que ia estoit creue & grant.
Et bien poeit auoir enfant.
Le roi en ont a raison mis.
Et de sa niece l'ont requis.
Q'a tiel home la mariast.
Q'is meintenist & conseillast.
Et si gardast son serement.
Qu'il s'en aquitast leaument.
Li rois oit qe cil disoient.
Et la requeste qe cil fesoient.
Vn respit lur en demanda.
Et dist qu'il s'en conseillera.
Sauer voudra & demander.
A qui il la porra doner.
Terme lur mist & ior noma.
A repairer les comanda.
Quant il se serra conseillez.
Et il si fut mult veziez.

A ses priuez en ad parlé.
Et son corage tut demustré.
Consail lur quist & demanda.
De ceus qi requeroient ia.
Q'a sa niece donast seignur.
Q'is maintenist a honur.
Mes il vout mielz suffrir lur guerre.
Q'il ne soit dessaisi de la terre.
Ceo li dient si conseiller.
'Fetes la loignz enmener.
En Bretaigne dela la mer.
Et a vos parenz comander.
Nonaine seit en vne abbeie.
Si serue Dieu tote sa vie.'
'Seignurs, tut el enpensé ai.
Tut altrement m'en deliuerai.
Rois Ekenbright quant il fina.
[f. 127. b. col. 1.] Et sa fille me comanda.
Vn serement me fist iurer.
Veianz vus touz & affier.
Qe au plus fort home la dorroie.
Qe en la terre troueroie.
Leaument me pus acquiter.
A Cuaran la voil doner.
Celui qu'est en ma cuisine.
De chauderes serra reyne.
Quant li baron repaireront.
Et la requeste me feront.

Oianz touz lur voil mustrer.
Qe a mon quistron la voil doner.
Qui fort est & de grant vertu.
Ceo sieuent cil qi l'ont veu.
S'il ni ad qui le contredie.
Ne qi le mattourt a vileinie.
Dedenz ma prison le mettrai.
Et au quistron cele dorrai.'
Ansi ad li rois diuisé.
Au ior q'il out a ceus nomé.
Apparailla de ses priuez.
En sa chambre .vii. vinz armez.
Car il quidoit auer mellée.
La ou ele serroit esposée.
A la curt vindrent li baron.
Li rois lur mustra sa raison.
'Seignurs,' fet il, 'ore m'escotez.
Puis qe ci estes assemblez.
Vne requeste me feistes.
L'autrer quant a moi venistes.
Q'a ma niece seignur donasse.
Et sa terre li otriasse.
Vus sauez bien & ieo le vus di.
Quant Ekenbright le roi fini.
En ma garde sa fille mist.
Vn serement iurer me fist.
Q'au plus fort home la dorroie.
Qe el reaume trouer porroie.

Assez ai quis & demandé.
Tant q'en ai vn fort troué.
[col. 2.] Vn valet ai en ma quisine.
A qui ieo dorrai la meschine.
Cuaran ad cil a non.
Li dis plus fort de ma maison.
Ne se poent a lui tenir.
Son giu ne sa liute suffrir.
Veritez est desq'a Rome.
De corsage n'ad si grant home.
Si garder voil mon serement.
Ne la pus doner autrement.'
Quant li baron ont escuté.
Qu'il out dite sa volenté.
Entre eus dient en apert.
Qe ceo n'ert ia par eus suffert.
Ia ienst granz coups donez.
Quant il fet venir les armez.
Sa niece lur fet amener.
Et a Cuaran esposer.
Pur lui auiler & honir.
La fist la nuit lez lui gisir.
Quant couché furent ambedui.
Cele out grant honte de lui.
Et il assez greindre de li.
As deuz se geut, si se dormi.
Ne voloit pas q'ele veist.
La flambe qe de lui issist.

Mes puis s'asseurerent tant.
Et par parole & par semblant.
Qu'il l'ama & od lui geut.
Come od s'espouse fere deut.
La nuit qe primes en parla.
Tiel ioie en out q'il l'ama.
Qu'il se dormit & oblia.
Enuers se geut, ne se garda.
Et la meschine s'endormi.
Ses braz getta sus son ami.
Iceo li auint en auision.
Q'ele ert alée a son baron.
Outre la mier en vn boscage.
La troeuent vn ors sauuage.
[fol. 128. col. 1.] Goupilz auoit en sa compaigne.
Tut fut couerte la champaigne.
Cuaran voleient assaillir.
Quant d'autre part virent venir.
Chiens & senglers qui le defendoient.
Et des goupilz mult occioient.
Quant li goupil furent venu.
Vn des senglers par grant vertu.
Ala vers l'ours si l'enuait.
Iloeqes l'occit & abatit.
Li goupil qi od li se tindrent.
Vers Coarun ensemble vindrent.
Deuant li se mistrent a terre.
Semblant firent de merci querre.

Et Coaran les fist lier.
Puis vout a la mier repairer.
Mes li arbre qi el bois erent.
De totes parz li enclinerent.
La mier crut & flot monta.
De si qa lui grant poour a.
Deus leons vist de grant fierté.
Vers lui vindrent tut effrée.
Les bestes del bois deuoroient.
Celes q'en lur voies trouoient.
Coaran fut en grant effrei.
Plus pur s'amie qe pur sei.
Sur vne halte arbre monterent.
Pur les leons q'il doterent.
Mes li leon auant aloient.
Desouz l'arbre sagenuilloient.
Semblant li firent d'amour.
Et qu'il le tenoient a seignur.
Par tut le bois out si grant cri.
Qe Argentille s'en esperi.
Mult out del sunge grant poour.
Puis out greindre de son seignur.
Pur la flambe q'ele choisit.
Qe de la bouche li issit.
En sus se trest & si cria.
Si durement q'ele esueilla.
[col. 2.] ‘ Sire,’ fet ele, ‘ vus ardez.
Lasse tut, estes allumez.’

Cil le braca & estreinst vers soi.
' Bele amie,' fet il, ' purquoi.
Estes vus issi effreie?
Qui vus ad issi espoentee?'
' Sire,' fet ele, ' ieo sungai.
L'auision vus conterai.'
Conte li ad & coneu.
Del feu li dist q'ele ad veu.
Qui de sa bouche venoit fors.
Ele quidoit qe tut son cors.
Fust allumé, pur ceo cria.
Cuaran la reconforta.
' Bele,' fet il, ' ne dotez rien.
C'est bon au vostre vs & au mien.
L'avision qe auez veue.
Demain poet estre conue.
Li rois doit sa feste tenir.
Touz ses barons i-fet venir.
Veneison i-auera assez.
Ieo dorrai hastes & lardez.
As esquiers a grant plenté.
Et as valez qui m'ont amé.
Li esquier sont li goupil.
Et li garcon qi sont plus vil.
Et li ours fut deshier occis.
Et en nostre quisine mis.
Deus tors fist hui le roi beiter.
Pur les leons le purus[2] conter.

[2] *Qu.* purums, *i. e.* pourrons.

Les ploms poom mettre pur mier.
Dont le feu fet l'ewe monter.
Dite vus ai l'auision.
Ne soiez mes en suspecion.
Le feu qi ma bouche getta.
Bien vus dirrai quei ceo serra:
Nostre quisine ardera, ceo crei.
Si en ert en peine et en effrei.
De porter fors nos chaudrons.
Et nos pieles & nos ploms.
[f. 128. b. col. 1.] Et ne puroec ne quier mentir.
De ma bouche soelt feu issir.
Quant ieo me dorm ne sai purquei.
Issi m'auient ceo prise mei.'
Del sounge lessent atant.
Puis s'endorment li enfant
Mes lendemain la matinée.
Quant Argentille fut leuée.
Vn chamberlenc qui fut od li.
Qui son piere auoit nurri.
L'avision dist & conta.
Icil a bien la tourna.
Puis li ad dit, ' en Lindesie.
Estoit vns homs de seinte vie.
Heremite fut, en bois manoit.
S'a lui parlast, il lui dirroit.
Del sounge quei ceo porroit estre.
Car Dieu l'amoit, si ert prestre.'

‘ Amis,’ fet ele, ‘ mult te croi.
Pur amour Dieu vien od moi.
A cel heremite voil parler.
Si tu i-voels od moi aler.’
Cil li otrie bonement.
Qe od lui irra priueement.
Vne chape li affubla.
Al heremitage la mena.
Al seint home la fist parler.
Et son corage tut mustrer.
Del songe dont ele out poour.
Et de la bouche son seignour.
Dont ele auoit le feu veu.
Mes ne sauoit quei ceo fu.
Par charité li quiert et prie.
Q'il la conseilt, si l'en die.
Son auis & sa volenté.
Li heremites ad suspiré.
A Dieu comence s'oreison.
Puis li dist de l'auision.
‘ Bele,’ fet il, ‘ ceo qe sunge as.
De ton baron tu le verras.
[col. 2.] Il est né de real lignage.
Oncore auera grant heritage.
Grant gent fra vers li encline.
Il serra roi & tu reyne.
Demande li qi fut son piere.
Et s'il ad sorour ne frere.

Puis si meint en lur contrée.
Iloec orras la destinée.
Dont ert nez & dont il est.
Et Dieu del ciel vertu te prest.
Et te dount tieu chose oir.
Que te pusse a bien reuertir.'
Argentille congé demande.
Et li seinz homs a Dieu la comande.
Ele s'en uet a son seignur.
Priuement & par amur.
Le demande ou il ert nez.
Et ou estoit sis parentez.
'Dame,' fet il, 'a Grimesby.
La les lessai quant ieo vinc ci.
Grim le peschere est mon piere.
Saburc ad non ceo quid ma mere.'
'Sire,' fet ele, 'aloms querre.
Si deliuerom au roi sa terre.
Dont il m'ad exillé a tort.
Et vus & moi, s'il si demoert.
Mieuz voil aillors estre mendiue.
Qe entre les miens estre cheitiue.'
Coaran li ad respondu.
'Dame, tost i-serroms venu.
Volenters vus merrai od moi.
Alom prendre congé au roi.'
Si firent il par matin.
Puis se mistrent au chimin.

Les .ii. fiz Grim amenerent.
A Grimesby s'en alerent.
Mes li prodoms estoit finiz.
Et la Dame q'is out nurriz.
Kelloc sa fille i-ont trouée.
Vn marchant l'out esposée.
[fol. 129. col. 1.] Il saluerent le seignur.
Si parlerent a lur sorour.
Il li demandent de lur piere.
Coment le fesoit lur miere.
Ele lur ad dit qe mort estoient.
Et li entrant grant doel fesoient.
Kelloc appella Coarant.
Si li demanda en riant.
'Amis,' fet il, 'par ta foi.
Ceste femme qu'est od toi.
Qui est ele, mult par est bele.
Est ele dame ou Damoisele?'
'Dame,' fet il, 'Rois Alsi.
Qe ai lungement ai[3] serui.
La me dona des l'autre ior.
Sa niece est fille de sa sorour.
Fille est au roi de grant parage.
Mes il la[4] tout son heritage.'
Kelloc oit qe cil li dist.
Merueillouse pité li prist.
De ceo qe fiz a Roi estoit.
Et de la femme q'il auoit.

[3] *Sic.* [4] *Qu.* il a.

Haueloc auant appella.
Et a consail li demanda.
Qui fiz il ert s'il le sauoit.
Si son parente conoissoit.
Il li respont, ' Grim fut mon piere.
Tu es ma soer, cist sont mi frere.
Qui sont ci od moi venu.
Bien sai qe nostre soer es tu.'
Kelloc li dist, ' n'est pas issi.
Bien te ciele si ieo le te di.
Fai ta femme auant venir.
Et toi & lui ferai ioir.
Qui fiz tu es ieo le te dirrai.
La verité t'en conterai.
Ton piere fut Gonter li rois.
Qui sire fut sur les Danois.
Hodulf l'occist par traison.
Qui tuz iors out le queor felon.
[col. 2.] Li rois Arthur Hodulf feffa.
Et Danemarche li dona.
Grim vostre piere s'enfuit.
Pur toi garrir terre guerpit.
Ta miere fut en mier perie.
Car nostre nief fut assaillie.
De outlaghes qe nus saisirent.
Li plus de nostre gent i-perirent.
Nous eschapames de la mort.
Ci ariuames a cest port.

Ne vout mon piere auant aler.
Ici li estoet demorer.
Sus cest hauene se herberga.
Sile vendit et achata.
Mult se pena de toi nurrir.
Et de celer & de couerir.
Pouerement estoit vestuz.
Qe ne fussez aparceu.
N'out si hardi en sa maison.
Qui osast dire ton droit non.
Haueloc auez a non, amis.
Si aler voillez en vostre pais.
Mon seignur vus i-condiuera.
Dedenz sa nef vus passera.
L'autrer en vint, n'ad mie vn mois.
Assez oit qe li Danois.
Vus voudroient entre eus tenir.
Car mult se fet li rois hair.
Vn prodome ad en la terre.
Qui touz iors ad vers li guerre.
Sigar l'estal est appellez.
A lui looms qe vus alez.
Il ad vne vostre parente.
Que pur vus est souent dolente.
Q'ele ne poet nouele oir.
Car desq'a eus porrez venir.
Oncore auerez vus vos heritez.
Ces .ii. valez od vus merrez.'

Argentille quant ele l'oit.
Mult durement s'en esioit.
[f. 129. b. col. 1.] A eus promet foi & amur.
Si Dieu la mette a honur.
Grant bien lur fera ceo dit.
Puis ni out gaires de respit.
Lur nief tost apresterent.
Vers Danemarche mer passerent.
Quant il sont el pais venu.
Et de la nief a terre issu.
Li marchant q'is amena.
De bons draz les atourna.
Puis lur enseigne q'il feront.
Et a quiele ville il turneront.
A la cité del seneschal.
Qe l'om appelle Sigar l'estal.
'Haueloc,' fet il, 'beaus amis.
Quant tu vendras a son pais.
En son chastel va herberger.
Et a sa table va manger.
Par charité quier le conrei.
Ta femme meine ensemble od tei.
Assez tost te demanderont.
Par la beauté q'en lui verront.
Qui tu es, & de quiele contrée.
Et qi tiele femme t'ad donée.'
Il s'en partent del marchant.
Si tienent lur chemin auant.

Tant ont trauaillé & erré.
Qu'il paruienent a la cité.
La ou le seneschal manoit.
Au chastel alerent tut droit.
Le riche home en la curt trouerent.
Par charité li demanderent.
Le conroi q'il lur ottriast.
Et q'a nuit les herbergast.
Li senescaus le lur granta.
Dedenz la sale les mena.
Quant fut houre del manger.
Et qe tuz alerent lauer.
Li prodoms a manger s'assist.
Les .iii. valez seeir i-fist.
[col. 2.] Argentille lez son seignur.
Serui furent a grant honur.
Li bacheler & li esquier.
Qui seruirent au manger.
La bele Dame ont esgardée.
Et sa beauté forment loée.
En vne part se turnent sis.
Ensemble ont lur consail pris.
Q'au valet sa femme toudront.
S'il s'en coruce, si le bateront.
Quant il leuerent del manger.
Li valez se vont herberger.
Li senescaus les fet mener.
A vn ostel pur reposer.

Cil qui la dame ont coueitée.
Qui mult ert bele & enseignée.
Apres eus vont en vne rue.
Au valet ont sa femme tolue.
Od eus l'eussent enmenée.
Quant Haueloc ad recouerée.
Vne hache trenchante & dure.
Ne sai par quele auenture.
Vn de ceus la tint & porta.
Il li tolit, si s'en ala.
Les cink en ad tue & occis.
Li vns est eschapez vifs.
Mes qe le poign out coupé.
Le cri lieue en la cité.
Cil s'enturnerent en fuiant.
A vn mouster vindrent currant.
Pur garison i-sont entré.
Les huis ont sus eus fermé.
Haueloc monta en la tour.
Cil del burg l'asseent entour.
De totes parz l'ont assailli.
Et il bien se defendi.
Desur le meur la piere prent.
Aual la gette igniielement.
La nouele vint au chastel.
Au seneschal, qui n'est pas bel.
[fol. 130. Qe cil qu'il auoit herbergé.
col. 1.] Cinc de ses homes ont tué.

Et li sistes est afolez.
Et il s'en est eschapez.
En la tour del mouster s'est mis.
Et li burgois l'ont assis.
Mult par l'assaillent durement.
Et il se defent asprement.
Les quareus de la tour enrue.
Mulz en mahaigne, plus en tue.
Li senescaus cheual demande.
A touz ses cheualers comande.
Qe od li augent a la meslée.
Q'en la cité est leuée.
Tut primerain vet au mouster.
Et vist celui si bien aider.
Qu'il les fet tuz trere arere.
Chescun se doute q'il n'esfiere.
Li senescaus ala auant.
Vist Haueloc & creu & grant.
Et a sa table auoit mangé.
Ensemble od lui out esté.
Gent cors & bele feture.
Lungs braz & grant furcheure.
Ententiuement l'esgarda.
De son seignur li remenbra.
Del roi Gunter q'il tant ama.
Anguissousement suspira.
Cil le resembloit de visage.
Et de grandour & de corsage.

Il ad fet remaneir l'assaut.
Et defent qe nuls ni aut.
Le valet ad a reson mis.
'Ne gettez mes,' fet il, 'amis.
Triues te doun, parole a moi.
L'achaison me di & purquoi.
Tu as mes homes issi morz.
As quieus de vus en est li torz.'
'Sire,' fet il, 'ieo vus dirrai.
Qe ia d'un mot n'en mentirai.
[col. 2.] Quant nus del manger turnames.
Oreinz & al ostel alames.
A leisir de vostre meson.
Me pursuirent li garcon.
Ma femme me voudrent tolir.
Et deuant moi od lui gisir.
Une de lur haches saisi.
Et moi & li en defendi.
Verité est qe ieos occis.
Mes sur moi defendant le fis.'
Li seneschaus quant il oit.
Le surfet do seus, li respondit.
'Amis,' fet il, 'venez auant.
Si ne dotez tant ne quant.
Gardez qe pas ne vus celez.
Dites moi dont estes nez.'
'Sire,' fet il, 'de cest pais.
Ceo me conta vns mis amis.

Vn riche home qi Grim out a non.
Qui me nurrit en sa maison.
Puis qe le regne fut conquis.
Et nus pieres fut occis.
Ensemble od moi & od ma mere.
M'en fui, puis la mort mon piere.
Mult enporta or & argent.
Par mier errames lungement.
De outlaghes fumes assailli.
Ma mere occistrent & ieo garri.
Et li prodoms s'en eschapa.
Qui me nurrit & mult m'ama.
Quant nostre nief fut ariuée.
En vne sauuage contrée.
Li prodoms mansion i-leua.
Tut primerement si herberga.
Assez nus troua a manger.
Par vendre siel & par pescher.
Puis i-ad tant de gent herbergé.
Qe ville i-est et marché.
Purceo qe Grim l'appelloit l'om.
Grimesby ad la ville a non.
[f. 130. b. col. 1.] Quant ieo fui grant ieo m'en parti.
En la maison le roi Aelsi.
Fui souz le keus en la quisine.
Il me dona ceste meschine.
Sa parente ert, ne sai pur quei.
Il assembla & lui & mei.

Jeo l'enmenai fors de la terre.
Ore sui venu mes amis quere.
Ne sai ou pusse nul trouer.
Car ieo ne sai nul nomer.'
Li senescaus li respondi.
' Beaus amis, ton non me di.'
' Haueloc, sire, sui nomez.
Et Coaran fui r'appellez.
Quant en la curt le roi estoie.
Et de sa quisine seruoie.'
Li senescaus se purpensa.
En son corage se remenbra.
Qe si out non li fiz le roi.
Qe Grim en out mene od soi.
Purpoi q'il nel ad coneu.
Mes ne pur quant en doute fu.
Par triues l'ad asseuré.
Et el chastel l'ad amené.
Sa femme & ses compaignons.
Il les appelle ses prisons.
Mult les fist bien seruir.
La nuit en sa chambre gisir.
Quant li enfant [furent][5] cuché.
Vn son priué i-ad mandé.
Pur saueir quant cil dormira.
Si flambe de lui istra.
Car ceo auenoit au fiz le roi.
Qe Grim out mene od soi.

[5] Cf. v. 381.

Haueloc fut mult las.
Endormi s'est igniel pas.
Meisme l'ure qu'il dormit.
De sa bouche le feu issit.
Le chamberlenc out grant poour.
Conter le vait a son seignur.
[col. 2.] Et il en ad Dieu mercie.
Qe le dreit heir ad recoueré.
Ses chapeleins fet demander.
Ses briefs escriure & enseeler.
Par ses messages les manda.
Et pur ses amis enuoia.
Pur ses homes pur ses parenz.
Mult i-assembla granz genz.
Tuz ceus qi el pais estoient.
Qui le roi Hodulf haoient.
Par matin fet les baigns temprer.
Et celui baigner & lauer.
De riches draz l'ad reuestu.
Et sa femme qe od lui fu.
En sa sale les ad menez.
Haueloc fut mult effreez.
De la grant gent q'il veoit.
Haueloc nill'[6] se cremoit.
Pur les homes q'il out occis.
Qe ceo fust vs de cel pais.
Qe l'om le deust issi seruir.
Baigner lauer & reuestir.

Qu. mult.

Et puis iuger pur le mesfet.
Et auant amener au plet.
N'est merueille s'il se dota.
Vne grant hache recouera.
El paleis pendit par vn croc.
As .ii. poigns l'ad pris Haueloc.
Vigerousement se voudra defendre.
S'il le voelent iuger a pendre.
Li seneschaus se regarda.
Vers lui se trest, si l'acola.
'Sire,' fet il, 'n'eiez effrei.
Cele hache rendez a mei.
N'eiez garde, ieo le vus di.
Ma leauté vus en affi.'
Il li ad la hache rendue.
Et cil l'ad au croc pendue.
A vne part le fet seeir.
Qe bien le poent tuz veeir.
[fol. 131. col. 1.] De son tresor fet apporter.
Le corn qe nul ne poet soner.
Si dreit heir n'est de lignage.
Sur les Danois par heritage.
Sauoir si soner le porroit.
Dist lur qu'il essaieroit.
Cil qui porra soner le cor.
Il lui dorra son anel dor.
N'out en la sale cheualier.
Sergant, valet, n'esquier.

Q'a sa bouche n'el mist.
Onques nuls soner n'el fist.
Le senescal ad le corn pris.
Haueloc l'ad en la main mis.
'Amis,' fet il, 'car essaiez.
Si le corn soner porrez.'
'Parfoi,' fet il, 'sire, ne sai.
Onques mes corn ne maniai.
Jeo n'en uoudroie estre gabez.
Mes puis qe vus le me comandez.
A ma bouche le corn mettrai.
Et si ieo puis ieo le sonerai.'
Haueloc est leué en piez.
Et del corner apparaillez.
Le corn ben esquit & seigna.
Hautement & bien le sona.
A grant merueille le tenoient.
Tuit cil q'en la sale estoient.
Li senescaus les appella.
A tuz ensemble le mustra.
'Seignurs, purceo vus ai mandez.
Qe Dieu nus ad reuisitez.
Veez ci nostre dreit heir.
Bien en deuom grant ioie aueir.'
Tut primerain se desafubla.
Par deuant lui s'agenuilla.
Sis homs deuint, si li iura.
Qe leaument le seruira.

Li autre sont apres alé.
Chescuns de bone volenté.
[col. 2.] Tuit si home sont deuenu.
Puis qu'il li eurent receu.
La nouele fut recontée.
Ne pout estre lunges celée.
De totes parz i-accurroient.
Et riche & pouere qui l'oeient.
De lui firent lur auowé.
A cheualier l'out adubbé.
Tant li aida le senescal.
Qui prodome fut & leal.
Qe merueillous ost assembla.
Au roi Hodulf par brief manda.
Qe la terre li deliuerast.
Hastiuement si s'en alast.
Li Rois Hodulf quant ceo oi.
Mult s'en gaba & escharni.
Ceo dist q'a lui combatera.
De totes parz gent auna.
Et li valez en reout assez.
Au iour q'entre eus fut nomez.
Qe li dui ost s'assembleroient.
Et ensemble se combateroient.
Haueloc vist la gent menue.
Q'en s'aide estoit venue.
Ne voelt qu'il soient occis.
Au roi Hodulf par ses amis.

Manda q'a lui se combatist.
Cors contre cors, & si le venquist.
Les genz a lui touz se venissent.
Et a seignur le tenissent.
Ne sai purquei se combateroient.
Qui nule culpe n'en auoient.
Li rois n'el deigna refuser.
Tote sa gent fist desarmer.
Et cil la sue de l'autre part.
Mult durement li sembla tart.
Qu'il soient ensemble venu.
Et qu'il eust gaigné ou perdu.
Ensemble vindrent li baron.
Requistrent soi come leon.
[f. 131. b. col. 1.] Haueloc fut de grant vertu.
Le Roi Hodulf ad si feru.
D'une hache q'il apporta.
Qu'il l'abatit, puis né leua.
Iloec l'occist deuant sa gent.
Qe touz li crient hautement.
'Sire, merci, qe ni moroms.
Car volenters te seruiroms.'
Cil se sont a lui tourné.
Et il lur ad tut pardoné.
Apres cest fet ad receu.
Le regne q'a son piere fu.
Par la terre bone pees mist.
Et des felons iustise prist.

Sa femme creut & l'amoit.
Et ele mult bien le seruoit.
Mult fut eincois desesperée.
Mes ore l'ad Dieus reconfortée.
Quant Haueloc est rois pussanz.
Le regne tint plus de .iiii. anz.
Merueillous tresor i-auna.
Argentille li comanda.
Qu'il passast en Engleterre.
Pur son heritage conquerre.
Dont son oncle l'out en gettée.
A grant tort desheritée.
Li rois li dist qu'il fera.
Ceo q'ele li comandera.
Sa nauie fet a turner.
Ses genz & ses ostz mander.
En mier se met quant orrea.
Et la reyne od lui mena.
Quatre vinz & quatre cenz.
Out Haueloc pleines de genz.
Tant out nagé & siglé.
Q'en Carleflure est ariué.
Sur le hauene se herbergerent.
Par le pais viande quierent.
Puis enuoia li nobles rois.
Par le consail de ses Danois.
[col. 2.] A Alsi qu'il li rendist.
La terre qe tint Ekenbright.

Q'a sa niece fut donée.
Dont il l'out desheritée.
Et si rendre n'el voleit.
Mande qu'il le purchaceroit.
Av roi uindrent li messager.
Mult le trouerent fort & fier.
Quant il li ont ceo conté.
Et il en out ris & gabé.
Par orgoil lur respondi.
'Merueille,' fet il, 'ai oi.
De Coaran cel mien quistron.
Qe ieo nurri en ma maison.
Qe me vient terre demander.
Mes keus ferai a lui iuster.
Ot trepez & od chaudrons.
Od paeles & od ploms.'
Li messager s'en sont turné.
A lur seignour ont conté.
Le respons qe le roi lur fist.
Et del terme qe le roi lur mist.
Dedenz le iour q'il eurent pris.
Alsi manda ses amis.
Et touz ceus q'il pout aueir.
Nul ni lessa remaneir.
A Theford les ostz assemblerent.
Et del ferir se conreierent.
Rois Alsi primes s'arma.
Sur vn cheual ferant monta.

Ses enemis vet surueeir.
Combien de gent poent aueir.
Quant il ad les Danois veuz.
As enseignes & as escuz.
Ne li remembra des caudrons.
Ne des paeles ne des ploms.
Dont il les auoit manacez.
Arere s'en est repairez.
Sa gent enseigne q'il feront.
Et coment se combateront.
[fol. 132. col. 1.] Entre eus fut dure la meslée.
Dissi qe vint a la vesprée.
Qu'il ne poient plus suffrir.
La neire nuit les fist partir.
Mult i-out des Danois maumis.
Et des autres assez occis.
Haueloc fut irascuz.
Pur ses homes q'il out perduz.
Od ses Danois s'en fust alez.
Et a sa nauie retournez.
Si la reine li suffrisist.
Mes vn engin ele l'aprist.
Dont il veincroit son enemi.
Remist le roi, si la crei.
Tote la nuit fist granz peus trencher.
Et de .ii. parz bien aguisser.
Les homes morz i-enficherent.
Et entre les vifs les drescerent.

Deus escheles en ont rengées.
Les haches sus les cols leuées.
Av matin quant il aiourna.
Rois Alsi primer s'arma.
Si firent tuit si cheualer.
Pur bataille comencer.
Mes quant il virent ceus dela.
Tote la char lur herica.
Mult fut hidouse la compaignie.
Des morz q'il virent en la plaine.
Contre vn home q'il auoient.
De l'autre part .vii. estoient.
Au roi dient si conseiller.
Qe bataille ni ad mester.
Li Danois sont de genz creuz.
Et il ad multz des soens perduz.
A la Dame rende son droit.
Et face pees einz qe pis soit.
Au roi l'estret tut granter.
Car il ne poet par el passer.
Par le consail de ses priuez.
Au roi Danois s'est acordez.
[col. 2.] Par fiance l'asseura.
Et saufs hostages li dona.
Tote sa terre li rendit.
Qe Ekenbright tint tant come il vesquit.
De Holande desq'en Gloucestre.
Furent Danois seignur & mestre.

Mes Haueloc sa feste tint.
A la cité quant il vint.
Des barons receut les homages.
Si lur rendre lur heritages.
Enpres cest fet Rois Aelsis.
Ne vesquit mes qe quinze dis.
Il n'out nul heir si droiturel.
Come Haueloc & sa muiller.
Li baron les ont receuz.
Et citez & chasteus renduz.
Haueloc tint en sa baillie.
Nicole & tote Lindesie.
.xx. anz regna, si en fut rois.
Assez conquist par ses Danois.
Mult fu de li grant parlance.
Li auncien par remenbrance.
Firent vn lai de sa victoire.
Qe touz iors en soit memoire.
Ceo fut le lai de Coarant.
Qui mult fut prouz & vaillant.

Explicit Haueloc.

THE

FRENCH ROMANCE

OF

Havelok

AS ABRIDGED AND ALTERED BY

GEFFREI GAIMAR.

[E Mss. Bibl. Reg. sign. 13. A. xxi. supplet. e Codd. Eccl. Cathed. Dun. C. iv. 27. et Linc. No. 50.]

I comence l'estorie des Engles solum la translacion Maistre Geffrei Gaimar.

[fol. 112. col. 1.]

Ca en arere el liuere bien deuant,
Si vus en estes remembrant,
Auez oi com faitement
Costentin [1] tint apres Artur tenement;
E com Iwain [2] fu feit reis
De Muref, e de Loeneis.
Mes de co veit mult malement,
Mort sunt tut lur meillur parent,
E li Seisne se sunt espanduz,
Ki od Certiz furent venuz.
Des Humbre tresk'en Cateneis
Doné lur out Modret li reis.
Si vnt saisi e purpris
La terre que ia tint Hengis.
Cele claiment en heritage,
Car Henges estoit de lur linage.
Este vus ci [3] acheson
Dunt en grant trauail entrent Breton.

[1] *ot ceste casement*, Ms. Dun. [2] *refait fu*, Ms. D.
[3] *une chancon*, Ms. D.

Si funt Escoz, e les Pictais,
Li Gawaleis, e li Combreis;
Tel guere funt la gent estrange,
En grant dolur entra Bretaigne.
Li Angleis tuz iurs acreisserent,
Car de ultre mer souent venaient.
Cil de Seissoigne, e de Alemaigne,
S'aiustent a lur compaigne;
Pur dan Hengis, lur ancessur,
Les altres firent d'els seignur.
[col. 2.] Tuz iurs si com il conqueraent,
Des Engleis la reconuissaient;
La terre [4]k'il vont conquerant,
Si l'apelent Engeland.
Este vus ci [5]vn acheson,
Par quel Bretaigne perdi son nun.
E les neuoz Artur regnerent,
Li encontre Engleis guereierent.

Ci perdi Bretaigne son non, e fu apelé Engeland

Meis li Daneis mult les haeient,
Pur lur parenz, ki morz estaient
Es batailles ke Artur fist
Contre Modret, k'il puis oscist.
Si co est veir ke Gilde dist,
En la geste [6]troua escrit,
Ke dous reis out ia en Bretaigne,
Quant Costentin estait cheuetaigne.
Cil Costentin, li nies Artur,
Ki out l'espée Caliburc.

[4] *ke vunt querant*, Ms. D. [5] *une chancon*, Ms. D. [6] *qu'il*, Ms. D.

Reis Adelbrict. Nortfolc.

[7]Adelbrit aueit a nun li vns des reis,
Riches hom fu, si ert Daneis;

Reis Edelsie. Nicole e Lindeseie.

Li altres out nun Edelsie,
Sue ert Nicole e Lindeseie.
Des Humbre desk'en [8]Roteland
Ert le pais en son comant.
Li altre ert reis de la contrée
Ki ore est Nortfolc apelée.
Tant s'acointerent cil dui rei,
K'il furent compaignon par fei,
E k'entre els [9]dous out tel amur,
[1]Edelsi dona sa sorur
A Adelbrit, cel riche reis,
Ki ert del linage as Daneis.
Li altre rei estait Breton,
Ki Edelsi aueit a nun.

La reine Orwain.

Sa sorur out nun Orwain,
Mult ert franche, e de bone main.

La fille Argentille,

De son seignur out vne fille,
Ke l'om apela Argentille.
La pucele crut e [2]tahit,
Car asez fu [3]ki la norit.
Si auint [4]trestut pur veir,
Ke son pere n'out nul altre eir.

[7] *Achebrit*, Ms. D. *passim*. In the same Ms. *a* and *li* are omitted.

[8] *orient*, Ms. D.

[9] Om. Ms. D.

[1] *Qu'a Edelsi*, Ms. D. and *a* om. in the next line. We should probably read, *Qu'Edelsi*.

[2] *tehid*, Ms. D.

[3] *suef*, Ms. D.

[4] *ore tut*, Ms. D.

[fol. 112. b. col. 1.]

En Denemarche le regnez
Aueit quatre riches contez,
E en Bretaigne aueit conquis
Cair Coel, od tut le pais;
De Colecestre tresk'en Hoiland
Durout son realme en vn tenant.
Tant cum il fu si poestis
Edelsi fu bien sis amis.

Mort est Adelbrict li reis.

Mes donc [5]auint ke Adelbrict fu mort
[6]Enz en la cité de [7]Teford.
A Colecestre fu portez,
Iloc fu li reis enterrez.
E Orewain, e Argentille,
Co fu la raine, e sa fille,
En sunt alé en Lindeseie.
A son frere, reis Edelsie.
Li regnes ke Adelbrict teneit
Li vnt liueré, que guarde en seit.
Car la raine ert enfermée,
Ne mais [8]vint iurs ad durée.
Apres Albrict quant fu finie,
Vnt la raine en sepelie.
E Argentille fu norie
A Nicole, e en Lindeseie.
Si com dit l'antine gent,
Ele n'out nul che ual parent,

[5] *fud Achebricht mort*, Ms. D.
[6] Om. Ms. D.
[7] *Tiedfort*, Ms. D.
[8] *Oit iurs n'en ad*, Ms. D.

De par l'un [pere][9] des Daneis:
Oiez ke fu cel felons reis.
Pur l'erité k'il coueitat,
Sa nece mesmariat.
Il la donat a vn garcon,
Ki Cuheran aueit a nun,
Pur co k'abeisser la voleit,
Se purpensa k'il li durreit.

Cist Coheran estait Haueloc.

Cil Cuheran estait quistrun,
Mes mult par ert bel valetun.
Bel vis aueit, e bele mains,
Cors [1]escheui, suef, e plains.
Li sons semblanz ert tut tens lez,
Beles iambes out, e bels piez.
Mes pur co que hardi estait,
E volunters se combateit,

[col. 2.]

N'aueit valet en la meison,
Si lui feseit ahatai son,
E sur lui comencast mellées,
K'il n'el [2]rueit, iambes leuées.
E quant il ben se corucout,
De la ceinture le hout;
E si cil dous n'aueit guarant,
Bien le bateit a vn vergant.
E [3]nepurhoc tant frans esteit,
Si lui vallez li prometteit,

[9] Ms. D.

[1] *eschiroid*, Ms. D.

[2] *ruast*, Ms. D.

[3] *nepurquant*, Ms. D.

Ke pur ico mains n'el amast,
[4]Ignel vre le deliast.
Quant il se erent entre baisez,
Donc estait Cuharan haitez.
E li reis, e li cheualer,
Li donouent de lur manger.
Asquanz li denouent gastels,
Asquanz quarters de simenels,
Les altres, hastes e gelines,
Ki lur veneint des quisines.
Ke tant aueit pain e conrei,
Ke douz vallez aueit od sei;
E as vallez de la meisons
Feseit souent mult larges dons,
De simenels, e de canestels,
E de hastes, e de gastels.[5]
Pur co estait si ben amez,
E si preisez, e si loez.
N'aueit frans hom en la meison,
Si Cuheran en voleit don,
K'il ne lui donast volunters:
Mes il n'aueit soing de luers.
De tant doner com il aueit,
Co lui ert vis ke poi estait.
E quant il n'aueit de doner,
Volunters l'alout enprunter.

[4] *Senes l'ure*, Ms. D.

[5] Vers. 137. 138. are om. in Ms. D.

Puis le donout, e despendeit,
Co k'en promtout tres ben [6]soldout.
Quant k'il aueit, trestut dunout,
Mes nule rien ne demandout.
Il ert issi en la meison
Esqueler [7]a vne quistron.
[fol. 113. col. 1.] Dous valez out, k'il nurisout:
[8]Seignurs, oiez pur quei il le fesout.
Il quidout k'il fussent si frere,
Mes ne lur apartint son pere,
Ne sa mere, ne son linage,
Ne n'estait de lur parage.
Pur hoc s'il estait en tel despit,
[9]Venuz esteit de gentil lit,
E si li reis s'aperceust,
Ne quid ke ia sa nece eust.
Dunt il ert nez pas ne saueit,
De lui son iugleur feseit.

Pur la terre Albrict tolir,
Feseit sa nece od lui gisir.
La fille al rei [en][1] pouere lit:
Ore est mesters ke Deus ait.
Car ci out feit grant crueltë,
Pur coueitise de cel regné.
Quant pur le regné sul aueir,
Honist sa nece a son espeir;

[6] *rendout*, Ms. D. [7] *cume*, Ms. D. [8] *Or*, Ms. D.
[9] *Se nuls*, Ms. D. [1] Ms. D.

E la dona a son quistrun,
Ki Cuheran aueit a nun.
Cil ne saueit ke femme estait,
Ne k'il fere [2]li deueit.
Tresk'l vnkes el lit veneit,
Adenz giseit, si se dormeit.
Argentille ert en grant purpens,
Pur quei il giseit si adenz.
E mult forment s'esmerueillout,
Ke vnkes vers lui ne se turnout.
Ne ne la voleit aprismer
Com home deit fere sa muller.
La nece al rei se compleigneit,
Souent son vncle maldisseit,
Ki si l'aueit desherité,
E a vn tel hom donée.
Tant k'il auint a vne nut,
K'il firent primes lur deduit.
Apres ico si s'endormirent,
Mult s'entreamerent, e ioirent.

Songe Argentills.

La fille al rei en son dormant
Songat, k'ele ert od Cuherant

[col. 2.]

Entre la [3]mer e vn boscage,
V conuersout vn vrs saluage.
Deuers la mer veait venir,
Pors e senglers [4]prist asaillir.

[2] *ne li*, Ms. D.
[3] *veie*, Ms. D.
[4] *prestz de saillir*, Ms. D.

Icel grant vrs, ke [5]si ert fier,
Ki voleit Cuheran manger.
Od l'urs aueit asez gopillz,
Ki puis le iur eurent perilz;
Car les senglers les entrepristent,
Mult en destruistrent e oscistrent.
Quant li gopil furent destruit,
Cel vrs, ki demenout tel bruit,
Vn sul sengler fier e hardi,
L'ad par son cors sul asailli,
Tel lui dona del vne dent,
En dous meitez le [6]quer li fent.
Quant l'urs se sent a mort feru,
Vn cri geta, puis est chay[ius,][7]
E li gopil vindrent corant
De tutes parz vers Cuherant.
Entre lur quisses lur cuetes,
Les chefs enclins [8]agenuletes,
E funt semblant de merci quere,
A Cuheran, a ki firent guere.
Quant il les out feit tuz [9]leuer,
Envers la mer volt repairer.
Li grant arbre, ki el bois erent,
De totes parz l'enclinerent.
La mer montout, e li floz vint,
De si k'al bois [unc][1] ne se tint.

[5] *tant*, Ms. D.
[6] *cors*, Ms. D.
[7] Ms. D.
[8] *enchatouettes*, Ms. D.
[9] *Lier*, Ms. D. Cf. Ms. Coll. Fec. v. 415.
[1] Ms. D.

Li bois se chaeit, la mer veneit,
Cuheran ert en grant destreit.
Apres veneient dous leons,
Si chaeient a ganillons;
Mes des bestes mult oscieient
El bois, ki en lur veie estaient.
Cuheran pur pour k'il out
Sur vn des granz arbres montout,
E les leons vindrent auant,
Envers cel arbre agenullant.
Par tut le bois out si grant cri,
Ke la dame s'en [2]eueilli;
[f. 113. b. col. 1.] E cum ele out ico sungé,
Son seignur ad fort enbracé.
Ele le troua gisant envers,
Entres ses braz si l'ad aers.
Pur la pour ses oilz ouerit,
Vne flambe vit, ki [s'en][3] issit
Fors de la buche son marri,
Ki vncore ert tut endormi.
Merueillat sei del auision,
E de la buche son baron,
E de la flambe k'ele vit:
Ore entendez k'ele dit.
'Sire,' fet ele, 'vus ardez,
Esueillez vus, si vus volez!
De vostre buche vne flambe ist,
Io ne sai vnkes ki i-mist.'

[2] *esperi*, Ms. D. Cf. Coll. Fec. v. 434. [3] Ms. D.

Tant l'enbrasca, e irest vers sei,
K'il il s'esueilla, e dist, ' pur quei,
Pur quei m'auez eueillé, bele amie?
Pur quei estes [4]espoutie?'
Tant la preia, e tant la blandist,
K'ele li conta tut, e [5]regehit,
De la flambe, e del auision
K'ele out veu de son baron.
Cuheran [l'en][6] respondi
Del auision k'il oi.
Selum son sens espeust le songe,
Kank'il dist, tut ert mencongе.
' Dame,' dist il, ' co serra bien
Anbure a vostre oes e al mien.
Ore m'est auis, ke co pot estre:
Li reis tendra demain sa feste.
Mult i-auera de ses barons:
Cerfs, e cheuerels, e veneisons,
E altres chars, tant i-auera,
E en la quisine tant remaindra,
Tant en prendrom a espandant,
Les esquiers ferai manant
De bons lardez, e de brauns,
[E][7] des esqueles as baruns.
Li esquier me sunt aclin
Ambure al vespre e al matin.
[col. 2.] Cil signefrent li gopil,
Dunt vus songastes, co sunt il.

[4] *espourie*, Ms. D. [5] *gehid*, Ms. D. [6] Ms. D. [7] Ms. D.

E l'urs est mort, hier fu oscis,
En vn bois fu saluage pris.
Dous tors i-ad pur les leons,
E pur la mer pernum les pluins,
V l'ewe monte come mer,
De si que freit la feit cesser.
La char des tors i-serra quite :—
Dame, l'avision est dite.'
Argentille quant ot co dire :
'Vncore auant me dites, sire.
Quei icel fu put espeleir,
K'en vostre buche vi ardeir?'
'Dame,' dist il, 'ne sai ke dait,
Mes en dormant si me deceit.[8]
Treske io dorm ma buche esprent,
De la flambe nient ne me sent.
[9]Veires, io en ai hunte mult grant,
Ke co m'auient en dormant.'
Dist Argentille, 'a moi entent :
Nus sumus u hontusement.
Mielz nus vendreit estre exillez,
Entre aliens, e [1]enpairez,
Ke ci gisir en tel hontage.
Amis, v est li ton linage?'
'Dame,' fet il, 'a Grimesby,
D'iloc turnai quant io vinc ci.

[8] Vers. 295. 296. are om. in Mss. Dun. and Linc.

[9] *Vers tei*, Ms. D. [1] *Enperrez*, Ms. D. *enterrez*, Ms. L.

Si la ne crois mun parenté,
Suz ciel ne sai dunt io sui né.'
'Amis,' feit ele, 'car i-alom
Sauer si ia [i-][2] trouerom.
Nuls hom ki mai ne tei amast,
V mieldre conseil nus donast.'
Dist Cuheran, 'la uraie amie!
V seit sauer, v seit folie,
Io ferai co ke vus volez.
La vus merrai, si vus me loez.'
La nut iurent tresk'al cler iur,
Lendemain vont a lur seignur.
Al rei vindrent, querent congé.
Quant il co ot, si en fu heité,
[fol. 114. col. 1.] [Tut en riant le lur dunad,
A tuz ses humes s'en gabad;
E dit, s'il unt un poi de faim,
V al tierz ior, v al demain,
Tut se mettrunt al repairier,
Quant ne purrunt mielz espleiter.
Ore s'en vunt cil a Grimesbi,
La trouerent un bon ami.
Pescheur ert, iloc maneit,
La fille Grim celui aueit.
Quant recunut les tres meschiens,
Cuaran, e les douz fiz Grims,][3]

[2] Ms. D.

[3] Ms. D. Hiatus in Ms. Reg. Some lines are also evidently wanting in Mss. D. L.

* * * * * *
* * * * en la lei
* * * peants en son corage,
Dist a sa femme, que mult ert sage:
‘ Dame,’ dist il, ‘ que ferom?
Si vus loez, descouerom
A Haueloc, le fiz le rei,
Nostre conseil, e le segrei.
Dimes li tut ouertement,
[4]Dum il est nez, e de quel gent.’
Dist la dame, ‘ s’il le saueit,
Io quid k’il le descouereit
En tel liu, par son folage,
V tost [5]l’en auendreit grant damage.
Il [6]n’e mie si sanant,
K’il sace couerir son talent.
S’il saueit ke des reis fu nez,
Curtes vres serreit celez.
E nepurhoc ore l’apelom,
Dunt il est nez [7]li demandom,
E si sa femme vent od lui:
Bien li poum dire co qui,
[8]Dum il est nez, e de quel terre,
[E][9] com il exillat par la guere.’
Atant apelent Haueloc,
E Argentille vint auoc.

[4] *Dunt*, Ms. D. [5] *li vendreit*, Ms. D. [6] *n’en est*, Ms. D.
[7] *ore*, Ms. D. [8] *Dunt*, Ms. D. [9] Ms. D.

E li prodom e sa mulier
L'unt pris mult bel aresuner.
' Amis,' funt il, dunt [1]es tu nez?
En quel liu est tis parentez?'
[col. 2.] [' Dame,' fait il, ' ci laissai
Mun parente, quant m'en turnai.
Tu es ma suer, io suis tis frere,
Ambure de pere e de mere.
Grim fud mis pere, un pescheur,
Ma mere ot nun Sebruc, sa uxor.
Quant furent mort, d'ici turnai,
Mes dous freres od mei menai.
Ore imes granz, reuenuz sumes,][2]
[M]es nos parenz ne conussumes,
Ne mais sul tai, e ton seignur:
Bien sai tu es nostre sorur.'
Respont Kelloc, tut i-ad el.
Vnc ton pere ne vendi sel,
Ne ta mere ne fu salnere.
Grim vendi sel, si fu peschere.
De mes freres grant gré te sai,
De co k'es as nuri te mercierai.
Hier ariuat [3]leus al port
Vn grant kenart, e bon, e fort.
Pain e char [4]menied, e vin, e blé,
Di cel vnt il mult grant plenté.
Vltre la mer volent passer,
Si vus volez od els aler.

[1] *estez*, Ms. D. [2] Ms. D. [3] *lays*, Ms. D. [4] *meine*, Ms. D,

Io quid k'il irrunt el pais
V sunt voz parenz e vos amis.[5]
Si vus volez od els aler,
Nus les vus purrum bien aluer.
Dras vus durrum a remners,
Si porterez de nos deners,
E pain, e char, e bon cler vin,
Pur prendre al vespre e al matin.
Conrei auerez tant cum voldrez,
Vos dous vallez od vus merrez.
Mes celez ben vostre segrei:
Vus fustes fiz a vn bon rei.
Danemarche out par heritage,
Si out son pere, e son linage.[6]
Li vostre pere out nun Gunter,
Si prist la fille al rei Gaifer.
Aluiue out nun, ele me nuri,
Maint ben me fit tant cum vesqui.
[f. 114. b. col. 1.] [Ele me leuad, co dist ma mere,
Fille sui Grim, un sun cumpere.
Mes co auint en vostre terre:
Li reis Arthur la mut conquerre.
Pur sun treu, que li detint,
Od mult grant gent el pais vint.
Al rei Gunter semblad contraire,
E iuste la mer li tint bataille.][7]

[5] Vers. 389—392. om. Ms. D. and in marg. Ms. Reg. is noted (a pr. m.) *Defec.*

[6] Vers. 401. 402. om. Ms. D. [7] Ms. D.

Oscis i-fu li reis Gunter,
E d'ambes parz maint cheualer,
Ki Artur [8] volt dona la terre.
Mes la reine, pur la guere,
Ne pout [9] en la terre remaneir:
Si s'en fui, od le dreit air.
Co estes vus, si cum io crei,
Danz Haueloc, le fiz le rei.
Mis pere aueit mult bon nef,
La reine amenout suef:
Vers cest pais [1] l'amenout,
Quant si auint, cum Deu plout,
De vtlaghes fumes encontrez,
En mer furent trestuz ruez;
Nos cheualers, e nostre gent,
E la raine ensement.
Vnc ne guari home fors mun pere,
Ne nule femme fors ma mere.
Mis pere estait lur conussant,
Pur co guarirent li enfant.
E io, e vus, e mi dui frere,
Par la priere de mun pere.
En cest pais quant ariuames,
Nostre grant nef par mi trenchames.
Car tute fu freite, e malucise,
Quant la raine fu oscise.
De nostre nef meison feimes;
Pur vn batel ben guarismes,

[8] *plot*, Ms. D. [9] *al pais*, Ms. D. [1] *l'en amenat*, Ms. D.

Dunt nostre pere ela pescher;
Peison eumes a manger.
Turbuz, salmuns, e muluels,
Graspeis, porpeis, e makerels;
A grant plenté, e a fuison,
Eumes pain e bon peison.
[col. 2.] [Del peissun cangium le pain,
Hom nous esportout a plain.
E cum nous eumes deniers,
Mis peres dunc devint salniers.
Tant cum vesqui, il e ma mers
Bien vus nurrit, mielz que mi freres.
E io remis si pris seignur,
Al m'ad tenud a grant onur.
Marchant ert, mer sot passer,
E set bien vendre e achater.
En Danemarche fud le autreer,
E a plusurz oid preier,
Si hom vus trouot, que venissiez,][2]
E le pais chalengissez.
Bien vus loum ke turnez,
Vos dous vallez od vus menez;
Pur vus seruir sarent od vus,
Si bien vus prent, mandez le nus.
Nus [vus][3] siwerons, si vus volez,
Si Deu vus rent vos heritez.'
Dist Haueloc e sa mulier:
'Nus vus rendrum mult bon luer.

[2] Ms. D. For *Si hom*, v. 461. Ms. Reg. has *S'il.* [3] Ms. D.

[4]Plus vus ferum ke ne [5]querez,
Si Deus nus rent nos heritez.
E les vallez od nus merrum,
Par Deu bien enpenserom.'
Respont la dame, 'veirement,
Ci remaindrez tant kaiez vent.
E si io puis, ainz ke passez,
De meillur dras vestuz serrez.'
Cil remistrent donc a suiur,
Vestuz furent [6]par honur.
Tant si iurnent ke vint l'oré;
E puis si sunt en nef entré.
E danz [7]Algers, li marchanz,
Ad fet pur els li couenanz.
Lur froc dona il e Kelloc
Pur la meisné Haueloc;[8]
E asez lur [9]i-mist vitaille,
Tresk'a treis meis ne volt ke faille.
[fol. 115. Pain, e vin, e char, e [1]bon peisson,
col. 1.] Lur mist el nef, a grant fuson.
E tresk'es la nef flota,
Li esterman bien se dresca.
Dous niefs i-ont tut verement,
Lur [2]sigles drescent [3]al vent.

[4] *E pus vus rendrums*, Ms. D.
[5] *quidez*, Ms. D.
[6] *a grant*, Ms. D.
[7] *Algres.* Ms. D.
[8] Vers. 485. 486. om. Ms. D. nor do they appear in Ms. Coll. Fec.
[9] *mist ent*, Ms. D.
[1] Om. Ms. D.
[2] *viels*, Ms. D.
[3] *contre*, Ms. D.

Tant vnt nagé, e gouerné,
K'en Denemarche sunt ariué.
En la contrée v ariuerent,
A vne vile s'en alerent.
La quistrent somers e carrei;
Mener i-firent lur conrei.
Les marchanz sunt tuz remes,
[4]Od lur herneis es dous nefs,
E Haueloc e sa moillier,
Vont a la vile herberger.
Illoc maneit vns riches hom,
Sigar [5]estalre aueit nun.
Seneschal fu al rei Gunter,
E de sa terre iustiser.
Maes ore [6]ert tels k'en peis teneit,
E icel [7]riche rei forment haeit,
Ki donc ert reis poistifs
Sur l'altre gent de cel pais,
[8]Pur son seignur k'il aueit mort,
[9]Par la vertu de Artur le fort,
K'il out par treison mandé,
E cel pais li out doné.
Pur co k'il ert traitres e fel,
[Plusurs vnt tenud le conseil,
Que ia od lui ne se tendrunt,
Ne de li terre ne prendrunt,

[4] *Enz es dous nefs od lur herneis*, Ms. D. [5] *l'estarle*, Ms. D.
[6] *est*, Ms. D. [7] Om. Ms. D. [8] *Sur*, Ms. D.
[9] *Par Artur le rei, qui mult fud fort*, Ms. D.

Deci qu'il sachent del dreit eir,
De sa vie, v de sa mort le veir.
Cist reis ki doné ert el pais,
Il ert frere al rei [1]Aschis,
Qui pur Arthur suffrid la mort,
La v Modret li fist tel tort.
Il ot a nun Odulf le reis,
Mult fud haiz de ses Daneis.
Si cum Deu plut e auenture,
Deus mist en Aveloc sa cure,][2]
[col. 2.] Pur sa moiller, ke trop ert bele,
La fille al rei, dame Argentele.[3]
* * * * *
* * * * *
Sis bachelers donc l'assaillirent,
Pristrent [4]la dame, lui ferirent,
E ses vallez mult lei dengerent,
En plusurs lius lur [5]chef bruserent.
Si cum il s'en [6]vnt od s'amie:
Danz Hauelocs en out envie.
Prent vne hache mult trenchant,
[7]K'en vne meison troua pendant,

[1] *Saschis*, Ms. L. *Aschil*, Wace. [2] Ms. D.

[3] Argentelcie, Ms. Here follows a blank of six lines, left designedly in the Ms. which the Durham and Lincoln copies do not supply. Cf. Ms. Coll. Fec. v. 670—698.

[4] *s'amie*, Ms. D. [5] *chefs*, Ms. D. [6] *vont*, Ms. D.

[7] *Qu'il troua en la meisun gisant*, Ms. D.

Cels ad ateint en la ruele,
Ki menouent dame Argentile ;
Treis en oscist, dous en tua,
E al siste le poinz trencha.
Prent sa femme, vint al ostel,
Esvers le cri mult criminel.
Prist ses vallez, e sa moiller,
Si s'en entra en vn muster,
Ferma les vs pur la pour,
Puis monterent sus en la [tur.
Iloec aueit tel defensail,
Ia ni fust pris senz grant trauail.
Kar cil tresbien se defendirent,
Blesciad i-erent cels k'is esailirent.
Quant dan Sigar vint puignant,
Veit cum les pieres vait ruant.
Danz Auelocs, qui mult ert fort,
Les cinc bricuns aueit il mort.
Sigar le vit, sil auisat
Del rei Guntier, dunc li membrat ;
Tresqu'il il unques l'ot choisid,
Vnc pur ses humes n'el haid.
A sun seignur resemblot,
Que quant il vit tel pitied en ot,
Qu'a mult grant paine pot parler ;
Tut l'asalt ad fait cesser.][8]
[f. 115. b. col. 1.] Peis e trues lui afia,
[E][9] en sa sale l'en amena ;

[8] Ms. D. [9] Ms. D.

Lui, e sa femme, e ses compaienz,
Les dous vallez, dunt dis ainz.
E quant furent aseurez,
Li riches hom ad demandez,
Ki il estait, e com ad nun,
E dunt erent si compaignon.
E de la dame demanda,
Dunt ele vint, e ki li dona.
'Sire,' fet il, 'ne sai ke sui,
En cest pais quid ke nez fui.
Vn mariner, ki Grim out nun,
M'en menat, petit valetun.
En Lindeseie [en][1] volt aler:
Com venimes en halt mer,
De vthlages [2]sumes asailliz,
Par ki sui si mal bailliz.
Ma mere i-ert, si fu oscise,
Io guari, ne sai en quele guise,
E li prodom en eschapa,
Ki me nuri, e mult m'ama.
Il e sa femme me nurirent,
E mult [3] me nurirent, e [en] [4]cherirent.
Quant furent mort, si m'en turnai,
[Un rei serui v io alai;
E douz vadlez furent od mei,
Tant cum io fui od cel rei.

[1] Ms. D.
[2] *fumes*, Ms. D.
[3] *m'aimerent*, Ms. D.
[4] Ms. D.

Tant fui od lui en ma iuuente,
E cest dame i-ert sa parente.
Si cum lui plut, la me donad,
E ensemble nus espusad.
Ci sui venud en cest pais;
Ne cunuis nul de mes amis,
Ne io ne sai a l'escient,
Si io ai un sul parent,
Mais per le bos de un marchant,
A Grimesbi est remanant;
Mult est prodom, nun ad Algier,
Il me load e sa muiller
Ci a venir mes amis querre,
E mes parenz en ceste terre.][5]
[col. 2.] Mes io ne sa[i] vn sul nomer,
Ne [6]ne sai com [7]les puise trouer.'
Dist li prodom, 'cum as tu nun?'
[8]'Sire, ne sai sil li respon.
Mes [tant][9] cum io sui en la curt grant
Si m'apelerent Cuherant,
E tant cum io sui valleton
Sai ben que Haueloc [1]eut nun.
A Grimesby [fui][2] l'altrer,
Haueloc m'apelat Alger;
Ore sui ici, quel ke voldrez
De ces dous nuns m'apelerez.'

[5] Ms. D. [6] Om. Ms. D. Cf. v. 185. [7] *ios*, Ms. D.
[8] *Ne sai, respunt le vadletun*, Ms. D.
[9] Ms. D. [1] *ei a*, Ms. D. [2] Ms. D.

Sygar s'estut, si escultat,
Del fiz le rei [3]bien li membrat,
[4]E icel nun dunt il diseit,
Le fiz Gunter cel non aueit.
Si li membrat de vn altre vice,
K'il [5]vit iadis par la nurice,
De la flambe ki ert issant
De sa buche, quant ert dormant.
La nuit le fit tres bien guaiter
La v il iust od sa muller.
Pur co k'il ert forment lassé
De la bataille, e del pensé,
K'aueit ev le ior deuant,
Sil s'endormi, nuls n'el demant.
Ignel pas com il dormi
De sa buche la flambe issi,
[E li sergant qui l'unt gaited,
A lur seignur l'unt tost [6]cunted.
E li prodom leuat del lit,
Quant il i-vint, la flambe vit.
Dunc sot il bien que veirs esteit
Co que de lui pensez aueit.
Mais tant li ert cel pensé chier,
Vnc n'el volt dire a sa muillier,
Tresqu'al demain qu'il leuad,
Dunc per ses humes enueiad.

[3] *si*, Ms. D.
[4] *A*, Ms, D.
[5] *sot*, Ms. D.
[6] *nuncié*, Ms. Reg.

Li mandat pur ses cheualiers,
Pur geldons, e pur peoniers.[7]
De tutes parz i-vienent asez;
Quant il en ot mult asemblez,][8]
[fol. 116. col. 1.] Donc vait a Haueloc parler,
Baigner le feit, e conreier,
De nouels dras l'ad feit vestir,
En sa sale le feit venir.
Com en la sale est entrez,
V vist tant homes asemblez,
Pour out grant ke cele gent
Ne li fascent mal iugement,
Pur les cinc homes k'out tuez,
Quidat ke fussent asemblez.
Pur vne hache volt aler,
Ke iloc teneit vn bacheler;
Saisir la volt, pur sei defendre:
[9]Sigar le vait, si l'ad fet prendre.
Com il le tindrent de tuz leez,
Sigar li dist, 'ne vus dotez;
N'aiez guarde, li mien ami,
Bien le vus iure, sil vus afi,
K'ore vus aim plus ke ne fis hier
Quant vus asis a mon manger.'
Puis si la fist delez sei,
Aporter feit le corn le rei.

[7] *pnigneres*, Ms. L. [8] Ms. D.
[9] *La prist de sa main tendre*, Ms. D.

Co fu le corn al rei Gunter;
Suz ciel n'aueit nul cheualer
Ke ia cel corn pust soner,
Ne venur, ne bacheler,
Si ke nuls ia corner l'oist,
Si rei v dreit air le feist,
De Denemarche le dreit air,
Le pot ben soner pur vair.
Mes altre home ia nel cornast,
Nuls hom pur nient s'en traueillast.
Cel corn aueit Sygar guardé,
Li reis Gunter li out liueré.
Quant le tint n'el pout soner,
A vn cheualer le feit liuerer;
K'il soncrat, k'il seit cornant:
'Si ke io en saie oiant,
Io li durrai vn bon anel,
[Qui a bosuin volt vn chastel.
Cil qui en sun dei l'aurad,
Si chiet en mer, ne meierad;][1]
[col. 2] Ne feu n'el pot de ren damager,
Ne nul arme n'el pot nafrer.
Tels com di est li anel:'
Ore vont corner le mainel,
Li cheualer, e li sergant,
Ne volt soner, ne tant ne quant.
Vnc pur nuls dels ne volt soner,
Donc l'out baillé al bacheler

[1] Ms. D.

K'il apelouent le prison,
Ki Auelocs out non.
Quant cil le tint, sil egardat,
E dist, ke vnkes ne cornat.
'Al seignur,' dist, 'lerrai ester,
Quant altre home nel pot corner.
Tut vus claim quite vostre anel.
Ne rois pener le meinel.'
Respont Sigar, 'nun ferez,
A vostre buch ele metez.'
'Sire,' feit cil, 'co ne vus vé,
De mai serra ia aseie.'
Donc prist le corn, si l'ad seigné,
A sa buche l'ad asaie.
Tresk'a sa buche le tuchat,
Le corn tant gentement sonat,
Ke vnc ne fu ainz oi son per,
Nul hom ne sout si bien corner.
Sygar l'entent, sailli en piez,
Entre ses braz l'ad enbracez.
Puis s'escriat, 'Deu seit loez!
Ore ai mon dreit seignur trouez.
Ore ai celui ke desirai,
Pur ki la guere maintendrai.
Co est li draiz airs, e la persone
Ki deit porter d'or la corune.
Tuz ses homes ad donc mandé,
Lores li firent felté.

Il meismes s'agenulla,
De fai tenir l'ascura.
Puis enveia pur les barons,
A ki cel reis aueit tencons;
Tuz sunt ses homes deuenuz,
E a seignur l'unt receuz.
[f. 116. b. col. 1.] Quant co vnt fet asemblent gent,
En quatre iurs en ont maint cent;
E al quint ior, des cheualers
Ourent il bien trente millers.
Li reis Edulf donc deffierent,
En vn plein s'entre contrerent.
Asez i-out granz colps feruz,
Li reis Edulf fu dunke vencuz,
Car Haueloc si se contint,
Il sul en oscist plus de vint.
Dous [2]p̄lices aueit el pais,
Ki ainz erent ses enemis,
E od Edulf serent tenuz,
Ore sunt a sa merci venuz.
Del pais la menue gent
Vindrent a merci ensement.
E Haueloc lur fist pardons,
Par le conseil de ses barons.
Tuz iurerent sa felté,
Li cheualer de cel regné,
E li prodome, e li burgeis,
De lui firent seignur e reis.

[2] *Qu.* palices, *i. e.* palasins. V. Roquef.

Grant feste tint, e grant baldoire,
Si cum nus dit la verai estoire.
Apres sumond tute sa nauire,
De son realme tute l'empire.
Od sa grant ost la mer passa,
Li reis Edelsi donc deffia.
Co li manda, k'il le defie,
S'il ne li rend le drait s'amie.
Li reis Edelsi li remandat,
Ke contre lui se combaterat.
Combatirent sei en vn plain,
Del matin tresk'al serain.
Mult i-out homes afolez,
D'ambedous parz, e mort rueiz.
Quant naire nuit les deseuera
Tresk'al demain k'il aiurna.
Mes par conseil de la reine,
Ki enseignat vne mescine,
Par ki remist le mal e la bataille,
Sen regne out sanz grei . . . . .
[col. 2.] Tute nuit fist en terre ficher pels,
Plus gros e granz ke tonels;
Les morz homes en sus ficherent,
E tute nuit sus les drescerent.
Dous escheles en firent granz,
Ke veirement estait semblant,
K'il fuissent combatanz, e vifs,
Le ior deuant erent oscis.

Home ki de loinz les esguardout,
Tute la char l'en hericout;
Ambure de loinz e de pres,
Hydus semblent, morz, desconfes.
Lendemain se reparillerent,
De combatre mult s'aficherent.
Les veors vindrent deuant
Veher la gent dan Cuherant.
Quant vnt veu que tant en i-a,
Tute la char l'en herica.
Car encontre vns hom k'il aueient,
D'altre part set en uaient.
Arere en vont al rei nuncier,
Li combatre n'i-ad mester:
'Rende la dame son dreit,
E fasce peis, ainz ke pis seit.'
Li reis ne pout par el aler,
Donc li estut co granter,
Car baron li ont loé:
Rendu li fu tut li regné,
Des Hoiland tresk'a Colecestre:
Rei Haueloc la tin[t] sa feste.
Les homages de ses barons
Recuz par tut ses regions.
Puis apres co ke quinz dis
Ne vesqui li reis Edelsis.
Il n'out nul eir si dreiturel
Com Haueloc e sa muiller.

Il out enfanz, mes morz esteient,
[Li barnages tres bien otreient,
Que Haueloc e sa amis
Ait la terre rei Edilsis.
Ia si ot il, vint anz fud reis,
Mult conquist par les Daneis.][3]

[3] Ms. D.

NOTES

TO

THE ENGLISH TEXT

OF THE

Romance of Havelok.

V. 9. *He was the wicteste man at nede*
That thurte riden on ani stede.]

This appears to have been a favorite expression of the poet, and to have comprehended, in his idea, the perfection of those qualifications required in a knight and hero. He repeats it, with some slight variation, no less than five times, viz. V. 25. 87. 345. 1757. and 1970. The lines, however, are by no means original, but the common property of all our early poetical writers. We find them first in Layamon's translation of Wace, made probably during the reign of Henry II. i. e. between 1155. (when Wace completed his work,) and 1189. where he is speaking of Dunwallo Molmutius.

This wes the feiruste mon
The æuere æhte ær thusne kinedom,
Tha he mihte beren wepnen,
& his hors wel awilden.

Ms. Cott. Cal. A. IX. f. 23. c. 1.

So also in the Romance of *Guy of Warwick:*

He was the best knight at neede
That euer bestrode any stede.
Coll. Garrick, K. 9. sign. Ll. ii.

Again, in the *Continuation of Sir Gy*, in the Auchinleck Ms.

God grant him heuene blis to mede
That herken to mi romaunce rede
Al of a gentil knight;
The best bodi he was at nede
That ever might bestride stede,
And freest found in fight.

And again, in the *Chronicle of England*, published by Ritson from a copy in the British Museum, Ms. Reg. 12. C. xii.

After him his sone Arthur
Hevede this lond thourh and thourh.
He was the beste kyng at nede
That ever mihte ride on stede,
Other wepne welde, other folk out-lede,
Of mon ne hede he never drede.—v. 261.

The very close resemblance of these lines to those in Havelok, v. 87-90. would induce a belief that the writer of the *Chronicle* had certainly read, and perhaps copied from, the Romance. The Ms. followed by Ritson was undoubtedly written soon after the death of Piers Gaveston, in 1313. with the mention of which event it concludes; but in the Auchinleck copy it is continued, by a later hand, to the minority of Edward III. It only remains to be observed, that the poem in Ms. Reg. 12. C. xii. is written by the same identical hand as the Ms. Harl. 2253. (containing *Kyng Horn*, &c.) whence some additional light is thrown on the real age of the latter, respecting which our antiquaries so long differed.

V. 31. *Erl and barun*, dreng *and kayn.*] The appellation of *Dreng*, and, in the plural, *Drenges*, which repeatedly occurs in the course of this poem, is uniformly bestowed on a class of men who hold a situation between the rank of *Baron*, and *Thayn*. We meet with the term more than once in Doomsday Book, as, for instance, in Tit. Cestresc: "Hujus manerii [Neuton] aliam terram xv. hom. quos *Drenches* vocabant, pro xv. maneriis tenebant." And in a Charter of that period we read: "Alger Prior, et totus Conventus Ecclesiæ S. Cuthberti, Edwino, et omnibus Teignis et *Drengis*, &c." Hence Spelman infers, that the Drengs were military vassals, and held land by knight's service, which was called *Drengagium*. This is confirmed by a document from the Chartulary of Welbeck, printed in Dugdale, *Mon. Angl.* V. II. p. 598. and in Blount, *Jocular Tenures*, p. 177. where it is stated, "In eadem villa [Cukeney, co. Nottingh.] manebat quidam homo qui vocabatur Gamelbere, et fuit vetus *Dreyinghe* ante Conquestum." It appears from the same document, that this person held two carucates of land of the King *in capite*, and was bound to perform military service for the same, whenever the army went into Wales. In the Epistle also from the Monks of Canterbury to Henry II. printed by Somner, in his Treatise on Gavelkind, p. 123. we find: "Quia vero non erant adhuc tempore Regis Willelmi Milites in Anglia, sed *Threnges*, præcepit Rex, ut de eis Milites fierent, ad terram defendendam." Spelman quotes another document, which would ascribe the origin of the term to the Conqueror himself, who is said to have bestowed it on the family of the Sharneburnes, in reward for their fidelity. But this story has too apocryphal a character to be admitted. In Layamon's translation of Wace the term is frequently used in the acceptation of thayn, and spelt either *dringches*, *drencches*, or *dringes*,

He cleopede alle his *dringches*,
That heo comen to hustinge,
Heore kinge to ræden.
fol. 59. c. 2.

We have not met with the term in any other early English composition, and it would seem to afford an additional proof of the priority of Havelok, in point of antiquity, to any of the numerous

Romances yet existing. Spelman derives the etymology of the word from the Teut. *draugh*, stipatio, but without any probability. It is to the Danes we are undoubtedly indebted for this, as for many other terms. In the Isl. and Su. Goth. *Dreng* originally signified *vir fortis, miles strenuus*, and hence Olaf, King of Norway, received the epithet of *Goddreng*. See Wormii Lex. Run. p. 26. Ihre, Vet. Cat. Reg. p. 109. Langebek, Script. Rer. Danic. V. I. p. 156. The term subsequently was applied to persons in a servile condition, and is so instanced by Spelman, as used in Denmark. In this latter sense it may be found in Hickes, Diction. Isl. and in Sir David Lyndsay's Poems,

> Quhilk is not ordanit for *dringis*
> But for Duikis, Empriouris, and Kingis.
> V. Pink. S. P. R. ii. 97.

V. Jamieson, Dict. in voce.

V. 45. *In that time a man that bore*
[*Wel fyfty pundes, Y woth, or more.*]

This insertion receives additional authority from a similar passage in the Romance of *Guy of Warwick*, where it is mentioned as a proof of the rigorous system of justice pursued by Earl Sigard,

> Though a man bore an hundred pound,
> Upon him of gold so round,
> There n'as man in all this lond
> That durst him do shame no schonde.
> V. Ellis, *Metr. Rom.* V. II. p. 9. Ed. 1803.

Many of the traits here attributed to Athelwold, appear to be borrowed from the praises so universally bestowed by our ancient historians on the character of King Alfred, in whose time, as Otterbourne writes, p. 52. "armillas aureas in bivio stratas vel suspensas, nemo abripere est ausus." Cf. *Annal. Eccl. Roffens.* Ms. Cott. Nero, D. II. The same anecdote is related of Rollo, Duke of Normandy, by Guillaume de Jumieges, and Dudon de Saint Quentin.

V. 91. *Sprong forth so sparke of glede.*] Cf. v. 869. It is a very common metaphor in early English poetry.

He sprong forth an stede,
  swa sparc ded of fure.
        Layamon, f. 136. c. 1.

He spronge forth, as sparke on glede.
        Sir Isumbras, f. 130. b.

He spronge as sparkle doth of glede.
        K. of Tars, v. 194.

And lepte out of the arsoun,
  As sperk thogh out of glede.
        Ly Beaus Desconus, v. 623.

Cf. Chaucer, Cant. Tales, v. 13833. and Tyrwhitt's note.

V. 110. *Of his bodi*, &c.] Compare the French text, v. 208. *Mes entre eus*, &c.

V. 114. *Than him tok*, &c.] Comp. the Fr. v. 211. *Rois Ekenbright*, &c.

V. 136. *He sende* writes *sone onon*] We must here, and in v. 2275. simply understand *letters*, without any reference to the official summonses of parliament, which subsequently were so termed, κατ' ἐξοχην. The word *briefs* is used in the same sense by the old French writers, and in Layamon we meet with some lines nearly corresponding with the present,

The king læi on bure,
  særiliche on beadde;
He sende his sonde
  zeond his kinelonde,
Lette lathien him to
  al his leod theines;
Mid wurden and mid *writen*,
  he dude heom wel to witen,
That ne mihte he no lengere
  libben on eærthe.—f. 37. c. 2.

V. 89-203. *Ther on he garte*, &c.] Compare the French Romance, v. 217-230.

V. 263. *Justises dede he maken newe,*
Al Engelond to faren thorw.]

The earliest instance produced by Dugdale of the Justices Itinerant, is in 23. Hen. II. 1176. when by the advice of the Council held at Northampton, the realm was divided into six parts, and into each were sent three Justices. *Orig. Judic.* p. 51. This is stated on the authority of Hoveden. Dugdale admits however the custom to have been older, and in Gervasius Dorobernensis, we find in 1170. certain persons, called *inquisitores*, appointed to perambulate England. Gervase of Tilbury, or whoever was the author of the *Dialogus de Scaccario*, calls them *deambulantes, vel perlustrantes judices.* See Spelman, *in voc.* The office continued to the time of Edward III. when it was superseded by that of the Justices of Assize.

V. 280. *The kinges douther*, &c.] Comp. the Fr. v. 283. *La meschine*, &c.

V. 433. *Crist warie him with his mouth!*
Waried wrthe he of north and suth!]

So, in the Romance of Merlin, Bishop Brice curses the enemies of Arthur,

> Ac, for he is king, and king's son,
> Y curse alle, and y dom
> His enemies with Christes mouth,
> By East, by West, by North, and South!
>
> V. Ellis, *Metr. Rom.* V. I. p. 260.

V. 591. *Of hise mouth*, &c.] Comp. the Fr. v. 71. sq. *Totes les houres*, &c.

V. 644. *Pastees and* flaunes, *al with suilk.*] Lye derives this term from the Sax. *flena*, which occurs in the Collection of medical receipts in the British Museum, cited under the title of *Liber Medic.* It is defined " Mistura quædam farinacea, nostræ quam *batter* dicimus, analoga, unde *flawn*, placentæ genus." The more obvious derivation is from the Fr. *flan,* which Le Grand tells us was a species of *patisserie,* used in France from the earliest period of the monarchy, and esteemed a dish fit for kings. *Vie Privée des Francois,* Tom. II. p. 280. Ed. Roquef. In the 13th century, the *Flan* was one of the articles commonly sold at Paris, as we learn from the curious poem of Guillaume de Villeneuve:

> Les *flaons* chaus pas nes oublie.
>
> *Crieries de Paris,* ap. Barbaz. v. 149.

And in France preference was given to the *Flans de Chartres,* above those of any other place, as appears from a string of Proverbs preserved by Le Grand. These dishes are termed in base Latinity *Flatones* or *Fladones,* of which several instances are produced by Du Cange. Thus, in the year 1316. a charter was granted by the Bishop of Amiens to the Commune of Montreuil, allowing them two ovens, *pro coqui faciendo pastillos et flatones.* From the Ordinary of the Church of Rouen, cream also appears to have been one of the ingredients of which they were composed. Chaucer, in his translation of the *Romaunt of the Rose,* writes:

> With tartes, or with chesses fat,
> With daintie *flaunes* brode and flat.

From this, the Flaun would seem to have been a sort of *pancake,* which is confirmed by a Proverb used in the Northern Counties, *As flat as a flaun,* Ray. Cotgrave, Menage, Minshieu, and Skinner, all interpret the word in question, *Custard,* and in that, or nearly a similar sense, it is used by Drayton, in his *Nymphidia,* 6. p. 1496. and by Ben Jonson, in *The Sad Shepherd,* Act I. Sc. 2. By Kersey it is defined "a kind of dainty, made of fine flower, eggs, and butter." Those who wish to investigate the subject further, may find in Pegge's *Form of Cury,* p. 120. (written about A. D. 1390.) a receipt *For to make Flownys in Lent,* and in Warner's *Antiquitates Culinariæ,* another for *A flaune of Almagne,* p. 73. from both which the Flaun appears to have been a fruit tart, baked in the manner of a raised pie. In addition to these we are enabled to add a third, taken from the very curious metrical work entitled *Liber cure Cocorum,* written in the reign of Hen. VI. and preserved in Ms. Sloane, 1986. fol. 87.

For Flaunes.

Take new chese, and grynd h[t] fayre
In morter w[t] eggis w[t] out dyswayre,
Put powder therto of sugar I say,
Coloure h[t] w[t] safrone ful wele thu may,
Put h[t] in cofynes th[t] ben fayre,
And bake h[t] forth Y the pray.

V. 676. *And with thi chartre make fre.*] Instances of the manumission of villains or slaves by charter may be found in Hickes, *Diss. Epistol.* p. 12. Lye's Dict. *ad calc.* and Madox's *Formulare Anglicanum,* p. 750. The practice was common in the Saxon times, and existed so late as the reign of Henry VIII.

V. 706. *Hise ship,* &c.] Comp. the Fr. v. 89. *Grim fet niefs,* &c.

V. 715-720. *Hauelok the yunge,* &c.] Comp. the Fr. v. 98-108. *Dedenz fist,* &c. Instead of the storm, in the French text Grim's ship is attacked by pirates, who kill the whole of the crew, with the exception of himself and family, whom they spare on the score of his being an old acquaintance.

V. 733-749. *In Humber,* &c.] So in the Fr. *Ceo fut al north,* &c. Cf. v. 125-135.

V. 753. *He took the sturgiun and the qual,*
And the turbut, and lax withal,
He tok the sele, and the hwel, &c.]

The list of fish here enumerated may be increased from v. 896. and presents us with a sufficiently accurate notion of the different species eaten in the 13th century. Each of the names will be considered separately in the Glossary, and it is only intended here to make a few remarks on those, which in the present day appear rather strangely to have found a place on the tables of our ancestors.

The sturgeon is well known to have been esteemed a dainty, both in England and France, and specially appropriated to the King's service, but that the whale, the seal, and the porpoise should have been rendered palatable, excites our astonishment. Yet that the whale was caught for that purpose, appears not only from the present passage, but also from the Fabliau intitled *Bataille de Charnage et de Caresme*, written probably about the same period, and printed by Barbazan. It is confirmed, as we learn from Le Grand, by the French writers; and even Rabelais, near three centuries later, enumerates the whale among the dishes eaten by the Gastrolatres. In the list of fish also published by Le Grand from a Ms. of the 13th century, and which corresponds remarkably with the names in the Romance, we meet with the *Baleigne*. See *Vie Privée des Francois*, T. II. sect. 8. That the seal was eaten during the 12th century we have the express testimony of Layamon, who inserts in his translation of Wace the following curious lines:

Islazene weoren to thon mele
twælf thusend rutheren *sele*,
& thritti hundred hærtes,
& al swa feole hinden.—f. 45. b. c. 2.

To descend to a later æra, among the articles at Archbishop Nevil's Feast, 6. Edw. IV. we find, *Porposes and Seales* XII. and at that of Archbishop Warham, held in 1504. is an item: *De Seales & Porposs. prec. in gross* XXVI. *s.* VIII. *d.* Champier asserts that the Seal was eaten at the Court of Francis I. so that the taste of the two nations seems at this period to have been nearly the same. For the courses of fish in England during the 14th and 15th centuries, see Pegge's *Form of Cury*, and Warner's *Antiquitates Culinariæ*, to which we may add Ms. Sloane, 1986.

V. 839. *And seyde, Hauelok, dere sone.*] Comp. the Fr. v. 166. *Beau fiz, fet il* &c. but the reasons assigned are very different.

V. 903. *The kok stod*, &c.] Comp. the Fr. v. 242. *Et un keu*, &c.

V. 939. *He bar the turues, he bar the star.*] The meaning of the latter term will be best illustrated by a passage in Moor's

Suffolk Words, where, under the word *Bent*, he writes, "*Bent* or *Starr*, on the N. W. coast of England, and especially in Lancashire, is a coarse reedy shrub—like ours perhaps—of some importance formerly, if not now, on the sandy blowing lands of those counties. Its fibrous roots give some cohesion to the silicious soil. By the 15. and 16. G. II. c. 33. plucking up and carrying away *Starr* or Bent, or having it in possession within five miles of the sand hills, was punishable by fine, imprisonment, and whipping." The use stated in the Act to which the Starr was applied, is, "making of Mats, Brushes, and Brooms or Besoms," therefore it might very well be adapted to the purposes of a kitchin, and from its being coupled with *turves* in the poem, was perhaps sometimes burnt for fuel. The origin of the word is Danish, and still exists in the Swed. *Starr*, Isl. *staer*, a species of sedge, or broom, called by Lightfoot, p. 560. *carex cespitosa*. Perhaps it is this shrub alluded to in the Romance of *Kyng Alisaunder*, and this circumstance will induce us to assign its author to the district in which the Starr is found.

> The speris craketh swithe thikke,
> So doth on hegge *sterre-stick.*—v. 4438.

V. 945. *of alle men*, &c.] Comp. the Fr. v. 254. *Tant estoit franc*, &c.

V. 959. *Of him ful wide the word sprong.*] A phrase which from the Saxon times occurs repeatedly in all our old writers. A few examples may suffice.

> Beowulf wæs brim,
> Blæd wide sprang.
> *Beowulf*, p. 4.
> Welle wide sprong thas eorles word.
> *Layamon*, f. 153. c. 2. Cf. f. 35. c. 2.
> And zet Alured seide an other side
> A word that is isprunge wide.
> *Disp. of the Hule and Niztingale*,
> Ms. Cott. Cal. A. ix. f. 232, c. 1.

Of a knight is that y-mene,
His name is sprong wel wide.
Sir Tristrem, p. 12.

The word of Horn wide sprong,
How he was bothe michel and long.
Horn Childe, ap. Rits. *Metr. Rom.* V. III. p. 291.

See also the *Kyng of Tars,* v. 19, 1007. *Emare,* v. 256. *Roland and Ferragus,* as quoted by Ellis, Ly *beaus Desconus,* v. 172. and *Chronicle of England,* v. 71.

V. 984. *In armes him no man nam*
That he doune sone ne caste.]
The same praise is bestowed on Havelok in the French text, v. 265. and it was doubtless in imitation or ridicule of the qualities attributed to similar heroes, that Chaucer writes of Sir Thopas, " Of wrastling was ther non his per." Cant. Tales, v. 13670.

V. 1006. *To ben ther at the parlement.*] Cf. v. 1178. If we examine our historical records, we shall find that the only parliament held at Lincoln, was in the year 1300. 28. Edw. I. and the writs to the *Archbishop of York,* and other Nobles, both ecclesiastical and secular, are still extant. The proceedings are detailed at some length by Robert of Brunne, Vol. II. p. 312. who might have been in Lincoln at the time, or at all events, was sufficiently informed of all that took place, from his residence in the county. If we could suppose that the author of the Romance alluded to this very parliament, it would reduce the period of the poem's composition to a later date, than either the style, or the writing of the Ms. will possibly admit of. It is therefore far more probable the writer here makes use of a poetical, and very pardonable license, in transferring the parliament to the chief city of the county in which he was evidently born, or brought up, without any reference whatever to historical data.

V. 1022. *Biforn here fet thanne lay a tre,*
And pulten with a mikel ston, &c.]
This game of *putting the stone,* is of the highest antiquity, and

seems to have been common at one period to the whole of England, although subsequently confined to the Northern counties, and to Scotland. Fitzstephen enumerates casting of stones among the amusements of the Londoners in the 12th century, and Dr. Pegge, in a note on the passage, calls it " a Welch custom." The same sport is mentioned by Geoffrey of Monmouth, among the diversions pursued at King Arthur's feast, as will appear in a subsequent note (v. 2320.) By an edict of Edward III. the practice of casting stones, wood, and iron, was forbidden, and the use of the bow substituted, yet this by no means superseded the former amusement, which was still in common use in the 16th century, as appears from Strutt's *Popular Pastimes,* Introd. pp. xvii. xxxix. and p. 56. sq. In the Highlands this sport appears to have been longer kept up than in any other part of Britain, and Pennant, describing their games, writes, " Those retained are, throwing the *putting-stone,* or stone of strength *(Cloch neart)* as they call it, which occasions an emulation who can throw a weighty one the farthest." *Tour in Scotl.* p. 214. 4to. 1769. See also *Statist. Account of Argyleshire,* xi. 287. In the French Romance of Horn, preserved in Ms. Harl. 527. is almost a similar incident to the one in Havelok, and would nearly amount to a proof, that Tomas, the writer of the French text of Horn, was an Englishman. After Horn's arrival in Ireland, (who is disguised under the name of Godmod) a game of *putting the stone* takes place, at which, says the writer,

> Iloec ben se pura ki fort est esprouer,
> Mut se peinent forment par trestut de essaier,
> Ki de force pura les autres surmunter.

After some trials on the parts of Egfer and Eglof, sons of the King Gudereche, Horn is requested by Egfer to take his part against his brother. Horn replies that he is (like Havelok) a stranger to the game, but is willing to try his strength at it.

> E la piere li fu portée a atant,
> Godmod la recut, mes unc n'en fist semlant

K'ele pesante fust le uaillant d'un gant;
Unc pur coe sun mantel ne fu desaffublant:
Il l'en point un petit, e cele fu uolant
Trestut dreit en cel cop, ou Eglaf fu ietant.

By a second cast he surpasses that of Eglaf the distance of six feet, and is consequently declared victor. To the above illustrations may be added the lines in the Romance of *Octavian Imperator*, where it is said of Florent,

At *wrestelyng*, and at *ston castynge*
He wan the prys, without lesynge;
Ther n'as nother old ne yynge
  So mochele of strength,
That myght the ston to hys *but* bryng,
  Bi fedeme lengthe.—v. 895.

It is singular enough, that the circumstance of Havelok's throwing the stone, mentioned in the Romance, should have been founded on, or preserved in, a local tradition, as attested by Robert of Brunne, p. 26.

Men sais in Lyncoln castelle ligges zit a stone,
That Hauelok kast wele forbi euerilkone.

V. 1077—1088. *The king Athelwald*, &c.] Comp. the Fr. text, v. 319—328. and 354—370.

V. 1103. *After Goldeborw*, &c.] Comp. the Fr. v. 378. *Sa niece*, &c. The French Romance differs here very considerably from the English, and in the latter, the dream of Argentille, her visit to the hermit, and the conversation relative to Havelok's parents, is entirely omitted.

V. 1203. *Thanne he komen there*, &c.] Comp. the Fr. v. 557. The marriage of Kelloc, Grim's daughter, with a merchant is skilfully introduced in the French, and naturally leads to the mention of Denmark. The plot of the English story is wholly dissimilar in this respect.

V. 1247. *On the nith*, &c.] Comp. the Fr. v. 381. *Quant couché*, &c. The voice of the angel is completely an invention of the English author, and the dream, (which is transferred from Argentille to Havelok,) is altogether different in its detail.

V. 1260. *He beth heyman*, &c.] Comp. the Fr. v. 521. *Il est né*, &c.

V. 1430. *Hauede go for him gold ne fe.*] Cf. v. 44. So in Layamon:

> Ne sculde him neother gon fore
> Gold ne na gærsume,
> Hæh hors no hære scrud,
> That he ne sculde beon ded,
> Other mid horsen to drazen.—fol. 131. b. c. 2.

V. 1632. *A gold ring drow he forth anon,*
An hundred pund was worth the ston,
And yaf it Ubbe for to spede :—
He was ful wis that first yaf mede.]

A similar incident, and in nearly the same words, occurs in Sir Tristrem.

> A ring he raught him tite,
> The porter seyd nought nay,
> In hand :
> He was ful wise y say,
> That first gave gift in hand.—st. 57. p. 39.

So also Wyntoun, who relates the subsidy of 40,000 moutons sent from France to Scotland in 1353. and adds,

> Qwha gyvis swilk gyftyis he is wyse.

V. 1646. *Hw he was wel of bones*, &c.] Comp. the Fr. v. 743. *Gent cors*, &c.

V. 1722. *Thanne he were set*, &c.] This is an amplification of the Fr. v. 677. sq.

V. 1725. *Kranes, swannes, veneysun,*
Lax, lampreys, and gode sturgun,
Pyment to drinke, and god clare,
Win hwit and red, ful god plente.]

We have here the principal constituents of what formed the

banquets of our ancestors. The old Romances abound with descriptions of this nature, which coincide exactly with the present, as will appear from one or two instances selected at hazard. In *Richard Cœur de Lion* a feast is thus detailed:

Plenty ther was offe bred and wyn,
Pyment, clarry, good and fyn;
Off *cranes,* and *swannes,* and *venysoun,*
Partryches, plovers, and heroun.—v. 4221.

At the banquet of Arthur, as described in the Romance of Merlin, *swans* and *cranes* are again enumerated, and in another passage:

Of *venisoun,* and flesch, and brede,
Of brown *ale,* and win *white and rede.*

Thus too in *Guy of Warwick:*

He shall you welcome, and your barons,
With *swans, cranes,* and *herons.*

And more at length in the *Squyr of Lowe Degre:*

With partryche, pecoke, and plovere,
With byrdes in bread y bake,
The tele, the duck, and the drake,
The cocke, the curlew, and the *crane,*
With fesauntes fayre, theyr was no wane,
Both storkes and snytes ther were also,
And *venyson* freshe of bucke and do.—v. 317.

"Wine is common," says Dr. Pegge, speaking of the entertainments of the 14th century, "both red and white. This article they partly had of their own growth, and partly by importation from France and Greece." A few examples will illustrate this:

He laid the cloth, and set forth bread,
And also wine, both *white and red.*
Sir Degore, ap. Ellis, *Metr. Rom.* V. 3. p. 375.

And dranke wyn, and eke pyment,
Whyt and red, al to talent.
Kyng Alisaunder, v. 4178.

Compare also *Horn Childe,* in Ritson, Metr. Rom. V. 3. p- 293. and *Ywaine and Gawaine,* v. 2048. In the *Squyr of Lowe Degre* is a long list of these wines, which has received considerable illustration in the curious work of Dr. Henderson. See also the Fabliau entitled *La Bataille des Vins,* and the Notes of Le Grand, T. II. p. 141. For the mode of preparing *piment* and *clarré* consult the same writer's Notes on the Fabliau *De la Dame qui fut corrigée,* T. II. p. 357. and in the *Vie privée des François,* T. III. p. 63—67. Ed. Roquef. Tyrwhitt also gives a receipt to make Piment and Clarré in his Glossary to Chaucer, and so does Weber, Metr. Rom. V. III. p. 310.

V. 1749. *And sende him unto the greyues.*] In the Fr. v. 694. Havelok is simply sent to an *ostel,* and the *greyve* does not appear in the story.

V. 1806. *Hauelok lifte up,* &c.] Comp. the Fr. v. 700. All the amusing details relative to Robert and Huwe Raven are omitted, and Havelok is made to retire to a monastery, where he defends himself by throwing down the stones on his assailants.

V. 1839. *And shoten on him, so doth on bere*
Dogges, that wolden him to tere.]

The same comparison is made use of in the Romance of Horn Childe:

> The Yrise folk about him yode,
> As hondes do to bare.
>
> Rits. *Metr. Rom.* V. III. p. 289.

See Note on v. 2331.

V. 1926—1930. *Sket cam tiding,* &c.] Comp. the Fr. v. 719. *La nouele uint,* &c. and also v. 1942. of the Engl. with v. 781. of Fr.

V. 2045. *That weren of Kaym kin and Eues.*] The odium affixed to the supposed progeny of Cain, and the fables engrafted on it, owe their origin to the theological opinions of the Middle Ages, which it is not worth while to trace to their authors. In the singular and highly interesting Dano-Saxon poem of Beowulf (which it is yet hoped will be given to the world in a better form than that in which it at present appears) the tradition is thus stated.

In Caines cynne	On Cain's kin (descendants)
Thone cwealm gewræc	This sin [homicide] avenged
Ece Drihten,	The Eternal Lord,
Thæs the he Abel slog.	Of him who Abel slew.
Ne gefeah he	He rejoiced not
Thære fæhthe,	In that act of hatred;
Ac he hine feor	But him afar off
Forwræc metod.	The Creator exiled.
For thy mane man cynne	Therefore many kinds of men
Fram thanon untydras	From thence, unfruitful
Ealle onwocon;	All arose. (took their origin;)
Eotenas and ylfe	Eotenes, and Ylfs,
And orcneas	And Monsters.
Swyke gi [gant] as	Such (were the) giants
Tha with Gode wunnon	That against God strove
Lange thrage,	A long period:
He hem thæs lean forgeald.	He them this loan requited.

Beowulf, fol. 132. Ms. Cott. Vit, A. xv.

The same fiction is related by the author of *Pier's Plouhman*, as follows:

Cayin the cursed creature. conceyved was in synne
After that Adam and Eve hadden ysynyed
With oute repentaunce. of here rechelessnesse
A rybaud thei engendrede. and a gome unryghtful.—
Alle that come of Cayin. caytives were evere
And for the synne of Cayines seed. seyde God to Noe,
Penitet me fecisse hominem.—p. 177. Ed. Whitak.

In the ancient Romances, both French and English, the Saracens are always termed part of Cain's race. So in the Fragment of Horn, in the possession of F. Douce, Esq.

Cum puis l'unt treit li felun Sarasin,
Vn en iot guaigna *del lignage Chain.*—v. 5.

Again, in the Romance of *Kyng Alisaunder:*

Of Sab the duk Manryn,
He was of *Kaymes kunrede.*—v. 1932.

In *Ywaine and Gawaine,* v. 559. the Giant is called "the karl of *Caymes kyn,*" and so also in a poem printed by Percy, intitled *Little John Nobody,* written about the year 1550.

Such caitives count to be come of *Cain's kind.*
Anc. Reliq. V. II. p. 130. Ed. 1765.

V. 2067. *For nou wile Y,* &c.] Comp. the Fr. v. 755.

V. 2076. *It ne shal no thing ben bitwene*
Thi bour and min, also Y wene
But a fayr firrene wowe.]

These lines will receive some illustration from a passage in Sir Tristrem, where it is said,

A borde he tok oway
Of her bour.—p. 114.

On which Sir W. Scott remarks, "The bed-chamber of the queen was constructed of wooden boards or shingles, of which one could be easily removed." This will explain the line which occurs below, 2106. "He stod, and totede in at a bord."

V. 2092. *Aboute the middel,* &c.] In the Fr. a person is placed by the Seneschal to watch, who first discovers the light. Comp. v. 830. sq.

V. 2132. *Bi the pappes he leyen naked.*] "From the latter end of the 13th to near the 16th century, all ranks, and both sexes, were universally in the habit of sleeping quite naked. This custom is often alluded to by Chaucer, Gower, Lydgate, and all our ancient writers." Ellis, *Spec. Metr. Rom.* V. I. p. 324. 4th Ed. In the *Squyr of Lowe Degre* is a remarkable instance of this fact:

How she rose, that lady dere,
To take her leue of that squyer;
Al so naked as she was borne
She stod her chambre-dore beforne.—v. 671.

So in the *Kyng of Tars*, v. 436. " On hire bed heo sat al naked." From this practice, says Le Grand, arose the expression *coucher nu à nue*, so common in the old Romances. See his Notes to *L'Ordene de la Chevalerie*, T. I. p. 145. In all the delineations of English costume given by Strutt, between the reigns of Edward I. to Henry VII. the figures represented in bed are pictured quite naked. See Plates 7. 50. and 58. " This may appear still more strange," adds Strutt, " when on the examination of the Saxon, Danish, and Norman æras, we find the figures in bed with close garments, like sheets." *Manners and Customs*, V. II. p. 88. It need scarcely be remarked, that this circumstance, united to many others, will afford solid reasons for assigning the composition of our Romance to the end of Henry III. reign or beginning of Edward I. The custom subsisted both in England and France to a very recent period, and hence probably was derived the phrase *naked-bed*, illustrated so copiously by Archdeacon Nares in his Glossary.

V. 2240-2265. *Lokes, hware he stondes her*, &c.] Comp. the Fr. v. 913-921. *Veez ci*, &c.

V. 2314. *Vbbe dubbede him to knith,*
With a swerd ful swithe brith.]

So likewise in the Fr. v. 928. *A cheualier l'out adubbé*. The ceremony of knighthood is described with greater minuteness in the Romance of *Ly beaus Desconus*, v. 73. and in *Kyng Horn*, the last of which passages we transcribe from the copy in Ms. Laud. 108. as being much fuller than in Ritson's printed text:

The day bygan to springe,
Horn cam biforn the kinge.
Wit swerde Horn he girde,
Rit honder hys herte;
He sette him on a stede
Red so any glede,
And sette on his fotes
Bothe spores and botes;
And smot a litel with,
And bed him ben god knict.—fol. 222. b. c. 1.

In the Fr. text of Horn, this occurs at v. 1438. For more particular information respecting this ceremony, Selden's *Titles of Honor* may be consulted, p. 438. sq. Ed. fol. 1631. The investiture of an Earl by girding a sword, which is alluded to subsequently, in v. 2922. is discussed by Selden, p. 676. whence it appears, that the earliest instance on record, is found in the reign of Richard I. when Hugh de Percy was created Earl of Northumberland. From the time of King John to Edward VI. this custom continued, after which the cap of maintenance, coronet, &c. were introduced into the ceremony.

V. 2320. *Hwan he was king, ther mouthe men se*
The moste ioie that mouhte be :
Buttinge with sharpe speres,
Skirming with taleuaces, &c.]

Ritson has justly remarked, Notes to *Ywaine and Gawaine,* v. 15. that the elaborate description of Arthur's feast at Carlisle, given by Geoffrey of Monmouth, l. IX. c. 12. has served as a model to all his successors. The original passage stands thus in a fine Ms. of the 13th century, Ms. Harl. 3773. fol. 33. b. "Refecti autem epulis diversos ludos acturi campos extra civitatem adeunt. Tunc milites simulachra belli scientes [*l. cientes,*] *equestrem ludum* componunt, mulieribus ab edito murorum aspicientibus. Alii *cum cestibus,* alii *cum hastis,* alii *gravium lapidum jactu,* alii *cum facis,* [*saxis,* Edd.] alii *cum aleis,* diversisque alii alteriusmodi jocis contendentes." In the translation of this description by Wace we approach still nearer to the imitation of the Romance before us.

A plusurs iuis se departirent,
Li vns alerent *buhurder,*
E lur ignels cheuals mustrer,
Li altre alerent *eskermir*
V *pere geter,* v *saillir;*
Tels i-aueit ki *darz lanconent,*
E tels i-aueit ki *lutouent :*
Chescon del gru s'entremetait
Dunt entremettre se saueit.—Ms. Reg. 13. A. XXI.

The parallel versions from the French of Layamon, Robert of Gloucester, and Robert of Brunne, may be read to great advantage in Mr. Ellis's *Specimens of Early English Poets.* At the feast of Olimpias, described in the Romance of *Kyng Alisaunder*, we obtain an additional imitation.

Withoute the toun was mury,
Was reised ther al maner pley;
There was knyghtis *turnyng*,
There was maidenes carolyng,
There was champiouns *skyrmyng*,
Of heom and of other *wrastlyng*,
Of liouns chas, of *beore baityng*,
And *bay of bor*, of *bole slatyng*.—v. 193. Cf. v. 1045.

Some additional illustrations on each of the amusements named in our text, may not be unacceptable.

1. *Buttinge with sharpe speres.* This is tilting, or justing, expressed in Wace by *buhurder.* See Strutt's *Sports and Pastimes*, p. 96. sq. 108.

2. *Skirming with taleuaces.* This is described more at large by Wace, in his account of the feast of Cassibelaunus.

Li chiualer wnt *bourder*,
Asquans se peinent de *lancer*,
Li vns volt la pere *geter*,
Tuz se peinent de bel iuer.
Vn giu amanent el pais,
Li mestres en aueit grant pris,
Co est le gius del eschermie,
Li vns al altre en porte enuie.
Ms. Reg. 13. A. XXI.

In Layamon it is somewhat varied:

Heo ferden zeond the feldes,
Mid scæftes & mid sceldes,

Summe heo gunnen æruen,
& somme heo gunnen eornen,
& summe heo gunnen pleien,
pliht com on ueste.
Summe *pleoden on tæuel-brede,*
& summen *ærnden heore stede.*—
Theos tweien cnihtes bigunnen
und sceldes to skirmen,
Ærst heo pleoweden,
And seoththe pliht makeden.—f. 45. b. c. 2.

In Fitzstephen this sport is mentioned, as practised by the Londoners in the 12th century, p. 77. Ed. Pegge, and is called by Stowe, *Survey*, p. 77. "practising with *wasters and bucklers.*" In Strutt's *Sports and Pastimes*, is a representation of this game, taken from Ms. Bodl. 264. illuminated between 1338. and 1344. in which the form of the *talevas* is accurately defined. It appears to have been pursued to such an excess, as to require the interference of the crown, for in 1286. an Edict was issued by Edward I. prohibiting all persons *Eskirmer au bokeler.* This, however, had only a temporary effect in restraining it, and in later times, under the appellation of *sword and buckler play,* it again became universally popular. See Strutt, ib. Maitland, V. I. p. 989. Stowe, V. I. p. 303. The still more modern *prize-fighting* is well known from the Papers in the Spectator.

3. *Wrastling with laddes, puttinge of ston.* See the Notes on v. 984. and 1022.

4. *Harping and piping.* This requires no illustration.

5. *Leyk of mine, of hasard ok.* Among the games mentioned at the marriage of Gawain, in the Fabliau of *Le Chevalier à l'Epée,* we have:

Cil Chevalier jeuent as tables,
Et as eschés de l'autre part,
O à la *mine,* o à hazart.

Le Grand, in his Note on this passage, T. I. p. 57. Ed. 1779.

writes: "Le Hasard était une sorte de jeu de dez. Je ne connais point la *Mine;* j'ai trouvé seulement ailleurs un passage qui prouve que ce jeu était très-dangereux, et qu'on pouvait s'y ruiner en peu de tems." Roquefort adds nothing to our knowledge of the game of *Mine,* nor is it noticed in the Essay contained in the *Collect. des Dissertat. &c. relatifs à l'Hist. de France,* Livr. 3. p. 221. We do not find it either in the curious Tract on the different games of dice or Tables, preserved in Ms. Reg. 13. A. XVIII. Sæc. XV. fo. 163. wherein are enumerated, 1. *Longus ludus,* or *ludus Anglicorum* (Backgammon.) 2. *Paume carie.* 3. *Ludus lumbardorum.* 4. *Imperial.* 5. *Provincial.* 6. *Baralie.* 7. *Faylys.* 8. Not named. It appears however from the Fabliau of *Du Prestre et des deuz Ribaus,* to have been certainly a species of *Tables,* or *Backgammon,* and to have been played with dice, on a board called *Minete.* The only passage we recollect in which any further detail of this game is given, is that of Wace, in the account of Arthur's feast, Harl. Ms. 6508. and Ms. Cott. Vit. A. x. but it must be remarked, that the older copy 13. A. XXI. does not contain it, nor is it found in the translations of Layamon, or Robert of Gloucester. Robert of Brunne, however, follows a similar copy, as quoted by Mr. Ellis, *Spec. Early English Poets,* V. I. p. 417. Ed. 1803. and as the original is extremely curious, it is here annexed.

Li vus disoent contes & fablez,
[1]Auquant demandoent dez & tablez,
Tielx ioient av *hasart,*
C'estoit vn giev de male part.
As eschiez ioient plusors,
Ou a la *mine,* [2]au gieu maiors.
Dui & dui au gieu s'escompaignent,
Li vns perdent, li autres gaignent.
Cil eniuent qui plus getent,
As autres dient qu'il i-metent.

[1] *Alquanz,* Vit. A. x. [2] *Val greinur,* Vit.

Sor gages emprestent deniers,
Vnze por xii. volantiers.
Souent iurent, souent affichent,
Gages prenent, gages plenissent.
Mult estriuent, mult se corrocent,
Souent mescontent, souent grotent.
Dous & ii. getent & quarnes,
Ambes as, & le tierc ternes,
A la fiee getent quines,
Et a la fie getent sixnes,
vi. v. iii[j]. iij. ii. as,
Ont a plusors tolleit lor dras.

The lines in Rob. of Brunne which express the preceding passage, are these:

Dysours ynowe tolde them fables;
& somme *pleide wyth des & tables;*
& somme pleide at hasard fast,
& lost & wonne with chaunce of cast.
Somme, that wolde nought of the tabler,
Drewe forthe meyne for the cheker, &c.

We quote from the Lambeth Ms. No. 131. f. 50. b. for the passage, as given by Ellis, is not transcribed correctly, and we have not had an opportunity of correcting it by the Ms. in the Inner Temple. It is evident that the words *pleide wyth des & tables,* &c. refer to the game of *mine,* which is also undoubtedly the one meant in the *tæuel-brede* of Layamon, in the passage above quoted, and in the version of Rob. of Gloucester,

Wyth pleyynge at tables, other atte chekere—p. 192.

6. *Romanz reding.* See Sir W. Scott's Note on Sir Tristrem, p. 290. and the Dissertations of Percy, Ritson, and Ellis.

7. *Ther mouhte men se the boles beyte,*
And the bores with hundes teyte.]

Cf. v. 1838. 2438. Both these diversions are mentioned by Lucianus, in his inedited tract *De laude Cestriæ.* Ms. Bodl. 672. who is supposed by Tanner to have written about A.D. 1100. [but who must probably be placed near half a century later.] They formed also part of the amusements of the Londoners in the 12th century, as we learn from Fitzstephen, p. 77. and are noticed in the passage above quoted from the Romance of *Kyng Alisaunder.* In later times, particularly during the 16th century, these cruel practises were in the highest estimation, as we learn from Holinshed, Stowe, Laneham, &c. See Strutt's *Sports and Pastimes,* p. 192. and the Plate from Ms. Reg. 2. B. vii. Also Pegge's Dissertation on Bull-baiting, inserted in Vol. ii. of Archæologia.

8. *Ther mouthe men se hw Grim greu.* If this is to be understood of scenic representation (and we can scarcely view it in any other light), it will present one of the earliest instances on record of any attempt to represent an historical event, or to depart from the religious performances, which, until a much later period were the chief, and almost only, efforts towards the formation of the drama. Of course, the words of the writer must be understood to refer to the period, in which he lived, i. e. according to our supposition, about the end of Hen. III. reign, or beginning of Edw. I. See Le Grand's Notes to the *Lai de Courtois,* V. i. p. 329. and Strutt's *Sports and Pastimes,* B. 3. ch. 2.

V. 2344. *The feste fourti dawes sat.*] Cf. v. 2950. This is borrowed also from Geoffrey, and is the usual term of duration fixed in the Romances.

> Fourty dayes hy helden feste,
> Ryche, ryall, and oneste.
> *Octauian Imperator,* v. 73:
>
> Fourty dayes leste the feste.
> *Launfal,* v. 631.
>
> With mykele myrthe the feest was made,
> Fourty dayes it abode.
> *Syr Eglamoure of Artoys,* sign. E. iv.

And certaynly, as the story sayes,
The revell lasted forty dayes.
Squyer of Lowe Degre, v. 1413.

V. 2384. The French story here differs wholly from the English. Instead of the encounter of Robert and Godard, and the cruel punishment inflicted on the latter, in the Fr. is a regular battle between the forces of Havelok and Hodulf (Godard.) A single combat takes place between the two leaders, in which Hodulf is slain.

V. 2450.] Conf. v. 2505. and 2822. This appears to have been a common, but barbarous, method in former times of leading traitors or malefactors to execution. Thus in the Romance of *Kyng Alisaunder*, the treatment of the murderers of Darius is described:

He dude quyk harnesche hors,
And sette theron heore cors,
Hyndeforth they seten, saun faile;
In heore hand they hulden theo tailes.—v. 4708.

V. 2513. *Sket was seysed*, &c.] Comp. the Fr. v. 971. *Apres cest fet*, &c.

V. 2516. *And the king ful sone it yaf*
Vbbe in the hond, wit a fayr staf.]

So in *Sir Tristrem:*

Rohand he gaf *the wand*,
And bad him sitte him bi,
That fre;
'Rohand lord mak Y
To hald this lond of me.'—p. 52.

The Editor is clearly mistaken in explaining the *wand* to be a *truncheon*, or *symbol of power*. For the custom of giving seisin or investiture *per fustim*, and *per baculum*, see Madox's *Formul. Anglican.* pref. p. IX. and Spelman, Gloss. in v. *Investire*, and *Traditio*. The same usage existed in France, *par rain et par baton*.

V. 2521. —— *of monekes blake*
A priorie to seruen inne ay.]
The allusion here may be made either to the Abbey of Wellow, in Grimsby, which was a monastery of *Black Canons*, said to have been built about A. D. 1110. or, (what is more probable,) to the Augustine Friary of Black Monks, which is stated in the *Monumental Antiquities of Grimsby*, by the Rev. G. Oliver, to have been "founded *about* the year 1280." p. 110. No notice of it occurs in the Tanner till the year 1304. Pat. 33. Edw. I. Some old walls of this edifice, which was dissolved in 1543. still remain, and the site is still called "The Friars." If the connection between this foundation, and the one recorded in the Poem, be considered valid, the date of the composition must be referred to *rather* a later period, than we wish to admit.

V. 2531. The Fr. supplies what is here omitted, viz. that Havelok sails to England by the persuasion of his wife. The remainder of the Fr. Poem altogether differs in its detail from the English.

V. 2927. *Hire that was ful swete in bedde.*] Among Kelly's Scotch Proverbs, p. 290. we find: "*Sweet in the bed,* and sweir up in the morning, was never a good housewife;" and in a ballad of the last century quoted by Laing, the editor of that highly curious collection, the *Select pieces of Ancient Popular Poetry of Scotland,* we meet with the same expression:

A Clown is a Clown both at home and abroad,
When a Rake he is comely, and *sweet in his bed.*

NOTES

TO

THE FRENCH TEXT

OF

Havelok.

The variations of Sir Thomas Phillipps' Ms. are numerous, but of little importance, being chiefly verbal. No complete collation has been attempted, on account of the Ms. itself having unfortunately been mislaid, and only a portion of the Text communicated from a transcript. The more essential differences will be noticed, so far as this transcript extends.

V. 10. *Vilein* m. 11. *s'en gart.* 18. *Curan rest.* 28. *En* Danem. 32. *tuz les* v. 41. *Tant* par *destresce tant* p.p. 46. *guere mener.* 64. En *la* b. *ou il irreit.* 66. *s'enfuist.* 70. *dous* ans. 73. *De sa* b. 75. 76. Desunt. 79. kil *saveent.* 85. *sur* eus *preisseist.* 89. *sa nef.* 99. *Ses chamberlencs.* 100. *ameine.* 112. Qui *laidement.* 114. Deest. Between v. 116. and the succeeding one, are inserted two lines:

La nef unt robé e mal mise,
E la reine i-fu oscise.

After v. 118. is an hiatus to v. 158. inclusive. 168. *e* od poure.

170. de *lur*. 172. *Ne ia ne* g. r. 177. les *servanz*. 178. *mult forz*. 179. *ben* g. f. 186. *noves* draps. 197. *E le* p. 199. Out *ausi* en. 203. *Eschebrit*. 208-209. *Mes il n'aveient* enfant, *Fors une sule* f. b. 210. la *damaisele*. 211. *Echebrit chai en fermete*. 212. *fu mult*. g. 213. qu'*il ne porra* g. 214. *Edelsi*. 215. Sa *nece*. 225-227. *K'en la terre trouer poreit, Pus li bailla les fermetez, Les chasteux e les citez*. 232. *le reis Echebrit* f. 236. av. *traiter*. 237. *Edilsi*. 239. *mult ot* g. g. 242. *Vn des ceus*. 244. Et m. *esteit*. 248. m. *de co serueit*. 251. M. *par les dona*. 256. *Le teneint entre els a* s. 260. *pur* qu. 262. et *servant*. 269. *les* b. Here the transcript ends.

V. 1. *Volenters deueroit*, &c.] The *Lai de Gugemer*, by Marie of France, commences with the same line.

V. 867. So, in the Romance of *Sir Guy*,

> Raynburne went and the swerde tooke,
> There as it hong vpon a *crooke*.—sign. Ll. i.

Gaimar.—V. 4.] See Galf. Mon. lib. viii. c. 1. Ed. Par. 1517. Constantine is said to have succeeded to Arthur, A. D. 542. Ywain was son of Urian, king of Murray, the brother of Augusel, king of Albany, or Scotland, and of Loth, Consul of *Loudonesia*, or Lothian. His accession to the crowns of Murray and Lothian is not mentioned by Geoffrey, nor by his translator Wace, but only his nomination by Arthur to the kingdom of Albany, on the death of his uncle Augusel. Lib. vii. c. 7. He is the hero of the well known and beautiful Romance of *Ywaine and Gawin*, on which see Ritson's Notes.

V. 38. The names of the northern sovereigns who were slain whilst fighting on Arthur's side against Mordred, are called by Geoffrey of Monmouth, lib. vii. c. 7. Olbrictus, King of Norway, and Achilles, King of Denmark. This latter is called Aschis, v. 524. and by Wace Aschil. Robert of Gloucester mentions their death, p. 223. but does not give any names. The additional circumstances stated by Gaimar and the Romance, of Hodulf's being the brother of Aschis, and his gaining the throne of Denmark by the treacherous murder of Gunter, are not to be found in Geoffrey, nor Wace, and proceed from some other source.

V. 689. sq. In the same language is described the ring given to Horn by Rimenil, who says:

> Vn meillur porterez, meillur al men auir,
> V seit al chastun un entaille suffrir.
> Home k'il ad sur sei, ia ne purrat ferir,
> En euue u en fu mar crendrat de murrir.—v. 2051.

Compare the similar lines in *Richard Cœur de Lion*, v. 1633.

Glossary.

GLOSSARY.

ABBREVIATIONS.

A. Bor. Anglia Borealis, the Northern Parts of England.—Ælf. Gl. Ælfrici Glossarium.—Bann. P. Bannatyne Poems.—Barb. Barbour's Bruce.—Chauc. Chaucer.—Doug. Gawin Douglas's Transl. of the Æneid.—Ellis, M. R. Ellis's Specimens of Metrical Romances.—Gl. Glossary.—Jam. Jamieson's Dictionary.—Jun. Etym. Junii Etymologicon.—Lan. Lancashire dialect.—Layam. Layamon's Transl. of Wace, Ms. Cott. Cal. A. ix.—Lynds. Chalmers' Ed. of Sir D. Lyndsay's Works.—Percy, A. R. Percy's Reliques of Ancient English Poetry.—P. Plouhm. Piers Plouhman.—R. Br. Robert of Brunne, edited by Hearne.—R. Gl. Robert of Gloucester, by the same.—Rits. A. S. Ritson's Ancient Songs.—Rits. M. R. Ritson's Metrical Romances.—Sc. Scotch, Scotland.—Sir Tr. Sir Tristrem.—Somn. Somner's Saxon Lexicon.—Wall. Wallace.—Web. Weber's Metrical Romances.—Wilb. Wilbraham's Cheshire Glossary.—Wynt. Wyntoun's Chronicle.—B. Lat. Barbarous Latin.—Belg. Belgic.—Fr. French.—Isl. Islandic.—Lat. Latin.—Sax. Saxon.—Su.G. Suio-Gothic.—Teut. Teutonic.—*q. v.* Quod vide.—The Romances separately cited are sufficiently indicated by the Titles.—The numbers refer to the line of the Poem.

A, 610. 956. Apparently an error of the scribe for *Al,* but written as pronounced. A. Bor. and Sc. *aw.* V. Jam.

A before a *noun* is a corruption of the Sax. *on,* as proved clearly by the examples in Tyrwhitt's Gl. Jam. Dict. and Gl. Lynds. It is surprising Johnson and Todd should not have admitted it. Cf. Pegge's *Anecd. of Engl. Lang.* p. 172. sq. 8vo. 1803. *A-two,* 1413. 2643. See On.

Aboven, *prep.* Sax. Above, 1700.

Abouten, *prep.* Sax. [*on-butan*] About, 521. 670. 1010. &c. *Abuten,* 2429.

Adoun, *adv.* Sax. Down. 567. *Adune,* 2735. *Doun,* 901. 925. &c. *Dun,* 888. 927. *Dune,* 1815. 2654.

Adrad, *part. pa.* Sax. Afraid, 1048. 1163. 1682. 2304. *Adradde,* 1787. *Adrede,* 279. 1258. *Odrat,* 1153. Sir Tr. p. 174. K. Horn, 124. 1170. R. Gl. Web. Chauc. Gl. Sibb. Gl. Lynds. See Dred.

Agen, *prep.* Sax. [*on-gean*] Against, 1792. *Ageyn,* 493. 569. 2024. &c. *Ageynes,* 2153. 2270. &c. *Ayen,* 489. 1210. 2799. *Yen,* 2271. *Ageyn,* Toward, 451. 1696. 1947. Upon, on, 1809. 1828. *Ageyn him go,* 934. Opposite, by his side, so as to bear an equal weight. *Ageyn hire,* 1106. At her approach. *Ageyn the lith,* 2141. Opposed to the light, on which the light shines. V. R. Gl. R. Br. Chauc. Wynt. Doug. Gl. Lynds.

Ageyn, *adv.* Sax. Again, 2426. *Ayen,* 1207.

AL, *adv.* SAX. Wholly, entirely, 34. 70. 139. 203. &c.

AL, ALLE, *adj.* SAX. All, 2. 264. &c. Every one, 104. Every part, 224.

AL-BIDENE, *adv.* By and by, forthwith, 730. 2841.

> Rohand told anon
> His aventours *al bidene.*
> *Sir Tristr.* p. 45.

The etymology is not known. See Rits. Gl. M. R. and Gl. to Minot, Jam. Dict. and Gl. Lynd. in voc. BEDENE.

ALINLAZ, *n.* Anelace, 2554. "A kind of knife or dagger, usually worn at the girdle." Tyrw. Note on Chauc. v. 359. So in Matth. Paris, "Genus cultelli, quod vulgariter *Anelacius* dicitur." V. Gl. in voc. and Todd's Gl. to Illustr. of Chauc. In *Sir Gawan and Sir Galoran,* ii. 4. an *anlas* signifies a sharp spike fixed in the chanfron of a horse. Probably from the Fr. *Anelaz, Analeze.* V. Jam.

ALS, ALSO, AL SO, *conj.* SAX. [*Al-swa*] As, so. 306. 319. &c. *Als*, 1912. As if. *Al so foles than birthe-men*, 2101. More like fools than persons of condition. *Als* is merely the abbreviation of *Al so.* In Layamon it is often written *alse.*

> And he hæfde a swithe god wif
> & he heo leouede *alse* his lif.
> Ms. Cott. Cal. A. IX.

Cf. Havelok, v. 1662. *Als* and *Also* are used indifferently, and universally by the old English and Scotch Poets.

ALTHER-BESTE, *adj.* SAX. Best of all, 182. 720. 1040. 1197. 2415. ALTHER-LEST, ALTHER-LESTE, 1978. 2666. Least of all. It is the gen. c. pl. of *Alle*, joined to an adj. in the superl. degree, and is extensively employed. *Alre-leofust, Alre-hendest, Alre-kenest,* Layamon, *Althe-werste,* K. Horn, Ms. *Alder-best, Aldermost,* R. Br. *Alther-best, Altherformest,* &c. Web. *Alther-furste, Alther-next, Alther-last,* Rits. M. R. *Alder-first, Alderlast, Alderlevest,* Chauc. *Alder-liefest,* Shakesp.

AMIDEWARD, *prep.* SAX. In the midst, 872. *Amiddewart,* K. Horn, 556. *Amydward,* K. Alisaund. 690. *A mydward,* Ly Beaus Desc. 852. *Amydwart,* Doug. Virg. 137. 35.

AN, *conj.* SAX. And, 29. 359. 371. &c. So used by Layamon, and still in Somersetsh. V. Jennings. *Ant,* 36. 557. K. Horn, 9. &c. AND, If, 2862. Sir Tr. and all the Glossaries.

ANDELONG, *adv.* SAX. Lengthways, i. e. from the head to the tail, 2822.

> Ovyrtwart and *endelang*
> With strenges of wyr the stones hang.
> *R. Cœur de Lion,* 2649.

Chauc. *endelong,* C. T. 1993.

ANILEPI, *adj.* SAX. [*anlepig*] One, a single, 2107. *Onlepi,* 1094. In the very curious collection of poems in Ms. Digb. 86. (written in the Lincolnshire dialect temp. Edw. I.) we meet with this rare word, which does not appear in any of the Glossaries.

> A! quod the vox, ich wille the telle,
> *On alpi* word ich lie nelle.
> *Of the vox and of the wolf.*

ANOTHER, *adj.* SAX. *Al another,* 1395. In a different way, on another project.

> Ah al hit iwrath *on other*
> Sone ther after.
> *Layamon,* f. 121. c. 1.

> Ac Florice thought al *another.*
> *Flor. and Blauncheft.* ap. Ellis, M. R. V. 3. p. 125. Ed. 1803.

ANUYE, *v.* FR. To trouble, weary, 1735. R. Gl. K. Alisaund. 876. Chauc. Melib. 219. *Noye*, Lynds. Gl. q. v.

AR, *n.* SAX. Oar, 1776. *Are*, Sir Tr. p. 27. Rits. M. R. See ORE.

ARE, *adv.* SAX. Former, 27. Sir Tr. p. 32. Rits. M. R. Web. R. Gl. R. Br. Minot, p. 31. *Air, Ayr*, Sc. V. Jam. See ER, OR.

AREN, 3. *p. pl.* SAX. Are, 619. 1321. &c. *Arn*, Chauc.

ARKE, *n.* SAX. LAT. A chest or coffer, 2018. R. Br.—Sc. Lanc. V. Jam.

ARMES, *n. pl.* LAT. Arms, armor, 2605. 2613. 2925.

> To *armes* knight and swayn.
> *Sir Tr.* p. 49.

ARUM for ARM, 1982. 2408.

ARWE-MEN, *n. pl.* SAX. Bowmen? 2115.

As for HAS, 1174.

ASAYLEDEN, *pa. t. pl.* FR. Assailed, 1862.

ASKEN, *n. pl.* SAX. Ashes, 2841. *Aske*, R. Gl. *Askes*, R. Br. *Ashen*, Chauc. *Assis*, Doug.

ASTIRTE, *pa. t.* Leaped, 893. *Astert*, King's Quair, ap. Jam. See STIRT.

AT, *prep.* SAX. Of, or to, 1387. Yw. and Gaw. 963. Still existing in Scotland. *Ath*, 59. At.

AT-SITTE, *v.* SAX. Contradict, oppose, 2200. It corresponds with the term *with-sitten*, 1683. In R. Gl. it is used synonymously with *at-stonde*.

> For ther nas so god knygt non no wer aboute France,
> That in joustes scholde *at sitte* the dynt of ys lance.—p. 137.

See SAT.

AUCTE, AUCHTE, AUHTE, AUTHE, *n.* SAX. Possessions, 531. 1223. 1410. 2215.

> And all the *ahten* of mine londe.
> *Layam.* f. 146. b. c. 1.

Aughtte, K. Alisaund. 6884. *Aucht*, Doug. Virg. 72. 4. Bann. P. p. 176. Lynds. Gl.

AUCTE, AUHT, AUHTE, *v. imp.* (originally *pa. t.* of AW, or OWE,) SAX. [*Agan-ahte*] Ought, 2173. 2787. 2800. *Aught*, Sir Tr. p. 44. *Ohte*, K. Horn, 418. *Aght*, Yw. and Gaw. 3229. *Aute*, R. Gl. *Aught*, Chauc. Troil. 3. 1801. *Aucht*, Doug. Virg. 110. 33.

AUTE, AWCTE, *pa. t.* of the same verb. Possessed, 207. 743. *Aught*, Sir Tr. p. 182. Ly Beaus Desc. 1027. *Oght*, Le bone Flor. 650. *Auht*, R. Br. p. 126. Wynt. Lynds. Gl.

AUEDEN, See HAUEDEN.

AUTER, *n.* FR. LAT. Altar, 389. 1386. 2373. Sir Tr. p. 61. Octavian, 1312. R. Br. Chauc. *Awter*, Barb.

AY, *adv.* SAX. Ever, aye, always, 159. 946. 1201. &c. *Ae*, Sc. V. Jam.

AYEN, See AGEN.

AYSE, *n.* FR. Ease, 59.

AYTHER, *pron.* SAX. [*Aegther*] Either, each, 2665. *Ether*, 1882. *Athir*, Sc. V. Jam. See OTHER.

AWE, *v.* SAX. To owe, own, possess, 1292. It may also very possibly be a corruption of *Have*. Cf. v. 1188. 1298.

B.

BAC, *n.* SAX. Back, 1844. 1950. &c. BACKES, *pl.* 2611.

BALDELIKE, *adv.* SAX. Boldly, 53. *Baldeliche*, R. Glouc. *Baldely*, R. Br. Minot, p. 20.

BALE, *n.* SAX. Sorrow, misery, 327. Sir Tr. p. 15. and in all the Glossaries.

BAR, See BEREN.

BARET, *n.* ISL. [*baratta*, prælium] Contest, hostile contention, 1932.

> Ther nis *baret*, nothir strif,
> Nis ther no deth, ac euer lif.
> *Land of Cokaygne*, ap. Hickes, Thes. 1. p. 231.

In alle this *barette* the kynge and Sir Symon
Tille a lokyng tham sette, of the prince suld
it be don. *R. Brunne*, p. 216. Cf. p. 274.
That mekill bale and *barete* till Ynglande
sall brynge. *Awntyrs of Arthure*, st. 23.

Barrat, Wallace, ii. 237. This is one of the words which Jamieson (most absurdly) instances in proof of the Scots having derived their language from the N. of Europe, and not from the Saxons. His other examples are *Bar*, *Bathe*, *Blout*, *Brade*. V. Jam. Pref. p. 23. Although of Gothic original, yet as these words are found in use among the early English writers, there is every reason to believe they passed into Scotland by the same channel which conveyed the mass of their language. V. Chalmer's Introd. to Gl. Lynds. The Fr. *Baret* is from the same root.

Barfot, *adj*. Sax. Barefoot, 862.

Barnage, *n*. Fr. Barons or Noblemen, collectively viewed, Baronage, 2947. Yw. and Gaw. 1258. Web. Doug. Virg. 314. 48. Wall.

Barre, *n*. Fr. Bar of a door, 1794. 1811. 1827. Synonymous with dore-tre, q. v. Chauc. C. T. 552.

Barw, See Berwen.

Bathe, *adj*. Sax. Both, 1336. 2543. *Bethe*, 694. 1680.

Be, See Ben.

Bede, *n*. Sax. Prayer, 1385.

Bede, *v*. Sax. To order, to bid, 668. 2193. 2396. To offer, 1665. 2084. 2172. Beden, *pa. t. pl.* Offered, 2774. 2780. Bedes, Bids, 2392. Of common occurrence in both senses. See Bidd.

Bedden, *v*. Sax. To bed, put to bed, 1235. Bedde, Bedded, Beddeth, *part. pa.* Put to bed, 421. 1128. 2771.

Bedels, *n. pl.* Sax. Beadels, 266. V. Spelm. in v. *Bedellus*, and Blount, *Joc. Ten.* p. 120. Ed. 1784.

Beite, Beyte, *v*. To bait, set dogs on, baited, 1840. 2330. 2440. *Bayte*, R. Br. From the Isl. *Beita*, incitare, Goth. *Beita biorn*, To bait the bear. V. Jam. and Thomson's Etymons.

Bem, See Sunne-bem.

Ben, *v*. Sax. To be, 19. 905. 1006. &c. Ben, *pr. t. pl.* Are, 1787. 2559. Be, Ben, *part. pa.* Been, 1428. 2799. Bes, Beth, *imp.* and *fut.* Be, shall be, 1261. 1744. 2007. 2246. *Lat be*, 1265. 1657. Leave, relinquish. A common phrase in the Old Romances. *Lat abee*, Sc. V. Jam.

Benes, *n. pl.* Sax. Beans, 769.

Beneysun, *n*. Fr. Blessing, benediction, 1723. R. Br. Web. Chauc. C. T. 9239. Lynds. Gl.

Bere, *n*. Sax. Bear, 573. 1838. 1840. 2448.

Bere, Beren, *v*. Sax. To bear, carry, 581. 762. 805. Bar, *pa. t.* Bore, 557. 815. 877. *Ber* (?) 2557. *Bere*, 974. Beres, *pr. t. pl.* Bear, 2323.

Bermen, *n. pl.* Sax. Bar-men, Porters to a kitchin, 867. 876. 885. The only author in which this term has been found, is Layamon, in the following passages.

Vs selve we habbet cokes,
to quecchen to cuchene,
Vs selue we habbet *bermen*,
& birles inowe.—f. 18. b. c. 2.

Tha the seruuinge wes idon,
That hit to the mete com,
Ther of ich wulle the tellen
Seleuthe spelles.
Weoren in theos kinges cuchene
twa hundred cokes,
& ne mai na man tellen
for alle tha *bermannen*.—f. 45. b. c. 2.

Bern, *n.* Sax. Child, 571. *Barn, bearne,* R. Br. *Bairn,* Sc. V. Jam. and Gl. Lynds.

Berwen, *v.* Sax. [*beorgan*] To defend, preserve, guard, 697. 1426. Barw, Burwe, *pa. t.* 2022. 2679. 2870. The original word is found in Beowulf:

Seyld wel *gebearg* The shield well defended
Life and lice. Life and body.—p. 191.

So in K. Horn, Ms. Laud, 108.

At more ich wile the serue,
And fro sorwe the *berwe.*—f. 224. b. c. 2.

The verb *to borrow,* so frequently used in the ancient writers, both English and Scotch, and signifying *to become surety for,* is apparently from a different root. V. Jam. See Serf-borw.

Bes, see Ben.

Bes for Best, 354.

Best, Beste, *n.* Fr. Beast, 279. 574. 944. 2691.

Bete, *v.* Sax. [*beutan,* Lye.] To beat, fight, 1899. 2664. 2763. Beten, *pa. t. pl.* Beat, strike, 1876. Chauc. C. T. 4206. to which Tyrwh. gives a Fr. derivation.

Betere, *adj. comp.* Sax. Better, 1758.

Beye, *v.* Sax. To buy, 53. 1654. *Byen,* 1625.

Beyes, *pr. t.* for Abeyes, Sax. Suffers, or atones for, 4560.

His deth thou *bist* to night,
My fo. *Sir Tristr.* p. 146.
We shulden alle deze
Thy fader deth to *beye.*
K. Horn, 113.
An of you schal *bye* thys blunder.
Le bone Flor. 1330.

See Jam. in v. Aby. Web. Gl. and Lynds. Gl. Also Nares, v. Bye.

Bicomen, *pa. t. pl.* Became, 2257. *part. pa.* Become, 2264. Bicomes, *imp. pl.* Become (ye) 2303.

Bidd, Bidde, *v.* Sax. Offer, 484. 2530. Order, bid, 529. 1733. *Ut-bidde,* 2548. Order out. Biddes, *pr. t.* Bids, orders, 1232. Bidde, To ask, 910. R. Glouc. Lynds. Gl. See Bede.

Bifalle, *v.* Sax. To happen, befall, 2981. Bifel, *pa. t.* 824. *Fel,* 1009. Appertained, 2359.

Bifor, Biforn, *prep.* Sax. Before, 1022. 1034. 1364. &c. *Biforen,* 1695. In front, 1812. 2406.

Bigan, *pa. t.* Began, 1357. Bigunnen, *pl.* 1011. 1302. Biginnen, *pr. t. pl.* Begin, 1779.

Bihalue, *v.* Sax. To divide into two parts, or companies, 1834. It occurs as a *noun* in Chauc. Troil. 4. 945.

Bihel for Beheld, 1645. Bihelden, *pa. t. pl.* Beheld, 2148.

Bihetet, *pa. t.* Sax. Promised, 677. *Behight,* Sir Tr. p. 105. *Behet, Bi het,* R. Gl. *Be hette,* R. Br. *Behete,* Web. Rits. M. R. *behighte,* Chauc. Bihoten, *part. pa.* Promised, 564. *Behighten,* Chauc.

Bihoue, *n.* Sax. Behoof, advantage, 1764. R. Gl. R. Br. Chauc.

Bikenneth, *pa. t.* Sax. Betokens, 1268. *Bikenne,* R. Br.

Bileue, *imp.* Tarry, remain, 1228. Bilefte, *pa. t.* Remained, 2963. From *v.* Sax. *belifan,* superesse.

Winde thai hadde as thai wolde,
A lond *bilaft* he.
Sir Tristr. p. 29. Cf. p. 38. 60.

He schal mid me *bileue,*
Til hyt be ner heue.
K. Horn, Ms. 367.
Horn than, withouten lesing,
Bilaft at home for blode-leting.
Horn Childe, ap. Rits. M. R. V. 3. p. 298.

Sojourn with us evermo,
I rede thee, son, that it be so.
Another year thou might over-fare,
But thou *bilere*, I die with care.
Guy of Warw. ap. Ellis, M. R. V. 2. p. 23.

See also the Gl. to R. Gl. R. Br. and Web. to which add *Emare*, 496. and Gower, Conf. Am. This is sufficient authority for the reading adopted in the text, and it may hence be reasonably questioned, whether *bilened* in Lye, and *belenes* in *Sir Gawan and Sir Galoran*, i. 6. quoted by Jamieson in v. BELENE, be not the fault of the scribe, or of the Editors.

BIMENE, *v.* SAX. Mean, 1259.

BINDEN, *v.* SAX. To bind, 1961. Used passively, 2820. as BYNDE, 42. BOUNDEN, BUNDEN, *part. pa.* Bound, 545. 1428. 2442. 2506. &c.

BINITHER, See NITHER.

BINNE, *prep.* SAX. Within, 584. *Byn*, Rits. M. R. *But and ben*, Doug. Virg. 123. 40. Without and within. V. Jam. in v. BEN.

BIRDE, *n.* SAX. Lady, damsel, 2761. A word often applied to a young female in old English Poetry. By metathesis it is *brid* in Sir Tr. p. 88. Hence the modern term *bride*. See Jam. and the Glossarists, for further illustration.

BIRTHE-MEN, *n. pl.* SAX. Men of birth, or condition, 2101.

BIRTHENE, *n.* SAX. Burden, 900.

BISE, *n.* FR. A North wind. *Bise traverse*, a North West or North East wind. *Cotgr.*

Après grant joie vient grant ire,
Et après Noel *vent bise*.
Rom. de Renart, 13648.

The term is still in common use.

BISEKEN, *v.* SAX. To beseech, 2994.

BISTODE, *pa. t.* SAX. Stood by, or near, 476. 507. Chron. of Engl. 763.

BISWIKE, *part. pa.* SAX. Cheated, deceived, 1249.

Hu thu *biswikest*
Moni ne mon. *Layam* f. 19. c. 2.

Byswyke, K. Horn, 296. Yw. and Gaw. 2335. *bisuike*, R. Br. *Beswyke*, R. Cœur de L. 5918. It is doubtful however whether *swike* be not here a noun. See SWIKE.

BITAKEN, *v.* SAX. [*bitæcan, tæcan*] To commit, deliver, give in charge, 1225. BITECHE, BITECHEN, 203. 384. 395. Layam. f. 29. b. *Bitake*, Sir Tr. p. 87. *Byteche*, K. Horn, 578. *Biteche*, Web. *Betake, Beteche*, Chauc. Barb. Wall. BITAUCTE, *pa. t.* Delivered, 206. 558. *Bitauhte*, 2212. 2317. 2957. *Bitawchte*, 1224. *Bitawte*, 1408. *Tauhte*, 2214. *Bitæht*, *Bitachet*, Layam. *Bitaught*, Sir Tr. p. 85. *Bitoke*, K. Horn, 1103. *Betok*, Ly Beaus Desc. 82. *Betauht, bitauht, tauht, bitechcd*, R. Br. *Bitake*, R. Gl. *Betake*, Sir Guy. *Betaught*, Chauc. *Betaucht*, Doug. Lynds.

BITE, *v.* SAX. To drink, 1731.

Horn toc hit hise yfere,
Ant seide, Quene, so dere,
No beer nullich *bite*,
Bote of coppe white.
K. Horn, 1129.

BITH for BY THE, 474.

BITUENE, BITWENE, BITWENEN, *prep.* SAX. Between, 748. 2668. 2967.

BLAC, *adj.* SAX. Black, 555. 1008. *Blake*, 1909. 2181. &c. *Bleike*, 470.

BLAKNE, *v.* SAX. To blacken in the face, grow angry, 2165.

And Arthur sæt ful stille,
Ane stunde he wes *blac*,
And on heuwe swithe wak,
Ane while he wes read.
Layam. f. 114. c. 2.

Tho Normans were sorie, of contenance gan *blaken*. *R. Brunne*, p. 183.

Blawe, *v.* Sax. To blow, 587. Blou, *imp.* Blow, 585.

Blede, *v.* Sax. To bleed, 2403.

Bleike, See Blac.

Blenkes, *n. pl.* Blinks, winks of the eye, in derision, 307. R. Br. p. 270. Sc. V. Jam. Suppl. Derived from Sax. *blican.* Su. G. *blaenka,* Belg. *blencken,* to glance. See Gl. Lynds.

Blinne, *v. n.* Sax. To cease, 2367. 2374. Sir Tr. p. 26. Rits. M. R. Web. R. Gl. Chauc. So in Sc. V. Jam. Gl. Lynds. Blinne, *pa. t. pl.* Ceased, 2670. Blinneth, *pr. t.* Ceases, 329.

Blissed, *part. pa.* Sax. Blessed, 2873.

Blithe, *adj.* Sax. Happy, 632. 651.

Blome, *n.* Sax. Bloom, flower, 63.

Bloute, *v.* To bloat, or swell out? 1910. V. Thoms. Etymons, who derives it from Sax. *blowan.* Jam. has *Bloute,* bare, naked, from Su. G. *blote,* but it does not here seem to apply.

Bode, *n.* Sax. Command, 2200. 2567. Sir Tr. p. 121. Web.

Bok, *n.* Sax. Book, 1173. 1418. &c. See Messe-bok.

Bole, *n.* [Isl. *bauli,* Br. *bwla.* The Sax. is lost.] Bull, 2438. Boles, *pl.* 2330.

Bon, Bone, See O-bone.

Bondemen, *n. pl.* Sax. Husbandmen, 1016. 1308. R. Gl.

Bone, *n.* Sax. [*bene*] Boon, request, 1659. Sir Tr. p. 31. and all the Gloss.

Bor, *n.* Sax. Boar, 1867. 1989. Bores, *pl.* 2331.

Bord, *n.* Sax. Table, 1722. K. Horn, 259. Rits. M. R. Web. Chauc. A board, 2106. See the Note on v. 2076.

Boren, *part. pa.* Sax. Born, 1878.

Boru, Borw, *n.* Sax. Borough, 773. 847. 1014. 1757. 2086. 2826. Borwes, *pl.* 1293. 1444. 1630. *Burwes,* 55. 2277. Sir Tr. p. 12. 99. Chalmers is certainly mistaken when he says it does not signify *boroughs,* but *castles.* Introd. Gl. p. 200. n. In Layamon the word is always clearly distinguished from *castle,* as it is in many other writers. V. Spelm. in v. *Burgus.*

Bote, *adv.* Sax. But, only, 720. See But.

Bote, *n.* Sax. Remedy, help, 1200. Layam. Sir Tr. p. 93. Web. Rits. M. R. Rob. Gl. R. Br. Minot, Chauc. Doug. Lynds. Gl. *Boote,* R. Hood, i. 118.

Bothen, *adj. pl.* Sax. Both, 173. 697. 958. *g. c.* Of both, 2223.

Bounden, Bunden, See Binden.

Bour, Boure, Bowr, *n.* Sax. [*bur,* cubiculum, *Ælf. Gl.*] Chamber, 239. 2072. 2076. &c. In Beowulf the apartment of the women is called *Bryd-bur,* p. 71.

> Ygarne beh to *bure,*
> & lætte bed him makien.
> *Layam.* f. 109. c. 2.

Honder hire *boures* wowe. *K. Horn,* 982. Ms. where Rits. Ed. reads *chambre wowe.* Cf. Sir Tr. p. 114. Rits. M. R. Web. R. Br. Doug. V. Jam. *Boor,* A. Bor. Ray, Brockett. See Note on v. 2076.

Bouthe, *pa. t.* Sax. Bought, 875. 883. 968. Cf. Sir Tr. p. 104.

Boyes, *n. pl.* Sax. Boys, men, 1899.

Brayd, *pa. t.* Sax. Started, 1282. Chauc. Gaw. and Gal. iii. 21. R. Hood, ii. p. 83. Drew out, 1825. A word particularly applied to the action of drawing a sword from the scabbard.

> Sone his sweord he ut *abræid.*
> *Layam.* 155. c. 1.

Cf. Am. and Amil. 1163. Sir Ferumbras, ap. Ellis, M. R. V. 2. p. 387. Rauf Coilzear, ap. Laing, and Wall. i. 223.

Bred, Brede, *n.* Sax. Bread, 98. 1879.

Breken, *v.* Sax. To break, 914. Broken, *pa. t. pl.* Broke, 1238.

Brennan, Brenne, *v.* Sax. To burn, 916. 1162. Rits. M. R. Rob. Gl. R. Br. Chauc. Brenden, *pa. t. pl.* Burnt, 594. 2125. Brend, *part. pa.* Burnt, 2832. 2841. &c. Sir Tr. p. 93.

Brenne, See On-brenne.

Brigge, *n.* Sax. Bridge, 875. Sir Tr. p. 148. and all the Gloss. Still used in Sc. and A. Bor.

Brihte, See Brith.

Brim, *adj.* Sax. Furious, raging, 2233. R. Br. p. 244. Chauc. Parl. Lad. 244. *Breme,* Rits. M. R. It originally signified the sea itself, and afterwards used for the raging of the sea. Beowulf, p. 113. Compl. of Scotland, p. 62. V. Jam.

Bringe, Bringen, *v.* Sax. To bring, 72. 185. &c.

Brini, Brinie, *n.* Sax. Cuirass, 1775. 2358. 2551. Brinies, *pl.* 2610. Sir Tr. p. 20. *Burne,* Layam. *Brenye,* K. Horn, 719. Ms. See Merrick's Gl. to Ess. on Anc. Armor. The *Brini* then worn was of *mail,* as appears from v. 2740. *Of his brinie ringes mo.* Hence in Beowulf it is termed *Breost-net,* p. 117. *Here-net,* p. 118. *Hringed-byrne,* 95. So in the French K. Horn, Ms. Douce, *Mes vnc de sun halberc maele ne falsa.* See Rits. Gl. M. R.

Brisen, *v.* Sax. To bruise, beat, 1835. See To-brised.

Brith, *adj.* Sax. Bright, 589. 605. &c. *Brihte,* 2610. *Bryth,* 1252. Brithter, *comp.* Brighter, 2141.

Brittene, *part. pa.* Sax. Cut in pieces, 1700. R. Br. p. 244. *Pistill of Sussan,* ap. Laing. In Doug. Virg. p. 76. 5. 296. 1. the verb has the sense of *to kill,* which it may also bear here.

Brod, *adj.* Sax. Broad, 1646.

Broucte, *pa. t.* Brought, 767. *Brouht,* 1979. *Broute,* 2868. *Brouth,* 336. 648. *Browt,* 2412. *Browth,* 2052. *Brouct of liue,* 513. 2412. 2829. Dead. Brouthen, *pl.* Brought, 2791.

Brouke, *v.* Sax. Brook, enjoy, use, 311. 1743. 2545.

> So *brouke* thou thi croune!
> K. *Horn,* 1041.

Cf. Rits. Gl. M. R. Rich. C. de Lion, 4758. Chauc. C. T. 10182. 15306. R. Hood, V. i. 48. ii. 112. Lynds. Gl. Percy, A. R. In Sc. *Bruike.* With these numerous instances before him, it is inconceivable how Jamieson, except from a mere love of his own system, should write: "There is no evidence that the Engl. *brook* is used in this sense, signifying only to bear, to endure."

Broys, *n.* Sax. Broth (?) 924. *Brouwys,* R. Cœur de L. 3077. Sc. V. Jam. and Brockett's North Country Words, v. Brewis, also Nares.

Brune, *adj.* Sax. Brown, 2181. 2249.

Bulder, *adj.* or *n.* 1790. In the North a *Boother* or *Boulder,* is a hard flinty stone, rounded like a bowl. Brockett's Gl. So also in Grose, *Boulder,* a large round stone. *Bowlders,* Marsh. Midl. Count. Gl. The word has a common origin with Isl. *ballotur,* Fr. *boulet,* Sc. *boule,* in Doug. V. Jam.

Bunden, See Binden.

Burgeys, *n.* Sax. Burgess, 1328. *Burgeis,* 2466. *pl.* 2012. Burgmen, 2049. *Burhmen, Bormonnen,* Layamon. V. Spelm. in v. Burgarii.

Burwe, See Berwen.

Burwes, See Boru.

But, Bute, *adv.* Sax. Except, unless, 85. 690. 1149. 1159. 2022. 2031. 2727. *Buton,* 505. Except. *Butand,* Sc. *But yif,* 2446. Unless.

But, *n.* Probably the same as Put, q. v. The word *Bout* is derived from the same source.

But, *part. pa.* Contended, struggled with each other, 1916. Buttinge, *part pr.* Striking against with force, 2322. From the Fr. *Bouter*, Belg. *Botten*, to impel, or drive forward. V. Jam. Suppl. in v. Butte. See Putten.

Butte, *n.* 759. It may mean either the *Hali-but*, or *Tur-bot*. "What in the North they call the Halibut, in the North [South] they call the Turbot, and the Turbot the Bret, nay in some parts of the West of England they call the Turbot Bret, and the Halibut Turbot." Ray, *Coll. Engl. W.* p. 99.

Byen, See Beye.

Bynde, See Binden.

Bynderes, *n. pl.* Sax. Binders, robbers who bind, 2050.

C

Caliz, *n.* Sax. Chalice, 187. 2711.

> Lunet than riche relikes toke,
> The *chalis* and the mes boke.
> *Yw. and Gaw.* 3907.

Callen, *v.* Sax. To call, 747. 2899.

Cam, See Komen.

Canst, *pr. t.* Sax. Knowest, 846. Cone, 622. Can. Kunne, *pl.* 435. V. Gl. Chauc. in v. Conne, Jam. and Gl. Lynds. See Couthe.

Carl, *n.* Sax. Churl, slave, villain, 1789. Cherl, 682. 684. 2533. Cherles, *g. c.* Churl's, 1092. Cherles, *pl.* Villains, bondsmen, 262. 620. Sir Tr. p. 39. V. Spelm. in v. Ceorlus, and Jam. and Gl. Lynds.

Casten, See Kesten.

Catel, *n.* Fr. Chattels, goods, 27. 225. 2023. 2515. 2906. 2939. Web. Gl. R. Br. P. Plouhm. Chauc.

> Nowe hath Beuis the treasure wone,
> Through Arundell that wyll runne,
> Wherefore with that and other *catel*,
> He made the castle of Arundel.
> *Syr Bevys*, O. iii.

Cauenard, *n.* Fr. [*cagnard, caignard*] A term of reproach, originally derived from the Lat. *canis*, 2389. V. Roquef. Menage.

> This crokede *caynard* sore he is adred.
> *Rits.* A. S. p. 36.
> Sire *olde kaynard*, is this thin aray?
> *Chauc.* C. T. 5817.

Cayser, Caysere, *n.* Lat. Emperor, 977. 1317. 1725. *Kaysere*, 353.

Cerges, *n. pl.* Fr. Wax tapers, 594. *Serges*, 2125. Chauc. Rom. R. 6248. V. Le Grand, *Vie privée des F.* V. 3. p. 175.

Chaffare, *n.* Sax. Merchandise, 1657. R. Cœur de L. 2468. R. Gl. Sir Ferumbras, ap. Ellis, M. R. V. 2. p. 412. Chauc. R. Hood, i. 87. *Chaffery*, Sc. V. Lynds. Gl.

Cham for Came, 1873.

Chambioun, *n.* Fr. Champion, 1007. Sir Tr. p. 97. Chaunpiouns, *pl.* 1015. 1031. 1055. V. Spelm. in v. Campio.

Chapmen, *n. pl.* Sax. Merchants, 51. 1639. R. Gl. R. Br. Chauc. In Sc. Pedlars. V. Jam. and Gl. Lynds.

Charbucle, *n.* Fr. Lat. A carbuncle, 2145. *Charbocle*, Syr Bevys. *Charbokull*, Le bone Flor. 389. *Charboucle*, Chauc. C.T. 13800. *Charbukill*, Doug. Virg. 3. 10.

Cherl, See Carl.

Chesen, *v.* Sax. To choose, select, 2147. Sir Tr. p. 27. K. Horn, 666. Rits. M. R. Web. R. Br. Chauc. V. Jam. in v. Cheis.

Chinche, *adj.* Fr. Niggardly, penurious, 1763. 2961.

> Bothe he was scars, and *chinche*.
> *The Sevyn Sages*, 1244.

So in Chauc. Rom. de la R. 5998. and Gower, *Conf. Am.* 109. b.

CHIST, *n.* SAX. LAT. Chest, 222. *Kiste*, 2018. *Kist*, Yorksh. and Sc. V. Jam. and Lynds. Gl.

CITTE, *pa. t.* SAX. Cut, 942. *Kit*, Web. M.R. *Kyt*, Syr Eglam. B. iv. *Kette*, Syr Bevys, C. iii. So Chauc. C. T. 6304.

CLADDES, *pr. t. 2. p.* SAX. Claddest, 2907.

CLAPTE, *pa. t.* SAX. Struck, 1814. 1821.

CLARE, *n.* FR. Spiced wine, 1728. See the Note on v. 1725.

CLEF, *pa. t.* SAX. Cleft, 2644. 2730.

CLEUE, *n.* SAX. Dwelling, 557. 596. V. Somn.

CLEUEN, *v.* SAX. To cleave, cut, 917.

CLOTHE, CLOTHEN, *v.* SAX. To clothe, 1138. 1233.

CLUTES, *n. pl.* SAX. Clouts, shreds of cloth, 547. *Clottys*, Huntyng of the Hare, 92. Cf. Chauc. C. T. 9827. and Lye Dict. in v. CLUT.

CLYUEDEN, *pa. t. pl.* SAX. Cleaved, fastened, 1300.

COK, *n.* LAT. Cook, 967. *Kok*, 903. 921. 2898. COKES, KOKES, *g. c.* Cook's, 1123. 1146.

COMEN, COMES, COMETH, See KOMEN.

CONE, See CANST.

CONESTABLE, *n.* FR. Constable, 2286. CONESTABLES, *pl.* 2366.

CONSEYL, *n.* FR. Counsel, 2862.

COPES, See KOPE.

CORPORAUS, *n.* FR. LAT. The fine linen wherein the sacrament is put. *Cotgr.* V. Du Cange, and Jam. in v. CORPERALE.

After the relics they send;
The *corporas*, and the mass-gear,
On the handom they gun swear,
With wordes free and hend.
Guy of Warw. ap. Ellis, M. R. V. 2. p. 77.

CORUNE, *n.* LAT. Crown, 1319. 2944.

CORUNING, *n.* LAT. Coronation, 2948.

COTE, *n.* SAX. Cot, cottage, 737. 1141.

COUEL, *n.* Coat, garment, 768. 858. 1144. *Cuuel*, 2904. *Keuel*, 547. 637. *Kouel*, 964. The word is probably connected with SAX. *Cugle*, BELG. *Kovel*, from the LAT. *Cucullus*. V. Jun. Etymol. in v.

COUERE, *v.* FR. To recover, 2040.

And prayde to Marie bryght,
Kevere him of his care.
Ly Beaus Desc. 1983.
Hyt wolde *covyr* me of my care.
Erl of Tol. 381.

COUPE, *v.* 1800.

COUTH, See QUATH.

COUTHE, *pa. t.* of CONNE, *v. aux.* SAX. Knew, was able, could, 93. 112. 194. 750. 772. KOUTHEN, *pl.* 369.

More he *couthe* of veneri,
Than *couthe* Manerious.
Sir Tristr. p. 24.

See CANST.

CRAKE, CRAKEDE, See KRAKEN.

CRAUEDE, *pa. t.* SAX. Craved, asked, 633.

CRICE, *n.* 2450. Perhaps from SAX. *crecca*, crepido maris. In Barb. x. 602. *Crykes* is used for *Angles*, corners. See KRIKE.

CRIST, *n.* LAT. GR. Christ, 16. &c. CRISTES, *g. c.* 153. *Kristes*, 2797.

CROIZ, *n.* FR. LAT. Cross, 1263. 1268. 1358. &c. *Croice*, Sir Tr. p. 115.

CROUD, *part. pa.* Crowded, oppressed (?) 2338. K. Alisaund. 609.

CROUN, CROUNE, *n.* FR. Crown, head, 568. 902. 2657. *Crune*, 1814. 2734.

Fykenildes *crowne*
He fel ther doune.
K. Horn, 1509.

Cf. K. of Tars, 631. Le Bone Flor. 92. and Erle of Tol. 72.

CRUHSSE, See TO-CRUHSSE.

CUNNRICHE, *n.* SAX. Kingdom, 2318. *Kinneriche*, 976. *Kuneriche*, 2400. *Kunerike*, 2804. *Kunrik*, 2143. In the last instance it means *a mark of royalty, or monarchy*. Web. *Kyngriche, Kynryche.*

CURT, *n.* FR. Court, 1685.

CURTEYS, CURTEYSE, *adj.* FR. Courteous, 2875. 2916.

CURUEN, *v.* SAX. To cut, or carve off, hence, to skin, 918. In Sir Tr. p. 33. it is expressed of the hide of a deer.

CUUEL, See COUEL.

D.

DAM, *n.* 2468. Here used in a reproachful sense, but apparently from the same root as the FR. *Dam, Damp, Dan,* and *Don,* i. e. from *Dominus.*

DAME, *n.* FR. LAT. Mistress, Lady, 558. 1717. V. Gl. Chauc.

DANSHE, *n. pl.* Danish men, 2689. 2945. &c. See DENSHE.

DATHEIT, *interj.* 296. 300. 926. 1125. 1887. 1914. 2047. 2447. 2511. *Datheyt*, 1799. 1995. 2604. 2757. An interjection or imprecation, derived from the FR. *Deshait, dehait, dehet,* explained by Barbazan and Roquefort, *affliction, malheur.* It may be considered equivalent to Cursed! Ill betide! In the old Fabliaux it is used often in this sense:

> Fils à putain, fet-il, lechiere,
> Vo jouglerie m'est trop chiere,
> *Dehait* qui vous i aporta,
> Par mon chief il le comparra.
>
> *De S. Pierre et du Jougleor*, 381.

The term was very early engrafted on the Saxon phraseology. Thus in the *Disputation of Ane Hule and a Niztingale*, Ms. Cott. Cal. A. IX. f. 230. b. c. 1.

> *Dahet* habbe that ilke best,
> That fuleth his owe nest!

It occurs also frequently in the Old English Romances. See Sir Tristr. pp. 111. 191. Horn Childe, ap. Rits. V. 3. p. 290. Amis and Amil. 1569. Sevyn Sages, 2295. R. Brunne, where it is printed by Hearne *Dayet.* To this word, in all probability, we are indebted for the modern imprecation of *Dase you! Dise you! Dash you!* still preserved in many counties, and in Scotland. V. Jam. Suppl. v. DASH YOU.

DAWES, *n. pl.* SAX. Days, 27. 2344. 2950. DAYES, 2353.

DED, DEDE, *n.* SAX. Death, 149. 167. 332. 1687. 2719. &c.

DED, *part. pa.* SAX. Dead, 2007.

DEDE, *n.* SAX. Deed, action, 1356.

DEDE, DEDEN, DEDES, See DO.

DEIDE, See DEYE.

DEL, *n.* SAX. Deal, part, 218. 818. 1070. &c. Web. R. Gl. R. Br. Chauc. *Deil,* Sc. V. Jam.

DELED, *part. pa.* SAX. Distributed, 1736. See TO-DEYLE.

DEMEN, *v.* SAX. To judge, pass judgement, 2468. DEME, DEMEN, *pr. t. pl.* Judge, 2476. 2812. DEMDEN, *pa. t. pl.* Judged, 2820. 2833. DEMD, *part. pa.* Judged, 2488. 2765. 2838. Used in all the old English writers.

DENSHE, *adj.* Danish, 1403. 2575. 2693. See DANSHE.

DEPLIKE, *adj.* SAX. Deeply, 1417. Synonymous with GRUNDLIKE, q. v.

DERE, *n.* SAX. Dearth, scarcity, 824. 841. It is so interpreted also in Hearne's Gl. to R. Gl. but we have not found any other instance. The common, and primary signification, is *Hurt, damage.*

Dere, *v.* Sax. To harm, injure, 490. 574. 806. 2310. Dereth, *pr. t.* Injures, 648. K. Horn, 147. R. Br. p. 107. K. of Tars, 192. Sir Guy, Cc. ii. Minot, p. 3. Chauc. *Deir*, Sc. Doug. Virg. 413. 52. Lynds. Gl.

Dere, *adj.* Sax. Dear, 1637. 2170. &c.

Deuel, *n.* Sax. Devil, 446. 496. 1187. Deueles, *g. c.* Devil's, 1409.

Deus, *adj.* Fr. Sweet, 1312. *Douce, Douse*, Sc. V. Jam.

Deus. This is undoubtedly the vocative case of the Lat. *Deus*, used as an interjection, 1650. 1930. 2096. 2114. Its use was the same in French as in English. Thus in King Horn:

Enuers Deu en sun quer a fait grant clamur,
Ohi, *Deus!* fait il, ki es uerrai creatur,
Par ki deuise, &c.
Harl. Ms. 527. f. 66. b. c. 2.

It was probably introduced into the English language by the Normans, and its pronunciation remained the same as in the French.

And gradde "as armes," for *Douce* Mahons!
K. Alisaunder, 3674.

It is curious to remark, that we have here the evident and simple etymology of the modern exclamation *Deuce!* for the derivation of which even the best and latest Lexicographers have sent us to the *Dusii* of St. Augustine, the *Dues* of the Gothic nations, *Diis* of the Persians, *Teus* of the Armoricans, &c. Thomson very justly adds, that all these words, "seem, like dæmon, to have been once used in a good sense," and in fact are probably all corruptions of the same root. Cf. R. Brunne, p. 254. and Gl. in v. Deus. For the first suggestion of this derivation the Editor is indebted to Mr. Will. Nicol.

Deye, *v.* Sax. To die, 840. Deide, *part. pa.* Died, 402.

Dide, Diden, Dides, See Do.

Dike, *n.* Sax. Ditch, 2435. Dikes, *pl.* 1923. A. Bor. and Sc. V. Jam. and Brockett.

Dine, *n.* Sax. Din, noise, 1860. 1868.

Dinge, *v.* Sax. To strike, scourge, 215. 2329. Dong, *pa. t.* Struck, 1147. Dungen, *part. pa.* Beaten, or scourged, 227. Sc. and A. Bor. See Jam. Gl. Lynds. and Ray.

Dint, *n.* Sax. Blow, stroke, 1807. 1811. 1969. &c. *Dent*, Sir Tr. p. 92. Chauc. *Dynt*, R. Br. Dintes, *pl.* 1437. 1862. 2665. *Duntes*, K. Horn, 865. *Dentys*, Rits. M. R. *Dyntes*, R. Gl. *Dintes*, Minot, p. 23. V. Gl. Lynds.

Dunten, *pa. t. pl.* Sax. Struck, beat, 2448.

Do, Don, *v.* Sax. The various uses of this verb in English and Scotch, in an auxiliary, active, and passive sense, have been pointed out by Tyrwhitt, Essay on Vers. of Chauc. Note (37) Chalmers, Gl. Lynds. and Jamieson. It signifies: to do, *facere*, 117. 528. 1191. To cause, *efficere*, 611. *Do casten*, 519. *Do hem fle*, 2600. To put or place, q. *do in*, or *do on*, 535. 577. 587. &c. *Dones* (?) 970. Dos, *pr. t.* 2. *p.* Dost, 2390. Dos, *pr. t.* 3. *p.* Does, 1994. 2698. Dos, Doth, Don, *pr. t. pl.* Do, 1838. 1840. 2434. 2592. Doth, *imp.* Do, cause (ye) 2037. Dede, Dide, *pa. t.* Caused, 970. 2978. &c. Dede, Dide, *pa. t.* Put, placed, 659. 709. 859. Dedes, Dides, *pa. t.* 2. *p.* Didest, 2393. 2903. Deden, Diden, *pa. t. pl.* Caused, 241. 953. Did, performed, 1176. 2306. Don, *part. pa.* Caused, 1169. Don, *part. pa.* Done, 667. *Of liue haue do*, 1805. Have slain.

Dom, *n.* Sax. Doom, judgement, 2473. 2487. 2813. &c. Sir Tr. p. 127.

Dore, *n.* Sax. Door, 1788.

Dore-tre, *n.* Sax. Bar of the door, 1806. See Tre.

Doughter, *n.* Sax. Daughter, 2867. *Douhter*, 120. 2712. *Douthe*, 1079. *Douther*, 2914. Douhtres, *pl.* 2982. *Douthres*, 2979. *Doutres*, 350. 717.

Doun, See Adoun.

Doutede, *pa. t.* Fr. Feared, 708.

Douthe, *n.* Fr. Doubt, 703. 1331. 1377.

Douthe, *pa. t.* of Dow, *v. imp.* Sax. [*dugan*, valere, prodesse] Was worth, was sufficient, availed, 833. 1184. It is formed in the same manner as *Mouthe*, Might. See Sir Tr. p. 91. Jam. and Gl. Lynds. in v. Dow.

Drad, See Dred.

Drawe, Drawen, See Drou.

Dred, *imp.* Dread, fear (thou) 2168. Dredde, Dredden, *pa. t. pl.* Dreaded, feared, 2289. 2568. Drad, *part. pa.* Afraid, 1669. See Adrad.

Drede, *n.* Sax. Dread, 1169. Doubt, care, 828. 1664. Chauc.

Dremede, *pa. t.* Sax. Dreamed, 1284. 1304.

Dreinchen, Drenchen, Drinchen, *v.* Sax. To drown, 553. 561. 583. 1416. 1424. &c. Drench, Drenched, *part. pa.* Drowned, 520. 669. 1368. 1379. V. Gl. Web. R. Gl. Chauc.

Dreng, *n.* See Note on v. 31.

Drepe, Drepen, *v.* Sax. To kill, slay, 506. 1783. 1865. &c. Drop, *pa. t.* Killed, slew, 2229. Dreping, *part. pr.* Slaying, 2684. None of the Glossaries contain this word, nor is it in Jam. The derivation however is clear, for in Cædmon, 35. 20. we read *drepen on gemynd*, deficere animo, and in Lye, *Drepe*, is *Lethi causa*.

Drinchen, See Dreinchen.

Drinken, *v.* Sax. To drink, 459. 800.

Drinkes, *n. pl.* Sax. Drinks, liquors, 1738.

Drit, *n.* Isl. Belg. [*dryt*] Dirt, 682. A term expressing the highest contempt. K. Alisaund. 4718. Wickliffe. So, in an ancient metrical invective against Grooms and Pages, written about 1310.

> Thah he zeue hem cattes *dryt* to huere
> companage,
> Zet hym shulde arewen of the arrerage.
> Ms. Harl. 2253. f. 125.

Cf. Jam. Suppl. in v. Dryte, and Gl. Lynds.

Driuende, See Drof.

Drou, Drow, *pa. t.* Sax. Drew, 502. 705. 719. &c. Vt-drow, *pa. t.* Out-drew, 2632. Drowen, *pl.* 1837. 2508. Ut-drowen, Out-drew, 2659. Drawe, Drawen, *part. pa.* Drawn, 1925. 2225. 2477. 2603. &c. Ut-drawe, Ut-drawen, Out-drawn, 1802. 2631. See To-drawe.

Drof, *pa. t.* Sax. Drove, 725. 1793. 1872. Driuende, *part. pr.* Driving, riding quickly, 2702.

Drurye, *n.* Fr. Courtship, gallantry, 194. Web. Rits. M. R. P. Plouhm. Chauc. Lynds.

Dubbe, *v.* Fr. Sax. To dub, create a knight, 2042. Dubbede, *pa. t.* Dubbed, 2314. *Dubban to ridere*, Chron. Sax. An. 1085. *To cnihte hine dubban*, Layam. f. 129. Hickes, Hearne, Gl. R. Gl. and Tyrwhitt, Gl. Chauc. all refer the word to the Saxon root, which primarily signified *to strike*, the same as the Isl. *at dubba*. Todd on the contrary, Gl. Illustr. Chauc. thinks this questionable, and refers to Barbazan's Gl. in v. *Adouber*, which is there derived from the Lat. *adaptare*. Du Cange and Dr. Merrick give it also a Latin origin, from *Adoptare*, and by corruption *Adobare*. See Note on v. 2314.

Duelle, *v.* Sax. To dwell, give attention, 4.

A tale told Ysoude fre,
Thai *duelle:*
Tristrem that herd he.
Sir Tristr. p. 181.

Cf. Sir Otuel, v. 3. and Sevyn Sages, 1. DWELLEN, To dwell, remain, 1185. To delay, 1350. DWELLEN, *pr. t. pl.* Dwell, 1058. DWELLEDEN, *pa. t. pl.* Dwelt, 1189. DWELLING, *part.* or *n.* Delay, 1352.

DUN, See ADOUN.

DUNGEN, See DINGE.

DURSTEN, *pa. t. pl.* SAX. Durst, 1866.

E.

EIE, *n.* SAX. Eye, 2545. *Heie,* 1152. *Yhe,* 1984. EYEN, EYN, EYNE, *pl.* Eyes, 680. 1273. 1340. 1364. 2171.

EIR, *n.* FR. LAT. Heir, 410. 506. 2539. *Eyr,* 110. 239. &c. Jam. gives it a Northern etymology, in v. AYR.

EK, *conj.* SAX. [*eac*] Eke, also, 1025. 1038. 1066. &c. OK, [SU. G. *och, ock,* BELG. *ook*] 187. 200. 879. 1081. &c. V. Jam. in v. Ac.

ELD, *adj.* SAX. Old, 546. *Helde,* 2472. HELDEST, *sup.* 1396.

ELDE, *n.* SAX. Age, 2713. *Helde,* 128. 174. 387. 1435.

Ælde hæfde heo na marc
Buten fihtene zere.
Layam. f. 151. c. 1.

R. Br. In Sc. *Eild.* It was subsequently restricted to the sense of *old age,* as in Chauc.

ELLES, *adv.* SAX. Else, 1192. 2590.

EM, *n.* SAX. Uncle, 1326. Sir Tr. p. 53. Properly, says Sir W. Scott, an uncle by the father's side. It appears however to have been used indifferently either on the father's or mother's side. See Hearne's Gl. on R. Gl. and R. Br. Web. Erle of Tol. 988. Chauc. Troil. 2. 162. and Nares. A. Bor. *Eam.*

ER, *adv.* SAX. Before, 317. 681. 1261. *Her,* 229. 541. *Ere,* 2680. Sir Tr. p. 169. K. Horn, 130. See ARE, OR.

ERL, *n.* SAX. Earl, 189. &c. ERLES, *g. c.* 2898. Earl's. *Herles,* 883. ERLDOM, 2909.

ERN, *n.* SAX. Eagle, 572. Rits. M. R. Octavian, 196. R. Gl. p. 177. Doug. 416.

ERTHE, *n.* SAX. Earth, 740. Ground, 2657.

ETE, ETEN, *v.* SAX. To eat, 791. 800. 911. &c. *Hete, Heten,* 146. 317. 457. 541. ET, *imp.* Eat (thou) 925. ET, HET, *pa. t.* Eat, 653. 656. ETES, *fut.* 2. *p.* Shalt thou eat, 907. ETETH, *fut.* 3. *p.* Shall eat, 672. ETEN, *part. pa.* Eaten, 657.

ETHEN, *adv.* SAX. Hence, 690. *Hethen,* 683. 845. 1085. 2727.

ETHER, See AYTHER.

EUERE, EURE, *adv.* SAX. Ever, 207. 424. 704. &c. *Heuere,* 17. 327. 830.

EUEREICH, *adj.* SAX. Every, 137. *Euere il,* 218. 1334. 1644. *Euere ilc,* 1330. *Eueri,* 1070. 1176. 1383. *Eueril,* 1764. 2318. &c. *Euerilk,* 2258. 2432. *Euerilkon,* 1062. 1996. 2197. Every one. See IL.

EUEREMAR, *adv.* SAX. Evermore, 1971.

EYEN, EYN, EYNE, See EIE.

EYR, See EIR.

F.

FADER, *n.* SAX. LAT. Father, 1224. 1403. 1416. Sir Tr. p. 35. K. Horn, 114. The cognate words may be found in Jam. *Faderles,* 75.

FADMED, *pa. t.* SAX. Fathomed, embraced, 1295. From *fæthmian,* Utraque manu extensa complecti, Cod. Exon. p. 89. It has the same meaning in Sc. V. Jam.

FALLE, *v.* SAX. To fall, 39, &c. FALLES, *imp. pl.* Fall ye, 2302. FEL, *pa. t.* Fell, appertained, 1815. 2359. Fellen, *pa. t. pl.* Fell, 1303.

Fals, *adj.* Sax. False, 2511.

Falwes, *n. pl.* Sax. Fallows, fields, 2509. Chauc. C. T. 6238. where Tyrwh. explains it *harrowed lands.*

Fare, *n.* Sax. Journey, 1337. 2621. R. Gl. p. 211. R. Br. Minot, p. 2. (left unexplained by Rits.) Barb. iv. 627. *Schip-fare,* A voyage, Sir Tr. p. 53.

Fare, Faren, *v.* Sax. To go, 265. 1378. 1392. &c. Fare, *pr. t. 2. p.* Farest, behavest, 2705. Fares, *pr. t. 3. p.* Goes, flies, 2690. Ferde, *pa. t.* Went, 447. 836. 1678. &c. Behaved, 2411. *For,* 2382. 2943. Foren, *pa. t. pl.* Went, 2380. 2618. Used by all the old English writers.

Faste, *adv.* Sax. Attentively, earnestly, 2148.

> Tristrem as a man
> *Fast* he gan to fight.
> *Sir Tristr.* p. 167.

> Bidde we zeorne Ihũ Crist, and seint Albon wel *faste,*
> That we moten to the Ioye come, that euere schal i-laste.
> *Vita S. Albani,* Ms. Laud. 108. f. 47. b.

Fastinde, *part. pr.* Sax. Fasting, 865.

Fauth, See Fyht.

Fawen, *adj.* Sax. Fain, glad, 2160. *Fawe,* K. of Tars, 1058. Octavian, 307. R. Gl. p. 150. Chauc. C. T. 5802.

Fe, *n.* Sax. Fee, possessions, or money, 386. 563. 1225. &c. See Jam. and Lynds. Gl.

Feble, *adj.* Fr. Feeble, poor, scanty, 323.

Feblelike, *adv.* Feebly, scantily, 418. *Febli,* Sir Tr. p. 179. for *meanly.*

Feden, *v.* Sax. To feed, 906. Feddes, *pr. t. 2. p.* Feddest, 2907.

Fel, See Bifalle, Falle.

Felawes, *n. pl.* Sax. Fellows, companions, 1338.

Feld, *n.* Sax. Field, 2634. 2685. 2910.

Felde, Felede, *pa. t.* Sax. Felled, 67. 1859. *Felden* (?) 2698. Felde, *part. pa.* Felled, 1824. 2691.

Fele, *adj.* Sax. Many, often, 778. 1277. 1737. &c.

Fele, *adv.* Sax. Very, 2442. Sir Tr. p. 19.

Fend, *n.* Sax. Fiend, 506. 1411. 2229.

Fer, *adv.* Sax. Far, 359. 1863. 2275. &c. Ferne, Far, 1864. 2031. Foreign, 2031.

> Tha kingges buh stronge,
> And of *ferrene* lond.
> *Layam.* f. 29. b. c. 2.

Ferd, Ferde, *n.* Sax. Army, 2384. 2535. 2548. &c. Layam. R. Gl. R. Br. Web. Ferdes, *pl.* 2683.

Ferde, See Fare.

Fere, *n.* Sax. Companion, wife, 1214. Sir Tr. p. 76. K. Horn, Web. R. Gl. R. Br. Minot, Chauc. *Feir,* Sc. V. Jam. and Gl. Lynds.

Ferlik, Ferlike, *n.* Sax. Wonder, 1258. 1849. Sir Tr. p. 21. Originally in all probability an *adj.* See the various Glossaries.

Ferthe, *adj.* Sax. Fourth, 1810.

Feste, *n.* Fr. Feast, 2344. &c.

Feste, *v.* Fr. To feast, 2938.

Festen, *v.* Sax. To fasten, 82. 1785. (used passively) Fest, *pa. t.* Fastened, 144.

Fet, See Fot.

Fete, *v.* Sax. To fetch, bring, 642. 912. 937. &c. Used passively, 316. 2037. Fetes, *pr. t. pl.* Fetch, 2341. V. Pegge's Anecd. of Engl. Lang. p. 135.

Fetere, *v.* Sax. To fetter, chain, 2758. Used passively.

Feteres, *n. pl.* Sax. Fetters, 82. 2759.

Fey, *n.* Fr. Faith, 255. 1666. *Feyth,* 2853.

Fiht, *n.* Sax. Fight, 2668. 2716.

FIKEL, *adj.* SAX. Fickle, inconstant, 1210. 2799.

FILE, *n.* LAT. ? Vile, worthless person, 2499.

> Men seth ofte a muche *file*,
> They he serue boten a wile,
> Bicomen swithe riche.
> *Hending the hende*, Ms. Digb. 86.

So in R. Br. p. 237.

> David at that while was with Edward the kyng,
> Zit auanced he that *file* vntille a faire thing.

It is used for *coward* by Minot, pp. 31. 36.

FINDE, FINDEN, *v.* SAX. To find, 220. 1083. *Fynde*, 42. FUNDEN, *pa. t. pl.* Found, 602. 1427. FUNDE, *part. pa.* Found, 2376.

FIR, FYR, *n.* SAX. Fire, 585. 915. 1162. &c.

FIRRENE, *adj.* SAX. Made of fir, 2078. *Firron*, Doug. Virg. 47. 34.

FLAUNES, *n. pl.* FR. Custards, or pancakes. See Note on v. 644.

FLEDDEN, *pa. t. pl.* SAX. Fled, 2416.

FLEMEN, *v.* SAX. To drive away, banish, 1160. R. Gl. R. Br. Chauc. Rits. A. S. So in Sc. V. Jam.

FLETE, *v.* SAX. To float, swim, 522. Sir Tr. p. 27. K. Horn, 159. Chauc. *Fleit*, Sc. V. Jam.

FLEYE, *v.* SAX. To fly, 1791. 1813. 1827. 2751. FLEY, *pa. t.* Flew, 1305.

FLO, *v.* SAX. To flea, 612. 2495. K. Horn, 92. FLOW, *pa. t.* Flead, 2502. FLOWE, *pa. t. pl.* 2433.

FLOK, *n.* SAX. Flock, troop, 24. See TROME.

FLOTE, *n.* SAX. Fleet, 738. It is here applied to the persons composing the crew of the ship.

FLOUR, *n.* FR. Flower, 2917.

FNASTE, *v.* SAX. To breathe ? 548. [*Fnæstian*, the wind-pipe, *Fnæstan*, puffs of wind. *Lye.*]

FO, *n.* SAX. Foe, 1363. 2849.

FOL, *n.* FR. Fool, 298. FOLES, *pl.* 2100.

FOLC, FOLK, *n.* SAX. Men collectively, people, 89. 438. &c.

FOLWES, *imp.* SAX. Follow ye, 1885. 2601.

FONGE, *v.* SAX. To take, 763. 856. In common use from Layam. to Chauc. and much later.

FOR, *prep.* SAX. Is prefixed to the Inf. of verbs in the same manner as the Fr. *pour*, or Sp. *por*. It is so used in all the old writers, and in the vulgar translation of the Scriptures, and is still preserved in the North of England. Cf. 17. &c. On account of, 1670. Sir Tr. p. 62. In order to, for the purpose, 2724.

FOR, FOREN, See FAREN.

FORBERE, *v.* SAX. Spare, abstain from, 353. Chauc. Rom. R. 4751. FORBAR, *pa. t.* Spared, abstained from, 764. 2623.

FORFAREN, *part. pa.* SAX. Destroyed, caused to perish, 1380. R. Br. *Forfard*, Ly Beaus Desc. 1484. The inf is also used in Web. P. Plouhm. Chauc. In Sc. *Forfair*. V. Compl. of Scotl. p. 100. and Gl. Lynds.

FORGAT, FORYAT, *pa. t.* SAX. Forgot, 249. 2636. &c.

FORLOREN, FORLORN, *part. pa.* SAX. Utterly lost, 580. 770. 1424. R. Br. Rits. M. R. Chauc. Used actively, Sir Tr. p. 35.

FORTHI, *adv.* SAX. On this account, therefore, because, 1194. 1431. 2043. 2500. 2578. Sir Tr. p. 14. and in all the Gloss.

FORTHWAR, *adv.* SAX. Forthwith, 731.

FORW, *n.* SAX. Furrow, 1094.

FORWARD, *n.* SAX. Promise, word, covenant, 486. 554. Layam. f. 26. b. Sir Tr. p. 13. Rits. M. R. Web. R. Gl. R. Br. Minot, Chauc.

FOSTRED, *part. pa.* SAX. Nourished, 1434. 2239.

FOT, *n.* SAX. *Euerilk fot*, 2432. Every foot,

or man. Fet, *pl.* 616. 1022. 1303. 2479. *Fote*, 1054. 1199.

Fouhten, See Fyht.

Fourtenith, *n.* Sax. Fortnight, 2284.

Fremde, *adj.* (used as a *n.*) Sax. Stranger, 2277.

> Vor hine willeth sone uorgiete
> Tho *fremde* and tho sibbe.
> Ms. Digb. 4.
> Ther ne myhte libbe
> The *fremede* ne the sibbe.
> K. Horn, 67.

See also R. Gl. p. 346. Chron. of Eng. 92. P. Plouhm. 79. Chau. Jam. and Gl. Lynds.

Freme, *v.* Sax. To perform, 441.

Fri, *adj.* Sax. Free, liberal, 1072. Chauc.

Frie, *v.* To blame (?) 1998. [Isl. *Frya*, querela, *Frya*, *Frygia*, carpere, vilipendere.]

Fro, *prep.* Sax. From, 265. &c.

Frusshe, See To-frusshe.

Ful, *adv.* Sax. Very, much, completely, 6. 82. &c. *Ful wo*, 2589. Much sorrow.

Ful, Fule, *adj.* Sax. Foul, 506. 555. 626. 965. &c. *Foule*, 1158.

Fulike, *adv.* Sax. Foully, shamefully, 2749.

Fulde, *part. pa.* Sax. Filled, complete, 355.

Funde, Funden, See Finde.

Fyht, *v.* Sax. To fight, 2361. Fauth, *pa. t.* Fought, 1990. Fouhten, *pa. t. pl.* Fought, 2661.

Fyn, *n.* Fr. Lat. Ending, 22. R. Br. Minot, Chauc. &c.

G.

Ga, *v.* Sax. To go, 314. Sir Tr. p. 26. Sc. V. Jam.

Gad, *n.* Sax. Goad, 279. Gaddes, *pl.* 1016. In Gl. Ælfr. among the instruments of husbandry occur *Gad*, stimulus, and *Gad-iron*, aculeus. So in *The Fermeror and his Docter*, printed by Laing:

> Quhen Symkin standis quhisling with ane
> quhip and ane *gaid*,
> Priking and zarkand ane auld ox hide.

V. Jam. in v. Gade, 4. and Nares.

Gadred, *part. pa.* Sax. Gathered, 2577.

Gadeling, *n.* Sax. An idle vagabond, low man, 1121.

> Tha wes æuerale cheorl
> Al swa bald alse an eorl,
> & alle tha *gadelinges*
> Alse heo weoren sunen kinges.
> Layam. f. 70. b. c. 1.

Cf. K. Alisaund. 1733. 4063. *Gadlyng*, Rob. of Cicyle, Ms. Harl. 1701. R. Gl. p. 277. 310. Chauc. Rom. de R. 938. The word originally meant *Vir generosus*. See Beowulf, f. 188. Ms. Cott. Vit. A. xv.

Gaf, See Yeue.

Galwe-tre, *n.* Sax. The gallows, 43. 335. 695. Le Bone Fl. 1726. Erle of Tol. 657. Galwes, Galewes, 687. 1161. 2477. 2508. R. Br. Chauc. Cf. Ihre Gl. Suiog. in v. ab Isl. *gayl*, ramus arboris.

Gamen, *n.* Sax. Game, sport, 980. 1716. 2135. 2250. 2577. Joy, 2935. 2963. *Gamyn*, Barb. iii. 465. V. Jam.

Gan, *pa. t.* Sax. Began, 2443. V. Jam.

Gange, Gangen, *v.* Sax. To go, walk, 370. 796. 845. &c. *Gonge*, *Gongen*, 855. 1185. 1739. &c. Gonge, *pr. t. 2. p.* Goest, 690. 843. Gangande, *part. pr.* On foot, walking, 2283. Wynt. V. Jam.

Gart, Garte, *pa. t.* Sax. Made, 189. 1001. 1082. 1857. &c. *Gert*, Sir Tr. p. 147. V. Jam. and Gl. Lynds.

Gat, Gaten, See Gete.

Gate, *n.* Sax. Way, road, 846. 889. Sir Tr. p. 27. Manner, fashion, 783. 2419. 2586. Tyrwhitt derives the latter sense from Fr. *Geste*.

GENGE, *n.* SAX. Family, company, 786. 1735. Retinue, 2353. 2362. 2383.

> The king of than londe
> Mid muchelere *genge*.
> Layam. f. 34. c. 2.

Hence *Gang*. V. Todd's Johns.

GENT, *adj.* FR. Neat, pretty, 2139. Sir Tr. p. 87. R. Br. Chauc.

GERE, See MESSE-GERE.

GEST, *n.* FR. Tale, adventure, 2984. See Note in Warton's Hist. E. P. V. I. p. 78. Ed. 8vo.

GETE, GETEN, *v.* SAX. To get, take, 792. 1393. 2762. 2960. GAT, YETE, *pa. t.* Got, 495. 730. GATEN, GETEN, *pa. t. pl.* Begot, 2893. 2934. 2978. GETES, *f. t. 2. p.* Shalt get, 908.

GHOD for GOOD, 255.

GISARM, *n.* FR. A bill, 2553. See Gl. Rits. M. R. Spelm. in v. Jam. Dict. and Merrick's Gl. in v. GESA, GESUM.

GIUE, See GAF.

GIUE, *n.* SAX. Gift, 2880. *Gyue*, 357. *Yeft*, 2336.

GIUELED, 814. *Qu.* from SAX. *gifeolan*, insistere.

GLADLIKE, *adv.* SAX. Gladly, 805. 906. 1760.

GLEDE, *n.* SAX. A burning coal, 91. 869. Rits. M. R. Web. R. Br. Chauc. See Note on v. 91.

GLEIUE, GLEYUE, FR. A spear, lance, 1770. 1844. 1981. GLEIUES, GLEYUES, *pl.* 267. 1748. 1804. Dr. Merrick explains it, "A weapon composed of a long cutting blade at the end of a staff." See R. Gl. p. 203. Guy of Warw. R. iii. Chauc. Court of Love, 544. Percy, A. R.

GLEM, *n.* SAX. Gleam, ray, 2122. See STEM.

GLEU, *n.* SAX. Game, skill, 2332. Properly, says Sir W. Scott, the joyous science of the minstrels. Cf. Sir Tr. p. 24. 35. 150.

GLEYMEN, *n. pl.* SAX. Gleemen, 2329. *Gleweman*, Sir Tr. p. 110.

> Whar bin thi *glewmen* that schuld thi *glewe*,
> With harp and fithel, and tabour bete.
> *Disp. betw. the bodi & saule*, ap. Leyd. Compl. of Scotl.

GLOTUNS, *n. pl.* FR. Gluttons, wicked men, 2104.

> Va *Glutun*, envers tei nostre lei se defent.
> K. Horn, 1633. Ms. Douce.

Cf. K. Horn, 1124. ap. Rits. Yw. and Gaw. 3247. R. Cœur de L. 5953. and Chauc.

GOD, GODE, *n.* SAX. Gain, wealth, goods, 797. 1221. 2034. R. Gl. R. Br. Chauc.

GOD, GODE, *adj.* SAX. Good, excellent, 7. &c.

GODDOT, GODDOTH, *interj.* God wot! (?) 606. 642. 796. 909. 1656. 2543. Cf. 2527. It is formed probably in the same manner as *Goddil*, for God's will, in Yorksh. and Lanc. V. Craven dialect, and View of Lanc. dialect, 1770. 8vo. The word before us appears to have been limited to Lincolnshire or Lancashire, and does not appear at all in the Glossaries. One similar instance only has occurred to us, in a very curious translation of a French Fabliau, written in Lincolnshire, in the reign of Edw. I.

> *Goddot!* so I wille,
> And loke that thou hire tille,
> And strek out hire thes.
> *La fablel & la cointise de dame Siriz*, Ms. Digb. 86.

GOME, *n.* SAX. Man, 7. Common to all the old Eng. and Sc. writers.

GON, *v.* SAX. To go, walk, 113. 1045. GOTH *imp.* Go ye, 1780. GON, *part. pa.* Gone, 2692.

GONGE, GONGEN, See GANGE.

GORE, 2497. Cf. *Guy of Warw.*

ap. Ellis, M. R. V. 2. p. 81. This phrase is here unintelligible.

Gos, *n.* Sax. Goose, 1240. Gees, *pl.* 702.

Gouen, See Yeue.

Goulen, *pr. t. pl.* 2. *p.* Sax. Howl, cry, 454. Gouleden, *pa. t. pl.* Howled, cried, 164.

> An *yollen* mote thu so heye,
> That ut berste bo thin ey.
> *Hule and Nihtingale*, Ms. Cal. A. ix. f. 237.

Used also by Wickliffe. In Scotland and the North it is still preserved, but in the South *Yell* is used as an equivalent. See Jam. and Gl. Lynds.

Gram, *adj.* Sax. Angry, incensed, 2469. Am. and Amil. 214. As a noun it is very common.

Graten, *v.* Sax. [*grædan*] To weep, cry, 329. Grede, 96. Grede, Gredde, Gret, Grete, *pa. t.* Cried out, wept, 454. 615. 1129. 1259. 2414. 2703. Greten, *pa. t. pl.* Wept, 164. 415. 2796. Grotinde, *part. pr.* Weeping, 1390. Graten, *part. pa.* Wept, 241. *I-groten*, 285. See Jam. and Gl. Lynds.

Grathet, See Greythe.

Graue, *v.* Sax. To bury, 613. Grauen, *part. pa.* Buried, 2528. Web. Sir Guy, Ii. iv. Chauc.

Greme, *v.* Sax. To irritate, revile, 442. In R. Br. *Gram* is used as a verb, in the same sense.

Grene, 996. *Qu.* from Sax. *georнan*, concupiscere. V. Jam. in v. Grene.

Greting, *n.* Sax. Weeping, 166.

Gres, *n.* Sax. Grass, 2698.

Gret, Grete, *adj.* Sax. Great, heavy, loud, 807. 1437. 1860. 1862. *Greth*, 1025. Grettere, *comp.* Greater, 1893.

Grette, *pa. t.* Sax. Accosted, greeted, 452. 1811. 2625. Gret, *part. pa.* Accosted, greeted, 2290. *Grethede*, 2003.

Greu, *pa. t.* Sax. Grew, prospered, arose, 2333. 2975.

Greue, *v.* Sax. To grieve, 2953.

Greythe, *v.* Sax. [*gerædian*] To prepare, 1762. Greythede, *pa. t.* Prepared, 706. Greythed, *part. pa.* Prepared, made ready, 714. *Grathet*, 2615. Layam. f. 24. b. Sir Tr. p. 33. Sc. *Graith*, V. Jam. and Gl. Lynds.

Greyue, *n.* Sax. [*gerefa*] Greave, magistrate, 1771. Greyues, *g. c.* Greave's, 1749. Greyues, *pl.* 266. V. Spelm. in v. Grafio, and Hickes, Diss. Epist. p. 21. n. p. 151.

Grim, *adj.* Sax. Cruel, savage, fierce, 155. 680. 2398. 2655. 2761. *grim or gore*, 2497. R. Br. Rits. M. R. See Beowulf, p. 12.

Grip, *n.* Lat. Griffin, 572. Web. *Graip*, Sc. V. Jam. The plural is in Layam. *Gripes*, f. 165. c. 2. and K. Alisaund. 4880.

Grip, *n.* Sax. [*græp*] Ditch, trench, 2102. Gripes, *pl.* 1924. V. Jam. in v. Grape, and Skinner, v. Groop.

Gripen, *pr. t. pl.* Sax. Gripe, grasp, 1790. Gripeth, *imp.* Gripe ye, 1882. Grop, *pa. t.* Grasped, 1775. 1871. 1890. &c.

Grith, *n.* Sax. Peace, 61. 511. Grith-sergeans, 267. Legal officers to preserve the peace. These must not be confounded with the *Justitiarii Pacis* established in the beginning of Edw. III. reign, and called *Gardiani Pacis*. V. Spelm. in v.

Grom, *n.* Male child, youth, 790. Young man, 2472. Leyden, Gl. Compl. of Scotl. derives it from Sax. *gruma*, a servant, but no such word appears in Lye. Jamieson thinks the original is *Gome*. In Belgic *grom* has the same sense of *boy*. V. Jun. Etym. So in *Sir Degore*,

He lyft up the shete anone
And loked upon the lytle *grome.*—A. iv.

It generally elsewhere signifies *lad, page.*

GRONGE, *n.* SAX. Grange, (?) 764.

GROP, See GRIPEN.

GROTES, *n. pl.* SAX. [*grut*] Small pieces, grit, dust, 472. 1414.

GROTINDE, See GRATEN.

GRUND, *adj.* 1027. See GRUNDLIKE.

GRUNDE, *n.* SAX. Ground, 1979. 2675.

GRUNDEN, *part. pa.* SAX. Ground, 2503. Yw. and Gaw. 676. *Grounden,* Chauc.

GRUNDLIKE, *adv.* Heartily, 651. 2659. Deeply, 2013. 2268. 2307. where it is equivalent to DEPLIKE, q. v. The word is undoubtedly Saxon, but in the Lexicons we only find *Grundlinga,* funditus, from Ælf. Gl. It is used by Layamon:

Cnihtes heom gereden
Grundliche feire.—f. 55. b. c. 1.

GUEDE, *adj.* 98. This term is clearly equivalent to *chinche,* 1763. and must be interpreted *sparing, niggardly.* The Glossaries have been searched in vain for an etymon. We meet with the same word however in *Horn Childe,* ap. Rits. M. R. V. 3. p. 285. where it is not noticed by the editor.

Sum baylis he made,
And sum he yaf londes brade,
His yiftes were nought *guede.*

And again, in a poem in Ms. Laud, 108. f. 200. b.

Thi faucouns that were nouzt to grede,
and thine houndes that thou ledde,
Me thinketh God is the to *guede,*
that alle thine frend beon fro the fledde.

See a later copy of these verses in the Auchinleck Ms. intitled *Disp. betw. the bodi & the saule,* ap. Leyd. Compl. of Scotl. In composition also, the word bears the same meaning:

Grete God of thy grace, and of gyfts *unguede,*
Thorow the help of the holy gost herde hyr preyer. *Sussan,* Ms. Cal. A. II.

There appears to be some connection between this word, and the expression in Sir Tristr. st. 49. "It nas to large no GUEDE," but the latter is explained very differently by the Editor, and Jam. q. v.

GYUE, See GIUE.

H.

HAL, 2370. All? Whole?

HALDE, *v.* SAX. To hold, take part, 2308. *Holden,* To keep or observe, 29. 1171. HALDES, *pr. t.* 3. *p.* Holds, 1382. HEL, *pa. t.* Held, 109. HELDEN, *pa. t. pl.* Held, 1201. HALDEN, *part. pa.* Held, Holden, 2806.

HALS, *n.* SAX. Neck, 521. 670. 2510. Sir Tr. p. 109. Common in old Engl. and Sc.

HALUE, *n.* SAX. Side, part, *Bi bothe halue,* 2682. See BI-HALUE.

HALUENDEL, *n.* SAX. The half part, 460. R. Gl. p. 5. R. Br. K. Alisaund. 7116. Emare, 444. Chron. of Engl. 515. R. Hood, I. 68.

HANDEL, HANDLEN, *v.* SAX. To handle, 347. 586.

HANGEN, *v.* SAX. To hang, 335. 695. *Hengen,* 43, &c. *Honge,* 2807. HENGED, *part. pa.* Hung, 1922. 2480.

HARUM for HARM, 1983. 2408.

HASARD, *n.* FR. Game at dice, 2325. See Note on v. 2320.

HATEDE, *pa. t.* SAX. Hated, 1188.

HAUEN, *v.* SAX. To have, 78. &c. *Haue, Hawe,* 1188. 1298. HAUES, HAUEST, *pr. t.*

2. *p.* Hast, 688. 848. Haues, Haueth, *pr. t.* 3. *p.* Haveth, hath, has, 1266. 1285. 1952. 1980. &c. Hauen, *pr. t. pl.* Have, 1227. *Hauenet*, 2005. Have it. Hauede, Hauet, *pa. t.* Hath, had, 564. 649. 775. &c. *Hauedet*, 714. Had it. Haueden, *pa. t. pl.* Had, 163. 236. &c. Haue, Hauede, Haueden, *subj.* Would have, 1428. 1643. 1687. 2020. 2675.

Haui for Haue I, 2002.

He, *pron.* Sax. Is often understood, as in v. 869. 1428. 1777. 2503. and hence might perhaps have been designedly omitted in v. 135. 860. 1089. 2311. He, *pl.* They, 54. &c.

Heie, *n.* See Eie.

Heie, *adj.* Sax. Tall, 987. *Hey, Heye*, 1071. 1083. High, 1289. *Heye se*, 719. *Heye curt*, 1685. *Heye and lowe*, 2431. 2471. &c.

Hel, Helden, See Halde.

Helde, Heldeste, See Eld.

Hele, Helen, *v.* Sax. [*hælan*] To heal, 1836. 2058. Hole, Holed, *part. pa.* Healed, 2039. 2075.

Helm, *n.* Sax. Helmet, 379. 624. 1653. &c. Helmes, *pl.* 2612.

Helpen, *v.* Sax. To help, 1712. Helpes, *imp. pl.* Help ye, 2595. Holpen, *part. pa.* Helped, 901.

Hem, *pron.* Sax. Them, 367. &c.

Hend for End, 247.

Hend, *n.* Sax. Hand, 505. 2069. &c. *Hon, Hond*, 1342. 2446. Hondes, *pl.* 214. 636. &c. *Hand-dede*, 92. Pure Saxon, like the *Hond-gewore* of Beowulf.

Hende, *n.* Sax. [*ened*, Ælf. Gl. Isl. *önd*] Apparently has the same meaning as *drake*. Anas, fulica, V. Lye.

Hende, *adj.* Courteous, gentle, 1104. 1421. 1704. 2793. 2877. 2915. Skilful, 2628. The derivation is uncertain. V. Jam. It certainly is the same word with *hendi, hendy*. See Tyrwh. on C. T. 3199. Gl. R. Glouc. Amis and Amil. 1393. Ly Beaus Desc. 333. Morte Arthur, ap. Ellis, M. R. V. i. p. 359. &c.

Hende, *adv.* Sax. Near, handy, 359. 2275. Web.

Henged, Hengen, See Hangen.

Henne, *adv.* Sax. Hence, 843. 1780. 1800. In the same manner is formed *Whenne*, K. Horn, 170. which Ritson thought a mistake for *whence*.

Henne, *n.* Sax. Hen, 1240. Hennes, *pl.* 702.

Her, See Er.

Her, *adv.* Sax. Here, 689. 1058. &c. *Her offe*, 2585. Here of.

Her, *n.* Sax. Hair, 1924. *Hor*, 235.

Herboru, *n.* Sax. Habitation, lodging, 742. *Herborowe*, Web. *Herbegerie*, R. Br. *Harbroughe*, Sq. of Lowe Degre, 179. *Herberwe*, Chauc. *Herbry*, Wynt. *Herberye*, Lynds. Gl. q. v. and Jam.

Herborwed, *pa. t.* Sax. Lodged, 742. Layam. Chauc. V. Jam. in v. Herbery.

Here, *pron.* Sax. Their, 52. 465. &c.

Here, *n.* Sax. Army, 346. 379. 2153. 2942. R. Br. K. Alisaund. 2101.

Here, Heren, *v.* Sax. To hear, 4. 732. 1640. 2279. &c. *Y-here*, 11. Herd, Herde, *pa. t.* Heard, 286. 465. 1640. &c. Herden, *pa. t. pl.* 150.

Herinne, *adv.* Sax. Herein, 458.

Herkne, *imp. s.* Sax. Hearken, 1285. Herknet, *imp. pl.* Hearken ye, 1.

Herles, See Erl.

Hernes, *n.* Fr. Armour, harness, 1917. R. Br. &c.

Hernes, *n. pl.* Sax. Brains, 1808.

Hern-panne, *n.* Sax. Skull, 1991. Yw. and Gaw. 660. R. Cœur de L. 5293. *Hardyn-pan*, Compl. of Scotl. p. 241. V. Gl.

Hert, *n.* Sax. Hart, deer, 1872.

Herte, *n.* Sax. Heart, 479. 2054. &c. *Herteblod,* 1819. Layam. f. 91. Sir Tr. p. 98. Chauc.

Hertelike, *adv.* Sax. Heartily, 1347. 2748. On the authority of this last line, *Hetelike* in v. 2655. was altered from conjecture, but perhaps without sufficient cause. See Hetelike.

Het, *pa. t.* Sax. Hight, named, 2348. Hoten, *part. pa.* Called, named, 106. 284.

Het, Hete, Heten, See Ete.

Hetelike, *adv.* Sax. Hotly, angrily (?) 2655.

> And Guy hent his sword in hand,
> And *hetelich* smot to Colbrand.
> *Guy of Warw.* ap. Ellis, M. R. V. 2. p. 82.

In Sir Tr. p. 172. *Hethelich* is explained *Haughtily* by the Editor, and by Jam. *reproachfully.*

Hethede, *pa. t.* 551. *Qu. commanded,* from Sax. *hetan.*

Hethen, See Ethen.

Heu, *n.* Sax. Hew, color, complexion, 2918. Very common. We may hence explain the " inexplicable phrase" complained of by Mr. Ellis, Spec. E. E. P. V. i. p. 109. " On *heu* her hair is fair enough"—occasioned by Ritson having inadvertently copied it *hen,* from the Ms. Anc. Songs. p. 25.

Heued, *n.* Sax. Head, 624. 1653. 1701. 1759. &c. Heuedes, *pl.* 1907.

Heuere, See Euere.

Heui, *adj.* Sax. Heavy, 808. laborious, 2456.

Hey, Heye, See Heie.

Heye, *adv.* Sax. On high, 43. 335. 695. &c.

Heylike, *adv.* Sax. Highly, honorably, 1329, 2319.

Heyman, *n.* Sax. Nobleman, 1260. Sir Tr. p. 82. Heymen, Heyemen, *pl.* 231. 958.

Hew, *pa. t.* Sax. Cut, 2730. Sir Tr. p. 20.

Hext, *adj. sup.* Sax. Highest, tallest, 1080. *Haxt,* Layamon, *Hext,* K. Alisaund. 7961. R. Gl. Chauc.

Hi, Hic, See Ich.

Hider, *adv.* Sax. Hither, 868. 885. 1431.

Hides, *n. pl.* Sax. Hides, skins, 918.

Hijs, *pron.* Sax. His, 47. 468. *Hise,* 34. &c. *Hyse,* 355.

Hile, *v.* Sax. [*helan*] To cover, hide, 2082. *Hele,* Sir Tr. p. 19. Web. Rits. M. R. Chauc. *Hilles,* Yw. and Gaw. 741. V. Jam. in v. Heild.—Somersetsh.

Him, *pron.* Sax. Them, 257. 1169.

Hine, *n. pl.* Sax. Hinds, bondsmen, 620. Web. *Hinen,* R. Gl. V. Jam. in v.

Hinne, See Ther-inne.

Hire, *pron.* Sax. Her, 127. &c. She, 2916.

His for Is, 279. 1893. 1973. 2692.

Hise, See Hijs.

Hof for Of, 1976.

Hof, *pa. t.* Sax. Heaved, 2750.

Hoh, *adj.* Sax. High, 1361.

Hok, *n.* Sax. Hook, 1102.

Hold, *adj.* Sax. Firm, faithful, 2781. 2816.

> Ant suore othes *holde,*
> That huere non ne sholde
> Horn never bytreye.
> *K. Horn,* 1259.

Cf. R. Glouc. p. 377. 383. 443. K. Alisaund. 2912. Chron. of Engl. 730.

Hold, Holde, *adj.* Sax. Old, 30. 192. 417. 956. &c. Former, 2460.

Holden, See Halden.

Hole, *n.* Sax. Socket of the eye, 1813.

Hole, Holed, See Hele.

Holpen, See Helpen.

Hon, Hond, Hondes, See Hend.

Honge, See Henge.

Hor, See Her.

Hore, See Ore.

Horn, 779.

Hors, *n.* Sax. Horse, 2283. Horse-knaue, Groom, 1019. So in a curious satirical poem, temp. Edw. II.

> Of rybaudz y ryme,
> Ant rede o my rolle,
> Of gedelynges, gromes,
> Of Colyn, & of Colle;
> Harlotes, *hors knaues*,
> Bi pate & by polle.
> Ms. Harl. 2253. f. 124. b.

Used also by Gower, Conf. Am. See Todd's Illustr. p. 279.

Hosen, *n. pl.* Sax. Hose, stockings, 860. 969. In Sir Tr. p. 94. trowsers seem to be indicated.

Hoslen, Hoslon, *v.* Sax. To administer or receive the sacrament, 211. 362. Hoseled, Hosled, *part. pa.* 364. 2598. Le bone Flor. 776. Chauc.

Hoten, See Het.

Houes, *pr. t.* Sax. Behoves, 582.

Hul, *n.* Sax. Hill, 2687.

Hund, *n.* Sax. Hound, 1994. 2435. Hundes, *pl.* 2331.

Hungred for Hunger, 2455.

Hungreth, *pr. t.* Hunger, 455. Hungrede, *pa. t.* Hungered, 654.

Hure, *pron.* Sax. Our, 338. 842. 1231. &c.

Hus for Us, 1217. 1409.

Hus, Huse, *n.* Sax. House, 740. 2913. *Hws*, 1141. *Milne-hous*, 1967.

Hyl, *n.* Sax. Heap, 892.

Hw, W, *adv.* Sax. How, 120. 288. 827. 960. 1646. &c. *Hwou*, 2411. 2946. 2987. &c.

Hwan, *adv.* Sax. When, 408. 474. &c. See Quan.

Hware, *adv.* Sax. Where, 1881. 2240. 2579. *Hwar of*, 2976. Whereof. *Hwere*, 549. 1083.

Hwat, *pron.* Sax. What, 596. 635. 1137. &c. For *that*, 2547. *Wat*, 117. 540. &c. *Wat is thw*, 453. *Hwat* or *Wat is the*, 1951. 2704.

Hwat, See Quath.

Hwel, *n.* Sax. Whale, or grampus, 755. *Hwæl*, balena, vel cete, vel cetus. Ælf. Gl. See Qual.

Hwether, *adv.* Sax. Whether, 294. 2098.

Hwi, *adv.* Sax. Why, 454. See Qui.

Hwil, Hwile, *n.* Sax. Time, 301. 363. 538. 722. 1830. 2437.

Hwil-gat, *adv.* Sax. How, in what manner, 836. *Howgates*, Skinner.

Hwit, *adj.* Sax. White, 1729.

Hwo, *pron.* Sax. Who, 296. 300. 368. 2605. &c. See Wo.

Hwor, *adv.* Sax. Whereas, 1119. Hwor so, Wheresoever, 1349.

Hwou, See Hw.

Hws, See Hus.

Hyse, See Hijs.

I.

Ich, *pron.* Sax. I, 167. &c. *Ihc*, 1377, *Hic*, 305. *Hi*, 487. *Ig*, 686. *Y*, 15. &c.

Id for It, 2424.

I-gret, See Grette.

I-groten, See Graten.

Il, Ilc, *adj.* Sax. Each, every, 818. 1056. 1740. 1921. 2112. 2483. 2514. *Ilke*, 821. 1861. 2959. 2996. *Same*, 1088. 1215. 2674. &c. Ilker, Each, 2352. Ilkan, Each one, 1770. 2357. *Ilkon*, 1842. 2108. See Everi.

Ille, *adj.* Sax. *Likede swithe ille*, 1165. Disliked it much. Sir Tr. p. 78. A common phrase. *Ille maked*, 1953. ill treated.

I-maked, See Make.

Inne, *adv.* Sax. In, 762. 807. See Ther-inne.

Inow, *adv.* Sax. Enough, 706. 911. 931. &c. *Ynow*, 563. 904. 1795.

Intil, *prep.* Sax. Into, 128. 251. &c. See Til.

Ioie, *n.* Fr. Joy, 1209. 1237. 1278. &c. *Ioye,* 1315. Ioyinge, Gladness, 2086.

Ioupe, 1762. Has this any connection with the v. to *Jaup,* used in the North? See Brockett's Gl. in v.

Is for His, 735. 2254. 2479.

Iuel, Iuele, *n.* Sax. Evil, injury, 50. 1689. *Yuel, Yuele,* 994. 2221. Sickness, 114. *Yuel,* 144. 155.

> Tha the wes ald mon,
> Tha com him *ufel* on.
> *Layam.* f. 110. b. c. 2.

Ful iuele o-bone, 2505. very lean.

Iuelelike, *adv.* Sax. Evilly, 132. *Yuele,* 2755.

K.

Kam, See Komen.

Kaske, *adj.* 1841.

Kaym, *n. p.* Cain, 2045. See note in loc.

Kayn, *n.* 31. 1327. Evidently a provincial pronunciation of *Thayn,* which in the Ms. may elsewhere be read either *chayn,* or *Thayn.* By the same mutation of letters *make* has been converted into *mate, cake* into *cate, wayke* into *wayte, lake* into *late* (R. Hood, i. 106.) &c. or *vice versa.* See Thayn.

Kaysere, See Cayser.

Keft, *part. pa.* 2005.

Keling, *n.* 757. Cod of a large size, Jam. q. v. The *kelyng* appears in the first course of Archb. Nevil's Feast, 6. Edw. IV. See Warner's *Antiq. Cul.* Cotgrave explains *Merlus,* A Melwall or *Keeling,* a kind of small cod, whereof stockfish is made.

Keme, See Komen.

Kempe, *n.* Sax. Knight, champion, 1036. V. Jam. in v.

Kene, *adj.* Sax. Keen, bold, eager, 1832. 2115. A term of very extensive use in old Engl. and Sc. poetry, and the usual epithet of a knight. See the Glossaries, and Jam.

Kesten, *v.* Sax. To cast in prison, or to overthrow, 81. 1785. (used passively.) Casten, *pr. t. pl.* Cast, throw, 2101. Keste, *pa. t.* Cast, 2449. Keste, *part. pa.* Cast, placed, 2611.

Keuel, See Couel.

Kid, *part. pa.* Sax. Made known, discovered, 1060. Sir Tr. p. 150. R. Br. Yw. and Gaw. 530. Minot, p. 4. Chauc. From *cythan,* notum facere.

Kin, Kyn, *n.* Sax. Kindred, 393. 414. 2045.

Kines, *n.* Sax. Kind, 861. 1140. 2691. V. Jam. in v. Kin.

Kinneriche, See Cunnriche.

Kippe, *v.* Sax. [*cepan*] To take up hastily, 894. Kipt, Kipte, *pa. t.* Snatch up, 1050. 2407. 2638.

> Horn in is armes hire *kipte.*
> *K. Horn,* 1208.

> *Kypte* heore longe knyues, and slowe faste to gronde. *Rob. Glouc.* p. 125.

Kept up, snatcht up, Gl. R. Br. Jamieson derives the word from Su. G. *kippa,* to take any thing violently. V. in v. Kip.

Kirke, *n.* Sax. Church, 1132. 1355. Kirkes, *pl.* 2583. V. Gl. Lynds. and Jam.

Kiste, See Chist.

Kisten, *pa. t. pl.* Sax. Kissed, 2162.

Kiwing, *n.* Carving (?) 1736.

Knaue, *n.* Sax. Lad, 308. 409. 450. &c. Attendant, servant, 458. *Cokes knaue,* 1123. Scullion.

> Heore cokes & heore *cnaues*
> Alle heo duden of lif dazen.
> *Layam.* f. 73. b. c. 2.

V. Jam. in v. Gl. Lynds. and Gl. Todd's Illustr. Chauc.

KNAWE, *v.* SAX. To know, 2785. KNAWE, *pr. t. pl.* Know, 2207. KNEU, *pa. t.* Knew, 2468. KNAWED, *part. pa.* Known, 2057.

KNICTH, KNITH, *n.* SAX. Knight, 77. 343. &c. KNICTES, KNIHTES, KNITHES, *pl.* 239. 1068. 2706.

KOK, See COK.

KOK, *n.* A small ship, cock-boat, 873. 880. 891. *Cogge*, Chauc. Leg. Wom. 1479. *Cogges*, R. Cœur de L. 4784. *Kogges*, Minot, p. 21. *Coggis*, Doug. Virg. 325. 47. The origin of the word may be sought in the BR. *cwch*, ISL. *kugge*, TEUT. *Kogghe*, *kogh*, B. L. *Cogo*. See Du Cange, and Spelm. Ritson's note on Minot, p. 98. Jam. Dict. and Gl. Lynds. in v. COG.

KOMEN, *v.* SAX. To come, 1001. COMES, COMETH, *imp. pl.* Come ye, 1798. 1885. 2247. CAM, KAM, KEME, KOM, *pa. t.* Came, 766. 863. 1208. 1309. 2622. COMEN, KOMEN, *pa. t. pl.* Came, 1012. 1202. 2790. COMEN, *part. pa.* Come, 1714.

KOPE, *n.* LAT. Cope, 429. COPES, *pl.* 1957.

KOREN, *n.* SAX. Corn, 1879.

KOUEL, See COUEL.

KOUTHEN, See COUTHE.

KRADEL-BARNES, *n. pl.* SAX. Children in the cradle, 1912.

KRAKE, KRAKEN, *v.* SAX. To crack, break, 914. 1857. *Crake*, 1908. CRAKEDE, *pa. t.* Cracked, broke, 568. *pl.* 1238.

KRIKE, *n.* SAX. Creek, 708.

KUNNE, See CANST.

KUNERICHE, KUNERIKE, KUNRIK, See CUNNRICHE.

KYNE-MERK, *n.* SAX. Mark or sign of royalty, 604. In the same manner are compounded *cine-helm*, *cine-stol*, &c.

& Cador the kene
Scal beren thas KINGES MARKE;
Hæbben haze thene drake,
biforen thissere duzethe.
Layam. f. 109. b. c. 1.

Thyll ther was of her body
A fayr chyld borne, and a godele,
Hadde a doubyll *kynges marke.*
Emare, 502.

L.

LAC, *n.* SAX. Fault, reproach, 191. 2219. Yw. and Gaw. 264. 1133. *Lak*, R. Br. Rom. of Merlin, ap. Ellis, M. R. V. I. p. 252. Sir Orpheo, 421. *Lakke*, P. Plouhm. Chauc. So in Sc. V. Jam. and Gl. Lynds. *v.* LAK, LACK.

LADDE, *n.* SAX. Lad, 1786. LADDEN, *pl.* 1038. *Laddes*, 1015. &c. A term subsequently applied to persons of low condition. "When *laddes* weddeth leuedis—" Prophecy of Tho. of Essedoune, Ms. Harl. 2253. f. 127.

LARGE, *adj.* FR. LAT. Liberal, bountiful, 97. 2941. R. Gl. Yw. and Gaw. 865. Sir Orpheo, 27. Sevyn Sages, 1251. Chauc.

LATE, *v.* SAX. [*lætan*, *letan*] To let, suffer, 17. 486. 2611. LATE, *pr. t.* Let, permit, 1509. LATE, *imp.* Let, suffer, 1376. 2422. LETH, *pa. t.* Let, suffered, 2651.

LATEN, *v.* SAX. [*lætan*, *letan*] To leave off, 328. LATE BE, *imp.* Leave, relinquish, 1657. 1265. LET, *pa. t.* Left, 2062. LATEN, *part. pa.* Left, abated, 240. 1925.

LATH, LATHE, *n.* SAX. Injury, 76. 2718. 2976.

LAUHWINDE, *part. pr.* SAX. Laughing, 946.

LAUTE, LAUTHE, *pa. t.* SAX. [*læccan-læhte*] Received, took, 744. 1673. LAUTH, *part. pa.* Received, taken, 1988. *I-lahte*, Layam. f. 172. b.

Horn in herte *laucte*
Al that men him taucte.
K. Horn, 249. Ms.

Laght, Yw. and Gaw. 2025. *Laught,* K. Alisaund. 685. 1109. *Lauht,* R. Br. (See Hearne's blundering Gl. in voc.) Rits. A. S. p. 46. *Laucht,* Wall. ix. 1964.

Laumprei, *n.* Sax. Lamprey, 771. Laumprees, *pl.* 897.

Lawe, Lowe, *adj.* Sax. Low, 2431. 2471. 2767. &c.

Lax, *n.* Sax. [*læx*] Salmon, 754. 1727. Laxes, *pl.* 896. V. Spelm. and Somn. in v. Jamieson says, it was "formerly the only name by which this fish was known."

Layke, *v.* Sax. [*lacan*] To play, 1011. *Leyke, Leyken,* 469. 950. 997. Leykeden, *pa. t. pl.* Played, 954. In the same sense the verb is found in P. Plouhman, and Sevyn Sages, 1212. So in Sc. and A. Bor. V. Jam. v. Laik, Ray, Brockett, and Crav. Dial. v. Lake.

Leche, *n.* Sax. Physician, 1836. 2057. Common in old Engl.

Lecchhe, *v.* 252. Perhaps from Sax. *læccan,* comprehendere, or *lecgan,* ponere. *Lacche* is so used in P. Plouhman, and *Leche* in Web. and Gower, Conf. Am.

Led, 924.

Lede, Leden, *v.* Sax. To lead, 245. &c. ut-lede, 89. Cf. 346. 379. Ledes, *pr. t.* 3. *p.* Uses, carries, 2573. Ledde, *pa. t.* Led, 1686. Ledden, *pa. t. pl.* Led, 2451.

Lef, *adj.* Sax. Agreeable, willing, *lef and loth,* 261. 440. 2273. 2313. 2379. 2775. A very usual phrase. See Beowulf, p. 41. Chauc. C. T. 1839. R. Hood, i. 41. Dear (?) 2606. *Leue,* 431. 909. 1888. Sir Tr. p. 187. K. Horn, 949. &c. Leuere, *comp.* More agreeable, rather, 1193. 1423. 1671. &c.

Leidest, See Leyn.

Leik, *n.* Sax. Body, 2793. *Liche,* K. Alisaund. 3482.

Leite, *adj.* Sax. Light, 2441.

Leme, *n.* Sax. Limb, 2555. *Lime,* 1409. Limes, *pl.* 86.

Leman, Lemman, *n.* Sax. Mistress, Lover, 1191. 1283. 1312. 1322. Used by all the old writers, and applied equally to either sex.

Lende, *v.* Sax. To land, 733. Sir Tr. p. 13. R. Br. See Jam. in v. Leind.

Lene, *v.* Sax. [*leanian*] To lend, grant, 2072.

> I sal *lene* the her mi ring.
> *Yw. and Gaw.* 737.

Lenge, *n.* The fish called *ling,* 832. [*Asellus longus,* or *Islandicus,* Ray.] It was a common dish formerly. Thus we have *Lynge in jelly,* in Archb. Nevil's Feast, 6. Edw. IV. and *Lyng in foyle,* in Warham's Feast, 1504. See Pegge's *Form of Cury,* p. 177. 184. and Ms. Sloane, 1986.

Lenge, *v.* Sax. To prolong, 1734. 2363. P. Plouhm.

Leoun, *n.* Lat. Lion, 573. *Leun,* 1867.

Lepe, *v.* Sax. Escape from (?) 2009. *Loupe,* To leap, 1801. Lep, *pa. t.* Leapt, 891. 1777. 1942. Lopen, *pa. t. pl.* 1896. 2616.

Lere, Leren, *v.* Sax. To learn, 797. 823. 2592. *Y-lere,* 12.

Lese, *v.* Sax. To loose, 333. Sir Tr. p. 110.

Leth, See Late.

Lette, *v.* Sax. [*lætan, letan*] To hinder, retard, 1164. 2819. 2253. To stop, cease, 2445. 2627. Let, *pa. t.* Stopped, 2447. 2500. Leten, *pa. t. pl.* Stopped, delayed, 2379.

Leue, *n.* Sax. Leave, 1387. 1626. 2952. &c.

Leue, *adj.* See Lef.

Leue, *v.* Sax. [*lyfan*] To grant, 334. 406. 2807. K. Horn, 465. Ms. R. Gl. Erle of Tol. 365. Emare, 4. Guy of Warw. ap. Ellis, M. R. V. 2. p. 77. where it is misprinted *lene.* It is very frequently used in the old Engl. Metrical Lives of the Saints, Ms. Laud, 108.

LEUED, *pa. t.* SAX. Left, 225.

LEUEDI, *n.* SAX. Lady, 171. &c. LEUEDYES, *pl.* 239. V. Hickes, Diss. Ep. p. 52. n.

LEUERE, See LEF.

LEUES, *pr. t.* 3. *p.* SAX. Believes, 1781. 2105. From *lefan.*

LEUIN, *n.* SAX. Lightning, 2690. R. Br. p. 174. Yw. and Gaw. Chauc. C. T. 5858. Doug. Virg. 200. 52.

LEWE, *adj.* SAX. Warm, 498. 2921.

> A' opened wes his breoste,
> Tha blod com forth *luke.*
> *Layam.* f. 161. b. c. 2.

LEYD, LEYDE, See LEYN.

LEYE, *n.* SAX. Lie, falsehood, 2117.

LEYE, *v.* SAX. To lie, speak false, 2010.

LEYKE, LEYKEN, See LAYKE.

LEYK, *n.* SAX. Game, 1021. 2326. So in Beowulf, p. 79. *sweorda-gelac,* and Sir Tr. p. 118. *love-laik.* In the pl. *laykes,* Minot, p. 10. In Lanc. a player is still called a *laker.*

LEYN, *v.* SAX. To lay, 718. *Lyen,* To lie down, 2134. LEYDE, *pa. t.* Laid, 50. 994. &c. Stopped, 229. *Leyd,* 1722. Placed. LEIDEST, *pa. t.* 2. *p.* Laidest, 636. LEYDEN, LEYEN, *pa. t. pl.* Laid, 475. 1907. LEYD, *part. pa.* Laid, 1689. 2839.

LICT, LITH, *n.* SAX. Light, 534. 576. 588. &c.

LIFT, *adj.* SAX. Left *(lævus)* 2130.

LIGGE, LIGGEN, *v.* SAX. To lie down, 802. 876. 882. 1374.

LIME, LIMES, See LEME.

LITE, *adj.* SAX. Little, 276. 1730. 1755. *Litel,* 1858. &c. *Litle,* 2014.

LITH, See LICT.

LITH, *imp.* SAX. Light (thou) 585.

LITH, *adv.* SAX. Lightly, (?) 1942.

LITH, *n.* SAX. Alleviation, comfort, 1338. *Lythe,* 147. We have met with no instance elsewhere of this word being used as a noun. As an adj. it occurs in Layam. f. 40. b. Sir Tr. p. 42. 82. R. Cœur de L. 2480. and Emare, 348. from the v. *lithian,* alleviare. Jamieson is here of no assistance.

LITH, *n.* SAX. [*hleoth, hlithe,* clivus ?] This word is explained by Ritson *plains,* by Hearne *tenements,* and by Jamieson a *ridge* or *ascent.* Its real signification seems unknown, but may be conjectured from the following passages.

> No asked he lond no *lithe.*
> *Sir Tristr.* p. 101.
>
> Ther wille not be went, ne lete ther lond ne *lith.* *R. Brunne,* p. 194.

where it answers to the Fr. Ne volent lesser tere ne *tenement.*

> Who schall us now geve londes or *lythe.*
> *Le Bone Flor.* 841.
>
> Here I gif Schir Galeron, quod Gaynour, withouten ony gile,
> Al the londis and the *lithis* fro laver to layre.
> *Sir Gaw. and Sir Gal.* ii. 27.

LITH for LICH, i. e. Like, 2155.

LITHES, *n. pl.* SAX. The extreme points of the toes, or articulations, 2163. *Fingres-lith,* extremum digiti, Luc. 16. 24.

LITHES, *imp. pl.* SAX. Listen, 1400. 2204. *Lythes,* 2576. The verb in the Sax. is *hlystan,* but in Su. G. *lyde,* and Isl. *hlyda,* which approaches nearer to the form in the poem. So also in K. Horn, 2. *wilen lithe,* Ms. R. Br. p. 93. Amis and Am. 3. R. Hood, I. p. 2. Minot, p. 1. Still used in Sc. and A. Bor. V. Jam. and Brockett.

LITTENE, *part. pa.* 2701. *Qu.* cut in pieces, from the same root as to *lith,* divide the joints. V. Jam. Suppl.

Liue, *n.* Sax. Life, 232. *brouth of liue,* 513. 2129. Dead. K. Horn, 183. *Of liue do,* 1805. Kill. Liues, Alive, 509. 1003. 1307. 1919. 2854. See On-liue.

Liuen, *v.* Sax. To live, 355. Liuede, Liueden, *pa. t. pl.* Lived, 1299. 2044.

Lof, *n.* Sax. Loaf, 653.

Loke, Loken, *v.* Sax. To look after, take care of, to behold, 376. 2136. Lokes, *pr. t.* 2. *p.* Lookest, 2726. Loke, *imp.* Look, 1681. 1712. Lokes, *imp. pl.* Look ye, 2240. 2292. 2300. 2579. 2812. Lokede, *pa. t.* Looked, 679. 1041.

Loken, Lokene, *part. pa.* Sax. Fastened, locked, closed, 429. 1957. So in the Const. Othonis, Tit. *de habitu Clericorum.* "In mensura decenti habeant vestes, et *cappis clausis* utuntur in sacris ordinibus constituti." V. Spelm. in v. Cappa clausa.

Lond, Londe, *n.* Sax. Land, 64. 721. &c. *Lon,* 340.

Long, *adj.* Sax. Tall, 987. 1063. So K. Horn, 100. Sir Orph. 22.

Longes, *pr. t.* 3. *p.* Sax. Belongs, 396. R. Br. Chauc. &c.

Lopen, See Lepe.

Loth, *adj.* Sax. Loath, unwilling, 261. 440. &c. See Lef.

Louede, *pa. t.* Sax. Loved, 71. Loueden, *pa. t. pl.* 955.

Louerd, *n.* Sax. Lord, master, 96. 483. &c. *Lowerd,* 621.

Louerdinges, *n. pl.* Sax. Lordings, masters, 515. 1401. See Note in Warton's Hist. Engl. Poet. V. i. p. 21. Ed. 8vo.

Loupe, See Lepe.

Low, *pa. t.* Sax. Laughed, 903. K. Horn, 1501. Lowen, *pa. t. pl.* 1056.

Lowe, *n.* Sax. [*hlæw*] Hill, 1291. 1699. Rits. M. R. Web. &c. V. Jam. and Brockett's Gl. v. Lawe.

Luue, *n.* Sax. Love, 195.

Lyen, See Leyn.

Lythe, See Lith.

M.

Maght, Mait, See Mowe.

Make, *n.* Sax. Mate, companion, wife, 1150. K. Horn, 1427. K. Alisaund. 3314. Le Bone Flor. 881. Chauc. *Maik,* Sc. V. Jam.

Maken, *v.* Sax. To make, 29. &c. *Make,* 676. To be made. Makeden, *pa. t. pl.* Made, 554. I-maked, *part. pa.* Made, 15.

Male, *n.* Fr. A budget, bag, wallet, 48. Layamon, f. 20. Web. Chauc. R. Hood.

Malisun, *n.* Fr. Malediction, curse, 426. Sir Tr. p. 179. Very commonly used.

Manred, Manrede, *n.* Sax. Homage, fealty, 484. 2172. 2180. 2248. 2265. 2312. 2774. 2816. 2847. 2850. Leg. of S. Gregori, ap. Leyd. Compl. of Scotl. See Jam. for further examples.

Marz, *n.* Lat. March, 2559.

Maugre, Fr. In spite of, 1128. 1789. Common to all the old writers. See Tyrwh. Gl. to Chauc. and Jam. in v.

Maydnes, *n. pl.* Sax. Maidens, 467. 2222.

Mayster, *n.* Fr. Master, 1135. Chief, 2028. 2385.

Mayt, Mayth, See Mowe.

Mede, *n.* Sax. Reward, 102. 685. 1635. 2402.

Mele, *n.* Sax. Oat-meal, 780.

Mele, *v.* Fr. To contend in battle, 2059. Gaw. and Gol. ii. 18. *Mellay,* Wynt. viii. 15. 19. V. Jam. and Cf. K. Horn, 2088.

Meme, *v.* 2201.

Mene, *v.* Sax. To mean, signify, 2114. Menes, *pr. t.* 3. *p.* Means, 597.

Meinie, Meynie, *n.* Fr. Family, 827. 834. This word is to be found in every Engl. writer from the time of Layamon to Shakespeare. Jamieson attempts to derive it from the North. V. in *v.* Menzie.

Mere, *n.* Sax. Mare, 2449. 2478. 2504.

Messe, *n.* Fr. Lat. The service of the Mass, 243. 1176. Messe-bok, Mass-book, 186. 291. 2710. Messe-gere, All the apparel &c. pertaining to the service of the Mass, 188. 389. 1078. 2217.

Mest, *adj. sup.* Sax. Greatest, 233. *Moste,* 1287. Tallest, 983.

Mester, *n.* Fr. Trade, 823. K. Horn, 234. Ms. &c.

Mete, *n.* Sax. Meat, 459. &c. Metes, *pl.* 1733.

Meynie, See Meinie.

Michel, *adj.* Sax. Much, 510. 660. *Mik,* 2342. *Mike,* 960. (Cf. Horn Childe, ap. Rits. V. 3. 292.) 1744. 1762. 2336. *Mikel,* 121. 478. &c.

Micte, Micten, Micthe, Mithe, Mithest, Mithen, See Mowe.

Micth, *n.* Sax. Might, power, 35.

Middelerd, *n.* Sax. The earth, world, 2244. *Middelærde,* Layam. Rits. Web. R. Gl. Minot, &c. So in Sc. V. Jam.

Mik, Mike, Mikel, See Michel.

Milce, *n.* Sax. [*mildse*] Mercy, 1361. A! me do thine *milce.* Layam. f. 26. c. 2. R. Gl. It is usually coupled with ore.

Milne-hous, See Hus.

Mirke, *adj.* Sax. Dark, 404. R. Br. Lynds. *merke,* Chauc. Still used in Sc. and A. Bor. V. Jam.

Misdede, *pa. t.* Sax. Did amiss, 337. Injured, 992. 1371. Misdo, *part. pa.* Misdone, offended, 2798.

Misferde, *pa. t.* Sax. Behaved, or proceeded ill, 1869. See Fare.

Misgos, *pr. t.* 2. *p.* Sax. Goest or behavest amiss, 2707.

Misseyde, *part. pa.* Sax. Spoken to reproachfully, 1688.

Mithe, Mythe, *v.* Sax. [*mithan*] To conceal, hide, dissemble, 652. 948. 1278. Sche might no lenger *mithe.* Horn Childe, ap. Rits. M. R. V. 3. p. 310.

Mixed, *adj.* Vile, base, 2530. Probably from Sax. *myx,* fimus. We have not found it elsewhere.

Mo, *adj. comp.* Sax. More, 1742. 1846.

Mod, *n.* Sax. Mood, humour, 1703.

Moder, *n.* Sax. Mother, 974. 1388. &c.

Mone, *n.* Sax. Moon, 373. 403.

Mone, *n.* Mind, say, opinion, 816. *Qu.* from Sax. *Monian,* monere, *monung,* monitum. Hence To *mone,* to *relate,* R. Cœur de L. 4636. and to *animadvert,* in Barbour. It appears to express the Fr. phrase *par le mien escient,* K. Horn, 467. Ms. Douce. In nearly the same sense *mone* may be found in K. Alisaund. 1281. R. Gl. p. 281. 293. Cf. v. 1711. 1972.

Mone, *v. pl.* [Isl. *mun*] Must, 840. *Maun,* Sc. *Mun,* Yorksh. Cumb. V. Jam.

Morwen, *n.* Sax. Morning, 811. 1131. 2669. &c. *To-morwen,* 530. 810. *Amorwe,* Sir Tr. K. Horn.

Moste, See Mest.

Mote, *v.* Sax. May, 19. 406. 1743. 2545. Moten, *pl.* 18.

Moun, See Mowe.

Mowe, *v.* Sax. May, be able, 175. 394. 675. Mowen, *pl.* 11. *Moun,* 460. 2587. Mait, *pr. t.* 2. *p.* Mayest, 689. *Mayt,* 845. 852. 1219. *Mayth,* 641. Maght, *pa. t.* 2. *p.* Mightest, 1348. *Mithe, Mithest,* 855. 1218. Micte, Micthe, Mithe, *pa. t.* 3. *p.* Might, 42. 233. 1030. 1080. Mouchte, Moucte, Moucthe, Mouthe, Mowcte, 145. 356. 376. &c. Micte, Micten, Mithen, *pl.* 232. 516. 1929. 2017. Mouhte, Mouthe, Mouthen, 1183. 2019. 2028. 2328. 2330. &c. V. Pegge's Anecd. of Engl. Lang. p. iii.

N.

Na, *adv.* Sax. No, 2363. 2530.

Nam, See Nime.

Nayles, *n. pl.* Sax. Nails, 2163.

Ne, *adv.* Sax. Nor, 44. &c.

Nede, *n.* Sax. Need, necessity, 9. &c. Nedes, *pl.* 1692.

Neme, See Nime.

Ner, *adv.* Sax. Near, 990. 1949.

Nese, *n.* Sax. Nose, 2450.

Nesh, *adj.* Sax. [*nesc*] Soft, tender, 2743. *Neys*, 217. Web. Rits. M. R. Rob. Br. Chauc. Still used in N. W. part of England.

Neth, *n.* Sax. Net, 752. 808. 1026.

Neth, *n.* Sax. Neat, cattle, 700. 1222. Netes, *g. c.* Neat's, 781.

Netheles, *conj.* Sax. Nevertheless, 1108. 1658.

Neue, *n.* Sax. Fist, 2405. Neues, *pl.* 1917. V. Jam.

Neuere, Neure, *adv.* Sax. Not, never, 80. 672. *neuere a polk*, 2685. *ne'er*, Vulg. *Neuere kines*, 2691. No kind.

Ney, *adv.* Nigh, near to, nearly, 464. 534. 640. 2619.

Neys, See Nesh.

Neythe, Neyther, *pron.* Sax. Neither, not either, 458. 764. 2970. &c. *Nother*, 2623. *Noyther*, 2697.

Newhen, *v.* Sax. [*nehwan*] To approach, 1866. In the more recent form to *neigh* it is used in several of the old Romances, Chauc. and Minot.

Nich, Nicht, Nicth, *n.* Sax. Night, 404. 533. 575. *Niht*, 2669. *Nith*, 1247. 1754. Nithes, *g. c.* Of night, 2100. Nihtes, Nithes, *pl.* 2353. 2999.

Nime, *v.* Sax. To take, 1931. Nim, *imp.* Take, 1336. Nam, *pa. t.* Took, 900. 954. Neme, received, 1207. Nomen, *pa. t. pl.* Took, 2790. Nomen, Numen, *part. pa.* Taken, 1265. 2581. Nime, Nimes, *imp. pl.* Go ye, 2594. 2600. Nam, *pa. t.* Went, 2930. In the first sense this verb is common in all the Glossaries, but in the latter sense *To go* it occurs no where but in the Gl. to Rob. Brunne, who, from being a Lincolnshire man, approaches nearer to the language of the present poem than any other writer.

Nis for Ne is, Is not, 462. 1998. 2244.

Nither, *adv.* Sax. Beneath, beyond, i. e. surpassing, 2025.

Noblelike, *adv.* Sax. Nobly, 2640.

Nok, *n.* [Belg. *Nock*] Nook, corner, 820. *nouth a ferthinges nok*, Not the value of a farthing.

Nomen, See Nime.

Non, *adj.* Sax. No, 518. 685. 1019. No one, 934. 974. *Nu*, 2421. 2460. 2650. &c.

Note, *n.* Sax. A nut, 419. *Nouthe*, 1332.

Nother, See Neythe.

Nou, *adv.* Sax. Now, 328. 1362. &c.

Nout, Nouth, Nouht, *n.* or *adv.* Sax. Not, naught, nothing, not at all, 249. 505. 566. 648. 1733. 2051. 2822. *Nowt*, *Nowth*, 313. 770. 2168. 2737.

Nouthe, See Note.

Noyther, See Neythe.

Nu, See Nou.

Numen, See Nime.

Nytte, *v.* 941. *Qu.* from Sax. *nydian*, urgere, abigere, *nit*, sustentabit, Ps. 36. 15.

O.

O, See On.

Of, *prep.* Sax. Off, 216. 603. 857. 1850. 2444. 2626. 2671. 2751. &c. *Of londe*, 2599. Out of the land, Sir Tr.

Offe, *prep.* Sax. Of, 435.

Offrende, Fr. Offering, 1386.

Ofte, *adv.* Sax. Often, 226. &c.

Ok, See Ek.

On, *adj.* Sax. One, 425. 1800. 2028. 2263. &c.

On, *adv.* Sax. Only, 962.

On, *prep.* Sax. In, on. *On-liue*, 281. 363. 694. 793. &c. *O-liue*, 2865. *On two*, 471. 1823. 2730. In two. *A-two*, 1413. 2643. *O-londe*, 763. On, or in land. *On-knes*, 1211. 1302. 2710. On knees. *O-knes*, 2252. 2796. *On-brenne*, 1239. In flame, on fire. *O-nith*, 1251. In the night. *On-nithes*, 2048. *O-worde*, 1349. In conversation. *O mani wise*, 1713. In many manners. *On-gamen*, 1716. In sport. *On lesse hwile*, 1830. In less time. *O-bok*, 2307. 2311. On the book. *Wel o-bon*, 2355. 2525. 2571. Strong of body. (*Wel-i-bon*, Layam. f. 32. c. 2.) *Iuele o-bone*, 2505. Lean. *On-hunting*, 2382. *O-stede*, 2549. On steed. *O-the dogges*, 2596. On the dogs. From these examples, added to those which occur in every Glossary, it is evident the Sax. prep. *On* was subsequently corrupted to *O* and *A*. See Tyrwh. and Jam. *A-nycht* in Barb. xix. 657. explained by the latter *one* night, is according to the above rule *In the night*, as confirmed by v. 1251. Sir Tr. p. 47. 114. R. Glouc.

One, *adj.* Sax. Alone, singly, 815. 936. 1153. 1710. 1742. 1973. 2433.

> Ther hue wonede al *one*.
> *K. Horn*, 80.

See Tyrwh. Gl. Chauc. v. On.

Ones, *adv.* Sax. Once, 1295.

Onfrest, *v.* Delay? 1337. *Qu.* from Su.G. *frest*, temporis intervallum, Sax. *firstan*, to make a truce. *Frest*, delay, Barb. vii. 447.

Onlepi, See Anilepi.

Onne, *prep.* Sax. On, 347. 1940.

Onon, *adv.* Sax. Anon, speedily, 136. 447. 1964. 2790.

Ontil, *prep.* Sax. Unto, 761.

Or, *adv.* Sax. Previously, before, 728. 1043. 1355. 1688. &c. *Or outh*, 1789. Before.

Ore, *n.* Favor, grace, mercy, 153. 211. 2443. 2797. Ich hadde of hire milse an *ore*. Hule and Nihtingale, f. 237. b. Ms. Cal. A. ix. Sir Tr. p. 24. K. Horn, 653. &c. See Tyrwhitt's Note on Chauc. C. T. 3724. and Ritson's Note, Metr. Rom. V. iii. p. 263. The derivation is uncertain, but probably Saxon. Jamieson's attempts to refer it to any other source are perfectly unsatisfactory.

Ore, *n.* Sax. Oar, 718. 1871. &c. Ores, *pl.* 711.

Osed for Hosed, 971.

Oth, *n.* Sax. Oath, 2009. 2272. &c. Othes, *pl.* 2013. 2231. &c.

Othe for Other, 861. 1986. 2970.

Other, *conj.* Sax. Either, or, 94. 674. 787. &c. See Ayther.

Other, *adj.* Sax. [*alter*] The other of two, second, 879. *The other day*, 1750. the following day.

> Day igo and *other*,
> Wituten seyl and rother.
> *K. Horn*, 195. Ms.

So also R. Br. p 169. and Wynt.

Other, *adj.* Sax. [*alius*] Other, 2490. *Othre*, 2413. Othre, *pl.* Others, 1784. 2416.

Ouer-fare, *v.* Sax. To pass over, cease, 2063. See Fare.

Ouer-go, *v.* Sax. To be disregarded, 2220.

Ouer-gange, *v.* Sax. To get the superiority, 2587.

Ouerthwert, *adv.* Sax. Across, 2822. *Ouerthuert*, R. Br. p. 241. *Overtwert*, Ly Beaus Desc. 1017. *Overthwarte*, Syr Eglamore, B. iii. Chauc. C. T. 1993.

Oune, *adj.* Sax. Own, 375. 2428.

Outh, *n.* Sax. [*awiht*] Any space of time, ought, 1189.

OUTH, *adv.* SAX. Without, 703. *Or outh long*, 1789. Before long.

P.

PALEFREY, *n.* FR. Saddle-horse, 2060. See Gl. on Chauc. in v. Pegge's Anecd. Engl. Lang. p. 289.

PAPPES, *n. pl.* LAT. Breasts, 2132.

PARRED, *part. pa.* Confined? 2439. We have met with this word only in one instance, where Ritson leaves it unexplained.

> Yn al this [tyme] was sir Ywayn
> Ful straitly *parred* with mekil payn.
> *Yw. and Gaw.* 3227.

PASTEES, *n. pl.* FR. Pasties, patés, 644.

> Ther beth bures and halles,
> Al of *pasteus* beth the walles.
> *Land of Cokaygne*, ap. Hickes.

PATEYN, *n.* LAT. The Plate used in the service of the Mass, 187.

PATHE, *n.* SAX. Path, road, 2381. 2390. PATHES, *pl.* 268.

PATRIARK, *n.* LAT. Patriarch, 428.

PAYED, *part. pa.* FR. Satisfied, content, 184. Rits. M. R. Web. R. Gl. R. Br. *Apaied*, Chauc.

PELLE, *v.* 810.

PENI, *n.* SAX. Penny, 705. 2147. PENIES, *pl.* 776. 1172.

PER, *n.* FR. Peer, equal, 989. 2241. 2792.

PIKE, *v.* To pitch, (used passively) 707. TEUT. *pecken*, LAT. *picare*. The verb in Saxon is not extant, but only the n. *pic*.

PINE, *n.* SAX. Pain, grief, 405. 540. 1374. Sir Tr. p. 12. V. Jam.

PINE, *v.* SAX. To grieve, 1958.

PLAT, See PLETTE.

PLATTINDE, *part. pr.* 2282. Has it any analogy with the Teut. *plotsen*, Germ. *pladern?* See Brockett's Gl. in v. PLOUTER.

PLAWE, *v.* SAX. To play, 950. *Pleye*, 951.

PLAYCES, *n. pl.* Plaice, 896.

PLEINTE, *n.* FR. Complaint, 134. *Pleynte*, 2961.

PLETTE, *v.* SAX. [*plættian*] To strike, 2444. 2613. PLAT, *pa. t.* Struck, 2755. *Plette*, 2626.

PLITH, *n.* SAX. [*pliht*] Harm, 1370. 2002. Layam. f. 22.

POKE, *n.* SAX. A bag, 555. 769. POKES, *pl.* 780.

POLES, *n. pl.* SAX. Pools, ponds of water, 2101.

POLK, *n.* SAX. Pool, puddle, 2685. *Pow*, Sir Tr. p. 171. *Pulk*, Somersetsh.

POUERE, POURE, *adj.* FR. Poor, 58. 101. 2457. &c.

POURELIKE, *adv.* Poorly, 323.

PRANGLED, *part. pa.* 639. *Qu.* from TEUT. *prangen*, comprimere, arctare, constringere.

PREI, *pr. t.* SAX. Pray, 1440. PREYE, *imp.* Pray (thou) 1343. PREIDE, *pa. t.* Prayed, 209.

PREST, *n.* SAX. Priest, 429. 1829. PRESTES, *pl.* 2583.

PRIKEN, *v.* SAX. To spur a horse, ride briskly, 2639.

PRUD, *adj.* SAX. Proud, 302.

PULTEN, *pa. t. pl.* So reads the Ms. v. 1023. instead of *putten*. Both have the same signification. So in the Romance of *Rob. of Cecyle*, Harl. Ms. 1701. f. 94. c. 1. *pulte* occurs for *put*, placed, and *pylt* in R. Cœur de L. 4085. *pelte*, Sir Tr. p. 95. In the *imp. Pult* for *put, place*, is used in *Hending the Hende*, Ms. Digb. 86. In the signification of *drove forward*, which is nearer to the sense we require, we find *pylte* in K. Horn, 1433. and R. Glouc. Hence the Engl. word *pelt*. See PUTTEN.

PUND, *n.* SAX. Pounds, 1633.

Put, *n.* Cast, throw, 1055. *But*, 1040.

Putten, *v.* To cast, throw, propel forward, 1033. 1044. *Puten*, 1051. Putte, *pa. t.* Cast, 1052. Putten, *pa. t. pl.* Cast, threw, 1023. 1031. 1842. Putting, Puttinge, *part. pr.* or *n.* Casting, 1042. 1057. 2324. From the Fr. *bouter*, Teut. *buitten*, or Belg. *botten*, to drive or propel forward, or, as others suggest, from the Br. *pwtiaw*, which has the same meaning, or Isl. *potta*. From the same root are derived both *Put* and *But*. Thus to *butt* in Sc. is to drive at a stone in curling, and to *put* in Yorksh. is to push with the horns. In the passage before us it is applied to a particular game, formerly in great repute. See Note on v. 1023. Cf. Ramsay's Poems, ii. 106. The word is still retained in the North, and Sc. V. Jam. and Brockett. See But, and Pulten.

Pyment, *n.* B. L. Spiced wine, 1728. See Note on v. 1726.

Q.

Qual, *n.* Sax. [*hwæl*] Whale or grampus, 753. See Hwel.

Quan, Quanne, *adv.* Sax. When, 134. 204. 240. &c. See Hwan.

Quath, *pa. t.* Sax. Quoth, 606. 642. &c. *Hwat*, 1650. 1878. *Wat*, 595. *Quod*, 1888. *Quodh*, 1801. *Quot*, 1954. 2808. *Couth*, 2606.

Queme, *part. pa.* Sax. Pleased, satisfied, 130. 393. Web. Rits. M. R. Rob. Br. R. Glouc. Gower, Chauc.

Quen, *n.* Sax. Queen, 2760. 2783. &c. Quenes, *pl.* 2982.

Qui, See Hwi.

Quic, Quik, *adj.* Sax. Alive, 612. 613. 1405. 2210. 2476. &c. *quik and ded*. This is the usual language of the Inquisitiones post mortem, which commence at the early part of Hen. III. reign. For the usage of the term, see Gl. to Sir Tr. p. 98. Yw. and Gaw. 668. Chron. of Engl. 760. &c. The word is preserved in the vulgar version of the Scriptures, and Creed. *Quike*, Quick, alert, 1348. *Al quic wede*, 2641. Cf. v. 2387.

Quiste, *n.* Sax. [*cwid*] Bequest, will, 219. 365. *Quede*, K. Alisaund. 8020.

Quod, Quodh, Quot, See Quath.

R.

Radde, See Rede.

Ran, See Renne.

Rang, *adj.* Sax. [*ranc*] Perverse, rebellious, 2561.

Rath, Rathe, *adv.* Sax. Speedy, ready, quickly, 75. 358. &c. (In v. 1335. I prefer considering it as a verb.) It seems, says Jam. to have been originally an *adj.* See Red.

Rathe, *v.* Sax. [*raedan*] To advise, 1335. A provincial pronunciation of Rede. In v. 2817. it is still broader, "Yf ye it wilen and ek *rothe*." In the same manner *Rode* is spelt, and was undoubtedly pronounced *Rothe*, Ly Beaus Desc. 425. and *Abode* is spelt *Abothe*, ib. 1118. Cf. v. 693. 1680. 2585. of the present poem, in all which instances the *d* has the sound of *th* in *rede*. See To-rede.

Recke, *pr. t.* Sax. Recks, regards, cares, 2047. 2511. Sir Tr. p. 124. &c.

Red, Rede, *n.* Sax. Advice, counsel, 180. 518. 826. 1194. 2871. &c. Perhaps *Rath*, 75. is only a broad pronunciation of this noun. V. supr.

Rede, *v.* Sax. To direct, advise, 104. 148. 361. 687. 693. &c. Radde, *pa. t.* Advised, 1353. V. Jam. in v. and Hearne's Gl. R. Glouc. See To-rede.

Reft, Refte, Reftes, See Reue.

Regne, *pr. t. pl.* Fr. Lat. Reign, assume the superiority, 2586. *Reng, Ring,* Sc. V. Jam. in v.

Renne, *v.* Sax. To run, 1161. 1904. *Ran on blode, pa. t.* 432. So in Sir Tr. p. 176. *His heued ran on blod,* and in Ms. Harl. 2253. f. 128.

> Lutel wot hit any mon hou loue hym haueth y-bounden,
> That for vs o-the rode *ron,* ant bohte vs with is wounde.

Reue, *n.* Sax. Magistrate, 1627. See Greyue.

Reue, Reuen, *v.* Sax. [*reafian*] To take away, bereave, rob, 480. 2590.

Reft, Refte, *pa. t.* Took away, bereaved, 1367. 1672. 2223. Spoiled, 2004. Reftes, *pa. t.* 2. *p.* Tookest away, 2394. Reft, Refte, Reuen, *part. pa.* Taken away, bereaved, 2483. 2485. 2991. Still used in the North.

Reures, *n.pl.* Sax. Robbers, bereavers, 2104.

> Alle bacbiteres wendet to helle,
> Robberes & *reueres* & the monquelle.
> *A lutel sermun,* Ms. Cal. A. ix. f. 246. b.

V. Jam. in v. Reyffar.

Reunesse, Rewnisse, *n.* Sax. Compassion, 502. 2227.

Rewe, *v.* Sax. To have pity, to compassionate, 497. 967. Rewede, *pa. t.* 503.

Riche, *n.* Sax. Kingdom, 133. 290. 407. See Cunnriche.

Richelike, *adv.* Sax. Richly, 421.

Ricth, Ricthe, See Rith, Rithe.

Riden, *v.* Sax. To ride, 10. &c.

Rig, *n.* Sax. Back, 1775. So in Layam. f. 37. b. Burne he warp on *rigge.*

Rim, Rym, *n.* Fr. Rhyme, poem, 21. 2995. 2998. So Chauc. *Rime of Sire Thopas.*

Ringen, *v.* Sax. To ring, 242. 1106. Ringes, *pr. t. pl.* Ring, 390. Rungen, *part. pa.* Rung, 1132.

Ringes, *n. pl.* Sax. Rings of mail, 2740. See Brini.

Rippe, *n.* Fish-basket, 893. Hence a *Rippar,* B. Lat. *riparius,* is a person who brings fish from the coast to sell in the interior. V. Spelm. in v. Nares prefers the etymology of *ripa,* but without reason. *Rip* is still provincial for an osier basket. See Jam. and Moore. So also in a curious Latin and English Vocabulary, compiled by Sire John Mendames, Parson of Bromenstrope [Brunham Thorp, Co. Norf.] in the middle of the 15th cent. and now preserved in the valuable Mss. library of T. W. Coke, Esq. *Cophinus* is explained *A beryng lepe, or ryppe,* terms still retained in the County.

Rirthwise, *adj.* Sax. [*rihtwis*] Righteous, just, 37. Rits. Web. M. R. Rob. Br. Minot, Lynds. R. Hood.

Rith, Ricth, *n.* Sax. Right, justice, 36. 395. 1099. 1383. 2717.

Rith, *adj.* Sax. Right (*dexter*). 604. 1812. 2140. 2545. 2725.

Rithe, Ricthe, *adj.* Sax. Right (*rectus*), 772. 846. 1201. 2235. 2473.

Rith, Rithe, *adv.* Sax. Rightly, 420. 872. 1701. 2611. &c. Exactly, just, 2494. 2506.

Ritte, *v.* To rip, make an incision, 2495.

> The breche adoun he threst,
> He *ritt,* and gan to right.
> *Sir Tristr.* p. 33.

V. Jam. in v. Rit, who derives it from Isl. *Reyte,* deglubo.

Robben, *v.* Sax. To rob, 1958.

Rode, *n.* Sax. The Rood, Cross, 103. 431. 1357. &c. V. Todd's Gl. Illustr. Chauc.

Rof, *n.* Sax. Roof, 2082.

Rome, *v.* Sax. To roam, travel about, 64.

Rore, *v.* Sax. To roar, 2496. &c. Rorede, *pa. t.* Roared, 2438.

Roser, *n.* Fr. Rose-bush, 2919. Chauc. Pers. Tale, 244.

ROTH, See RATHE.

ROWTE, v. SAX. [*hrutan*] To roar, 1911. R. Cœur de L. 4304. V. Gl. Lynds. and Jam. in v. The latter derives it from ISL. *rauta*, mugire, and Tyrwhitt from FR. *router*. The word is still retained in the provinces. V. Brockett and Wilbr.

RUNCI, *n.* B. LAT. A horse of burden, 2569. V. Du Cange and Spelm. The word is common both in Fr. and Engl. writers.

RUNGEN, See RINGEN.

RYM, See RIM.

S.

SA, *imp. pl.* Say (we) 338.

SAL for Shall, 628.

SAME for SHAME, 1941. V. Jam.

SAMEN, *adv.* SAX. Together, 467. 979. 1717. &c. Web. Rits. M. R. Rob. Br. So also in Sc. V. Jam.

SAMENED, *part. pa.* SAX. Assembled, united, 2890. Web. R. Br. p. 2.

SARE, *adv.* SAX. Sore, sorrowfully, 401.

SAT, *pa. t.* SAX. Opposed, 2567. See ATSITTE. In Sc. is *Sit*, *Sist*, to stop, from Lat. sistere. V. Jam.

SAUTRES, *n. pl.* FR. LAT. Psalters, Hymns for the Office of the Dead, 244.

SAWE, SAWEN, SAY, See SE.

SAYSE, *v.* B. LAT. To seise, give seisin or livery of land, 251. 2518. SEYSED, *part. pa.* Seised, 2513. 2931. Horn Childe, ap. Rits. M. R. V. 3. p. 309.

SCABBED, SKABBED, *adj.* SAX. LAT. Scabby, scurvy, 2449. 2505.

SCATHE, *n.* SAX. Harm, injury, 1352. SCATHES, *pl.* 269. R. Br. V. Gl. *Skaith*, Sc. V. Jam.

SCHE, SCHO, SHO, *pron.* SAX. She, 111. 126. 649. 1721. &c.

SCHIFTE for SHRIFT, Absolution, confession, 1829.

SCHOTEN, SHOTEN, *pa. t. pl.* SAX. Shoot or cast, 1838. 1864. *Scuten*, 2431.

SCHULLE, *n.* Species of fish, sole? 759.

SE, The Sax. art. *The*, but perhaps a mistake of the scribe, v. 534. as it is not elsewhere used.

SE, *n.* SAX. Sea, 535. &c. *Sei*, 321.

SE, SEN, *v.* SAX. To see, 1021. 1273. &c. SEST, *pr. t.* 2. *p.* Seest, 534. SEN, *pr. t. pl.* See, 168. 1217. SAWE, SOWE, *pa. t.* Saw, 1182. 1323. *Say*, 881. SAWEN, SOWEN, *pa. t. pl.* 957. 1055. 2255. SENE, *part. pa.* 656.

SECKES, *n. pl.* SAX. Sacks, 2019.

SEGGES, *n. pl.* FR. [*seches*] 896. In Cotgr. the *Seche* is explained the Sound, or Cuttle fish. The *Seches de Coutance* were held in the highest estimation. V. Le Grand. See also Jam. v. SYE.

SEI, *n.* See SE.

SEI, *v.* See SEYEN.

SEKEN, *v.* SAX. To seek, 1629. The reading is confirmed by an old poem in Ms. Digb. 86.

> Sire, we ben kniȝttes fer i-fare,
> For to *sechen* wide-ware.
>
> *La vie seint Eustace, qui out noun Placidas.*

SELCOUTH, *n.* SAX. Wonder, strange thing, 124. 1059. *Selcuth*, 2119. It was in all probability originally an *adj.* as *Selkuth*, 1284. Strange, wonderful. The word occurs in all the Glossaries.

SELE, *n.* SAX. Seal, 755.

SELI, *adj.* SAX. Simple, harmless, 477. 499. R. Gl. Chauc.

SELTHE, *n.* SAX. [*selth*] Advantage, benefit, 1338. Not met with elsewhere.

SEMBLING, *n.* FR. Assembling, 1018. It may also be derived from the SU. G. *samlung*, conventus.

SEMES, *pr. t.* Seems, 2916. SEMEDE, *pa. t.* Seemed, 976.

SEN, See SE.

Sendes, *pr. t.* Sendeth, sends, 2392. Sende, *pa. t.* Sent, 136. &c.

Serf-borw, *n.* Sax. Surety, pledge, 1667. In Ms. Soc. Antiq. No. 60. known by the name of *The Black Book of Peterborough*, is an instrument in which many names both of Saxon and Danish origin appear as the *Borhhanda*, or Sureties, otherwise called *Festermen*. See Jam. and the Glossaries, for further examples.

Serganz, *n. pl.* Fr. Attendants, officers, 2088. 2091. 2116. *Sergaunz*, 1929. 2361. 2371. *Serjaunz*, 2066. V. Spelm. in v. Servientes, and Hickes, Thes. T. i. p. 148.

Serges, See Cerges.

Serk, *n.* Sax. Shirt, 603. Emare, 501. R. Br.

Seruen, *v.* Sax. To serve, 1230.

Seruede, *pa. t.* Sax. Deserved, 1914. Web. M. R. So in Sc. V. Jam.

Sest, See Se.

Sette, *v.* Sax. To set, descend, 2671.

Sette, *pa. t.* Sax. Set, placed, 2405. Appointed, 2571. Setten, *pa. t. pl.* Set, 1211. Sitte, *part. pa.* Set, placed, 2612.

Seyen, *v.* Sax. To say, 2886. Seyst, *pr. t.* 2. *p.* Sayest, 2008. Sey, *pa. t.* 1. *p.* Said, 2993. Seyde, *pa. t.* 3. *p.* Said, 117. &c. Seyden, *pa. t. pl.* Said, 376. 1213. Seyden, 456. Have said.

Seysed, See Sayse.

Seyst, See Seyen.

Seyt, *pr. t.* Sit, or perhaps Say, q. say it, 647. So in Sir Tr. p. 117.
For mani men *seyt* ay whare.

Shaltou, Shalt thou, 1800. *Shaltow*, 1322. *Shaltu*, 2180. 2186. 2882. 2901.

Shamlike, Shamelike, *adv.* Sax. Shamefully, disgracefully, 2825. 4562. *Schamliche*, Sir Tr. p. 93.

Shankes, *n. pl.* Sax. Legs, 1903. *Sconke*, Layam. f. 87. b. See Rits. A. S. p. 16. and Diss. p. xxxi. *Schankis*, Sc. V. Jam.

Shar, *pa. t.* Sax. Share, cut, 1413. So in Am. and Amil. 2298. Her throtes he *schar atwo*.

Shauwe, Shawe, *v.* Sax. To shew, 2206. 2784. *Sheu*, 1401.

Shel, Sheld, *n.* Sax. Shield, 489. 624. 1654. &c.

Shende, *v.* Sax. To ruin, destroy, 1422. Bevis of H. ap. Ellis, M. R. V. 2. p. 99. Chauc. Shend, Shent, Shamed, disgraced, 2749. 2845. The more common sense of this verb is the latter. V. Jam.

Shere, Share, portion? 1250.

Sheu, See Shauwe.

Shides, *n. pl.* Sax. It here expresses pieces of wood cleft at the end, 917. In Doug. Virg. *Schide* signifies a billet of wood, 223. 10. or a chip, splinter, 207. 8. So in *Rauf Coilzear*, st. 39. Schaftes of schene wode they scheueride in *schides*. The word is preserved in Lanc. This custom of skinning eels by inserting the head in a cleft stick, is still practised, we are informed, in the fish markets.

Shir, *adj.* Sax. Bright, 588. 916. 1253. &c. In common use among the old writers.

Shireue, *n.* Sax. Sheriff, 2286. Schireues, *pl.* 266.

Sho, *pron.* See Sche.

Sho, *v.* Sax. To shoe, 1138.

Shof, *pa. t.* Sax. Shoved, pushed, 871. 892.

Shole, Shall, 562. 645. *Shul*, 328. Shole, Sholen, *pl.* 621. 1127. 1788. 1230. &c. *Shulen*, 731. 747. &c. *Shoren*, 1640.

Shol, Should, 1782. *Shude*, 1079. Sholdest, Shouldst, 2712. Sholden, *pl.* 1020. 1195. *Shulden*, 941. Sule, Should ye, 2419.

Sholdre, *n.* Sax. Shoulder, 2738. *Shuldre*, 604. 1262. *Shudre-blade*, 2644. Sholdres, *pl.* Shoulders, 1646. 1818. *Shuldren*, 982.

Shon, *n. pl.* Sax. Shoes, 860. 969.

Shop, *qu.* Shok, Shook, struck, destroyed, 1101.

Shotshipe, *n.* Sax. [*shot*, symbolum, *scipe*, societas] An assembly of persons who pay pecuniary contribution or reckoning, 2099.

> For al Sikelines quiden
> *Sotscipe* heo heolden,
> And swa longe swa beoth æuere,
> Ne scal hit stonde næuere.
> *Layam.* f. 133. b. c. 2.

See Nares, *v.* Shot-clog.

Shrede, *n.* Sax. Clothing, 99. *Schrede*, Web. Rits. M. R. See Shrud.

Shres, *n.* Sax. Sheers, 857.

Shride, *v.* Sax. To clothe, 963. Shrid, *pa. t.* Clothed, 978.

Shriue, Shriuen, *v.* Sax. To confess, make confession, 362. 2598. Shriue, Shriuen, *part. pa.* 364. 2489.

Shrud, *n.* Sax. Clothing, 303. See Shrede.

Shude, Shul, Shulen, See Shol.

Shuldre, Shuldres, See Sholdre.

Shuldreden, *pa. t. pl.* Sax. Shouldered, 1056.

Sibbe, *adj.* Sax. Related, allied, 2277. Sir Tr. p. 44. See Fremd.

Siden, *n. pl.* Sax. Sides, 371.

Sike, *v.* Sax. To sigh, 291.

Siking, *n.* Sax. Sighing, 234.

Sikerlike, *adv.* Sax. Surely, 422. 625. 2301. 2707. 2871. *Sikerly*, Sir Tr. p. 35. &c.

Sikernesse, *n.* Sax. Surety, security, 2856. R. Glouc. R. Br. Chauc.

Simenels, *n. pl.* Fr. A finer sort of bread, "q. a *simila* h. e. puriori farinæ parte." *Spelm.* Assis. pan. 51. Hen. III. *Symnellus* vero de quadrante ponderabit 2. sol. minus quam Wastellum. It elsewhere appears to be a sort of cake, or craknel. So in the *Crieries de Paris*, v. 163. Chaudes tartes et *siminiaus*. V. Nares, in v.

Sinne, *n.* Sax. Fault, 1976. *Ne for loue ne for sinne*, 2375. *Wolde he nouth for sinne lette*, 2627. Traces of this phrase may be elsewhere found:

> Neyther for *love* nor yet for *awe*
> Lyuinge man none than they saw.
> *Sir Degore*, c. iv.
>
> Maboun and Lybeaus
> Faste togedere hewes,
> And stente *for no synne*.
> *Ly Beaus Desc.* 1959.

Sire, Syre, *n.* Fr. The term in v. 34. 1229. is used not only to express respect, but command. A parallel passage is in R. Cœur de L. 2247. It simply means *Sir*, v. 909. 2009.

Site, *v.* Sax. To sit, 2709. 2809. Sittes, *pr. t.* 2. *p.* Sitteth, sits, 1316. Sitten, *pr. t. pl.* Sit, 2098.

Sithe, *pron.* Such? 1666.

Sithe, Sithen, *adv.* Sax. Then, afterwards, after, 399. 446. 472. 756. 1414. 1814. 1988. &c.

Sithe, *n.* Sax. Time, 1052. Sithe, Sithes, *pl.* 213. 778. 1737. 2189. *Sythe, Sythes*, 2162. 2843. Sir Tr. p. 55. &c.

Sket, *adv.* Quickly, soon, 1926. 1960. 2303. 2493. 2513. 2574. 2736. 2839. Sir Tr. p. 36. 40. &c. Ly Beaus Desc. 484. K. Alisaund. 97. R. Cœur de L. 806. Rom. of Merlin, ap. Ellis, M. R. V. i. p. 228. *Qu.* from Sax. *scytan*, irruere.

Skirming, *part. pr.* or *n.* Fr. Skirmishing, 2323. Web. M. R. See Note on v. 2320.

Slawe, Slawen, See Slo.

Slenge, *v.* Sax. To sling, cast out, 2435. Slenget, *part. pa.* Slung, 1923.

Slepes, *pr. t.* 2. *p.* Sleepest, 1283.

Sleie, Sley, *adj.* Skilful, expert, 1084. 2116. Sir Tr. p. 23. 28. Horn Childe, ap. Rits. M. R. V. 3. p. 296. Emare, 67. R. Glouc. p. 350. Barb. xix. 179. Doug. 137. 12. Jamieson derives it from Su. G. *sloeg*, Isl. *slaegr*.

Slike, *adv.* Slyly? 1157.

Slo, *n.* Sax. Sloe, berry, 849. 2051.

Slo, *v.* Sax. To slay, 512. 1364. 1412. &c. *Slou*, 2543. Slos, *pr. t.* 2. *p.* Slayest, 2706. Slos, *imp. pl.* Slay ye, 2596. Slou, Slow, *pa. t.* Slew, 501. 2633. Slowe, Slowen, *pa. t. pl.* Slew, 2414. 2427. 2432. 2683. Slawe, Slawen, *part. pa.* Slain, 1803. 1928. 2000. &c. In v. 2747. it has only the sense of *struck*, wounded, agreeably to the signification of the original word, *slæan*, *slægan*, Cædere, ferire.

Smerte, *adj.* Sax. Painful, 2055.

Smerte, *v.* Sax. To smart, 2647.

Smoth, *pa. t.* Sax. Smote, 2654.

So, 933.

So, *conj.* Sax. As, 278. 349. *et pass.*

Softe, *adj.* Sax. Of a mild disposition, 991.

Softe, *adv.* Sax. Gently, 2618.

Somdel, *adj.* Sax. Somewhat, in some measure, 240. 450. 497. 1054. *Sumdel*, 2305. 2950. Web. R. Gl. Chauc.

Sond, *n.* Sax. Sand, 708. 735.

Sone, *n.* Sax. Son, 660. 839. Sones, *pl.* 2980.

Sone, *adv.* Sax. Soon, 78. &c. so soon as, 1354.

Sor, *n.* Sax. Sorrow, 234. *Sorwe*, 1374. Pain, sore, 1988.

Sor, *adj.* Sax. Sore, detestable, 2229.

Sorful, *adj.* Sax. Sorrowful, 151. 2541.

Soth, Sothe, *n.* Sax. Truth, 36. 647. 2008. &c.

Sothlike, *adv.* Sax. Truly, 276.

Soupe, *v.* Fr. To sup, 1766.

Soure, *n.* Sax. Shore, 321.

Southe, *pa. t.* Sax. Sought, 1085.

Sowe, Sowen, See Se.

Sowel, *n.* 767. 1143. 2905. *Qu.* the same as Sc. *sawens*, flummery, from Sax. *seawe*, paste, glue.

Span-newe, *adj.* Quite new, 968. This is the earliest instance on record of the use of this word. For its disputed etymology see Jam. Nares, Todd's Johns. and Thoms. Etymons. It occurs in Chauc. Troil. 3. 1671.

Sparkede, *pa. t.* Sax. Sparkled, 2144.

Spede, *v.* Sax. To speed, prosper, 1634.

Speke, Speken, *n.* Sax. Speech, 946. 1070.

Speke, Speken, *v.* Sax. To speak, 326. 369. 548. &c. *Spak*, *pa. t.* Spoke, 2389. 2968. Speken, *part. pa.* Spoken, 2369.

Spelle, *n.* Sax. Story, relation, 338. K. Horn, 958.

Spelle, *v.* Sax. To relate, tell forth, 15. 2530.

Spen for Spent, 1819.

Sperd, Sperde, *part. pa.* Sax. Barred, bolted, 414. 448. Still common in the North. V. Brockett.

Spille, *v.* Sax. To perish, 2422. Of *limes spille*, 86. Suffer the loss of limbs. K. Horn, 203. Web. Chauc.

Spired, *part. pa.* Sax. Speered, inquired, 2620. V. Jam. in v.

Spore, *n.* Sax. Spur, 2569.

Sprauleden, *pa. t. pl.* Sax. Sprawled, 475.

Sprong, *pa. t.* Sax. Sprung, 959. See the Note. *Sprongen*, 869. Sprungen, *part. pa.* Risen, 1131.

Sprote, *n.* Sax. Sprout, 1142.

Spuse, Spusen, *v.* Sax. To espouse, marry, 1123. 1170. 2875. Spused, Spusede, *pa. t.* Espoused, 1175. 1266. 2887. *Spuset*, 2928.

Spusing, *n.* Sax. Espousals, marriage, 1164. 1177. 2886.

STAC, *n.* SAX. A stack, or, more properly, *stick* of fish, a term applied to eels when strung on a row, "sic dicta, quod trajecta vimine (quod *stic* dicimus) connectebantur." *Spelm.* A *stica* consisted of 25. eels, and 10. *Sticæ* made a *Binde.* Glanv. lib. 2. c. 9.

STALWORTHE, STALWORTHI, STALWRTHE, *adj.* SAX. Strong, valiant, courageous, 24. 904. 1027. &c. STALWORTHESTE, *sup.* 25. The term is found in nearly every English writer from the time of Thomas of Erceldoune to Holinshead.

STAN-DED, *adj.* SAX. Dead as a stone, completely dead, 1815. *Stille als a ston,* 928. Cf. K. of Tars, 549. Erle of Tol. 754. Launfal, 357.

STAR, *n.* ISL. [*starr*] Species of sedge, 939. See the Note.

STAREDEN, *pa. t. pl.* SAX. Stared, 1037. STARINDE, *part. pr.* Staring, 508.

STARK, *adj.* SAX. Stiff, stout, strong, 341. 380. 607. &c. Still used in the North. V. Jam. in v.

STEDE, *n.* SAX. Steed, horse, 10. &c.

STEDE, *n.* SAX. Place, 142. 744. STEDES, *pl.* 1846.

STEM, *n.* SAX. A ray of light, beam, 2122. It is equivalent to GLEM, q. v.

> Therewith he blinded them so close,
> A *stime* they could not see.
> *R. Hood,* i. 112.

Cf. Brockett's Gl. in v. STIME.

STERNES, *n. pl.* 1809.

STERT, *n.* SAX. Leap, 1873. Chaucer has *at a stert* for immediately, C. T. 1707. Cf. v. 1767.

STERTE, *n.* SAX. [*steort,* cauda] Tail, 2823. *Start* is still retained in the North.

STEUENE, *n.* SAX. Voice, 1275.

STI, *n.* SAX. Road, way, 2618. Sir Tr. p. 192. Yw. and Gaw. 599. Emare, 195. Sevyn Sages, 712. R. Br. Chaucer uses *stile* in the same sense, C. T. 12628. and Minot, p. 5. in both which passages the respective Editors have made the same mistake in explaining it.

STILLE, *adj.* SAX. Quiet, 955. 2309.

STILLE, *adv.* SAX. In a low voice, secretly, 2997. Sir Tr. p. 55. K. Horn, 315.

STIRT, STIRTE, *pa. t.* SAX. Started, leaped, 398. 566. 1049. &c. STIRTE, STIRTEN, *pa. t. pl.* Started, 1964. 2609. Derived by Skinner from SAX. *astirian,* movere, by Jam. from TEUT. *steerten,* volare. See ASTIRTE.

STITH, *n.* SAX. Anvil, 1877. Chauc. Still provincial. V. Moore, and Brockett.

STIWARDE, *n.* SAX. Steward, 666.

STONDEN, *v.* SAX. To stand, 689. STONDES, *pr. t.* 3. *p.* Standeth, stands, 2240. 2983. STOD, *pa. t.* Stood, 591. 679. STODEN, *pa. t. pl.* 1037. See BISTODE.

STOR, *adj.* SAX. Hardy, stout, 2383. Layam. f. 51. b. Yw. and Gaw. i. 55. Chron. of Engl. 462. Sq. of Lowe D. 658. Ly Beaus Desc. 1766. *Steir, Sture,* Sc. ap. Jam. Hence the Engl. word *Sturdy.*

STRA, *n.* SAX. Straw, 315. 466.

STRENES, *pr. t.* 3. *p.* SAX. Begets, 2983. From *streon,* gignere. Cf. K. Alisaund. 7057.

STRIE, *n.* 998.

STROUT, *n.* Dispute, contention, 1039. Qu. from SAX. *strith,* certamen.

STROUTE, *v.* To raise contention, 1779. To *strowte out* in Cotgr. is *Bouffer, s'enfler,* but does not here bear this meaning. V. Jam. where *to strout* is the same as *to strut.*

STUNDE, *n.* SAX. Short space of time, 2614. V. Gl. to R. Glouc. See UMBESTONDE.

STURGUN, STURGIUN, *n.* Sturgeon, 753. 1727.

STUTE, *pa. t.* Started? 873. STUTEN, *pa.t.pl.* 599.

SUERE, SWEREN, *v.* SAX. To swear, 388. 494. SUERETH, *pr. t. pl.* Swear, 647. SWEOR, *pa. t.* Swore, 398. *Swor*, 2367.

SUETE, *adj.* SAX. Sweet, 1388.

SUEYN, SWEYN, *n.* SAX. Swain, villain, 343. 1328. &c. SWEYNES, *pl.* 371. 2195. 3261. It is generally used in opposition to *knight.*

SVICH, *adj.* SAX. Such, 60.

SUILK, 644.

SULE, See SHOL.

SUMDEL, See SOMDEL.

SUNNE-BEM, *n.* SAX. Sun-beam, 592. 2123.

SWERD, *n.* SAX. Sword, 1759. &c. SWERDES, *pl.* 1769. 2659.

SWIKE, *n.* SAX. Deceiver, traitor, 423. 551. 626. 1158. 2401. 2451. &c. SWIKES, *pl.* 2834. 2990. Layam. f. 74. c. 1. R. Gl. p. 105. Perhaps, in v. 1249. it means *fraud, treachery*, as in R. Cœur de L. 4081.

SWIKEL, *adj.* SAX. Deceitful, 1108.

> For alle thene witien
> Beothe swithe *swikele.*
> *Layam.* f. 91. c. 1.
> Hoe beth of *swikele* kunne
> Ther mide the witherwinne.
> *The sawe of Seint Bede*, Ms. Digb. 86.
> He was *suikel*, fals, and fel.
> *Chron. of Engl.* 791.

SWILEN, *v.* SAX. [*Swilian*, Ps. 6. 6.] To wash, 919. Not found elsewhere.

SWILK, *adj.* SAX. Such, 1118. 1625. 2123. 2684. 2783.

SWINGE, *v.* SAX. To beat, chastise, (used passively) 214. SWNGEN, *part. pa.* Beaten, 226. Layam. f. 121. b. c. 1. So in *Syr Bevys*, C. ii. All at ones on him they *swonge.* In the North the verb retains the same meaning. See Brockett.

SWINK, *n.* SAX. Labor, 770. 801. 2456.

SWINKEN, *v.* SAX. To labor, 798. SWANK, *pa. t.* Labored, 788.

SWIRE, *n.* SAX. Neck, 311. Formerly in universal use, and still preserved in the provinces.

SWITHE, SWYTHE, *adv.* SAX. Very, exceedingly, 110. 216. 341. Quickly, 140. 682. 690. *ful swithe*, 2436. appears a pleonasm. *Swithe forth and rathe*, 4594.

SWOT, *n.* SAX. Sweat, perspiration, 2662. The word has the same meaning in Cædmon, f. 24. which seems to contradict Mr. Price's assertion to the contrary, in the new Ed. of Warton's Hist. Engl. Poetr. p. xcii. n. 9.

SWNGEN, See SWINGE.

SYRE, See SIRE.

SYTHE, SYTHES, See SITHE.

SYTHE, *n.* SAX. Scythe, 2553. 2699.

T.

TABOUR, *n.* FR. Tabor, 2329.

TALE, *n.* SAX. Number, 2025.

TALEUACES, *n. pl.* FR. Large shields, 2323. See the Note on v. 2320.

TARST, 2688.

TAUHTE, See BITAKEN.

TEL, *n.* SAX. Deceit, reproach, 191. 2219.

TELLE, *v.* SAX. To count, number, 2615. TOLDE, *part. pa.* Numbered, esteemed, 1036.

TENE, *n.* SAX. Grief, affliction, 729. In all the Gloss.

TERE, *v.* SAX. To tar (used passively) 707.

TETH, *n. pl.* SAX. Teeth, 2406.

TEYTE, *adj.* SAX. Speedily, 1841. 2331. Sir Tr. p. 22. 50. Rits. M. R. Web. R. Br. Ellis, M. R. V. 2. p. 81. 308. *Tyte*, Sc. V. Jam. in v.

THA, *adv.* SAX. Then, when, 175.

THAN, THANNE, *adv.* SAX. Then, 156. 1044. &c. When, 226. 248. *et sæpius.* Than if *(quàm)* 944. 1867.

THAR, 129.

THARE, *adv.* SAX. There, 2481. 2739.

THARNE, *v.* To lose, be deprived of, 2492. 2835. THARNES, *pr. t.* Loses, is deprived of, 1913. *Tharned the ded*, 1687. The verb only exists in the SAX. in the part. *thærnode*, Chron. Sax. p. 222. Ed. Gibs. which is derived by Lye from the Cimbr. *At thuerna*, or *thorna*, diminui, privari. V. Hickes Thes. I. p. 152. The term is not to be found in any of the Glossaries.

THAS, 1129.

THAT, *adv.* SAX. Appears to have the force of the Lat. *ut* for *utinam*, v. 16. 2009. See THET.

THAUE, *v.* SAX. [*thafian*] To give, 296. Bear, sustain, 2696. Not to be found in the Glossaries.

THAYN, *n.* SAX. Nobleman, 2184. *Thein*, 2467. THAYNES, *pl.* 2260. *Theynes*, 2194. See KAYN.

THE, *n.* SAX. Thigh, 1950. THES, *pl.* 1903. 2289. (?)

THE, *adv.* SAX. There, 142. 476. 863. 933. THE OF, Thereof, 544. THE WITH, Therewith, 639. See THER.

THE, *conj.* SAX. Though, 1682. *Thei*, 1966. *They*, 807. 992. 1165. 2501. See THOU.

THEDE, *n.* SAX. Country, dwelling, 105. Place, 2890. Web. Le Bone Flor. 246. R. Br. p. 18. V. Jam.

THEF, *n.* SAX. Thief, 2434. THEUES, *pl.* 1780.

THEI, *pron.* SAX. They, 1020. 1195. &c.

THEI, THEY, *conj.* See THE.

THENKE, *imp.* SAX. Think, 2394, THENKESTE, *pr. t. 2. p.* Thinkest, 578.

THENNE, *adv.* SAX. Then, 777. 1185. &c. See THAN.

THER, *adv.* SAX. Where, 318. 448. &c. There, *passim*. The place whence, 1780. Therefore, in that, 1740. THERINNE, Therein, 535. &c. *Therhinne*, 322. THER-OF, THEROFFE, Thereof, 372. 466. 1068. &c. THERTHORU, By that means, 1098. THERTIL, THERTO, Thereto, 396. 1041. 1045. THERWIT, THERWITH, Therewith, 1031. 1046. See THE, THOR.

THERE, *pron.* SAX. Their, 1350.

THERL, for THE EARL, 178.

THERTEKNE, 2878.

THET, *conj.* SAX. That (*quòd*) 330.

THET, *pron.* SAX. That, 879. *Thit*, 502. 997. 2990.

THETHE, THETHEN, *adv.* SAX. Thence, 2498. 2629.

THEU, THEW, *n.* SAX. [*theow*] In a servile condition, or station, 262. 2205. R. Gl.

THEWES, *n. pl.* SAX. Manners, 282. Layam. Rits. M. R. Web. P. Plouhm. Chauc. Gl. Lynds. Percy, A. R.

THI, See FORTHI.

THI for THY, 2725.

THIDER, *adv.* SAX. Thither, 850. 1012. 1021. &c.

THIGGE, *v.* SAX. [*Thigian*] To beg, 1373. This word is not found in the Old Engl. Glossaries, but is preserved in the Sc. writers. Wall. ii. 259. Doug. Virg. 182. 37. Evergreen, ii. 199. Bannatyne Poems, p. 120. V. Jam. in v. who derives it from SU. G. *tigga*, ALEM. *thigen*, petere.

THIS for These, 1145. 2021.

THISTERNESSE, *n.* SAX. Darkness, 2191.

> Dalden from than fihte
> Al bi *thustere* nihte.
> *Layam.* f. 42. b. c. 1.

THO, *art.* SAX. The, 1918. 2044.

THO, *pron.* See THU.

THO, *adv.* SAX. Then, 930. 1020. 1047. &c. *Thow*, 1669.

THORE, *adv.* SAX. There, 741. 922. 1014.

&c. THORTIL, Thereto, 1443. THORWIT, Therewith, 100. See THE, THER.

THORU, *adv.* SAX. Through, 627. 774. 848. &c. *Thoruth*, 1065. 2786. *Thorw*, 264. 367. 2646. *Thuruth*, 52.

THORUTHLIKE, *adv.* SAX. Thoroughly, 680.

THOU, *conj.* SAX. Though, 124. 299. &c. *Thouche*, 504. *Thouthe*, 1166. See THE.

THOUCTE, *pa. t.* SAX. Thought, 197. 507. &c. *Thouthte*, 1073. *Thowthe*, 1869. *That god thoucte*, 256. That thought it good. Cf. Sir Tr. p. 30. 36. And so in Ms. Vernon, Bodl.

> Riche metes was forth brouht
> To all men *that gode thouht.*
> *Disp. betw. a Crystene mon and a Jew*, f. 301.

THOUTH, *n.* SAX. Thought, 122. 1190.

THRAL, *n.* SAX. Slave, villain, 527. 684. 1097. 1158. 2564. 2589. In an opprobious sense, 1408. Sir Tr. p. 175.

THRAW, *n.* SAX. Space of time, 276. 1215. Web. Rits. M. R. Rob. Br. Doug. Virg. *Throw*, Chauc. Gower, &c.

THREDDE, THRIDDE, *adj.* SAX. Third, 867. 2633.

THRETTE, *pa. t.* SAX. Threatened, 1163.

THRIE, *n.* SAX. Trouble, affliction, 730. Apparently the same with *Tray*, R. Br. p. 235. 304. Minot, p. 22. R. Hood, I. 38. *Treye*, Am. and Amil. 1572.

THRINNE, *num.* SAX. Three, 716. 761. 1977. 2091.

THRIST, THRISTEN, *v.* SAX. To thrust, 1152. 2019. 2725. THRIST, *part. pa.* Thrust, 638.

THU, *pron.* SAX. Thou, 527. &c. *Tho*, 388. *Thw*, 453. 1316. *Tow*, 1322. *Tu*, 2903. It is often joined to the verb which precedes, as *Shaltow*, *Wiltu*, &c.

THURTE, *adv.* SAX. Across, astride, 10. *Athort*, Sc. *Athwart*, Engl. V. Jam.

THURUTH, See THORU.

THUS for THIS, 785. 2586.

TID, *n.* SAX. Time, hour, 2100. 2510.

TIL, *prep.* SAX. To, 141. 762. 864. &c. See INTIL, THERTIL.

TIL, *v.* SAX. To tell? 1348.

TILLED, *part. pa.* SAX. Obtained, acquired, 438. V. Gl. R. Br. in v. TILLE, and see Quotation under GODDOT.

TINTE, *pa. t.* SAX. Lost, 2023. Sir Tr. p. 104. V. Jam.

TIRNEDEN, *pa. t. pl.* SAX. Turned, 603.

TITHANDES, *n. pl.* SAX. Tidings, 2279.

TO, *adv.* SAX. Too, 303. 526. 689. 691. &c.

TO, in composition with verbs, is usually augmentative, but sometimes pleonastic. TO-BRISED, *part. pa.* Very much bruised, 1950. (See BRISEN.) TO-CRUHSSE, *inf.* Crush in pieces, 1992. TO-DEYLE, *inf.* Divide, 2099. (See DELED.) TO-DRAWEN, *part. pa.* Dragged or pulled to death, 2001. (See DROU.) TO-FRUSSHE, *inf.* Break in pieces, 1993. TO-HEWEN, *part. pa.* Hewn in pieces, 2001. TO-REDE, *inf.* Advise, 118. 693. *To rathe*, 2542. (See RATHE.) TO-RIUEN, *inf.* Torn in pieces, 1953. (See RIUE.) TO-ROF, *part. pa.* Burst open, shattered, 1792. TO-SHIUERE, *inf.* Shiver in pieces, 1993. TO-SHIUERED, *part, pa.* Shivered to pieces, 2667. TO-TERE, *inf.* Tear in pieces, 1839. TO-TORN, *part. pa.* Torn in pieces, 1948. 2021. TO-TUSEDE, *part. pa.* Entirely rumpled or tumbled, 1948. TO-YEDE, *pa. t.* Went through, 765. (See YEDE.)

TO, *n.* SAX. Toe, 1743. 1847. &c. TOS, *pl.* 898. 2163.

TO, *num.* SAX. Two, 2664.

TO-FRUSSHE, *v.* FR. [*froisser*] To dash or break in pieces, 1993.

The Sarezynes layde on with mace,
And al *to-frussched* hym in the place.
R. Cœur de L. 5032. Cf. 5083.

He suld sone be *to-fruschyt* all.
Barb. x. 597. So also Doug. Virg. 52. 41. and Wynt. vii. 10. 71.

V. Jam. in v. FRUSCH.

TOGIDERE, TOGYDERE, *adv.* SAX. Together, 1128. 1181. 2683. 2891.

TOK, TOKE, *pa. t.* SAX. Took, 354. 467. 537. 1216. &c. TOKEN, *pa. t. pl.* 1194. *Token under fote,* 1199.

TOLD, See TELLE.

TOTEDE, *pa. t.* Peeped, looked, 2106. This verb is twice found in P. Plouhman's Crede.

With tabernacles ytyght, to *toten* all abouten.

And again:

Whow myght thou in thy brothers eighe a bare mote loken,
And in thyn owen eighe nought a beme *toten.*

It is explained in the Gloss. *To espie.* Although it would appear a rare word from its not appearing in Hearne, Ritson, or Weber, yet in later times it occurs often, and is instanced by Jamieson from Patten's Account of Somerset's Expedicion, p. 53. and by Nares from Hall, Latimer, Spenser, and Fairfax. In Sc. it is pronounced *Tete,* which is derived by Jam. from the same stock as SU. G. *titt-a,* explained by Ihre, "Per transennam veluti videre, ut solent curiosi, aut post tegmina latentes." V. the authorities quoted, Todd's Johns. and Wilbr. Gl.

TO-TUSEDE, *part. pa.* Entirely rumpled or tumbled, 1948. See Nares, in v. TOSE, and TOUSLE, TOOZLE, in Jam. Brockett, &c.

TOUN, *n.* SAX. Town, 1750. &c. *Tun,* 764. 1001. &c. TUNES, *pl.* 1444. 2277.

TOUR, *n.* FR. Tower, 2073.

TRE, *n.* SAX. A bar or staff of wood, 1022. 1821. 1843. 1882. &c. *Dore-tre,* 1806. 1968. Bar of the door.

TREWE, *adj.* SAX. True, 1756.

TRISTEN, *v.* To trust, 253.

TRO, See TROWE.

TROME, *n.* SAX. [*truma*] A troop, company, 8.

Heo makeden heore sceld *trome.*
Layam. f. 53. b. c. 1.
Bisydes stondeth a feondes *trume,*
And waileth hwenne the saules cume.
Les Unze peyne &c. Ms. Coll. Jes. 29.

The same mode of expression used above occurs lower down, v. 24. 'A stalworthi man in a *flok,*' which is also found in Layamon,

Cador ther wes æc,
The kene wes on *flocke.*—f. 138. c. 1.

And in *Sir Guy,* H. iii.

Then came a knight that hight Sadock,
A doughty man in every *flock.*

TRONE, *n.* LAT. Throne, 1316.

TROWE, *v.* SAX. To believe, 1656. *Tro,* 2862. TROWEDE, *pa. t.* Believed, 382. Sir Tr. p. 41.

TRUSSE, *v.* FR. [*trousser*] To pack up, to truss, 2017. R. Gl. Hence to *make ready,* K. Alisaund. 7006. Minot, p. 50. which Rits. was unable to explain.

TUENTI, *num.* SAX. Twenty, 259.

TUMBEREL, *n.* 757. In Spelm. *Timberellus* is explained, a small whale, on the authority of Skene, Vocab. Jur. Scot. L.

Forest, *Si quis cetum*. In Cotgr. also we find "*Tumbe*, the great Sea-Dragon, or Quadriver; also the Gurnard, called so at Roan."

Tun, See Toun.

Turues, *n. pl.* Sax. Turf, peat, 939. Chauc. C. T. 10109. V. Spelm. in v. and Jennings' Somersetsh. Gl.

Twel for Twelve, 2455.

V.

Veneysun, *n.* Fr. Venison, 1726.

Vmbestonde, *adv.* Sax. Formerly, for a while, 2297.

> & heo seileden forth,
> Ther inne sæ heo comen,
> Ma *vmbestunde* ne sæge heo
> noht of londe.
> *Layam.* f. 68. c. 2.

It is equivalent to *umbe-while*, elsewhere. See Stunde.

Umbistode, *pa. t.* Sax. Stood around, 1875. See Bistode, Stode.

Vn-bi-yeden, *pa. t. pl.* Sax. Surrounded, 1842. See Yede.

Vnblithe, *adj.* Sax. Unhappy, 141. Sir Tr. p. 171.

Unbounden, *pa. t. pl.* Sax. Unbound, 601.

Underfong, *pa. t.* Sax. Understood, 115. This sense of the verb is not found elsewhere. It is in the present poem synonymous with Understod, (as Lat. *accipere, percipere*.)

Understod, *pa. t.* Sax. Received, 1760. Understonde, *imp.* Receive, 1159. 2814. So in K. Horn, 245. Ed. Rits.

> Horn child thou *vnderstond*,
> Tech him of harpe and song.

where the Ms. Laud, 108. reads *vnderfonge*.

Unker, *pron. g. c. pl.* Sax. Of you, 1882.

Vnkeueleden, *pa. t. pl.* Fr. Uncovered, 601.

Unkyndelike, *adv.* Sax. Unsuitably, 1250.

Vnornelske, *adj.* Sax. Lat.? Rudely, improperly, 1941. The only word in the Sax. remaining to which it can be referred, is *unornlic*, tritus, Ios. 9. 5. The following instances also approach the same stock.

> Ne speke y nout with Horne,
> Nis he nout so *vnorne*.
> *K. Horn*, 337.
> Mi stifne is bold & nozt *unorne*,
> Ho is ilich one grete horne,
> & thine to ilich one pipe.
> *Hule and Niztingale*, f. 232. c. 2.

Unride, *adj.* Sax. [*ungereod, ungeryde*] It is here used in various significations, most of which, however, correspond to the senses given by Somner. Large, cumbersome (of a garment) 964. Unwieldy (of the bar of a door) 1795. Deep, wide (of a wound) 1981. 2673. Numerous, extensive (of the nobility) 2947. Unrideste, *sup.* Deepest, widest, 1985. In the second sense we find it in Sir Tristr. p. 167.

> Dartes wel *unride*
> Beliagog set gan.

And in *Guy of Warwick*, ap. Ellis, M. R. V. 2. p. 79.

> A targe he had ywrought full well,
> Other metall was ther none but steel,
> A mickle and *unrede*.

In the fourth sense we have these examples:

> Opon Englond for to were
> With stout ost and *unride*.
> *Horn Childe*, ap. Rits. M. R. V. 3. p. 383.

Schir Rannald raugh to the renk ane rout wes *unryde*. *Sir Gaw. and Gol.* ii. 25.

The soudan gederet an ost *unryde*.
K. of Tars, 142.

Cf. also *Sir Guy*, Ee. iv. in Garrick's Collect. 'Ameraunt drue out a swerde *unryde*.' In the sense of huge, or unwieldy, we may also understand it in Sir Tr. p. 148. 164. Guy of Warw. ap. Ell. M.R. V. 2. p. 78. Horn Childe, ap. Rits. V. 3. p. 295. In R. Brunne, p. 174. it expresses loud, tremendous. Sir W. Scott and Hearne are both at fault in their Glossaries, and even Jamieson has done but little to set them right, beyond giving the true derivation, and then, under the cognate word *Unrude*, Doug. Virg. 167. 35. &c. errs from pure love of theory.

UNRITH, *n.* SAX. Injustice, 1369.

UNWRAST, UNWRASTE, *adj.* SAX. [*unwræste*] Vile, base, 547. 2821. This word occurs in the Saxon Chron. 168. 4. applied to a rotten ship, and this appears to have been the original meaning. The sense in which it was subsequently used may be learnt by comparing Layam. f. 175. c. 2. f. 80. c. 1. R. Gl. p. 586. Chron. of Engl. 661. 921. Ly Beaus Desc. 2118. (not explained by Rits.) K. Alisaund. 878. R. Cœur de L. 872. and Sevyn Sages, 1919. It is not found in Jam.

VOYZ, *n.* LAT. Voice, 1264.

VRE, *pron.* SAX. Our, 13. 596. &c.

VT, *prep.* SAX. Out, 89. 155. 346. &c. *Uth*, 1178.

UT-BIDDE, See BIDDE.

UT-DRAWE, UT-DRAWEN, VT-DROW, UT-DROWEN, See DROU.

UTEN, *prep.* SAX. Out, exhausted, 842. Without, foreign, *Uten-laddes*, 2153. 2580. Foreigners.

UT-LEDE, See LEDE.

UTRAGE, *n.* SAX. Outrage, 2837.

W.

W, See Hw.

WA, *n.* SAX. Woe, wail, 465.

WACNE, *v.* SAX. To wake, awaken, 2164.

WADE, *v.* SAX. LAT. To pass, go, 2645. *Wede*, 2387. 2641. Vid. Nares.

WAGGE, *v.* SAX. To wield, brandish, 89.

WAITEN, WAYTE, WAYTEN, *v.* FR. SAX. To watch, 512. 1754. 2070. Chauc.

WAKEN, *v.* Precisely the same word as the last, disguised by a different pronunciation, 630. WAKED, *part. pa.* Watched, kept awake, 2999. See R. Br. Sq. of L. D. 852. Chauc.

WAN, *adv.* SAX. When, 1962.

WAR, *adj.* SAX. Aware, wary, 788. 2139. Of very common use in the old writers.

WARIE, *v.* SAX. To curse, 433. WARIED, *part. pa.* Cursed, 434. Emare, 667. *Wery*, Minot, p. 7. *Warrie*, Chauc. See Gl. Lynds.

WARP, *pa. t.* SAX. Threw, cast, 1061.

Al swa feor swa a mon
Mihte *warpen* ænne stan.
Layam. f. 99. b. c. 2.

So in Sc. Doug. Virg. 432. and Barb. iii. 642. V. Jam.

WASHEN, *v.* SAX. To wash, 1233.

WASTE for WAS THE, 87.

WASTEL, *n.* FR. Cake, or loaf made of finer flour, 878. WASTELS, *pl.* 779. See Todd's Illustr. of Chauc. who derives the name from *wastell*, the vessel or basket in which the bread was carried. V. Du Cange, Spelm. Jam. In Pegge's Form of Cury, p. 72. 159. we meet with *Wastels yfarced.*

WAT, *pron.* See HWAT.

WAT, *v.* See QUATH.

WAWE, *n.* SAX. Wall, 474. 2470. The phrase

bith wawe, 474. is also found in Rits. A. S. p. 46. which is left unexplained by the Editor, and is badly guessed at by Ellis. By the aid of Moor's Suffolk Gl. we are enabled to ascertain the meaning of an expression which is not yet obsolete. "By the walls." Dead and not buried. "A' lie bi' the walls"—said, I believe, only of a human subject." *Wowe*, 1963. 2078. Still so pronounced in Lanc. &c.

WAXEN, See WEX.

WAYKE, *adj.* SAX. Weak, 1012.

WAYTE, WAYTEN, See WAITEN.

WE, 115. 287. 392. 772. Apparently an error of the scribe for *wel*, but its frequent repetition may cause it to be doubted, whether the *l* may not have been purposely dropped.

WEDE, *v.* See WADE.

WEDE, *n.* SAX. Clothing, garments, 94. 323. 861. In very general use formerly, and still preserved in the phrase, a widow's *weeds*.

WEDDETH for WEDDED, 1127.

WEI, WEIE, *n.* SAX. Way, road, 772. 952.

WEILAWA, WEILAWEI, *interj.* SAX. Woe! alas! 462. 570. See Gl. Sir Tr. Rits. M. R. and Chauc. Sir W. Scott and Ritson conjecture it to have been the burden of some old song, but this is quite unnecessary, as we find it commonly used by the Saxon writers.

WEL, *adv.* SAX. Full, *passim*. *Wel sixti*, 1747. *wel o-bon*, See ON. *Wel with me*, 2878. *Wol*, 185.

WEL, *n.* SAX. Weal, wealth, prosperity, 2777. *For wel ne for wo.* A very common expression in all the old Engl. poetry.

WELDE, *v.* SAX. To wield, govern (a kingdom) 129. 175. (a weapon) 1436. (possessions) 2034. WELDES, *pr. t.* 2. *p.* Wieldest, governest, 1359

WENDE, WENDEN, *v.* SAX. To go, 1346. 1705. 2629. 1344. WENDE, *pr. t. pl.* 2. *p.* Go, 1440. WEND, *part. pa.* Turned, 2138.

WENE, *v.* SAX. To ween, think, 655. 840. 1260. &c. WENES, *pr. t.* 2. *p.* Thinkest, 598. *Wenestu*, 1787. Thinkest thou. WEND, WENDE, *pa. t.* Thought, 374. 524. 1091. 1803. &c. WENDEN, *pa. t. pl.* 1197. 2547.

WEPEN, *pr. t.* or *pa. t. pl.* SAX. Weep, wept, 401.

WEPNE, *n.* SAX. Weapon, 89. 490. 1436. &c.

WER for Were, 1097.

WERD, *n.* SAX. World, 1290. 2241. 2335 2792. 2968.

WERE, *v.* SAX. [*werian*] To defend, 2152. 2298. Sir Tr. p. 156. Yw. and Gaw. 2577. Horn Childe, ap. Rits. M. R. V. 3. p. 289. K. of Tars, 189. Chauc. C. T. 2552. V. Note, p. 182. *Werye*, K. Horn, 791. Ms. Web. Minot, Gl. Lynds.

WERE, Should be, 2782. WEREN, 3. *p. pl.* Were, 156. &c.

WEREN for WHERE, 784.

WEREWED, *part. pa.* SAX. Worried? 1915. *Worewed*, 1921. *Qu.* from SAX. *Wurgan*, suffocare, strangulare. V. Jam. in v. WERY.

WERNE, *v.* SAX. To forbid, deny, 1395. WERNE, *pr. t.* 3. *p.* Refuses, forbids, 926. Sir Tr. p. 88. K. Horn, 1420. &c.

WESSEYL, SAX. Wassail, 1246. WESSEYLEN, *pr. t. pl.* Wassailed, 2098. WOSSEYLED, *part. pa.* 1737. See Rits. A. S. Diss. p. xxxiii. n. Hearne's Gl. to R. Glouc. in v. QUEME and WASSEYL, Selden, Notes on Drayton's Polyolb. p. 150. and Nares.

WEX, *pa. t.* SAX. Waxed, grew, 281. WAXEN, *part. pa.* Grown, 302. 791.

WICKE, WIKE, WIKKE, *adj.* SAX. Wicked, vile, 66. 319. 425. 665. 688. &c. *Swithe wicke*, 965. very mean. *Swithe wikke clothes*, 2457. very mean cloathing. *Wicke wede*, 2825. The same.

WICTH, WITH, *n.* SAX. [*wiht*] Whit, bit,

small part, 97. 1763. 2500. Layam. f. 86. b. c. 1. Sevyn Sages, 293. 'The loue of hire ne lesteth no *wyht* longe,' Ms. Harl. 2253. f. 128.

WICTH, WITH, *adj.* SAX. [*hwæt, hwate*] Courageous, stout, active, 344. 1064. 1651. 1692. &c. WICTESTE, *sup.* 9. An epithet used universally by the ancient poets, and to be found in every Gloss. merely differing in orthography, as spelt *Waite, Wate, Wight, Wich*, &c.

WIDDER, *adv.* SAX. Whither, where, 1139.

WIDUEN, WYDUES, *n. pl.* SAX. Widows, 33. 79.

WIF, *n.* SAX. Wife, 2860. Woman, 1713. WIUES, *pl.* 2855.

WIKE, WIKKE, See WICKE.

WIL, *adv.* SAX. While, 6. 15.

WIL, *adj.* Lost in error, uncertain how to proceed, 863. Wynt. vi. 13. 115. V. Jam. who derives it from Su. G. *will*, ISL. *vill-ur*. It is radically the same with *wild*.

WIL, *adj.* SAX. Willing, 1042.

WILE, Will, 352. 485. &c. *Wilte*, 528. 1137. Wilt thou, *Wiltu*, 681. 905. WILEN, *pl.* 732. 920. 1345. 2817. &c.

WILLE, *n.* SAX. Will, 528.

WIMMAN, *n.* SAX. Woman, 1139. 1168. &c. *Wman*, 281. *Wymman*, 1156.

WIN, *n.* SAX. Wine, 1729.

WINAN, *v.* SAX. To get to, arrive at, 174. V. Gl. Chauc. and Lynds.

WINNE, *n.* SAX. Joy, gain, 660. 2965. *Muchere winne*, Layam. f. 58. c. 1. Horn Childe, ap. Rits. M. R. V. 3. p. 294.

WIRCHEN, *v.* SAX. To work, cause, 510.

WIS, *adj.* SAX. Wise, prudent, 180. 1421. 1635. skilled, 282.

WISLIKE, *adv.* SAX. Wisely, 274.

WISSE, *v.* SAX. To direct, ordain, advise, 104. 361. Sir Tr. p. 29. K. Horn, Chron. of Engl. 499. Chauc. Gl. Lynds.

WISSING, *n.* SAX. Advice, or conduct, 2902.

WISTE, *pa. t.* SAX. Knew, 115. 358. 541. &c. WISTEN, *pa. t. pl.* 1184. 1187. 1200. &c.

WIT, *conj.* SAX. With, 52. 505. 701. 905. 1090. 2517. &c. WITUTEN, 179. 247. 2860. Without. *Withuten*, 425. Except. *With than*, 532. *With that*, 1220. If, so that.

WIT, *prep.* SAX. By, 2489.

WIT, WITE, *v.* SAX. [*witan*, decernere] To decree, ordain, 19. 517. 1316. WITE, *pr. t. pl.* 2. *p.* Decree, 2808.

WITE, *v.* SAX. To preserve, guard, defend, 405. 559. 694. R. Gl. p. 98. 102. So in the *Carmen inter Corpus & Animam*, Ms. Digb. 86.

The king that al this world shop thoru his holi miztte,
He *wite* houre soule from then heuele wiztte.

And in the French Romance of Kyng Horn, Ms. Harl. 527. f. 72. b. c. 2.

Ben iurez *Wite God*, kant auerez beu tant,
Kant le vin uus eschaufe, si seez si iurant.

WITE, WITEN, *v.* SAX. [*witan*, cognoscere] To know, 367. 517. 625. 2201. 2786. To recollect, 2708. WITEN, *pr. t. pl.* 2. *p.* Know, 2208. See WOT.

WITH, *conj.* See WIT.

WITH, *n.* See WICTH.

WITH, *adj.* See WICTH.

WITH, *adj.* SAX. White, 48. 1008. 1144.

WITH-COMEN, *pa. t. pl.* SAX. May either mean come with, or come against, from *with*, contra.

WITH-SITTEN, *v.* SAX. To oppose, 1683. R. Br. Web.

WLF, *n.* SAX. Wolf, 573.

WLUINE, *n.* SAX. She-wolf, or wolf's-cub? 573.

WMAN, See WIMMAN.

WNDEN, *part. pa.* SAX. Wound, 546.

Wo, *pron.* Sax. Who, whoso, 76. 79. &c. See Hwo.

Wo, *n.* Sax. Woe, sorrow, 510. &c.

Wod, *adj.* Sax. Mad, 508. 1777. 1848. &c. *Wode*, 1896. 2361. &c. To be found in all the Glossaries.

Wok, *pa. t.* Sax. Awoke, 2093.

Wol, See Wel.

Wole, Will, 1150. Wolde, Would, 354. 367. &c. *Wode*, 951. 2310. Wolden, *pl.* 456. 514. 1057.

Wombes, *n. pl.* Sax. Bellies, 1911.

Wom so, *pron.* Sax. Whomso, 197.

Won, Wone, Great number, plenty, 1024. 1791. 1837. 1907. 2325. 2617. 2729. R. Gl. Horn Childe, ap. Rits. M. R. V. 3. p. 308. 314. R. Cœur de L. 3747. K. Alisaund. 1468. K. of Tars, 635. Minot, p. 14. Chauc. *Wane*, Yw. and Gaw. 1429. *Wayn*, Wall. viii. 947. The derivation is unknown. Jam. conjectures from Su. G. *winna*, sufficere.

Wone, *n.* Sax. Probably the same as *ween*, Sir Tr. p. 59. 78. Opinion, conjecture, 1711. 1972. Cf. v. 816. and the Glossaries, in v. *Wene*.

Wone, *v.* Sax. To dwell, 247. 406. Woneth, *pr. t.* 3. *p.* Dwelleth, 105. Wone, *part. pa.* Wont, 2151. 2297. K. Horn, 36. R. Gl. Chron. of Engl. 632. Web. Chauc.

Wonges, *n. pl.* Sax. Fields, plains, 397. 1444. Cf. v. 1360. Spelman thinks arable land is meant by the term, rather than pasture.

Wore, 3. *p. s.* Were, 504. 684. &c. Wore, Woren, *pl.* 237. 448. &c. It is not merely a licentious spelling, as conjectured by Sir W. Scott.

Worthe, *v.* Sax. To be, 1102. 2873. *Wrth*, 434. 1102. 2873. *Wurthe*, 2221. Layam. f. 167. c. 1. Sir Tr. p. 49. and all the Gloss. including Lynds.

Wosseyled, See Wesseyl.

Wot, Woth, *pr. t.* 1. *p.* Sax. Know, 119. 213. 653. 1345. &c. Wost, *pr. t.* 2. *p.* Knowest, 527. 582. 1381. &c. Woth, *pr. t.* 3. *p.* Knows, 2527. Wot, *pl.* 1. *p.* Know, 2803.

Wowe, See Wawe.

Wrathe, *n.* Sax. Wrath, anger, 2719. 2977. See Wroth.

Wreieres, *n. pl.* Sax. Betrayers, spoilers, 39.

> The *wraiers* that weren in halle,
> Schamly were thai schende.
>
> *Sir Tristr.* p. 190.

Wreken, *v.* Sax. To avenge, revenge, 327. 544. 1884. (used passively,) 1901. Wreke, *imp.* Revenge (thou) 1363. Wreke, Wreken, *part. pa.* Revenged, 2368. 2849. 2992. Sir Tr. p. 190. &c.

Wringen, *v.* Sax. To wring, 1233.

Writ, *n.* Sax. Writing, 2486. Writes, *pl.* Writs, letters, 135. 2275. See the Note.

Wrobberes, *n. pl.* Sax. Robbers, 39.

Wros, *n. pl.* Corners? 68. So in the *Leg. of S. Margrete*, quoted by Dr. Leyden,

> Sche seize a wel fouler thing
> Sitten in a *wro*.

Which Jamieson aptly derives from the Su. G. *wra*, angulus.

Wroth, *adj.* Sax. Wrath, angry, 1117. *Wrothe*, 2973. See Wrathe.

Wrouht, *pa. t.* Sax. Wrought, 2810. *Wrouth*, 1352. *Wrowht*, 2453.

Wrth, See Worthe.

Wunde, *n.* Sax. Wound, 1980. 2673. &c. *Wounde*, 1978. Wundes, *pl.* 1845. 1898. 1986. *Woundes*, 1977. &c.

Wurthe, See Worthe.

Y.

Y, See Ich.

Ya, *adv.* Sax. Yea, Yes, 1888. 2009. 2607. See Rits. Note to Yw. and Gaw. v. 43.

Yaf, See Gaf.

Yare, *adj.* Sax. Ready, 1391. 2788. 2954. Sir. Tr. p. 28. Rits. M. R. Web. Chauc. Gl. Lynds.

Yaren, *v.* Sax. To make ready, 1350. This word in all the Gloss. has the form of *Yarken*.

Yede, *pa. t.* Sax. Went, 6. 774. 821. &c. Yeden, *pa. t. pl.* 889. 952.

Yeft, See Giue.

Yelde, *v.* Sax. To yield, reward, 803. 2712. Very common formerly in this sense. Yeld, *imp.* Yield (thou) 2717.

Yeme, *v.* Sax. To take charge of, govern, 131. 172. 182. 324. &c. Yemede, *pa. t.* Governed, 975. 2276. Sir Tr. p. 115. Rits. M. R. Web. R. Gl. Chauc. Hence probably is derived the term *Yeomen*.

Yen, See Agen.

Yerne, *adv.* Sax. Eagerly, anxiously, 153. 211. 880. 925. Web. Rits. M. R. Chauc. In the old Gl. to P. Plouhm. it is falsely rendered *ofte*.

Yerne, *v.* Sax. To desire earnestly, 299. Layam. f. 25. K. Horn, 1419. R. Br. Chauc. Gl. Lynds.

Yete, *adv.* Sax. Yet, 973. 996. 1043.

Yete, *pa. t.* See Gete.

Yeue, *v.* Sax. To give, 22. 298. &c. Yeueth, *pr. t.* 3. *p.* Giveth, 459. Yeueth, *imp.* Give (thou) 911. *Yif*, 674. Yaf, *pa. t.* Gave, 315. 419. &c. *Gaf*, 218. 418. 1311. &c. Gouen, *pa. t. pl.* 164. Sir Tr. p. 129. Yaf, *part. pa.* Given, 1174. *Youenet*, 1643. Given it. *Giue*, 2488. *Gouen*, 220.

Yhe, See Eie.

Y-here, See Here.

Yif, *prep.* Sax. If, 126. 377. 1974. &c. *Yf*, 1189.

Yif, See Yeue.

Y-lere, See Lere.

Ynde, *n. p.* Lat. India, 1085.

Ynow, See Inow.

Youenet, See Yeue.

Yuel, See Iuele.

Yuele, See Iuelelike.

Yunge, *adj.* Sax. Young, 368. &c.

Yure, *pron.* Sax. Your, 171.

SINCE the preceding sheets were printed, the Editor has had an opportunity (which did not before present itself) of revising the Romance by an ulterior collation with the MSS. and the following *errata*, (chiefly literal, proceeding from the transcript being originally made without an immediate view to publication,) deserve correction.

ENGL. TEXT. v. 38. 54. *oueral*, lege *ouer al.*
99. *sbrede*, l. *shrede*, and dele the *qu.*
156. *weten*, l. *weren.*
204. *Onanne.* In the Ms. it is *Ouanne*, by a mistake of the illuminator. Correct it *Quanne.* A fresh paragraph begins here.
223. *noman*, l. *no man.*
226. *swungen.* The Ms. reads *swngen*, not *swugen.*
259. *winti*, l. *winter.*
275. *castel*, l. *catel.* The *s* is expuncted in Ms.
371. *hete*, l. *here*, and d. the *qu.*
407. *wrth*, l. *with*, and d. the *qu.*
442. *queme*, l. *greme.*
507. *shod*, l. *stod*, and d. the *qu.*
581. *hem*, l. *him.*
601. *Vnkeuelede*, l. *Vnkeueleden.*
776. *peines*, l. *penies.*
820. *ne*, l. *he*, and d. the *qu.*
879. *he the ok.* Dele *the.* It is expuncted in Ms.
1011. *lake*, l. *layke.*
1023. *putten*, l. *pulten.*
1798. *Gomes*, l. *Comes.*
1872. *drof.* So also in Ms. the former *o* being expuncted.
1928. *slawen.* This is right. Dele the false reading.
2021. *This*, l. *His.*
2141. *Brither*, l. *Brithter.*
2219. *lat*, l. *lac.*
2377. *bunde.* So also in Ms. Dele the false reading.
2719. *dede dede.* Dele the last.
2781. *other*, l. *othes.*

Some few others of minor import, (together with most of the above) are corrected in the Glossary.

Fr. Text. v. 142. *lui*, l. *liu*.

248. *apris*, l. *apres*.

262. *& serg.* l. *& li serg.*

484. *prise*, l. *peise*.

722. *ont*, l. *out*.

759. *ieo vus*, l. *ieo le vus*.

782. *nus*, l. *mis*.

858. *nill'*, l. *mult*, and d. the *qu*.

991. *orrea*, l. *orré a*.

1017. *Ot*, l. *Od*.

Notes, p. 205. l. 1. *Tauner*, l. *Tanner*.

In illustration of the Proverb, v. 2461. *Old sinne makes newe shame*, may be added a passage taken from the *Histoire de Melusine, tirée des Chroniques de Poitou*, &c. 12mo. Par. 1698. in which Thierry, Duke of Bretagne, says to Raimondin: " Vous autorisez par votre silence *notre Proverbe*, qui dit *Qu'un vieux peche fait nouvelle vergogne*."—p. 72.

Gloss. p. 246. in v. Rippe. For *Brunham-Thorp*, read *Broomsthorp*, in the Hundred of Gallow. Sire John Mendames was not the Compiler of this Glossary (which is substantially the same with the *Ortus Vocabulorum*, printed by W. de Worde, in 1500.) but only the Scribe. He held the above living from 1529. to 1532. Vid. Blomf. Norf. V. iii. p. 726.